ISBN: 978-0998212777

Rune Awakening

BOOK ONE
THE NECROMANCER'S DAUGHTER

GENEVRA BLACK

PROLOGUE

THE DARK RIVER waves lapped at the sides of the boat as it approached the mouth of the cave. The sky was gray, and clouds roiled as thunder mumbled in the distance. The woman sitting in the boat, shivering, raised her face to the sky and closed her eyes as the rain covered her; her companion rowed, slow and deliberate, toward the sound that pierced even the growling clouds—the deep-throated, earth-shaking, unceasing howl of a wolf.

At last, they were close.

Hope lifted the woman's heart, but a contraction brought it to a stuttering halt.

She lowered her hands to her swollen abdomen, grimacing in pain as the beings inside of her writhed, spurred into a frenzy by the oncoming storm and the immense energy calling to them from the craggy breach ahead. The cave jutted out of the river's center, the slanted, jagged stone ebony with moisture. Standing guard before it were pillars of similarly jagged stone and sharp rocks just above the surface of the water, obscured by fog.

The woman's companion struggled for grip against the wet surface of the boat's stempost, clutching the jaws of the wooden serpent which adorned it. He dug his long oar into the riverbed and turned to look at her, brows knit. "Are you okay?"

She just nodded, giving him a reassuring smile, and pointed ahead. "We're so close...."

He smiled back, then eased into rowing position again, pushing them forward. The path was treacherous, the going slow as they navigated the maze of razor-sharp, black rock. Thunder growled, closer now—and, in the distance, lightning.

"Go faster," the woman breathed.

Her companion dug deeper and pushed harder, and the boat rocked as they veered off-course and grazed the slimy side of one of the pillars. The howling came again, long and low and mournful, from the mouth of the cave.

There was only sheer stone on either side of them as they finally disappeared into the thin breach, guarded at last from the rain. Inside, it was darker than anything.

The man let the boat drift as he raised his hand and lit the lantern clutched in the serpent's jaws. A blue-green light illuminated the close walls and low ceiling of the passageway; a quieter howl called to them from beyond.

Finally, they came to the end of the tight passageway, and the ceiling raised, the light following and filling the space. The hull of their boat bumped up against a rocky embankment.

Before them stood a great, circular stone door etched with ancient runes. The woman gripped the side of the boat as the beings inside of her grew agitated in the presence of the runes—runes enchanted with the blood of their father.

The door *would* open for her.

Her companion laid his stick down and pulled the boat ashore, then returned to help her from where she sat. Slowly, she rose and approached the door, taking heart in her children's excited reaction even through the pain. The sound of thunder roared through the passageway behind them and was answered with another, more agitated howl from beyond the stone slab.

"Are we sure this will work?" the man whispered.

"The door will open to the kinsblood."

The children stretched, pushing on her ribs and spine as though trying to escape her body. She felt like she might burst. With a groan, she closed her eyes and delved into her body, into the children, trying to grasp their agitated minds. She pulled at one, dug her fingernails into the silk of her robe.

"Give it to me," she demanded in a hiss.

One of them, the weaker, struggled and refused. The woman spread her roots deeper into the little thing's body, drinking of its veins until they were sunken and scarred.

The child stilled.

When the woman brought her hand away from her abdomen, a cloud of red mist followed it. Deep crimson flecks roiled there, tripping over each other like frenzied insects before swarming to the runes in the stone and pooling in the etchings like water in a basin. As the woman stepped closer, the stone absorbed the blood magic. The runes blazed gold.

Slowly, the circular door rolled to the side, rumbling and shaking the whole cavern. Gravel and fine dust rained down upon both their heads.

A fevered howl greeted the woman as she stepped into the enormous amphitheater beyond. From the darkness, two bright red eyes peered at her. The light from the passageway outside touched just the tip of the great wolf's muzzle and his slavering jaws. Hewn into the stone floor all around him, aqueducts of stinking river water glistened. His saliva dripped from the corners of his mouth and into the ducts, and in the distance, the woman could hear a steady stream of liquid flowing from the amphitheater into the river outside.

She raised her head to meet his eyes. "So, you are the Wolf of Ván."

The monster was so enormous that his arched back touched the ceiling of the cavern—there was barely room for him to lie where he was, bound to the floor with immense chains.

The wolf's red eyes drifted to her abdomen, then back up. He growled.

"I'm a friend," the woman said, "and I have much to tell you."

CHAPTER ONE
TWENTY-FIVE YEARS LATER

EDIE HOLLOWAY HAD NEVER TOUCHED a dead thing before.

Well, first time for everything, she thought as she stood in the doorway of her bedroom, staring at the hamster cage perched on her dresser. Beyond the wire mesh, a small, furry body lay stock still, four little legs sticking straight up toward the ceiling. *Dammit.*

It wasn't anything that could have been helped. Rodents were unpredictable, and Hervey's random illness had only taken a turn for the worse in the last day or so; sluggishness, aggression, lack of appetite, and refusal to drink. All things considered, Edie really *should* have been prepared for him to give up the ghost.

No one had ever told her that being in the same room as a dead body felt so *weird*, though.

I should have taken him to the vet right away. She sagged onto her bed across from the dresser, feet tired after a double shift of bussing tables and helping tend bar. A couple days ago, it had seemed a little ridiculous to take something as small as a hamster in to see a vet. Now, staring at the cage with shivers going up and down her spine, she felt bad for hesitating.

It was just that she had to consider the bill. Being recently fired from her second job at Weiner's Gas & Garage hadn't done a kindness to her bank account. "Nothing personal," Mr. Weiner had said, like *nothing personal* would pay her rent. She was pretty sure he had been trying to let her down easy. It was probably pretty ridiculous to see a pasty, raven-headed goth cleaning Nissan windows and handing out road maps—maybe even bad for business—but screw him. To add to that, having to pick up a bunch of new, super-late shifts at the downtown club that now served as her one remaining job hadn't done a kindness to her *schedule.*

Stretched as thin as she was, she knew she couldn't have spared the time *or* money to get Hervey to the vet. Still, her heart—and her wallet—ached.

Edie rose from her bed and went to stand in front of Hervey's cage, looking in. The poor little guy had made an admirable attempt at clinging to life the past few days, but he was so small and had gotten ill so quickly.

Maybe she should have done more. Or maybe she should have known that the most she could do, feasibly, was give him a comfortable death.

A sad sigh escaped her. *I could have dipped into the band fund,* she thought as she bent to observe him more closely. But DYSMANTLE's sole other member—her roommate, Mercy—probably wouldn't have been too keen on that idea. Edie usually left all that business to her. *She* was just the bassist, after all.

And when it came to asking Mercy for help directly, she'd still hesitated. Her odd (but charming) best friend would probably end up rubbing essential oils on Hervey or hanging crystals in his cage or something.

Besides, Mercy was in Salem with her boyfriend for the weekend. So, Edie was stuck here, alone, with a seemingly dead hamster and the persistent feeling that something ... *something* about this situation was *very strange.*

She'd never even been *near* anything that had died. She'd never even been to a family funeral. In fact, she barely knew her extended family, and Dad had been cremated hastily after his crash. Holding his urn was way different than having an entire body there, empty of anything. Even if that body was little and not human.

Maybe Hervey was sleeping? In shock? But no—somehow, Edie knew that wasn't the case. It was … odd. She could feel how utterly empty he was and she hadn't even touched him yet.

Oh, yeah. That part.

She couldn't just leave him lying there. After taking a moment to mentally prepare herself, she unlatched his cage and reached out to scoop him up.

"Whoa."

The air around him felt so weird, Edie actually said it out loud. Her fingers hovered over the small corpse for a moment, her whole arm suddenly thrumming with a strange energy. It was almost as if his hurt and sickness were tangible to her—and, wow, it really was uncomfortable. This must be why people hated being near dead bodies so much.

She hesitated, then scooped the hamster up, bringing him close to her chest. Definitely dead. She didn't need to be an expert to know that. His fur felt all wrong, and he was cold. That was a strange feeling in and of itself, to add to all the others. He must have been dead for a few hours.

"Shit," she whispered, shoulders sinking. She'd have liked to be there, even if that was silly.

No one who saw her on the street would have expected that, of course. Her overall style—all black everything, leather jacket, dark makeup— suggested she'd break the kneecaps of anyone who looked at her sideways. Yet here she was, cradling her sickly hamster and wishing she'd been there to comfort him in his last hours.

But no one deserved to die alone. That was a fact.

Edie's eyes began to water, though her emotions were all so jumbled that she couldn't tell if it was just because she was exhausted and overwhelmed or actually devastated. The hamster hadn't even been hers for very long, but it was still sad. He'd been all alone. Had he been scared?

Please get over yourself. Hamsters don't think like that. Trying to gather her thoughts, she thumbed him between the eyes, ruffling the fur there. After a few moments, she sat down on her bed and closed her eyes.

"Okay," she told herself in a breath. "Okay. I don't know where to put you. I don't know what to do." The freezer? The freezer could work until she found a better place. Did she have anything she could wrap him in, though? She really didn't want a dead hamster falling out the next time she reached for a frozen pizza.

The thrumming energy mounted. Edie was preoccupied, trying to think rationally about how to handle the current situation, but she kept losing focus to the unsettling feeling.

That heavy, cold feeling around the body—she could feel it, too, inside of her.

Her heart rate began to speed up as though she were approaching an anxiety attack. Her fingers and toes were numb, and heat rushed to her stomach, turning it unpleasantly slimy. He was just a hamster, but she'd put his care off because of money, and she hadn't been there. He'd been alone.

Like Dad.

Of course her emotionally exhausted brain would equate the two.

Sorrow broke in her chest even though she was aware of the absurdity of the comparison. Why did everything she cared for end up hurt or dead or gone? Dad dying, Mom pushing her away, all the failed friendships and relationships since. Mercy tried to understand, but Mercy hadn't known Edie before her father had died, and no one in Mercy's immediate family had ever died suddenly. *Mercy* was never lonely. In fact, she had a gaggle of good friends and a *huge* extended family always bugging her to visit.

Edie had few friends. No family contacting her just to check up or begging her to spend time with them. Even her own mother—who had moved across the country the second Edie had turned eighteen—hadn't called all year. It all weighed on her, and the sadness pushed her further. Her job, money, the hamster, the isolation. Everything was too much right now.

On top of all that, Mercy's own pet was just in the other room, perfectly healthy. Because of course it was. Stupid fish.

Edie knew it was wrong, but just for a second, she wished she could trade the fish for the hamster. Not because she wanted to cause Mercy pain, but because she was just *tired* of *striking out.*

And— She had no idea what happened next. Her body went stiff and, though she didn't close her eyes, her vision darkened. Misty, almost-human outlines of blue and teal and gray rushed at her from behind her eyelids, groping at her throat, emitting shrieks that vaporized into whispers.

In all, the flash of darkness probably lasted for less than a full second, but it felt like hours; it felt like she'd been sleeping, weightless, completely unaware of herself, who she was, or anything around her.

When she came to, she was in the exact same position she had been in: sitting on her bed with a dead hamster in her hands.

But something was different.

There was heat there, now, beneath the fur. A cool, blinding sting spread from the centers of her palms, through her veins, up her arms. It felt nice at first—fresh—and then it ached horribly.

She practically jumped when she felt movement in her hands.

Hervey squeaked quietly and snuffled at her fingers.

CHAPTER TWO

THERE WAS A LONG SILENCE. The hamster looked at Edie. Edie looked at the hamster.

"Hi, buddy," she managed, unsure of what else to say. The cold ache was fading through her shoulders and down her back, gradually lessening. "Were you sleeping?"

The hamster didn't say anything, so at least she knew this was still a reality she was somewhat familiar with. He just looked at her. She could see him inhale and exhale; his ears twitched, and his little black eyes were wide open.

"Okaaay…." She took a deep breath and slowly went to his cage, letting him down near the door. He hopped back in eagerly, retreating into his little hutch and hunkering down in the wood shavings. He looked scared, but alive. He had to be alive. He was moving and breathing. That was alive. He was alive.

But she'd been so sure—

Edie tried to shake the doubts from her head, latching the cage again. She sat back on her brocade bedspread and watched the hamster for a long while. *He was just in shock. That happens all the time with small pets. Maybe he was playing dead because he's in a lot of pain or something.*

She took her cellphone from her pocket, without taking eyes off the cage for too long. The browser was still open to the article on hamster illness that she'd found during her preoccupied shift. Technically, she wasn't supposed to have her phone out at work, but she'd told her boss there was a family emergency to keep track of.

It wasn't a *complete* lie. Hervey had come from a friend who simply hadn't wanted him anymore, and she'd felt sorry for the little guy, so she'd offered to take him in. Just her luck that he'd only gotten sick—or … whatever *this* was—when he'd come to live with her, after never needing medical attention in his life.

The internet said shocked hamsters would stop moving and feel cold to the touch. That was it. That was probably it.

"If he doesn't improve in thirty to sixty minutes, take your hamster in for veterinary care," she read aloud, if only to hear something besides him scratching at the wood chips in his cage and the thudding of her own heart.

Edie scrubbed her face with one hand. It was fine. It would all be fine. She just had to forget about that strange energy and her weird blackout. Life was stressful right now. She'd just made a mistake. Had panicked.

A loud *ping* from her phone startled her, numbing her already shocked system for a moment before she realized what it was. A message from Mercy had appeared in her notifications.

[Mercy Cedeno]: How is everything going?

The message appeared alongside Mercy's icon, a selfie: a woman a year or so older than Edie, with medium brown skin, round chocolate brown eyes, and voluminous, wavy pink hair that put Jem and the Holograms to shame.

[Edith Holloway]: Nice timing. Hervey just had an episode or something? …he was in shock, but he looks okay now.
[Mercy Cedeno]: really? :(Poor Hervey!! make sure he's nice and warm and tell me if you need anything from my room

Any herbal remedies Mercy might suggest would have to be a last resort. They might help a human feel better, but Edie wasn't sure they'd work on a small rodent.

[Edith Holloway]: How are things over there?
[Mercy Cedeno]: things are okay, just checking in before I go to bed <3

In Mercy-speak, that meant, *Don't bother me, I'm about to get laid.* Edie sent a thumbs up and set her phone aside.

One of her mom's old scarves hung over the towel rack on the back of her door. She grabbed it and draped it over the cage, hoping it would give Hervey some sense of security.

The texture of the scarf brought back memories of Mom. Should she call her? Did Mom even know she *owned* a hamster? She couldn't remember if she'd mentioned it, but probably not. They barely spoke.

Edie felt like she should talk to *someone*, but Mercy had gone to bed. There was no one else. Well, no one she felt comfortable texting in the middle of the night to talk to about her sick hamster. And even if there was, what would she tell them? *Hey, I'm totally not crazy or a weirdo but my hamster just came back to life and I'm kind of having a breakdown! How are you?*

She bundled up in bed, propping herself against the wall so she was facing the hamster cage. Though she tried to watch vigilantly, it wasn't long before she was almost too exhausted to even keep her head up.

It wasn't like she *wanted* to go to sleep—chills still ran up her spine, through her body. Maybe *Hervey* had just had an episode, but whatever had happened to *her* had been totally weird and definitely creepy. That blackout....

She'd passed out before, once. It had been at prom, and she'd been wearing a black velvet gown half her weight that she'd fasted all day to fit into. Turned out, humans needed food and water to live. She'd literally swooned in her date's arms, and he had promptly dropped her on the dance floor. She'd elected to skip prom the following year.

But this had been more than just passing out. The icy ache that had spread up her arms still stiffened her shoulders and neck. She felt sick herself. Surely, she couldn't have caught anything from the hamster. That was ridiculous. That was kooky 60s science fiction. *The Day the Hamsters Rose.*

Eventually, the gray and gold sunrise started to filter through her blinds. Edie realized with dull surprise that she hadn't slept in almost a full day, and with the light coming in, the empty apartment seemed less threatening.

Leaned against the wall at the head of her bed, she finally gave up and surrendered to sleep, those bobbing, hissing shadows still whispering behind her eyelids.

It wasn't until the next night that she noticed the smell.

When she got home from work, right away, she knew there was something off about the apartment.

To be fair, the apartment had never smelled *quite* right. Edie guessed that having a hundred different tenants over the years and no change of carpet would do that. Under Mercy's postmodern art and wreaths of flowers were cracking brick walls; under the smell of sandalwood and vanilla, a mildewy, musty scent lingered.

But this wasn't the slightly moldy smell Edie was used to. Sniffing her way through the house, she eventually traced the weird scent to her room. It was even worse there, though still vague enough for her to wonder what it was and where it came from.

As she approached Hervey's cage, the intensity of the smell mounted, and she coughed a little. It almost smelled like a mix of bad fish and very strong, cheap perfume. Edie peeked into the hamster cage, half-expecting to find him *really* dead this time.

But Hervey was there, awake and as alive as he'd been last night, sniffing at his water bottle and scratching at the wood chips under him. He looked fine, but the closer she got, the weirder he smelled.

"God, buddy, what did you get into?" After pausing a second to gather her courage, she opened the latch and carefully plucked him out. His fur still didn't feel right, and his eyes looked strangely glassy and gray. After last night, she had hoped he wouldn't still be sick, but she saw now that that was stupid.

She turned him over, noticing that he was flushed on his underside. It looked like he had a few open sores, too. She had no idea where they could have come from, but they looked nasty.

Holding Hervey close to her chest, Edie walked briskly down the hall, into the bathroom, and started to fill the sink with lukewarm water. Usually, the hamster loved baths, but as she moved to place him in the shallow water, he squealed and scrambled up her palm. Huddling against her wrist, he clung to her sleeve as if for dear life.

"Hey, it's okay! It's just water." She held two fingers under the running water, then brushed them over the fur of his back. His skin twitched in agitation, but eventually, he seemed to grow used to the feeling.

She helped him into the shallow pool, turned off the faucet, and got out the soft-bristled toothbrush she usually cleaned him with. She decided to forgo the hamster shampoo Mercy had concocted; since she didn't know what was wrong with him, it was probably best to avoid anything other than water.

The bath didn't go quite as expected.

Gently, she picked him up and turned him in her palm so she could brush his belly. But with the amount of skin that sloughed off of him, you'd think she was scrubbing him with industrial sandpaper. He didn't seem hurt, exactly, but was becoming increasingly annoyed as she handled him. He squirmed until she set him back in the water.

Between her fingers, there it was: a thin sheet of skin and hair.

It wasn't much; it wasn't his whole stomach, and she hadn't broken any of the weird blisters on his belly, but ... *holy shit. What the hell?*

Hervey was already scrabbling to get out of the water, so Edie quickly helped him out and wrapped him up in a hand towel. She rinsed off her shaking hands, drew out her cellphone, and called Mercy. They usually just texted, but she didn't think anything she tried to type right now would be comprehensible, especially not with still-wet fingers.

"Hello?"

Hearing her friend's soft, concerned voice relaxed Edie considerably, but she couldn't stop herself from shaking. Hervey was just a sick hamster, sure, but everything about the situation was ... off. And she was certain she'd just hurt him pretty badly, though he hadn't seemed to notice.

"Hi, um, so ... Hervey's, er ... skin is falling off?"

Mercy was quiet for a moment. *"What?"*

"Yeah, and he's got these sores on him, and ... I don't know what to do. Do I take him to the vet, or...?"

"Does it seem like he's in pain?" There was a shuffling noise and some distant voices, like Mercy had left a crowded room to move to a quieter one.

"Um, well, he— Probably? I brushed him and some came off. That had to have hurt...." Edie wrinkled her nose, never taking her eyes off the hamster, who was hunkered down on his hand towel, casually cleaning his face. Every so often, he'd look at her as if to say, *What? Why are you freaking out?*

"Oh, wow ... okay. How much came off?"

Edie looked down at the thin sheet of skin and hair in the basin. "Um, I don't know. Not that much. A couple layers?"

"Okay, and you said he has sores?"

"Yes, and his fur feels weird, and he smells really bad."

There was a long pause on the other end of the line. Edie even pulled away slightly to make sure she hadn't accidentally hung up, but then Mercy finally spoke. "Is— is he alive?"

What, did she think Edie couldn't tell the difference between a living and dead rodent? "He's moving around and breathing, so...."

Another long pause. "M'kay, he probably just has a skin condition.

Maybe that's why he's been acting so weird, because it was bothering him. Just make sure he's clean. And there should be some ointment in a little pink bottle behind the mirror." When Edie didn't say anything, Mercy added, flatly, "It's just antiseptic. You should use it."

Edie looked from the sink to Hervey. "Okay," she mumbled. "What if he gets worse?"

"Well." A sigh. "We can take him to the vet, but it's up to you. They'd probably give better advice than me. Oh, and don't forget to feed my fish, okay?"

Stupid fish. "Yeah, okay. I'll call later." After a second, Edie hung up.

She appreciated Mercy being there for her, but this was all a little much. She still couldn't spare more than maybe forty bucks; everything else had to go to her half of the rent, food, and utilities. At the moment, there wasn't any room for extras. She had to take care of herself. And after last night's weirdness, she wasn't even sure if she was fit to do *that*.

Like usual, she was stuck in a never-ending cycle of crap—a cycle she was at least partially responsible for. And it sucked.

Better feed the fish before I forget. It wasn't Mercy's or the fish's fault that life was coming at Edie a little too fast. She picked Hervey up, walked down the hall with him, and set him back in his cage.

She tried to shake off the feeling of creeping dread as she entered Mercy's room. Walls of pastel pink and deep blue greeted her, decorated with decals of purple cats, pentagrams, fish skeletons, and lots of stars. All the furniture was dark and modern, but the bedspread had Sailor Moon on it. Above the desk where Mercy kept her cacti garden was a wall of knives— mostly collector's pieces, made of out cool materials or intricately engraved, including a machete with a bone handle and a rainbow switchblade. It all amalgamated into an aesthetic Mercy liked to call "Mermaid Murder."

Edie called it confusing, but Mercy was happy, and that was all that mattered. At least Mercy knew who she was and what she liked, which was more than could be said for most people.

Edie crossed to the old-timey diving helmet her friend's betta fish called home, picking up the canister of fish food and crouching to sprinkle the flakes on the surface of the water.

She stopped short, almost dropping the canister.

The fish was floating belly-up.

CHAPTER THREE

FOR THE NEXT LITTLE WHILE, Edie kept to herself. She was withdrawn, almost paranoid after the last couple days, like she had a human body back at her apartment and not just a dead fish. As she rode the subway in to work, she tried to avoid eye contact with everyone else. *How many of these strangers know my dark, fish-murdering secret?*

Why were all the animals in her apartment getting sick and dying?

On top of everything, Nocturnem wasn't exactly a bright and happy place to be working. It was a dark, pretentious "draft haus" for dark, pretentious people—and it looked like an Addams Family fever dream, so Edie wasn't convinced going in would be conducive to a positive mental state. But it wasn't like she had a lot of choice.

At least she looked less out-of-place there than at Weiner's.

Nocturnem was below-ground, so it was nice and cool this time of year —late spring, when it was still breezy but the sun beat hot on the pavement. On the brick façade outside hung a sign with the name of the club in flowery gothic font. Below it was what looked to be the mouth of an alley that, when the sun set, would be lit up with eerie purple, red, and blue string lights.

But the "alley" wasn't as it seemed. Beyond the entryway was a thin, enclosed stairway leading from the main street down into a sort of switchback alley, its brick walls plastered with clear signage: NOCTURNEM DRAFT HAUS, 21 +, GIVE IN TO YOUR DARK FANTASY.

In online circles, it was considered to be one of the "realer" clubs in the area, clearly targeted to an overwrought goth audience. The entrance was way too sketchy for most "normal" clubbers, which was a draw for people who labeled themselves alternative. Nocturnem's preferred clientele liked the privacy—and probably the novelty—of a dark, underground den.

Live music wafted from the club as Edie pulled open the heavy door. A cool wave of air enveloped her as she stepped in, bracing herself for her double shift. First half, she was supposed to perform; second half, she'd be bussing, waitressing, and helping the bar. Maybe it wouldn't be so bad. Maybe she could even forget the craziness of the past couple days.

The club's main room looked like Alexander McQueen's "Horn of Plenty" and the Red Room from *Twin Peaks* had been thrown into a blender and then upended. Red velvet curtains lined and hid alcoves, lights were dim and obscured partially by cutouts made to look like the twisted limbs of dead trees. Everything was harsh and dark and sculptural. At the far end of the club, there was a stage where musicians or a DJ were usually on duty.

Even though Mercy was on vacation, Nocturnem's owner, Scarlet, expected DYSMANTLE to fulfill their obligation to perform—even if it meant Edie had to recruit another band to help her for the night. Mercy had told her that if she wasn't comfortable with it, they could try harder to cancel the gig. Truth be told, she *was* a bit nervous, but borrowing musicians wasn't anything new, considering it had been just the two of them for a while. And leading a performance would be a nice chance to prove she could carry herself.

Her heart sank when she saw only a handful of patrons milling around the club. But it was early. Maybe the crowd would fill out in the next half hour.

A girl could hope.

As she went to hang her leather jacket in one of the alcoves near the door, Edie threw a quick glance at the stage. Some guy in a sleeveless tailcoat was up on stage, crooning a Soap&Skin song into the microphone. She couldn't help but smile. As extra as the people here tended to be, it was sort of endearing. She watched, half amused and half embarrassed second-hand as the guy wailed at the crowd, brought to his knees by … some type of feeling. Kinda looked like indigestion.

Edie left the coat area and almost immediately bumped her guitar case against one of the creepy wicker mannequins that stalwartly guarded each alcove, another "charming" display of Scarlet's interior design skills. "S'cuse me," she mumbled, righting the mannequin and trotting behind the bar to shortcut her way backstage.

A person who called themself Klein was working the bar tonight. Edie wasn't sure of their gender, and frankly, she'd always been too embarrassed to ask. They were tall, thin, and androgynous in both build and manner, with long, platinum blond hair and myriad piercings and tattoos. Some people, Edie was sure, would have found them unsettling—but not here. Personally, she felt much more comfortable with them than she would have working retail with a bunch of soccer moms.

Klein gave Edie a knowing smile as she slipped by. "Some crowd tonight, eh, Edith? Scarlet is *so* generous."

She laughed and turned. "Shut up."

Klein shook their head, crouching to refill an ice bucket. "You're later than usual. Tsk."

Klein didn't co-own the bar or anything—they didn't even get along with Scarlet very well, from what Edie had seen—but they were here more than anyone else. Edie had never worked a shift where they weren't there. Actually, come to think of it, she'd never performed or visited on a night when they weren't there, either. If she didn't know any better, she'd have thought they were a sleepless vampire or something.

"I lost track of time. Family stuff." She paused. "I usually wouldn't take a second shift on a gig day, but I need the money."

Klein just raised their perfect platinum eyebrows and turned to hang up some martini glasses. They always had a way of prying details out of Edie without even saying a word.

"My hamster's sick, so I gotta take it to the vet."

"B'aww, poor guy. You better get moving, then. 'Mommy' won't be happy if her guests aren't entertained."

Edie cringed at the thought of her totally cringe-worthy boss and nodded. On the surface, Scarlet was quirky and interesting, though her latter-day Elvira aesthetic was campy at best (obviously, considering she'd named and furnished Nocturnem) and offensive at worst (who the hell wore overcoats made of Victorian straitjackets?). However, once you spent enough time with her—like, say, if you *worked* for her—you got to see another side. She was cold as ice, unforgiving, mean just for the sake of it, and vindictive like nothing Edie had ever witnessed before.

Her acrimoniousness seemed to have little basis in reality, but once her outer shell had been cracked, nothing she said could be untainted. God help Edie if she screwed up this performance.

"Go kick ass," Klein said, giving her a thumbs up with their right hand while they poured a shot of tequila with the other.

Well, at least Klein thinks I'll do a good job.

Guitar case bumping against her leg, Edie parted the thick velvet curtains that led to the employees-only area. It was dark, illuminated only by a porthole window on the kitchen door directly in front of her and a dim red light in the backstage area to her left.

Backstage was *cozy*, to put it politely, lit with tiny red lamps so the performers could see where they were going. There was enough room to store some props and change clothing if need be, but it wasn't big enough to loiter in. It extended beyond into a weakly lit, musty maintenance room containing a washer and dryer, a couple of industrial sinks, and cleaning supplies.

She made her way into the maintenance room and sat on the cement step in front of the washer and dryer. She didn't want to be in the way of the tailcoat singer when he exited stage.

Setting her guitar case next to her, she smoothed a hand over it—black leather with a little plaque inscribed with her name. It was the most expensive thing she owned. Dad had bought it along with her first bass guitar, a long time ago, but it didn't have a scratch on it. When she wasn't bumping into mannequins like an idiot, she took exceptional care of it.

Thinking of her dad always got Edie wrapped up in her own head. She went through the motions of getting ready for her performance: tuning up, looking over her set list without really reading it, taking out a compact to touch up her dark makeup. She was acutely aware of Richard Holloway's slate eyes, pointy nose and chin, and round cheekbones looking back at her in the mirror.

It had been an accident. He'd been driving too late, on a road he'd had no reason to be on. He'd crashed into a tree and died right there on the scene. Edie had always wanted to know more. Her mother had never allowed her to visit the crash site, had never allowed her to see Dad's body or even know the particulars of just *how* he'd died, thinking they'd only upset her further. Mom didn't understand that the things that gave *her* closure weren't the same things that gave Edie closure.

But then again, Mom didn't understand most things, especially when it came to Dad. One day, Edie had kissed him good night; the next morning, she'd been told she would never see him again, ever. That wasn't closure. That was raw loss.

There was so much about her that no one would ever know, so many memories only she and her father had shared. Now that he was gone, she was the only one. How could she explain what that felt like—to own memories that might as well have not even existed?

Nowadays, she was largely on her own. She tried to convince everyone that that suited her just fine. Mercy had plenty of family drama to revel in vicariously, anyway.

Edie was so distracted it took her a moment to notice that the mellow music drifting from the stage was no longer accompanied by the wailing tailcoat man. He retreated backstage, red-faced and dripping sweat, like a melting Robert Smith about to collapse and leave behind only flesh-goo and the remnants of his leather pants.

That meant she was up soon. Leading a band. Without Mercy.

Just because Edie wrote most of DYSMANTLE's original songs didn't mean she had the stage presence to carry a whole performance, but hopefully she'd do okay. Anyway, she couldn't back out now. The rest of the band—the one that had performed with Melting Robert Smith and had agreed to perform with her—was taking a break, but she only had a few minutes to prepare. Anxiety knotted in her stomach.

It was almost enough to make her forget the monstrosity waiting for her at home.

The crowd did not fill out. But by the time Edie's set was over, there was a decent wave of customers for a weekday night, so she was stuck waiting tables.

And, god help her, this week just kept getting weirder and weirder.

The two strangers had been there for a couple hours, now. There was something … out of place about them. The first was a young, tan white guy probably around her age, with a shaved head, a beard, and a seriously beefy build. The second was notably creepier: death-pale and skinny, ginger, wearing a T-shirt that was way too big for him and sagging jeans that he kept wiping his sweaty hands on.

They'd arrived about an hour into her shift and had been ordering drink after drink without ever seeming to get drunker. She'd had to stop serving them food when the kitchen closed for the night, and they'd only acted weirder since then—staring, mostly silent, and rude when she did get them to speak.

Edie was absolutely convinced that they were watching *her*, specifically.

The hamster, the fish, now this. It kind of made sense. If she was going to have a mental breakdown, of course it would come to a head at Nocturnem. The place didn't really lend itself to positive thought.

But she was starting to think the feeling that she was being watched was more than her brain stress-cannibalizing itself.

Working here, Edie saw all types of weirdos and freaks, and she got along great with most of them. But there was something different about these guys. They had an air about them that sent shivers up her spine. She had taken to retreating behind the bar whenever she could just to be away from them.

Klein didn't seem to mind her presence. As she clicked away on her phone, they were quiet, mixing and refilling drinks. Eventually, they turned to her and nodded over the bar. "Hey, those two creeps are looking around for you again."

"Great."

"I swear to god," Klein said, leaning against the back of the bar, "if they step out of line with you or one of the other customers, I'm going to kick their asses."

"Don't worry." Edie held a breath, rose, and turned to the shelf behind the bar.

There were a hundred bottles there, reflected in the diamond-shaped mirrors and twinkling in the dim light like a wall of stained glass. She grabbed a couple and prepared their drinks while trying to shake off their unwavering stares.

When the drinks were finished, she headed toward their table, dragging her feet at the thought of another uncomfortable exchange with them.

They were silent as Edie served them. Then she straightened up and looked between them. "Uh ... is there anything else I can get for you guys?"

They didn't say anything. They just stared at her.

"Oookay. Just let me know."

She was starting to back away from them when the skinny one made a strange noise deep in his throat, a sort of rumbling. She couldn't tell if it was a burp or a growl, but when she looked at him, his eyes were ... different than they had been. Something pale blue flashed in them, moved behind his glare like a living thing slithering through his skull.

Her heart began to thunder. On stage, the bass and the beat of the drums seemed to deepen and slow, stirring up a strange energy between her and the man sitting in front of her. It was as if time slowed around them. The room was getting darker, the shadows cast by the eerie tree cutouts becoming longer, raking over her.

A long, low note like a fog siren echoed in her mind, and in her peripheral vision, she could have sworn she saw the other man at the table ... change.

Was it just a trick of the light, or was his skin suddenly more like bone?

She jerked her head in his direction, but he looked as he had before. And with her gaze now broken from the other man, the yawning darkness subsided; the sounds of clinking glasses and the mellow beat of the music reached her again.

She didn't look at them. She couldn't. Turning tightly, Edie walked past the bar without acknowledging Klein and threw back the maroon curtains that led to the employees-only area.

She managed to make it to the adjacent wall before she sank down, clutching her head in her hands. Between this and what had happened the other night with Hervey, she was close to losing it. In fact, evidence would suggest she already had.

And she still hadn't told Mercy about her fish.

The anxiety was getting to her again. That had to be it. She'd been thinking a lot about Dad recently. The band wasn't going anywhere. Money was tight. She was exhausted and stressed, and she was starting to get confused.

"You feeling okay?"

Edie looked up to see Klein there, a bottle of water in one hand and a somewhat concerned look on their face.

After a moment of staring at them, she heaved herself to her feet. "Yeah, I'm fine. Just kind of stressed. And those guys aren't really helping. But I'm okay."

She averted her eyes when she noticed that Klein was looking her over with a quirked eyebrow, like they could see right through her. She was suddenly certain that if she looked them directly in the eyes, she'd die, like they were one of those cursed paintings or something.

Finally, with a sigh, they seemed to accept her answer. "Listen, why don't you go home early? Or at least go on your break." They glanced at their wristwatch and thrust the water bottle into her hand with a pat. "You know what, your shift's almost over, anyway."

She squeezed the bottle idly, trying to school her expression. Yep, totally fine. Nothing wrong at all. "You sure? You'd practically be alone."

Klein waved a hand. "Oh, phff. It's not likely to get any busier. I can handle myself. Besides, you look like you haven't slept in a decade. Go! Before I change my mind," they added teasingly.

Edie dropped her act. The sooner she could get out of here, the better. Wordlessly, she darted backstage to grab her guitar.

CHAPTER FOUR

THE NEXT NIGHT brought *another* long shift, but thankfully, the creepy strangers didn't show their faces.

At least, not at first.

It was around one in the morning when Edie finally started back home. The past couple nights had been a blur of working and taking sleep where she could get it. There was no reprieve from the bullshit in sight; Hervey wasn't getting any better, and her run-in with those creeps the night before had her looking over her shoulder at every little noise.

Noises really piled up when you lived in a city as big as Anster, Massachusetts. She was a wreck.

With the sun down, the pleasant heat of the spring day was gone, and her security had gone with it. The air was frigid as she walked, hugging herself around the middle to keep the broken zipper of her jacket closed.

Usually, if Mercy and her boyfriend Drake were free, they would meet her at the subway station and walk with her. But she was on her own tonight, and there were only so many groups of people she could follow before she got to her neighborhood. No city was exactly a safe haven—especially this late at night—and Edie didn't live in the friendliest neighborhood in the whole world, but she'd never felt uneasy like she did now.

She walked faster.

Her apartment entrance didn't face any main street; it was hidden a bit and could only be reached by an alley. The alley led into a yard that must have been a mews or garden a century earlier, and to what had once been the back door.

She lived at the end of a hallway with one other apartment, and that back door was the only way in. It was a nice set-up if you wanted some privacy, but the illusion of isolation in a big city gave her the creeps. It was like her apartment existed in a separate world.

Thinking about it as she walked alone unsettled her. She'd left behind the busy, taxi-filled streets, and her only thought was of getting home and locking the door.

Dread settled in her gut. Something was not right. Beyond her paranoia, something was ... wrong.

The feeling reminded her of Hervey's "episode," as she'd taken to calling it. It had been almost exactly three days since it had happened, and that short moment of time lost when she'd passed out still scared her. She slept with the blankets pulled up around her head; she'd started sleeping with a fan on to drown out the undertone of voices that babbled at her if she listened to the silence hard enough.

The more she listened, the louder the voices got, like they noticed that she could hear them.

She couldn't help but feel that what had happened with the fish hadn't been natural, either. Even worse, she couldn't help but feel that it was all her fault. The instinct didn't make a lot of sense, but she couldn't shake it. Dad had always said to follow her instincts. Though, to be fair, he probably hadn't meant, *Yeah, definitely reasonable to assume the reason your animals are all dying and going into shock is because everything you touch dies.*

The sense that she was just out of the reach of something—both in her subconscious and physically, there, on the sidewalk—made the hairs on the back of her neck stand up. She trotted a little faster in the direction of her apartment.

Eventually, she could see the building's front stoop sitting tantalizingly close, just across a paved playground. Normally, she wouldn't have cut through the playground—bushes and small maples lined one side, and it was pretty dark near the treeline—but she wanted to get inside as soon as possible.

She had almost reached the other side when something tore from the bushes behind her.

The sound of an animal's claws skittering on pavement broke the silence, and then a thud sounded as something fell heavily to the ground behind her. A wave of heat and foul breath followed and hit her in the back. She stumbled, caught herself, and froze.

Her instincts, if she could really trust those, told her a large predator had just dropped behind her.

But when she whipped around to face it, all she saw was the figure of a human man. He knelt on the ground as if to catch his breath, and a moment later, a second male figure sprinted through the bushes to meet him.

"Get up, he's coming!" the second man told the first urgently.

As the two turned, she could see them more clearly—and she recognized them.

The creeps from the bar.

Edie watched them, heart rate increasing. She couldn't just turn and run. They would notice and follow her, and her apartment was right there. No way she could lose them before she reached it.

It was a second before the first one recognized her. Something passed between them; recognition, anger, fear all shone in his eyes as he studied her. It was how she imagined she would look at her worst enemy. She returned the look with nothing but confusion, taking a few steps back.

The guy hoisted himself up with a little help from his ginger friend and muttered, "Don't worry. I held him up a mile or so back." He tossed his head in Edie's direction. "Look."

The ginger guy followed his motion and noticed Edie for the first time.

His face reflected a range of emotions similar to those of his friend, but his eyes looked hungrier, more frenzied. Out of control.

She didn't know why, but she knew they were after her.

They were coming closer. And as they approached, they seemed *taller* somehow, their eyes shadowed.

In that shadow, their faces ... changed. Their eyes darkened until only concentrated points of white light stared out at her, boring into her. A chattering sound like rattling bones rose with them as they became taller and thinner, their lengthening shadows throwing her into darkness. Limbs slimmed until they looked like the branches of dead trees; their faces were gaunt and ghastly, complexions sun-starved.

Edie was frozen, unable to comprehend what was happening. These weren't men anymore. They were completely different creatures.

Above her, something dripped from a mouth lined with long, razor-sharp needles. It oozed along her shoulder, and she moved only her eyes to watch the reeking substance glitter down her leather jacket.

Oh, god. It was *drool.*

She turned her eyes back to the things towering above her. They were morphing and changing and rasping, closing in.

And then a third figure—a figure glowing in the darkness—leapt over the bushes and touched down behind her.

CHAPTER FIVE

THE FIGURE behind Edie seized her by the arm and pulled her to the side. The quick movement caught her off guard, and she tripped over a curb, falling onto the concrete and smacking the back of her skull.

She didn't know if it was because of a head injury or the adrenaline that shot through her, but the few moments before she was able to pull herself upright felt more like a minute and a half. The world spun, bright light and white limbs streaking across her field of vision in a jumble. But even as things slowly came into focus, they still didn't make much sense.

The figure that had pulled her aside looked like a man and, unlike the monsters, stayed that way. He was tall and lean with smooth, cool brown skin. Dark hair, its auburn undertones evident in the light emanating from him, was slicked back out of his face—and he was dressed in what appeared to be armor: light-colored leather, chainmail, and silvery-white plates glistened back at her like a beacon in the night.

He was in a battle stance next to her fallen form, and as she gaped, he jerked forward like he was going to fling himself at the creatures.

"Hey!" She reached out and managed to catch his left hand.

When he whirled to snap, "Get out of my way!" she got a better look at his face. High cheekbones and narrow eyes—golden, brighter than she thought was humanly possible—with a long, downturned nose and a strong jaw.

"What are you *doing*?" she croaked, refusing to release him.

Even though the stranger was clearly positioned to defend her, he looked at her with hatred so pure it sent a shiver down her spine.

What the hell had she done to piss all these people off?

The monsters weren't blinded by the glowing man's arrival anymore and were starting to scramble away. He wrenched himself from Edie's grip with surprising strength. "I said get out of my way."

As she marveled at him, he flexed his now-free hand. A helix of light shot from it, coiling up his arm then back down to form a long, lucent blade of white-gold. He sneered as he looked her over one last time before throwing himself after the monsters.

She couldn't see him clearly—he and the beasts moved so quickly, tangled together—but she couldn't help but stare. He had confronted two seven-to-eight-foot-tall monsters without a moment's hesitation. And, from what she could make out, he was now *climbing* them, slashing at their spidery limbs with a chilling efficiency. They moved erratically with their new challenger, but he was fast.

Edie exhaled sharply. He was going to get himself killed. What they needed to do was *run*.

But the man didn't give her so much as a glance, and before she could cry out again, he and the creatures were engulfed in a blinding aura of light so bright it left black spots in her vision.

Her mind whirled. The light had come *from* the man.

Edie turned over and scrambled to get her legs underneath her, struggling with shaking knees until she was able to take off in the direction of her yard. She didn't dare look back, but she could hear and see more bursts of light. Each one stung her back, scorching choppy shadows onto the pavement and momentarily blinding her.

She found herself fleeing face-first into the brick wall of her apartment building. *Very graceful.*

There was no time to regroup. She ignored the throbbing pain all over her body and staggered into the alleyway. With shuddering breaths, she felt her way to her apartment door, leaving the sounds of battle behind.

And then, as soon as she slammed her door closed, the noises stopped.

The floorboards beneath her squeaked as she slid down her door and sat, curled against it in stunned silence. Her breath was raspy and labored like a half-drowned woman's; her hair, jostled from its bun, fell in a black curtain around her face. Her stomach ached, and her back and face burned like she'd just spent a couple hours at the beach without sunscreen. The black spots in her vision lingered as she looked around her apartment.

Everything was just as it was supposed to be. Everything was normal.

She wheezed again, coughed, and started to weep fearful tears.

I'm going crazy.

When Edie finally calmed down enough to check on Hervey, she found him in rough shape.

For one thing, his tail had fallen off, along with a good portion of his fur. His sores were an angry red, and the skin surrounding them was tinged with the beginnings of what looked like bruises. Foamy stuff was coming from … somewhere, and he smelled like low tide. It was awful.

As bad as she felt, she couldn't handle being in the same room as him. The smell was too overpowering. She laid a towel down on the coffee table in the living room and set the cage there, then knelt beside it to get a better look at her unfortunate little friend.

Though his balance had been thrown off by the loss of his stubby tail, he trundled around his habitat slowly, completely unbothered but perambulating like a heavy Jim Henson puppet. It would have been funny if the entire situation hadn't been completely fucked up.

Scrolling through her phone, she couldn't find anything online to explain his illness. Her best guess was that he had some kind of skin condition or … *ugh*, mites. By the time she was satisfied with her research, it was almost 2 a.m.

She would have to take Hervey to the vet clinic in the morning. Screw the band fund. Mercy would understand, and they'd save up more money eventually. She couldn't let Hervey suffer like this.

"You stay out here for now, buddy." Edie covered the cage with another towel, all the while holding her breath, and triple checked the front door lock before shutting herself up in her room. Hervey would have to stay in the living room for the night. No way she'd get any sleep if he stayed in her room.

Not that I'm likely to get much sleep anyway, she thought as she locked her bedroom door and shoved a box in front of it.

Though she had tried to distract herself from what had happened in the park by worrying over the hamster, she was still trembling. Nothing seemed to be making sense, and she was exhausted from working herself too hard, and Mercy would be back tomorrow, and they had a gig that night at some new bar she'd never even heard of—*and* Edie didn't particularly feel like going back to work and possibly getting attacked again.

She didn't know what those monsters—and that radioactive man—had against her, but she wasn't excited to find out.

Edie groaned and lay face-down on her bed, wishing it would swallow her up so she could become one with the mattress instead of dealing with her onslaught of problems, both mundane and batshit.

After a moment, she propped herself up and listened closely. The sounds of the fight she'd fled from earlier were long gone and the regular sounds of the city had replaced them: nighttime traffic, wind, the monorail that ran past her neighborhood.

Maybe she'd misunderstood what she'd seen. But how could that even be possible? How the hell could you *misunderstand* two giant monsters and a glowing guy coming out of nowhere to fight them?

It was hard to ignore the sting on her face and back, too. Physical proof.

Every bone in her body ached for sleep, but she was so shaken up she didn't know if she could. At least, not without a little help.

Edie glanced at the bottle of sleeping supplements on her bedside table.

The most she'd ever taken at once was two, and that had been more than enough.

She took three, turned off the light, and buried herself in blankets.

CHAPTER SIX

THERE WAS NOTHING. Then, all at once, she became aware of the feeling of something fluttering against her cheek.

Edie opened her eyes to a world thick with white. Little tufts fell from the sky, so slow and light that she thought they were cotton at first.

It took a moment for her to adjust and realize she was lying on her stomach in a small clearing. The darkness of the unknown beyond her patch of moonlight was palpable. Even though only a soft gray filtered through the flurries of snow, the trees closest to her, grotesquely gnarled and struggling to reach toward the sky, were as solid and black as ink in the foreground of her vision.

Under her fingers, she could feel the give of the freshly fallen snow, the way it stuck to the grooves of her palm as it melted. It was cool, but not frozen—not as cold as snow should be.

Slowly, she sat up. The snowflakes falling on her cheeks and in her hair melted once she moved, like they were living creatures she had scared away. Instead of leaving behind water, they almost seemed to move through her, like they had bored tiny holes into her skin.

Where am I?

Though her other senses were muted, everything *looked* so detailed, so real. Should she call out? Would anyone hear? The silence here was so pervasive and heavy she wasn't even sure the sound would reach her own ears.

Edie stood, wiping her numb hands down her front. What was she even wearing? Some kind of heavy, velvety cloak, it felt like. Definitely not the flannel pajamas she had gone to sleep in. She was about to investigate further when a startling noise cut through the silence.

A long, loud howl.

It *shattered* the silence, more accurately. As though the wolf's throaty call had ripped away a layer of haze over her mind, she was suddenly aware of the other sounds of the dark forest: Trees trembling under the weight of new-fallen snow, the weak whisper of a stream nearby, birds in the distance, her own ragged breathing, and the hissing of blood through her ears.

The clearing suddenly felt too small, like it was the mouth of a huge animal, slowly closing in on her. Edie whipped her head around, trying to find a path out. All the trees seemed to be uniformly packed, thinning nowhere. There was no road to where she stood.

She'd have to pick a direction and just *go*.

She had lived in the city all her life. The only forests she'd ever visited were national parks with carefully marked trails. Even when the trails were tough and the trees were thick, they were never like this. Edie struggled to weave between the inky sentinels, their bark so black she couldn't make out any grooves or knots.

The further she went, the harder it seemed to move at all, as though friction in the air itself was slowing her down. She worked her legs, unsure of where she was headed. No noise seemed to come from any specific direction. How was she even supposed to track how far she had traveled?

She finally called out, voice already raw with panic, desperate to hear something other than the crunching of snow and the vague whisper of water. *Am I even hearing a stream or is that people talking?* she wondered. "Hello?"

The second the sound left her lips, she felt a thousand gazes on her, as though she'd committed some forest faux pas by yelling and drawing attention to herself. Every knot in every tree was like an eye, watching her progress and judging her; some seemed amused at how lost and confused she was, some irritated that she was there at all, others impassive and emotionless.

"Hello?!"

Another howl, this one deeper. And closer.

You should find it. Edie wasn't sure where the idea came from. The only wolf she'd ever seen had been behind Plexiglass at some nature reserve when she was, like, eight. But the answer seemed so simple now that it had presented itself. *Find it.*

Her body moved without consulting her mind: She took a deep breath and tipped her head back, then loosed a howl of her own.

The foreign sound coming from her own chest frightened her even more than the wolf had, made her heart beat faster.

Fuck. Why the hell did I do that?

Complete silence answered her call. No snow fell from boughs, no branches creaked, no birds crowed, no whispers reached her ears. The gazes she had felt looked beyond her, now … as if they, too, waited for a response.

She was about to give up and start walking again when she noticed two points of light in the brush.

Fires? They flickered and slowly came closer, but the perspective was all wrong.

They changed rapidly, ducking, and she realized they were nested in the skull of something stalking her.

A white wolf bared its teeth.

Edie awoke in a cold sweat, looking around her dark room. Groggily, she pressed the home button on her phone, which was nestled in the covers near her side, and checked the time. It was around five in the morning, but it was still dark out.

She groaned and turned over in bed. Her throat ached, her mouth suddenly unbearably dry and thirsty. *Great. I'll never be able to get back to sleep with a sandpaper throat.* She glared at the ceiling for a while, trying to conjure up the will to get out of bed—and the courage, considering she ought to lock herself in her room and never come out after the night she'd had.

And she'd have to get up in a few hours to take Hervey to the vet. *Ugh.* Just the thought of it made her head ache. But the sooner she got up and went pee and got something to drink, the sooner she could get back to sleep.

She forced herself to sit up and swing her legs over the edge of the bed.

The moment her feet touched the carpet, she knew something was wrong.

A strange power rumbled within the floor, a vibration traveling into her body and through her nervous system. She was sure she'd never experienced it before, and yet it was oddly familiar.

It was *almost* the same feeling she'd had when she'd touched Hervey. When she'd passed out.

She sat for a moment, eyes wide, letting her body acclimate to the hum until it eventually faded into the background like a heartbeat. No matter how long she sat there and waited for it to go, it remained.

There was something in the apartment.

How she knew that was anyone's guess—but she *knew.* Trying not to make any noise, she slowly rose and crossed to the locked door. She could feel the same strange vibrations from the other side, getting stronger the closer she came. Listening at the door, she could hear shuffling ... the sound of Hervey moving around in his cage, faintly ... and...

Someone coughed. It was a hacking cough, distinctly male.

Edie covered her mouth, body going numb and cold in an instant. Was it the glowing man? One of the monsters?

I locked the door. I locked the freaking door. Whoever it was, they had forced their way in to get to her.

At least on the playground she'd had somewhere to run. Her room only had one door, and one window above her bed that was way too small for her to fit through.

She had to find a weapon.

She dropped silently to a crouch, trying not to trip on her sweatpants as she crawled across her bedroom floor, looking for something—anything— she could use to defend herself.

Looking around the room, she could only see a few things she was sure could at least keep her attacker at arm's length: her bass guitar, a plastic axe that had been sitting in the corner of her room since last Halloween, and ... a bottle of nail polish remover.

Oh, Jesus. If only she'd taken up knife collecting.

Although ... the nail polish remover wasn't that bad an idea, actually. If she could splash it in the guy's eyes, she could run into Mercy's room and get a proper weapon, or just straight up run out of the apartment.

Edie grabbed the bottle and tested the weight anxiously before carefully twisting the cap off.

Creeping to the door, she toed the box in front of it out of the way and reached out with her free hand. As she slowly lifted the hook-and-eye lock, metal scraped against wood, and she held her breath.

No reaction from the other side of the door. She could still hear the intruder moving around out there, clearing his throat, but he hadn't noticed that she was awake. Yet.

With her free hand, she gripped the doorknob, trying not to let it slip from her sweaty palm.

You've got this. Get a move on. It was only a matter of time before whoever was out there decided he was tired of waiting and tried to come into her room.

Okay. One—

Two—

She turned the knob, and it practically vibrated in her palm.

Three.

She flung the door open.

Almost immediately, any plan Edie had had for attacking the trespasser fell to the floor along with her bottle of nail polish remover.

She had never seen a decaying human body before, but there was no mistaking what she was looking at. Sitting on her couch, fully animated and glowering at the hamster cage in front of it, was a corpse.

CHAPTER SEVEN

THE CORPSE LEANED FORWARD, resting its elbows on its knees, and continued to glower at Hervey.

She thought it was male, but it looked like it had stepped right out of *The Walking Dead* season five: Sallow, stretched skin was pulled tight and peeling over the valleys of its face, and she could see the leathery red muscles of its substantial biceps; the larynx was visible, and there was nothing but wisps of dark hair on a flaking scalp. Its torn, chapped lips were twisted in a sneer, and the angry crease between its brow wrinkled the bridge of a nose that had long ago rotted away, leaving a torn and gaping hole.

After a second, the corpse stood, and she was able to get a better look at its body. It was well over six feet tall and built like a Marine. But despite its appearance, its clothes *weren't* tattered like it had just risen from the grave. It wore a tight white T-shirt with a pair of army-green cargo pants, and worn Carolinas with the thickest rubber sole she'd ever seen.

"The fuck'd you do to this hamster?" it asked, gesturing sharply to Hervey's cage. Its voice put Tom Waits to shame—the voice of someone who smoked twenty packs of cigarettes a day, ate nail sandwiches, and chased them down with cement-gravel cocktails.

The fact that it was talking was only the first problem in a string of at least fifty, however.

Edie pressed up against her bedroom door, glancing at the hamster cage. Her voice came out smaller than she anticipated, considering she felt like shrieking at the top of her lungs. "He's ... he's sick."

The zombie—what else could she call it?—looked at her like she had just said the stupidest thing it had ever heard. It rolled its milky eyes and grimaced. "Well, ain't you just the slickest little shit? When'd he die?"

"He ... didn't. He's ... I don't know, he has some kind of"—she winced, trying to keep her voice from rising in pitch—"skin condition." *Am I really getting chastised by a* Fallout *Ghoul right now?* "What— *Who* are you? What are you doing here, what do you want?"

As she asked, she was reminded of what she'd witnessed on the playground just a few hours ago. This had to be related. So many weird things couldn't just *happen* to one person for no reason. And now, here she was with a Romero reject in her living room, criticizing her ailing hamster.

Maybe this was a nightmare, too. She preferred the wolf, if she was honest.

The zombie looked at her for a moment before sitting back down, taking out a pack of Newports, and lighting one up. Judging by the look on what was left of its face, this was going to be a long night.

She dared to raise her voice. "This is a no-smoking apartment." The least of her worries, but it was the only sentence she could form coherently.

The zombie turned up its palms and raised its voice along with her: "Do you ever do anything besides bitch?"

Whatever this thing was doing in her living room, it was on the fast track to getting a kick in the ass.

As it ashed its cigarette directly on the glass coffee table, Edie noticed a few used butts there, too. How long had it been sitting there, waiting? It looked up at her, and their eyes met squarely for the first time.

The zombie was slightly wall-eyed, but then again, it was probably an achievement that it had eyes left in its head at all. They were also the bluest eyes she had ever seen, even as cloudy as they were—and there was something in the pits of them, like a little glowing light in the back of the skull.

He said, "My name's Calcifer."

Looking him in the face sent panic racing from Edie's gut and up her throat. The awful sight of him was catching up to her, making her slightly dizzy with shock.

And now that she was looking more closely, she noticed that he had a sawed-off shotgun strapped to his right thigh.

She choked back nervous bile, her heart speeding up. "Get— get out of my house."

Calcifer stood. She knew she would never be able to take him. Jogging was about all she had in her exercise repertoire, and she was only five foot five. This guy looked like he wrestled bears for sport.

"You can just call me Cal," he continued casually, as if she hadn't said a thing. "Actually, yeah, call me Cal. Edith, right?"

He knew her name.

She had to get him out of here.

Edie didn't give him any time to pull his gun. She kicked the coffee table forward, toppling Hervey's cage and hitting Calcifer in the shins, throwing him off balance. He staggered and fell backward onto the couch with a grunt.

It would only take him a moment to recover, but it gave her enough time to rush to Mercy's room and slam the door behind her. She scrambled for the lock before remembering that Mercy didn't have one.

"Piss off!" Edie shouted through the door as she crossed the pastel room and grabbed a bowie knife the size of her arm. "Whatever you are, get the hell out of my house!"

She didn't have to wait long for the zombie to follow her. He forced the door open, leading with a revolver she hadn't noticed before. When he saw her knife, however, he lowered it slightly. The bemused look on his face bordered on cartoonish.

"Huh. Where the hell'd you get that?"

"Go away!" Edie took another step back, holding the knife out with both hands. "I'm going to call the police if you don't leave right now!"

The zombie glared, baring his stained teeth. "Oh, cut the shit. What, did Daddy teach you to act like an idiot? You can manipulate people better that way?"

Daddy? *Her* dad? Edie felt herself begin to tremble. "Wh— What? He has nothing to do with this!"

"Ha! That's cute." Calcifer's grin was full of disdain. "The hamster's just the start, and we both know it, kid. Guess I shouldn't've expected you to be any better than him."

Click.

"I didn't haul my ass cross-country to have a tea party with a baby necromancer. The world'll be better off without you."

He raised the revolver, glaring down the barrel at her.

I'm going to die.

She'd never considered what dying might be like—which, now that she thought about it, wasn't very goth of her. Millennial ennui prevented her from imagining a life for herself beyond her twenty-somethings, but that wasn't quite the same thing.

As her thundering heartbeat drowned out all coherent thought, she realized that even at her most depressed, she'd never *really* wanted to die. It was just talk.

She wasn't ready.

Edie felt her anger and fear curl up in her chest and shake like a geyser about to burst. She looked past the barrel of the revolver, glaring at the points of light in the centers of the zombie's pupils. A strange energy built inside of her before finally culminating in a raw, angry shout like a punch:

"*Stop!*"

At that moment, pressure she hadn't even known was there was released. It was sudden and satisfying, like she'd just popped her spine after a long day at work.

Calcifer's arms went limp and dropped to his sides. Edie watched as his gaze became unfocused for a moment.

Then he straightened up, tucked his revolver at the small of his back, and shook his head hard.

"Okay ... fine," he finally muttered, backing up through the doorway with his eyes downcast and his jaw clenched tight. "I'm going."

Edie didn't move. Between the unfamiliar energy she felt inside and the fear, she couldn't. He still had time to pull his gun again and turn her into Swiss cheese, so she stayed on guard.

But he didn't make any move to attack her. He just kept backing up until he was out of her sight. After a few moments, she heard him shuffle out the front door and slam it behind him.

Edie stood still, silent, for what felt like an hour before she finally dared to creep out of the room. No one came, no one grabbed her from behind. She was alone.

Hurriedly, she locked the front door and retreated to the living room, not taking her eyes off the door except to check on Hervey. He had weathered his fall from the coffee table in no worse shape than he'd already been in—though that was very bad shape, indeed.

What ... the hell ... was that?

The zombie had looked so defeated. But that didn't make any sense; *he* had been the one waving the firearm around. All she'd had was a knife she didn't even know how to use. Sure, she'd been fired up, but she was short and noodle-armed. She'd never pose even a bit of threat to ... what was his name? ... *Calcifer*, no matter how angry she got.

The world will be better off without you, he'd said.

She was pretty sure he'd really meant to hurt her.

What had she done to change his mind?

Zaedicus Oldine swirled his heavy goblet, scanning the underbelly of The Ash Wyrm Club. He drummed his fingers impatiently on the arm of the high-backed chair in which he sat, occasionally pausing to dig his nails into the leather.

Where were those damned wraiths? Surely, Holloway could not have escaped them herself. And, surely, he had dispatched them too quickly for the Aurora to capture her first.

He sighed into his goblet and took a sip of the smooth liquid. Refreshing. Most other high-wights had to make do with feeding on the blood of humans and other lesser races. The blood of ljósálfar—light elves, the race he'd been in life—was much rarer, and so much more satisfying.

After several centuries of being confined principally to the indoors and the night, Zaedicus took simple pleasures where he could. He was barely recognizable as an elf anymore, and was often mistaken for a lowborn døkkálfr—dark elf—due to his ashen complexion and pale eyes.

Him, one of those tunneling savages? Ridiculous.

No one who made that particular mistake ever made it again, one way or the other. Death was cheap, and being a wealthy member of the Gloaming had its advantages.

The disadvantages, on the other hand, were numerous. Especially these days.

He brushed his sheet of silver hair over one shoulder and gazed around the club again, fresh disgust twisting his gaunt face. On display before him were the remnants of a faction that had once been magnificent. Clusters of the once-great races of the Nine Worlds—living and undead alike—were sprawled across velvet couches; they indulged in the libations and entertainment The Ash Wyrm provided, most of them occupied with a companion or thrall of some other race. It was a relaxed, almost sensual scene.

And it was *pitiful*.

There was nothing mighty about this. This was unrecognizable as the Gloaming he'd once known, and it had become even worse since Gloaming Lord Fahraad's death. These degenerates had simply holed up in their dens for fear of their Auroran enemies' opposition, with nothing to do but wallow in their decadence.

At least when Zaedicus indulged in such things, he knew he had earned the privilege. He doubted any of the beings surrounding him were thinking about the discovery of the Holloway girl—despite the announcement he had made regarding her. They cared more for personal gratification than moving forward.

Idiots. Didn't they remember what had happened to Richard Holloway, how close Lord Fahraad had been to swaying him to their side? And didn't they remember what had happened when he'd ultimately refused?

Didn't they understand how important this was?

How ironic that, ten years later, Fahraad had made the same mistake as Richard Holloway. Things were changing; there was a new player, someone more powerful than the Gloaming Lord could have comprehended.

The Wounded.

Fahraad had refused to turn with the tide, had refused the Wounded's generous offer—and now he was dead after an unfortunate, *opportune* run-in with the Aurora.

The thought brought a tight smile to Zaedicus's lips.

"Lord Oldine?"

He looked up to see someone standing there. It was a woman, dressed in a tight black dress that covered her up to her throat but afforded a surprising view of her long legs. She had the deathlike pallor and sloe-black eyes of a human-wight. *Vampire*, they called themselves. A lowly race compared to high-wights like himself, but they served their purpose.

He decided to hear her out. "Yes?"

"Someone's here to see you. They used the back door upstairs." She raised her brows.

He could see that she thought it strange. He had to agree. Anyone who had any *real* business seeing him would have used the entrance directly into the private, VIP floor of the club. "I see. And who is this person?"

She shrugged a shoulder. "Some wraith."

The wraiths. Zaedicus straightened up in his chair and set his goblet aside, signaling one of his enthralled human guards over. They exchanged words briefly, and with a wave of Zaedicus's hand, the room was cleared of guests.

Only he and the human-wight remained, for now. He studied her closer. Human aging had always baffled him, but if he had to guess, he'd say she had been approaching her mid-thirties when she'd died. Her hair was black, her lips red and smiling. Zaedicus couldn't help but feel a prickle of disgust at her appearance. *So human.*

"Thank you, vampire. You were brave to come down here and alert me." Either she was very brave or didn't know her place. The upper floor was for the common Gloaming, and she certainly was that. "What is your name?"

"Scarlet."

Scarlet. He waved a hand. "Begone, and I will see to it that you are compensated for delivering the message."

She said nothing, but as she turned and climbed the stairs to the main level, she glanced back over her shoulder at him. Her look was equal parts solemn and curious.

Odd woman.

Before he could ruminate further, his doorway was darkened once more.

The wraith struggled down the stairs. It was a pitiful sight, stuck halfway between its human and true form. Its skin was stretched and scarred and covered in pale, branch-like appendages which shot from pockets in the flesh. Its glassy eyes searched the darkness almost blindly; claws of bone protruded from finger- and toenail beds. Needle teeth cut through its twisted mouth, and, branching out from its chest like lightning … scorch marks.

The Aurora.

"My, but what have you done?" Zaedicus mumbled, staying seated as the thing limped its way over to prostrate itself before him.

"Master," it said, "I'm dying."

The high-wight sighed. "Let me see." He stood and took the wraith by its chin, lifting its head so he could examine its body more closely. What little human flesh wasn't torn was burnt and bubbling. Zaedicus's hand dropped to the strange scorch mark in the middle of the wraith's chest, just below the solar plexus.

"No!" croaked the creature. "Don't take it out. If you take it out, I'll die."

Zaedicus raised a brow, but indulged his thrall for now. He removed his hands, looking down at the pitiful creature. "Where is the girl? Don't tell me you lost her."

The wraith was either unable or unwilling to meet its master's eyes. It was looking at the floor, snarling and snapping in animal pain. It finally managed, "We found her, started to follow her home … but we met an Auroran looking for her, too.…"

"Did you recognize them?"

"No … but his eyes glowed like the sun. He … unleashed himself, burned us."

Zaedicus tilted his head and took the wraith by the chin again, checking its wounds once more. Clinically, he prodded the boils covering some exposed flesh. No, blisters. Indicative of the radiant magic of an Auroran vivid. The holy power of the sun.

"Keep going," he said over the wraith's whimpers of pain.

"He killed the other. I barely escaped."

Zaedicus doubted it had been much of an escape. More likely, the vivid had allowed the wraith to live so it could relay the tale. Nonetheless, there were more important things to deal with than the Aurora's arrogance. "And the girl? Focus!"

The wraith snarled at the ground. Its movements had become jerkier. The pain was overtaking its logical brain.

"Focus," the high-wight said again, gripping his thrall's deformed shoulders.

"She … ran. She had already left and run away.…"

Fear mounted in Zaedicus's chest. "Surely, you must have followed her. Even in this state, you could bring her to me. Surely, you know where she is, at least."

"I tried to wait, but.…"

"But what?" His voice was strained, betraying his fear. This worthless thing better not have lost the girl's trail—for both their sakes.

The wraith wheezed, grating out, "The again-walker. He came, he found her. I tried to come to you as soon as I could...."

No. That couldn't be. The zombie was supposed to be across the country, sucking the Holloway inheritance dry and staying out of the way. He had no business with Edith. Zaedicus would have thought he wouldn't *want* any business with her, considering how much he despised her father.

This had never been a consideration. There was no plan for this contingency. The Gloaming had let the rotter go because they had known he would never come back.

Now that he was here, what could it mean? Could it be—

Zaedicus laughed at the thought, dropping his thrall to the ground. No, it was impossible. Not even a necromancer could resurrect the Reach.

For over a millennium, the Gloaming's expansion had been impeded by the "neutral" Reach, but its fracturing and ultimate demise had brought on a new age. Reconstructing the faction had been Richard Holloway's pipe dream, and the experiment had died with him. There would be no coming back. There was no chance.

But there is, said something inside of him. There were good reasons he'd been tasked with capturing Edith. Her raw power alone.... But the Wounded wasn't the only one who could use her. If conscripted, she might revivify the Reach as surely as she could the Gloaming.

All at once, things made sense. The Reach—whomever that consisted of now—must have her.

The Wounded would be furious. Zaedicus had to set this right before his lord found out, or his punishment would be unspeakable.

"I will have someone scry for her again," he whispered, mostly to himself. "And I will send someone more competent to collect her."

The wraith's whimpering distracted his thoughts. He turned his attention to it sharply.

"What are you blubbering about?"

"It hurts, Lord Oldine."

Zaedicus had no doubt. He glanced down at the scorched fissure in the wraith's chest and thrust his fist inside.

The creature howled in pain as deep orange embers spurted from the fissure. He gripped the wraith by one shoulder and eased his hand further in, until his fingers wrapped around something smooth.

It was white-hot. Agony seared through Zaedicus as he touched it. It was as if the sun itself was lodged in this wraith's chest cavity.

A holy boon, like a bomb, meant to implode the creature. Meant to send a message.

Zaedicus steeled himself and tore it out.

CHAPTER EIGHT

WHEN MERCY ARRIVED HOME, Edie was bundled on the couch in a pile of blankets and pillows that resembled a snail's shell, fast asleep and drooling on herself. It was about five in the afternoon. Not exactly a normal time for anyone to sleep in till, but then again, she hadn't meant to fall asleep at all.

After that zombie had broken into the apartment, she'd refused to go to bed. Even when the sun had finally come up, she had stayed at her post, eyes on the locked door. She wasn't sure when she'd finally succumbed to exhaustion, but she remembered thinking about having lunch before she'd decided to "rest her eyes for a second," so it must have been around noon.

In her half-dreaming state, she could vaguely hear the TV, still on the same channel she'd been stalwartly watching all night: the local news. So far, no coverage of a zombie apocalypse.

The couch shifted as Mercy managed to negotiate a few inches of it for herself, and Edie felt a cool breeze brush her face as her friend reached out and shook her gently. "Edie … hey, Edie? I'm home!"

Edie groaned and sat bolt upright, her cave of blankets collapsing behind her. At once, she was tense and ready to run—but when she saw Mercy, she relaxed again, rubbing her face. "Oh. Yay. How was your trip?"

Mercy ignored the question, brushing her lion's mane of bubblegum pink hair over her shoulders. "Are you feeling okay? Your eyes are all bloodshot. And— ew, your blanket is soaking."

Edie looked down at her primary shell of duvet and cringed as she touched it. "Sorry."

"No! I'm not angry, I'm just worried. Are you sick?" Mercy sniffed the air. "What's that smell?"

Edie stiffened. *Hervey. Dammit.*

"Edie? What's with the smell?" Mercy persisted, waving to draw her friend's attention back to the matter at hand.

Edie was too exhausted to do anything but tell the truth. "Um ... it's Hervey."

Mercy wrinkled her nose. "That's *him*? Are you *sure* he's alive?"

Edie gestured to his cage, which still sat on the coffee table. "He's been up and moving around all night. I don't know what's wrong with him."

Well, she had an idea, but it was so crazy it wasn't even worth talking about.

Mercy shifted a little to take a closer look, pinching her nose. "Are you going to take him to the vet?"

"I was," Edie said, sighing and reaching back to reconfigure her messy bun. Compared to Mercy—who was travel-chic as hell with her wide-brimmed black hat, matching round sunglasses, and velvet leggings—Edie looked like she'd just escaped from a serial killer's basement. "I was going to do it today, but it's probably too late..."

"There's an emergency night vet a couple blocks away," Mercy said, shrugging one shoulder. She gave Edie another once over before quirking an eyebrow. "But you don't look so hot, girl."

"Thanks."

"I could take him?"

Edie took a deep breath, then pushed it out aggressively, flopping onto her best friend's lap with a groan. "I dunno. Maybe. I just really feel like shit."

"I can tell." Mercy smiled, patting her friend, and reached for the remote. She wrinkled her cute, round nose before changing the channel. "What were you doing watching the news all night?"

What was she even supposed to tell her? *Oh, I just got attacked by monsters only to be saved by a radioactive man. Also, a zombie broke into our house last night and I was too scared to go to bed. Oh, and my hamster maybe died and now his skin is falling off. By the way, I killed your fish.* Instead, she just shrugged. "I'm, uh, just really stressed out about Hervey."

"Mmm." Mercy looked at the hamster hunkered down in his cage and shook her head. "Edie, you didn't even ask for this. We were just supposed to watch him for a few weeks and then Kyle, like, forced him on you."

"I guess," Edie mumbled, though she knew Mercy was right. She'd never had a rodent before, so she had *always* kind of been guessing at how to take care of him.

Mercy slid off the couch, crouching in front of Edie and taking both of her hands. She'd always been the better friend, *and* she'd always been three steps ahead of Edie in terms of adult life, always prepared and independent and confident in herself. She was lucky on that front. Edie hoped she knew that.

"Listen," Mercy said, taking off her sunglasses. Her brown gaze was soft. "You're obviously stressed already, so I'll take him to the vet, okay? You just hang here, or go out and *do* something to try and get your mind off it, okay?"

Edie looked away, uncomfortable with the raw concern she saw in her friend's eyes considering she wasn't telling her the whole truth. She made a vague noise and chewed on her lip, which Mercy apparently decided to take as consent.

Mercy rose and turned to Hervey, throwing a discarded towel over his cage before taking out her cell and dialing the emergency vet's number. Her conversation with the secretary was a dull drone as Edie curled back up on the couch, pulling her cave of blankets back over her head.

If Mercy left, would the zombie be back? Edie's heart raced just thinking of that possibility. Her friend was right; she had to get out of here and do something. There was no way anyone could follow her all around the city. She'd take the subway across town and go to a park or something. She'd spend some time alone—truly alone, with no stalkers breathing down her neck.

"I'm heading out!" Mercy called from the door. Hervey's cage rattled as she maneuvered it through the doorway

Edie just moaned in response and closed her eyes.

She couldn't shake the feeling that the zombie would be back. She couldn't stand to be in this apartment anymore.

At least Mercy hadn't noticed the lingering smell of nail polish remover.

Edie was in the park when she got the call.

The sun was only just starting to go down, and she was starting to truly enjoy her time alone. And she was sure she *was* completely alone. That nagging feeling of being watched dissipated for the first time in a couple days.

And it damn well should have. She was in the most comfortable place she could think of outside of her apartment, or anywhere else a zombie might wait for her.

Hidden away in a section of her favorite park, the overgrown path was strewn with rusty playground equipment. The city had stopped paying to have it maintained a long time ago. It had been that way when she had come here as a kid, too—just a forgotten memory off the side of a dirt footpath. Together, she and Dad had made it into something more. A castle, a pirate ship, a dragon's roost....

Sat on a splinter-ridden bench, she had mostly been taking in her surroundings. She was still close enough to the street to hear faint sounds of traffic, but as a kid, her tiny self and wild imagination had always perceived this place as being in the middle of a forest. She had many memories of running through an endless forest that had really been—as she could see clearly, now—just a trail in a city park.

But as strangely secure as she felt in this forgotten place, she was gearing up to go home. She wasn't keen to be out *anywhere* after nightfall —especially after what had happened last time.

Mercy had texted her a bit ago, saying she'd had to take a detour on the way to the vet, so she probably wouldn't be back home for an hour or so. But that was fine. After coming here and clearing her head, Edie felt like she'd be okay if she ended up alone in the apartment.

That was, until the call came.

Her phone vibrated in her pocket, and Mercy's name appeared on the screen. Already expecting the worst, Edie tried to quell her nausea as she picked up. "Hello?"

"Edie? Where are you at right now?" Mercy sounded shaken up. *Not good news.*

"I'm just in the park. Why? Is everything okay?"

"Um ... it's Hervey."

Edie stood up and gathered her bag, starting along the footpath that led to the more public part of the park. "What's wrong?"

She heard Mercy turn away from the phone and talk to someone, then come back. "The vet isn't sure what's happening to him."

Dammit. "Of course not."

There was a pause. "They said it's almost like he's ... decomposing."

Dread set in. That only confirmed what the zombie had implied—that she'd brought Hervey back to life. But that was impossible. She'd never dealt with a dead thing before Hervey, but she didn't have to to know that when things were dead, they just *were*. Forever. She, of all people, would know that.

"Edie? Are you there?"

She was still hurrying along the footpath. "Yeah, I'm sorry. What?"

"They think maybe he has some kind of infection. They said we should leave him here for ... tests? To be honest, I don't think they know what's going on either. That's my sense, anyway."

"I'm sure it's just some freak thing," Edie said. It was definitely a freak thing, but she was starting to doubt it was an illness. "Did they say anything else?"

"Well ... yeah."

Edie jogged across the footbridge that separated the trail from the rest of the park. A group of teenagers hung out nearby, and a mom and her kid were walking up toward the nearest subway station, but other than that, it was relatively empty. Edie decided not to follow the mom, instead taking the long way around the park to give Mercy time to talk.

"They said he's probably in a lot of pain. Like, if they wanted to remove this necrotic flesh, they'd have to take most of his ... skin? ... off? I think they really want you to put him down."

Edie sighed and rubbed her forehead. Would that work? *If* she had somehow managed to ... *resuscitate* him, would they even be *able* to put him down again? "Yeah. I agree with them."

"I'm gonna go home, 'cause they said the tests might take a while, and they won't put him down without you signing a bunch of papers in person."

Edie passed a peeling gazebo and a little copse of trees, and Mercy's voice turned to a drone as something caught her attention from the corner of her eye. It looked like a group of all-white figures standing in the distance, and for a second, her heart threatened to leap from her chest and run for the hills.

Then she recognized the shapes: headstones. One of Anster's tiny graveyards.

She'd never been happier to see one. Anything but those monsters from the other night, whatever they had been.

"Edie? Are you gonna be okay?"

She'd been so startled that she'd forgotten Mercy was even on the line. "Yeah, I'm okay. Just text me when you get home, okay? I'll pick him up later. Gotta go."

"Okay. And remember, we have a gig at that new place tonight!"

Edie mumbled an okay, hung up, and pocketed her phone.

Poor Hervey. She didn't like the idea of putting him down. He was a cutie pie, usually, when he wasn't rotting and whatnot. But it had to be done, for his sake.

It was probably best that Mercy go home, anyway. She was sensitive when it came to the circle of life, and being there when Hervey passed— again?—wouldn't be a pleasant experience for her. Edie had never thought *too* deeply about those kinds of things. She'd never been very spiritual, but she knew it was a big deal for Mercy.

Edie adjusted her bag over one shoulder and continued down the path toward the subway station a couple blocks down. The dirt walkway passed right by the small graveyard that had freaked her out so badly before. Now that she got a closer look at the graves, she felt silly for being scared of them.

There were a lot of random little groups of headstones around this part of the city, usually in meandering clusters of five or six with no other plots for blocks. It was an antiquated detail speaking of years long past, when farms had thrived here and families had buried loved ones on their own land. Now, everything was so close together. The austere little graveyards were almost sweet. To her, anyway.

The last time she'd sat in one of these tiny plots had been on a date with a guy from out of town, and he had remarked that he'd never been in a city that simply built around old graves. They usually just moved them to a bigger cemetery.

Of course, then Edie had had to go into detail explaining that the city *had* moved some of them, and the ones that remained were there because of disputes over ownership, and had been allowed to stay where they were because it was easier than arguing and spending money. He hadn't called her for a second date.

Besides that disaster of a date—which most of her dates tended to be— she had a lot of good memories in graveyards. It seemed odd to most people, considering they were where humans went when they died, generally. The end of the line. Yet they had been her playgrounds as a child;

her father had always been taking her out grave reading, the older the better.

Mom always said that was why Edie had ended up so weird: because of Dad. And it was true; he had been weird. But he'd been a good father, there for Edie no matter what. Whenever she spoke to her mom about him, she got the feeling they hadn't had the best marriage, but Edie didn't understand it. She couldn't remember even one bad moment with him.

She stopped, walked across the grass until she reached the cluster of headstones, and knelt. The lights from the buildings and traffic nearby were still enough to make her feel safe, even as the sunset made way for twilight.

"End of the line," she mumbled as she scanned the graves.

The moment she spoke to the twilight, it was as though it came alive.

That feeling of finally being left alone was gone, and the watching eyes were back, stronger than ever. Rigidly, she turned and looked behind her. The park was completely empty now, and she suddenly realized she couldn't hear the traffic.

There was only the drum.

That same drum, the same whispering, the same skim of ghostly fingers against her. With a start, she pulled back from that which she couldn't see, hairs standing on end as she stepped away from the headstones.

Something was stirring beneath her; somehow, she could feel the very earth roiling with power as she stepped over it, and every step away from the graveyard somehow increased the feeling, rendering it more unbearable.

She felt hunted, and she couldn't even see what was hunting her. It was … *below* her, somehow. But what was there? Nothing but dirt and rocks. It was a park, for god's sake. It was—

She staggered as something caught her eye. She thought she saw something … no, some*one* … weaving through the trees of the nearby copse. She stared for a long time until, finally, the figure moved through the trees again. A hooded—

To her left, she heard something burst through the soil.

The sound of crumbling stone reached her, and the beating of the drum came louder, louder, *louder*, until it felt almost as though it was the heartbeat of whatever slumbered in the ground.

Or slumbered no longer.

She closed her eyes tight. *Please let this be another bad dream.*

The drum stopped.

For a few moments, everything was eerily silent and still. Edie opened her eyes wide, listening for a moment before tucking her arms across her chest and turning.

What in the hell?

She looked in the direction of the street, far off, still flooded with lights and beautiful civilization. The drums were gone; the dizziness was over, along with the strange power that had emanated from the ground. She looked to the copse of trees. No one there. Absolutely nothing.

Something rasped and dry-heaved behind her.

She didn't have to look. She knew what it was.

And she could feel that *she* hadn't raised it.

Edie scrabbled forward, trying to ignore the throaty moans behind her as she searched for something she could use to fight her assailant off. There had been a group of teenagers hanging around near here, and she'd seen one of them chasing the others with a huge stick. *Please, god, tell me they didn't take it with them.*

Edie trotted forward, fumbling with her phone flashlight and swinging it until she finally found the stick a few yards ahead.

The thing behind her groaned and wailed weakly as it noticed her— *fuck*—and she darted forward, the hair on the back of her neck standing at attention. She dropped her phone in her bag and dove for the stick.

Gripping her new weapon with two hands, like she was winding up to hit a home run, she turned toward the zombie.

Her courage faltered. She could feel herself start to freeze again.

The zombie was much closer than she had anticipated, first of all. And it was different from the one she'd met before, Calcifer. At least *he* had moved like a human, emoted. There had been a soul in his eyes. This ... was different.

It was nearly fleshless and moved loosely, like its limbs might pop off at any second. The eyeless hollows in its skull stared straight ahead, torn and bruised and expressionless. Its dusty jaw fell slack against its chest, and its limbs jerked and twitched like a puppet's. And when it started for her, nothing stopped it—neither the uneven ground nor its own crumbling joints.

It focused only on her.

She gripped the stick tighter and swung as hard as she could, aiming for anything that could slow it down. The stick connected with its side, staggering it, and Edie felt a kernel of hope blossom in her chest. She could take this thing on her own; all she had to do was knock it down and make sure it didn't get up again. Just keep hitting. Easy.

The zombie righted itself, its torso rolling on its hips, then turned to her sluggishly. Its stomach and chest were ... *convulsing*.

She stuttered. "What are you d—"

It vomited. It simply opened its mouth and spewed an acrid, greenish fluid onto the ground at her feet. Then it looked up at her, squawked, and heaved again.

She barely ducked in time. The zombie hurled, and the substance flew out like a projectile and missed her hair by an inch, so pungent her eyes watered. Another stream shot past her left side, and she stumbled back, falling on her butt. The vomit hit the grass next to her, hissing and turning it black and wilted.

Edie dropped her stick. No. Uh-uh. The living dead were one thing —*acid puke* was another.

She scrambled to her feet, leaving her shoulder bag behind, and booked it down the footpath and onto the paved walkway. The zombie staggered as it followed her, dragging its withered limbs, compelled by some otherworldly force to come get her.

She knew she could outrun it—the zombie was slow, and she could jog for a couple miles without stopping—but the thought of something slowly, surely following her was almost worse than something making a break to kill her.

She had to rest eventually. *She* had to sleep. Somehow, it knew where she was, and it would keep going. It would come.

A shriek built up in her throat—a primal reaction to being chased—but she couldn't let it out. She was already running full tilt through a metropolitan area; screaming was sure to get the cops called on her.

Edie barely knew where she was at this point, running blindly through the city. She'd long since passed the subway station, and she was starting not to recognize the street names. When she reached for her phone, hoping to get a clue, she found only an empty pocket.

Shit. It had been in her bag. It was possible to retrace her steps and find her way back to the apartment, but was it wise to go there? Would the zombie follow her that far?

Edie stopped for a moment and looked behind her. It was probably pretty far behind by now, but the dread of its presence still weighed her stomach down like lead. A zombie—an honest-to-god undead *thing*—had been summoned by someone in that park and was now chasing her.

Was it really possible that something long-dead had clawed its way out of the ground to ... what, kill her? She wasn't sure what it wanted with her, but the possibilities did not bode well. And who had raised it?

She must have been standing there, watching and waiting, for longer than she realized. Without warning, to her left, a moist screech cut the silence. It drew a yelp from her. What, had the walker found a second wind or something?

She turned toward the noise and found herself facing the mouth of an alley. At the end, there was a figure. *More than one? Are they trying to flank me or something?*

Then, another slithered into view.

And another.

All three were wiry-framed and hunched, off-balance, swaying slightly.

Oh, good, he brought friends.

Edie bolted without waiting another second, pumping her arms and legs like an Olympic runner. As she shouldered through thin crowds of people, she could hear the zombies behind her, their shrieks and moans growing fainter but no less haunting as she ran—more slow ones, but not as slow as their friend.

Her panic only increased as, at intervals, new shrieks greeted her. It was like someone had called ahead to every corpse in the city and told them where they could find a fresh girl dinner.

An executive decision had to be made.

She took an unexpected left turn at Veteran Street and jumped a low wall to run through the courtyard garden of some government building, effectively putting a few blocks between her and her new boyfriends. Her lungs were aching, and her legs were becoming weaker with each block. Where was even safe? Who could she go to that would believe her?

The answer had already dawned on her a couple streets back, but she refused to acknowledge it. Even if she had *wanted* to contact that gun-waving asshole, she didn't know how.

As she passed a courthouse, Edie glanced over her shoulder before slipping into one of the stout alcoves carved into the stone on either side of the stoop. They were only tall enough for her to fit in if she sat hunched over, but maybe that could be an advantage. Maybe they wouldn't find her.

With her knees pulled up to her chin, she tried to think of other solutions, but they all led back to Calcifer.

Edie would never in a million years have thought she would be counting on a zombie to save her from zombies, but nothing that had happened in the past few days made a whole lot of sense.

She balled her hands into fists and pressed them against her eyes, shaking all over. Tears slicked her wrists, and she pulled her sleeves up to wipe them away. She couldn't stay, she couldn't go. She couldn't fight, but she couldn't keep running. She just sat, listening to the booming of what she assumed was construction nearby.

Turned out, it wasn't.

Eventually, she heard footfalls. Heavy footfalls against the pavement. She froze mid-wipe, her eyes instantly drying. It had to be around eight o'clock. So who was coming to the courthouse?

The footsteps didn't drag or shuffle, but they still slowed as they reached her. She dared a peek past her fists and saw the thick rubber soles of a pair of brown Carolinas, trailing blood and buckshot. She watched as the stranger flicked a cigarette butt to the pavement and stamped it out.

"Get up," Calcifer said as he dragged her from her hiding place. His grip was iron. "Get in the fucking car."

CHAPTER NINE

Edie sat stiffly across from the zombie in a vinyl booth. Outside the window, a neon sign flashed: "Dolores' RESTAURANT," it said, only the lights in some of the letters had gone out, aptly making it "res' TAURANT."

Calcifer hadn't said a word on their way there, but he had burned through a good half pack of cigarettes. Thank god the top of the car—some kind of convertible—had been down. At any rate, he seemed a lot calmer now, and he wasn't waving a gun around. Him bringing her somewhere so public, with all these bright lights, was probably a good sign.

She hoped so, anyway.

Still, once in the diner, she'd refused to sit down until he convinced her he'd gotten the zombies off her tail. He hadn't gone into detail, but he'd made it clear that they wouldn't be coming after her—or going anywhere, considering most creatures needed functioning limbs to locomote.

Feeling a confusing mix of gratitude and terror, Edie had finally relented and taken a seat.

"So, I guess we're at an impasse," Calcifer said finally, after Edie had been awkwardly swirling her ice around in her soda for a few minutes. He hadn't even opened his menu, just tossed it aside and leaned forward with his elbows on the table.

She looked across at him, then glanced around the diner and leaned forward. "Um, Calcifer ... why are we here? Can't people see, you know... what you look like?"

"No. Magic isn't really my bag, but I have a glamour I control. It doesn't work great on anyone besides humans, and *you* won't see it at all, considering our *bond*." He said the word with disdain. "But they all see me as a regular guy." He gestured to the waitress and the few other late-night patrons, then added, "And don't call me Calcifer."

"Sorry. Cal." *Our bond?* Edie watched the waitress's feet as she came over to their table.

"All decided on what you want to eat?" The woman was young and cute, a brunette with dark eyes and pretty cupid's-bow lips.

Cal reached across the table and took Edie's menu, stacking it on top of his own discarded one. "Nothing for me, sweetheart, but get the kid a plate of fries." He flashed a grin that, from Edie's perspective, looked pretty horrifying.

The waitress, however, smiled like everything was normal. "Coming right up." She gathered the menus and made her way back to the kitchen with a spring in her step.

Edie couldn't help but snort. "Aren't you a charmer."

His grin died as he looked at her again. He grunted. "Cut the shit. You and I both know we had a pretty close call last time, but I'm hearin' you out. Against my better judgment." He folded his arms tightly across his chest. "Why did you raise the hamster? Think it'd be fun?"

Edie balked, almost snorting diet soda up her nose. "What— *No*. It was an accident. I came home and he was ... *prone*, but when I touched him, he ... wasn't, anymore." She didn't give Cal time to reply, pressing her question: "And what the hell are you supposed to be? You're like ... you're like a zombie?"

Cal growled and leaned back in his booth. "Come on, really?"

Okay. So *zombie* wasn't PC. "What are you, then? And why did you come for me?"

"You think they'll let me smoke in here?"

"Who *are* you?"

"Oh, for the love of god." Then, slowly, as if coming to a realization, he said, "You really don't know *anything* about what's going on, do you?"

She didn't know why that was such a surprise. What normal person would understand all of this? The only reason she had kept her composure this long was because she dreaded the alternative.

But, somehow, his presence ... helped. She got strange vibrations from him, like they were in sync somehow. It wasn't a bad feeling; it was almost soothing. It was like, even though she didn't know him, her soul did.

When she didn't answer, Cal grabbed the bowl of creamers and started to stack them. "Where the hell do I even start..." He stopped and considered her for a moment. "You remember anything about your father?"

What a loaded question. She remembered that he had loved her more than anyone in the whole world; he'd told her that all the time. She remembered that he'd really understood her. She remembered all her surprise birthday parties, special trips with just the two of them, and how he'd always seemed to know exactly what she was thinking. Their long walks, their adventures, how she could talk to him about anything.

She held on to those tightly. If she didn't remember them now, who would?

But now, thinking harder about it, she also remembered that he hadn't been around as often as she would have liked. She remembered long stretches of time where he would go away for work. She remembered him and Mom fighting when they thought she couldn't hear. She remembered the night he hadn't come home, and the morning after. She remembered the funeral.

Cal could apparently sense that the question had affected her. He simply waited for her to answer.

"You said that in the apartment, too," she said finally, voice soft. "What does this have to do with my dad?"

The dead man looked back up and held her gaze for a moment. He looked so *angry*—as angry as he had when they'd first met. She really hoped this wouldn't end in another stand-off.

He must have noticed her shrinking back from him, because he softened a bit. His jaw unclenched, and eventually, he spoke. "Whatever you thought—whatever *lies* he told you—your father wasn't who he said he was."

This was unreal. There was a stranger in front of her—a stranger who appeared to be deceased—presuming to know about her life and telling her she hadn't known her own father. It was too much. She avoided his eyes, propping her forehead against one fist. She didn't know whether to cry or launch herself across the table and punch him.

After another moment, Cal asked, "You feelin' all right?"

"What is happening to me?" Her voice finally cracked, betraying her fear.

When he heard it, his low brow wrinkled. He studied her for a while, expression equal parts confused and concerned.

Edie still didn't look at him. "Did you know my dad?"

He opened his mouth to speak, but the waitress approached with a plate full of fries. Edie mumbled a thank-you but didn't look at her. The thought of eating right now made her want to throw up.

"Thanks, darlin'." Cal picked up Edie's glass and handed it over. "How about another soda?"

"Sure thing!"

Once the waitress had gone, Edie dared a glance at the plate of fries. *Ugh.* "I don't want any. You can have them."

With a frown, he said, "No, I can't. You shoulda told me before I ordered them."

"Oh." She didn't say it out loud, but she doubted she wanted to know what he *did* eat.

"I know what you're thinking." Cal rolled his eyes. "I just can't digest *this* stuff." He gestured to the fries. "There are, uh, a few things I can digest … but I don't need them to survive."

Well, that's a relief.

"And, yeah, I knew your dad." He grunted and crossed his arms. "Better than I'd've liked." When that statement was met with a look of confusion, he became exasperated and said again, "You really *don't* know what's going on, do you? Fuck me."

"No thanks."

"Easy on the attitude, sister." Cal knocked over his pyramid of creams and started stacking them again. "Richard Holloway wasn't a, a ... auditor, or whatever you thought," he said, waving a hand.

"Accountant," she mumbled.

He either didn't hear her or ignored her. "He was a *necromancer*. Part of a faction called the Reach. I'm—I *was*—his revenant." A pause. "Since he's dead, and now that you've got your powers ... according to your blood, I'm yours. I'm bound to Holloway's lineage."

Reach? Revenant? Swimming in new jargon, she let her gaze drift out the window. Cal was quiet, just letting her think it all through. She was surprised to find that his company was actually sort of calming. The strange power flowing between them seemed to slow her heart rate, sharpened her focus.

Revenant. What did that entail, exactly? In what way was he "bound" to her lineage? And what had he meant when he'd said she had gotten her powers?

"Hervey. How did I...?"

He sighed and gestured to her. "I figure you'd never touched something dead before, right? Then you did. You must've been upset. Somehow, your body figured out how to make the power work, and then ... well, you know the rest."

She picked at the rubber siding of their table. "You're telling me that my dad was some kind of ... wizard?"

"Necromancer. Among other things. And so are you." He leaned forward and rested his elbows on the table again, then pointed to her bare arms. "Use the magic enough, and it'll start to show. When Holloway died, he was covered in runes."

Now that he said it, she thought she recalled her dad having some strange tattoos ... but when she was young, she hadn't questioned it. For her part, she didn't have any yet, magical or otherwise. Not because she didn't want one—most of her friends had at least two or three; Mercy had fish scales tattooed up her thighs and flanks—but because she had no idea what to get. It seemed silly to spend money on something she wasn't a thousand percent enthusiastic about, even for the aesthetic.

She was about to ask him more when she realized he wasn't carrying any of his weapons. "Do zombies usually pack heat? I thought you guys liked eating brains, not splattering them."

He grimaced. "What'd I say about the attitude?" When he continued what he'd been saying earlier, his tone was harsher: "Holloway raised me—from the grave, that is—before you were even born. I don't remember anything about who I was before, and if he knew, he didn't tell me. He was a bastard, and once he was dead, I could do whatever the hell I wanted."

Edie didn't know what to say. What he claimed was so completely the opposite of everything she'd ever known about her dad that it didn't seem like it could be possible. "My father was a good man," she said, though even to her own ears, she didn't sound convinced.

"Anyone who enslaves another person's soul for his bloodline ain't a *good man*, kid."

"If he was so bad, why did you come back?"

Cal clenched his jaw and looked away. "Well, 'cause ... better me than the other people who'll be looking for you. I thought about killing you—that'd be better, too, trust me—till I realized you really *didn't* know what the fuck you were doing."

"Why would anyone be looking for me?"

The revenant rolled his shoulders. "Necromancy is just the beginning. Some of the darker shit your dad could do ain't for everyone, and it's not stuff that can be learned like vanilla necromancy or pyromancy or whatever. People'll want you for different reasons. Because they want your power on their side, or because they think you're scum and wanna kill you."

"Listen, Cal." Edie rubbed the bridge of her nose. "The closest I've ever come to casting a spell is playing Bubble Witch Saga. Now I'm supposed to be some kind of specialized wizard?"

He turned one of the creams over and checked the expiration date. "I think *mage* sounds cooler, but all right."

"I can see why my dad kept you around. You're so helpful," she said sarcastically. "You said he was a member of some ... Reach?"

"Hmph. The way I've always understood, there's 'light' and 'dark' factions. The Reach is the in-between. Holloway always said balancing light and dark was what made the old Reachers so powerful." Cal huffed. "I think he was just jerking himself off. He was obsessed with bringing the Reach back. With him as its leader, of course. Always talking about how it used to be bigger than either the Aurora or the Gloaming, like, a thousand years ago or something."

"Aurora and ... what?"

"The Aurora. They'd have you believe they're the 'light' part of that equation. They're uptight SOBs who think they're better than everyone else. You could save their asses and they'd still call you evil 'cause of what you are. So you and I can go fuck ourselves. They're probably looking to kill you.

"The Gloaming suck, too, but at least they'll let anyone in. Wights, wraiths, undead, shifters. They're into some seedy shit, but they're organized, so if you're willing to give up your freedom and learn your place, you're at least guaranteed protection. Most are bastards and slavers." He spread his hands. "Your dad tried real hard to make the Reach an actual thing again. And he almost did it, but it died out once he was gone. As it is ... the Reach can't give nobody protection these days, so no one bothers."

Edie shut her eyes for a second. Two factions, light and dark—though that sounded oversimplified—and the space between. The space her father had been trying to bring out of extinction when he'd died. "So what do I do? I can't just keep running forever."

Cal looked her dead in the eye. His expression had become serious, and his face was so frightful anyway that she felt uncomfortable. "Trust me, I'd love to hop in the car, drive back across the country, and never see you again. But now we're here, and I don't have any choice but to stay and see this through. And neither do you."

Edie was quiet for a long time, still struggling. She could barely keep herself alive living a normal life; what the hell was she supposed to do with all of *this*? "So ... you're staying. Those people after me, they'll leave me alone now?"

Cal snorted. "Fuck no. They might have to regroup, but I'm only one guy." After a thoughtful pause, he said, "But—" before stopping again.

"What?"

"I guess I know someone who might be able to help," he finished with a shrug.

Edie took another look at her untouched fries and shook her head. "Let's just get out of here."

"Fine," he said, waving the waitress over and asking for the check. When he turned back to meet Edie's eyes, he looked angry again. "And one more thing...."

This time, he actually stood up, hands planted on the table as he leaned forward and got right in her face.

"When you made me leave your apartment, I couldn't resist. Because of what I am, I had to do what you said." He stabbed a finger at her, his voice dropping low. "Don't. *Ever.* Do that to me again. *I don't like it.*"

She heard the warning loud and clear. Even when he'd been pointing his gun at her, he hadn't sounded so serious. "Okay," she mumbled through sudden nausea. He'd *had* to do what she said? That was what she'd done in the apartment—forced him to comply?

But she didn't want that. She wasn't that kind of person. What kind of person would keep someone, even a dead person, like a slave? That was ... evil.

Edie crossed her arms over her turning stomach. But her Dad....

"Glad we have that settled." Cal sat back down, rolling his shoulders and relaxing a bit. "By the way, you're paying."

CHAPTER TEN

EDIE PAID for the food with some loose bills in her coat pocket and followed Cal outside to the car.

It was late—probably around eleven—and dark, but for some reason, she felt safer the more she got to know her new companion. That was unexpected, considering he'd almost killed her the first time they'd met, but nice.

She'd been a bit too traumatized to notice anything special about Cal's car before, besides the fact that it was a white convertible. Now, she saw that it was some type of muscle car, with long fins on the end, a glossy finish, and leather interior. It stood out in the dark like an apparition.

"You drove cross-country in this?"

"Yep. *This* is a '63 Cadillac Eldorado. Custom paint job and interior. A few modifications, but nothing major."

"Where did it come from?"

Cal picked at some flaking skin on his jaw. "She was Holloway's. He won her off some guy and was just letting her sit around and rust in a storage unit. So, when he died, I took her for a joyride to Vegas. I've been taking care of her ever since."

Edie ran a hand along the hood of the convertible. She didn't know much about cars, but it seemed to be in really good shape. "Cool."

The car beeped twice and flashed its lights, and the passenger door popped open.

Edie retracted her hand, her gaze flying to Cal. At first, she assumed he'd done it remotely somehow, but that was impossible; this car was way too old to have automatic locks or anything like that.

The revenant just smirked.

"Okay … mind telling me what's going on?"

"Meet Ghost." He gestured to the car like he was introducing her to a friend.

Edie looked back at the car uncertainly. "Uh … hi?"

The car flashed its lights two times, and the engine purred to life.

"Ghost, this is Edie." Cal opened the driver's side door and climbed in, then looked at Edie. "You coming?"

"Okay, so … possessed car." She couldn't believe she was thinking it, but that actually *wasn't* the craziest thing she'd experienced in the past couple days. "Have you ever seen *Christine?*" she asked skeptically, approaching the passenger door.

As if in response, the door slammed shut just as she reached it, and the engine sputtered.

Cal patted the dashboard affectionately, frowning at Edie. "Don't be like that. Ghost only runs people over if they deserve it. And she's not *possessed* … just really fuckin' haunted."

"Great. Remind me to stay on her good side."

Edie opened the passenger door herself and slid in, thankful when she saw that the car had seat belts. She was also happy to find her bag in the footwell. She'd been too busy looking over her shoulder and wondering if Cal was going to kill her to notice it on the ride here. He must have tracked her to the park and found it where she'd dropped it running from those zombies—uh, undead.

"Uh, so … where are we going?"

"We already talked about this, didn't we?" Cal said as he fiddled with the radio. "We're gonna go see someone who can"—he waved his hand, looking for the word—"orient you."

"You mean, like, train me?"

He pursed his torn lips almost disdainfully. "Slow your roll, jack. You ain't Luke Skyscraper yet."

"Skywalker."

"Eh?"

Edie sighed. "Nothing. So what is he gonna do?"

"She," he corrected, putting Ghost in reverse and peeling out of the parking lot. He turned west toward the highway. "I've been in Vegas the past ten years, so I haven't really been, uh, *keeping in touch*. I missed all the political bullshit out east, so you and I are almost in the same boat."

"Adjacent boats?" Edie offered.

"Adjacent boats. I can give you the big picture, but not much else."

"So, she's from the Aurora?"

He snorted. "Hell no. Weren't you listening to a thing I said? Those dickheads don't want anything to do with you. She's one of the last members of the Reach. Or was, last I knew. Kind of in the same business you are. Death, that is."

"So she's a..." The words still sounded so stupid when she said them out loud. "Necromancer?"

Cal scrunched up what was left of his nose. "No ... not really." He struggled to find the words to explain it for a few moments before shaking his head. "You'll just see, okay?"

Edie shifted in her seat and pulled her bag into her lap, opening it and trying to turn on her phone. It was dead; of course it was. She pulled out the charger and started to look for somewhere she could stick it in the console.

Cal watched her from the corner of his eye as they turned onto the highway. "Whatcha doin'?"

"I'm trying to find somewhere to plug..." She trailed off, realizing how stupid that was. Of course there wasn't anywhere to charge her phone. The car was older than *Gilligan's Island*, for god's sake. There was barely a radio.

Cal grinned wickedly. "We'll have to entertain ourselves the old-fashioned way," he said over the wind that whipped past their faces. He leaned forward and fiddled with the radio again, scanning through the channels with one hand while he steered with the other.

"I can't believe that thing still even works."

He grinned even wider, which was kind of a horrifying sight, if she was being completely honest. "It just takes a little elbow grease to keep her running, that's all." He stopped on a channel blaring Bon Jovi's "You Give Love a Bad Name" and leaned back in his seat, looking mightily satisfied. "That's more like it."

Edie stared at him for a moment before shaking her head and resting her chin in her hand, watching the world blaze by the passenger side. Eventually, once the song ended and the DJ switched to something more mellow, she turned toward him.

"So." She struggled to be heard over the wind. "You never told me how you got your name."

Again, he pursed his already pretty much non-existent lips and glanced at her. "How'd you get yours?"

"Um ... my dad named me?"

There was a pregnant pause as she digested the unspoken: her dad had named him, too. Nausea rolled through her, and she had to take a deep breath to steady herself.

Eventually, she spoke again. "Isn't Calcifer the name of the guy from that book, *Howl's Moving Castle*? Dad used to read that to me all the time when I was little."

"Yeah," he grumbled, barely audible. "*Cute*, isn't it? He raises a guy from the dead, erases everything about him, then names him after some asshole from a kids' book."

"I'm sure he just thought the name was cool," Edie tried, maybe more to reassure herself than him.

Cal's glare intensified, and for a moment, it looked like he might pull over and throw her out of the car. But his anger seemed to simmer and turn into a quiet agitation, his grip tightening on the steering wheel. "You can't just name another person like that, like you'd name a dog. Goes to show the kind of guy he was, playing with other peoples' lives like they were toys."

Clearly, she'd hit a sore spot, but it wasn't easy to hear someone talk about her father like that—even if he apparently deserved it.

"He thought he could do whatever he wanted. He was cocky, and in the end, that's what killed him."

What? Edie's brow furrowed. She wanted to say something in protest, but the words became lost in her throat.

Cal was quiet, too, his jaw clenched. She could tell by his silence that he hadn't meant to let that slip out, or maybe he hadn't known she was clueless to the truth—whatever that was. He did now.

"My father died in a car crash," Edie mumbled softly.

The revenant sighed and flexed his sinewy hands against the steering wheel. "Of course that's what they told you and your mom." He clenched and unclenched his jaw like he was chewing on his words, then glanced at the pack of cigarettes lying on the dashboard. After a while, he grumbled, "Sorry, kid."

She pulled her bag close to her chest. "So what's the truth, then?"

Cal seemed to waffle, probably trying to decide how much he should actually tell her. "I'm ... gonna be honest with you. I don't know the whole story. I know he went to meet with some Gloaming bastard and never came back." He paused, then added quietly, "Still remember when I felt the sever."

Edie knew she shouldn't ask; it would only upset her. But after so many years of wanting to know more about her dad's last moments, she couldn't stop herself. "Sever?"

"Yeah. When I knew he had died. It hurt for a second, then it was gone. He was gone out of me." He exhaled. "It felt fuckin' great. Like I could breathe."

In a way, she felt happy for him, but it still hurt to hear someone talk about her father's death like it had been a stroke of good luck. "So when he died, you were ... set free?"

Cal smiled a little. "I stole the car and was on the road within a week. I've been in Nevada ever since."

"But you came back. To kill me."

His smiled died, slowly turning into a grimace. "Yeah, well, like I said ... your powers were dormant until you touched something dead. It sent up a signal to anyone looking for someone like you, but especially to me. I was— It's just like...." He sighed. "When I arrived, I assumed you'd be some big, bad necromancer. Not a dumb kid."

"Thanks." She exhaled shortly. "And now the Aurora and the Gloaming are both looking for me, too?"

"Now that they know where and what you are, sure. Those husks you were running from in the park probably came off someone sent to fetch you." He glanced over as they exited the highway.

Edie looked at the exit signs and saw that they were driving out of the city, toward Shipshaven. She'd been there once or twice, usually with Mercy; it was a seaside town with a really good alternative night club and some occult shops on the wharf.

"Anything else weird happen to you, besides the hamster thing?"

"A couple things." She looked back at Cal. "Some ... things have been following me. They look like dudes when other people are around, but they chased me home the other day, and I thought I saw— They looked like ... I don't know. They were really long and white and skinny."

Cal frowned. "That's gonna be a wraith."

"Wraith?"

"They're what vampires leave behind when they bleed an enthralled human dry." He paused, making a vague gesture. "Sort of ... Class F—"

"*Vampires*? You can't be serious."

He looked over at her, brow raised, looking almost as skeptical as she did. "You're sitting next to a dead guy in a haunted Caddy and you're gonna stop me at *vampires*, lady?"

He had a point. But it was still hard to believe in something like *vampires.* She could only envision Dracula. Or Edward Cullen. "Okay, fine. So if a vampire eats a human they've mind-controlled or whatever, it makes a wraith?"

"Pretty much."

"So I'm seriously being hunted by vampires," she concluded flatly.

"Okay, *technically,* they're called wights—" Cal stopped himself and shook his head. "Look, it doesn't matter right now. What I'm getting at is, probably some Gloaming Lord is looking for you. Anyone else following you around?"

There had been that radioactive man—the one with the glowing golden eyes. She'd never forget the color. It had been like the sun was pouring through his irises, a pure yellow-white. He'd saved her from the wraiths, but he hadn't exactly been kind. She contemplated how to word the rest of her story as they turned down a side street, going about twenty-five past darkened storefronts.

Cal was surprisingly patient. Finally, Edie answered him: "Well ... there was this guy, the same night those things came after me. He sort of saved me from them. He had these glowing yellow eyes, and he pushed me on the ground and sort of ... exploded at the wraiths or whatever."

"I can guarantee you that was an Auroran vivid."

"What's that?" She looked back at him as they rolled to a stop outside of what appeared to be a book shop.

Cal nodded, gesturing to the shop. He killed the engine and slid out of the car. "I'll tell you later, but we gotta get a move on."

Edie followed suit, holding her bag close as she got a better look at the book shop, though it was too dark to read the sign.

It was a Victorian-style corner storefront made of real, old brick, with a second story that loomed over the arched doorway like an awning. Jewelry and heavy-looking medallions hung in the windows: some sort of hammer-looking thing woven from iron, a round medal with runes etched into the surface, necklaces and pins shaped like running wolves and bears and boars. The books laid out in the window looked strange, too: old, the covers sun-bleached and the bindings frayed.

There was a CLOSED sign in the front window, but Cal tried the handle. Unlocked.

Edie turned to ask him what kind of shop this was, but he was already halfway through the door, motioning for her to hurry up.

It was just as dark inside the shop as it was out, and it was musty, too. It must be filled with old stuff. Before either of them could get a better look around, though, they were both distracted by the sound of raised voices. The voices were muffled, and it was impossible to understand what they were saying, but they were coming from somewhere toward the back of the building—a man and a woman, it sounded like, broken up by short periods of silence. It seemed their argument was switching quickly between tense, quieter conversation and impassioned yelling.

Edie and Cal traded a look, and strangely, she could almost feel them exchange thoughts. Without speaking, they hurried deeper into the shop, Cal resting a hand on the revolver holstered at the small of his back.

"Probably in a back room or something," Edie suggested.

Cal simply nodded before motioning for her to follow him between the tall, old bookshelves.

At the ends of the aisles, wooden tables butted up against shelves set with displays of jewelry, wooden and iron figurines, and many other strange and almost otherworldly-looking trinkets of glass and gold, silver and blue and green. They intrigued Edie. It was the kind of place that compelled her to stop and look at every display, like these things were calling to her.

Maybe there would be time later, if they weren't about to stop a murder in progress or something. She took in as much of the space as she dared while she followed Cal to the back of the shop.

They came to a heavy curtain that, when Cal pushed it aside, revealed an ancient-looking door bound with worn iron straps and rivets, closed by a rusted latch.

Cal looked at Edie, catching her eye as he drew his revolver. He nodded between her and the latch, and she took position, poised to lift it when he signaled. He seemed pleased that she followed direction so easily.

"Ready?" he mouthed, before counting back from three on his mottled fingers.

On the last count, Edie lifted the latch and pulled the door open fast. The second the path could accommodate his beefy frame, Cal slipped through, gun drawn.

Should she follow? Edie had only ever seen a gun in person a couple of times, and those had been on policemen. She *definitely* hadn't ever been in the middle of a firefight. She hesitated in the doorway, but Cal glanced over his shoulder and nodded for her, looking a little irritated.

It wasn't a good look for him. She quickly slipped through after him.

The shortish hallway beyond was even darker than the shop, with no windows. There was a staircase going up to their immediate right, with cardboard boxes stacked several high beside and under it. At the far end of the hall was another doorway, leading to a room that glowed with soft lamplight. The smell of some sort of pleasant, wintery incense drifted from it.

The conversation drifting out with it, however, was anything but pleasant.

"I know that you know where she is," said the man's voice, rough with stress.

"You're *mistaken*," came the woman's voice, accented and irritated. "There hasn't been a hellerune in this area for years—"

"Her *father*."

"—and there isn't likely to be another for a long time, if ever. I don't have to explain that to you, Blade of Tyr."

Cal sidled up to the doorway, concealing himself near a stack of boxes. For a moment, it looked like he planned to wait out the argument and hide from the man as he left. But scuffling and a grunt from the other room spurred him into action, and he jumped around the doorway with Edie right behind.

As they entered the room, there was an unearthly shriek, and a cold, almost-blinding white light filled the room. A figure was thrown across the room by a blast of energy and hit a desk, splintering the wood, then crashed into the window beyond and cracked one of the glass panes.

Edie's gaze followed the figure as it sank to the floor. It was a man—a familiar man. She recognized the armor, the face, and of course, the golden eyes.

Standing—or, rather, levitating—at the end of the room closest to the door, hand outstretched, was a being made of wispy blue and white light. An enormous woman, taller than Cal—taller than anyone Edie had ever seen—and built like a warrior. The top half of her moon-white face was obscured by a winged silver helmet, and ghostly platinum braids tumbled down her shoulders. A pair of sharp, almost knife-like black wings erupted from her shoulder blades.

The blinding energy fled from the golden-eyed man and back to the specter. And then, in a flit of wings and another wave of light, the unearthly image was gone.

In its place stood a middle-aged woman of average height, in jeans and a long-sleeved tunic. Her outstretched hand trembled. Tattoos blazed azure across her tan, freckled skin as she lowered her arm with a deep breath. Her crystal-blue eyes were severe but tired as she gazed at the man she'd just thrown.

Cal lowered his weapon, also looking at him. The mysterious stranger—a member of the Aurora, Edie knew now—groaned as his body settled, no longer held by the woman's power.

After a second, the revenant cleared his throat and said, "Guess that handles that."

The woman—or whatever she was—finally acknowledged them. She looked to Cal, and in her eyes, recognition quickly turned to puzzlement. Her gaze stilled on him for a few moments before wavering and finally turning to Edie.

Something else filled her face then; an emotion Edie couldn't identify. The woman's eyes widened, her terse brows knitting and jaw clenching as she inhaled sharply.

"By the Allfather," she murmured, "how you've grown."

Cal holstered his revolver. "Hey, Astrid."

The woman tore her icy gaze from Edie and looked at Cal again, drawing in another breath. "Calcifer … you came back."

"Yeah. I did."

Edie hadn't known Cal for more than a few hours, but she'd never heard him sound so miserable. She hugged herself around the middle, suddenly feeling responsible for pulling him back to the East Coast. But it wasn't her fault, right? He'd chosen to come, after all.

Cal nudged Edie with a leathery arm. "This is the lady I was tellin' you about. Astrid Fengrave."

The woman—Astrid—nodded solemnly at Edie, coming closer. Her movements were hesitant, but Edie got the distinct feeling that this sensitivity and polite awkwardness were not usually the way she did things. In fact, there was something about her that really made Edie want to somersault away and run back down the highway at top speed.

Cal nudged Edie again, tipping his head and muttering, "It's okay."

"Yes, it's okay," Astrid said, stopping her advance toward Edie abruptly and offering her hand—large, freckled, worn from work. "I was wondering when, if ever, you might appear at my doorstep. You probably have no idea who I am, do you, Edith?"

Edie looked at her hand. It seemed like a lot of people had known who she was even before *she* had. "You know me?"

"How could she forget?" snapped the golden-eyed man, who had been silent until now. He'd pulled himself to his feet, observing their interaction with a glare. "You're a hellerune. A Holloway."

Astrid didn't look away from Edie as she reached forward, taking one of Edie's hands in both of hers. The moment their hands touched, an icy pain the likes of which Edie could never have imagined flew up her arm in an instant—and stabbed her in the heart.

CHAPTER ELEVEN

EDIE SANK TO HER KNEES, sputtering as something wormed its way inside her chest cavity. It squeezed her heart, cold as death, then burst from her ribcage with another soul-shaking explosion of pain.

Astrid let go, and Edie was left scrambling. She shoved a hand up her shirt to find the exit wound of whatever had just been torn from her.

There was nothing. Her skin was covered in goosebumps and cold to the touch, but completely unscathed.

She felt Cal's heavy hand on her shoulder as he crouched beside her and pulled her back firmly, steadying her. "Jesus Christ, kid, what the hell happened?"

Edie was speechless as he helped her to her feet. She looked at the strange woman with an open mouth.

"Apologies," Astrid said, looking almost as surprised as Edie. "It didn't occur to me that you are still a fledgling." She turned and looked at the golden-eyed man, nodding to a small range close to where she'd thrown him. "Marius, fetch her some tea? It's right there on the stove."

He snarled. "Go to Hel."

So much for the tea, Edie thought, her breath catching as she inhaled.

Her insides still felt like brittle ice, as though they might break if her lungs expanded too much.

Marius. At least she had a name now.

"If you're just gonna stand there like an asshole, maybe you should leave," Cal said, baring his teeth.

Marius looked to Cal, rolling his shoulders. "So, you're back. You never stood a chance, did you, again-walker? You ran back the first moment your master needed you?"

Cal made a hissing sound with his front teeth. "Fuck off."

"He's right, Marius," Astrid said tersely, folding her hands in front of her and standing her ground. "We've done no wrong; there is nothing for you to smite here,"

Cal waved him off. "So run along before someone chops off your other hand, kid."

Other hand? Edie's eyes flew over Marius in confusion. His left hand was there, clutching his injured side; but his pauldrons were asymmetrical, and on his right side, he had a full arm of gleaming steel plate, segmented to resemble a canine's bristling hackles. At the end, instead of a gauntlet with fingers, there was only the head of a wolf forged into a perpetual snarl. In the soft light, she could just barely see runes glinting across the surface as he shifted.

When her gaze reached his face, their eyes met. He drew his arm back, hiding it from view before looking back at Astrid. "The girl comes with me, Fengrave."

"She's staying here, Marius."

From the way Marius's expression twisted and his shoulders sank, Edie could tell there wasn't much he could do to defy this powerful woman's wishes.

Edie took a big gulp of air and shook Cal off half-heartedly. "I'm not going or staying or *anything* until someone tells me what's going on"—she shot a pointed look at Cal—"and what I'm doing here."

Marius gritted his teeth and came forward abruptly, shouldering his way between Cal and Astrid. He looked back when he reached the doorway, giving Edie another once-over. "I won't be questioned by a hellerune," he spat. "I'll capture her eventually."

Cal reached for the small of his back, but Astrid placed a hand on his arm, stopping him. Their eyes met, and she shook her head.

Marius left hastily, slamming the heavy wooden door behind him with enough force to shake the entire shop.

The remaining three said nothing as the structure shuddered.

Cal was the one to break the silence. "Fuckin' douche. He knew who I was, but I didn't recognize him."

Astrid pursed her lips and wordlessly crossed to the range she'd indicated earlier, rolling up the sleeves of her linen tunic. She checked the heat of the range's one coil, then grabbed a small wooden cup from the cupboard above it. Pouring in some water, she opened a clay jar resting on a sideboard nearby and sprinkled in a pinch of its contents. From Edie's vantage point, it looked like dirt, but she was sure it was some sort of loose-leaf tea.

Eventually, the strange woman crossed the room again and handed the cup to Edie. Their fingers brushed, but this time, Edie only bristled a little—not at all the violent reaction she'd had minutes ago. She gripped the cup tightly. Her body was cold all over, and the heat helped to stave off the bone ache a bit.

"You'd recognize his father," Astrid finally said to Cal. "The young man became a vivid within the last few years."

"Thought so." Cal crossed his arms. "Who's his father?"

"Eirik Sørensen."

The revenant was quiet for a few moments before saying, "Oh."

Edie was surprised to hear trepidation in his voice. "Is that someone important?" she asked.

Cal looked over. "He's the leader of the Aurora in this part of the country. Radiants, they're called. He'd be the ... Radiant of the Rising Divine, yeah? *Rising Divine* meanin' the East Coast."

"The first place in the country to see the morning sun." Astrid touched Cal's elbow, a gesture Edie was sure would elicit some sort of grumpy response. He didn't seem at all fazed, though. "Would you like some tea, too?"

"No, thanks. I try not to digest anything with an alcohol content below four percent."

Edie snorted, taking a big sip—

"Are you sure? It's grave moss."

And she choked, unfortunately managing to swallow most of the liquid still in her mouth. "*Grave moss?*"

"It's good for you," Astrid said mildly, smirking and shrugging a shoulder.

All of this was too weird. Wiping her mouth with the back of her hand, Edie finally asked the question she'd been wanting to ask since she'd set foot in the shop. "I don't mean to be rude, but ... what *are* you? What was that whole thing about?"

Astrid looked to Cal and raised a brow.

He gestured to Edie. "I only told her the basics. Figured it'd be better to have someone who's actually been *on* the East Coast give her the rundown."

Astrid raised her head a bit and looked at Edie. Something in her eyes glinted, a small blue light that reminded Edie of the one she'd often spotted coming from the back of Cal's skull—but this was in her irises, not her pupils.

Before Edie could ask another question, Astrid gestured with an open palm. "Sit."

To their left, up against a window that looked out on the adjacent street, was a wooden table. A linen cloth interwoven with purple and gold threads was thrown over it, and in the center of the table was an incense burner—circular, wooden, ringed with a steel serpent devouring its own tail. Edie took a seat, studying it.

"That is Jörmungandr, the World Serpent," Astrid said as she took a seat across from Edie. Her accent really came out when she said that word. Before Edie could ask what it meant, Astrid continued, "Son of Loki, great enemy of mighty Thor."

"Oh. Yeah ... I love Tom Hiddleston," Edie mumbled, pulling her bag onto her lap.

Cal snorted behind her, but Astrid didn't seem as amused. Her eyes glinted. "You are irreverent, like your father before you. That will change, in time."

Edie would usually have taken a comparison to her father as a compliment, but in light of recent discoveries, it didn't seem like such a good thing now. "You knew my dad, too?"

Astrid nodded grimly. "There isn't an attuned being in this area who doesn't know who he was. He almost succeeded in reviving the Reach in the years leading up to his death. A controversial figurehead."

"'Cause he was a necromancer," Cal cut in. "The Aurora weren't too pleased to see a hellerune in charge of a supposedly neutral party, and I guess the Gloaming saw it like there was another dark magic game in town."

Edie looked between them. "That guy, Marius. He called me a hellerune, too."

Astrid crossed her legs under the table. One of the charcoals in the incense burner popped, sending a puff of smoke up between her and Edie. "*Hellerune* roughly translates to *sorceress* or *necromancer*, but the meaning runs deeper than that. Hellerunan are descendants of the original sorcerers of the Circle of Hel. An ancient sect, even older than I and long gone."

"That sounds ... ominous."

Astrid chuckled. "Not quite as ominous as it sounds to young ears. Hel is the goddess of the dead, revered by the ancients. Long ago, she chose a small number of her worshipers—her Circle—and gifted them with innate mastery over powerful magics. The ebon magics, Edith, considered unholy by modern men: blood, plague, shadow, death. There used to be quite a few of you, over a millennium ago." Her expression turned to a weary glare. "But, like many of us, you've since been hunted—by the Aurora and the Christians alike. Reduced to a mere handful worldwide."

That didn't sound great. If she was going around being known as a sorcerer of dark magic, Edie wasn't surprised people didn't want to be associated with her. She was fairly certain this "goddess of death" was just a myth, but still. "So Hel's worshipers were ... evil?"

"Not evil but *powerful*. Power unchecked can corrupt a person, but fear of power can do the same. In the end, magic is only as good or as evil as the person wielding it."

Edie looked at Cal, who huffed. Apparently preferring not to be involved in this particular conversation, he crossed the room and started to pick up the splintered debris that had once been Astrid's desk.

The strange woman watched him affectionately. But Edie was still uneasy about her, and she hadn't forgotten what had happened when they'd first touched. The bone ache was still there, a chill that wouldn't leave.

As if reading her mind, Astrid said, "Drink your tea. It will help."

Edie tilted the small wooden cup, watching the grit at the bottom swirl around. "You said it was ... *grave* moss?"

"It has restorative properties to beings with innate death magic. It will heal that burn I gave you."

Edie touched her chest, remembering the feeling. She met Astrid's eyes. "You still haven't told me what you are."

The woman looked away, watching Cal. Finally, she said, her tone steady as a warrior's march, "I am a valkyrie."

"A valkyrie?" Edie asked. She'd seen paintings of those before, heard about them in stories. "Like an angel?"

"No, not exactly. We are choosers of the slain. After all battles, it is up to us to decide who will live and who will die, our hands guided by Fate."

"That seems like the sort of thing that should be up to, I don't know ... a god?"

Astrid pursed her lips. "One of our gods could not dictate every detail of life and death. As attuned to the flows of time as some of them are, they have limited sway over what may happen. Each of us decides on behalf of Odin and the Mother Valkyrie; we are their eyes and their hearts where they cannot be."

Edie said, "Okay...." But with all the talk of valkyries and Odin, Astrid conjured memories of when Mercy had gone through a soul-searching phase a few years back and gotten into the idea of Norse Paganism. It hadn't been worth it. Turned out, a lot of the groups still into that stuff didn't exactly welcome an outspoken bisexual Latina.

Astrid didn't miss a trick; she peered at Edie. "You have something on your mind?"

"I'm not really sure how to say it."

"I appreciate a direct approach."

Edie waved her hands awkwardly, as if she could dispel the tension by shooing it away like smoke, but only succeeded in waving actual smoke from the incense into her nose. Between sneezes, she said, "I dunno, just … a lot of white supremacist groups use Vikings and Norse stuff to make themselves seem cool and badass. This isn't … *that*, right?"

Astrid blinked, then paused to thank Cal as he passed with an armful of splintered wood. She shook her head. "No. This isn't that."

Edie wasn't exactly at ease yet, but she said, "Okay … good."

The valkyrie, though, wasn't done. She leaned forward, crossing her arms and planting her elbows on the table. "Let me make myself perfectly clear. The ancients were far from peaceful, perfect people. I should know; I was there. Like everywhere, horrible things happened. But the people of which you speak are *not* my brothers. They know little of the truth of the heritage they claim. They declare valor and courage where there is only insecurity, poison, and violence against the vulnerable."

"Yeah." Edie averted her eyes. "Uh, agreed." She was so intense that Edie felt almost embarrassed for asking the question, but at least they were on the same page now.

Astrid relaxed a bit. "I apologize. Valkyir have been around for longer than you can imagine, Edith. I'm relatively young compared to many of my sisters, but I've seen what men like that are capable of."

Edie hadn't considered that. If valkyir picked who lived and died in battle, Astrid must have been around for modern wars, too. Was it possible she'd been around for the World Wars? That thought made Edie shudder.

She changed the subject, looking into her tea and swirling it around.

"You said that, uh, gods don't actually decide much when it comes to Fate. So who does?"

"The Norns," Astrid answered simply. She traced the spiral pattern of the tablecloth before her, following the lines of gold thread. "The Mother Norns spin the tapestries of the gods and their heroes, and their lesser spirits deal with others. I am a daughter of the Mother Valkyrie. My sisters and I are expected to keep the balance, to bring about what has been foreseen. No matter how unpleasant."

Sounds like a shitty job, Edie thought. "How exactly do you become a valkyrie?"

Astrid looked up at the rear door as Cal returned from dumping the remainder of the desk debris out back. She sighed at him. "It's a shame. I loved that desk."

"You shouldn't have launched a dude into it, then," Cal said, rubbing his dusty hands on the thighs of his pants. He looked at Edie. "Feeling better?"

She shrugged. "I guess." Her question seemed to have been forgotten, but it could be answered later—if she didn't wake up from this nightmare first.

"Good." Cal looked to Astrid, raising a brow. "'Cause you got that look in your eyes like you got some big, world-changing news."

The valkyrie stood, moving to the nearby fireplace, and the air around Edie got quite a bit warmer as she did. She crossed her arms and looked down at the smoldering logs, silent. The fire rendered her wavy blond hair a glowing gold at the edges, the hard plains of her face casting stark shadows. Even in her jeans, Astrid looked like some kind of ancient war queen.

Finally, she spoke: "Things have … changed since Richard Holloway. Before, life was like it always had been. The tides of war would rise and ebb, of course; there were moments of chaos or strife. But the Aurora and the Gloaming were largely at a stalemate. Perhaps the trouble began when your father tried to revive the Reach in a meaningful way. His penalty for trying, after all, was death."

Edie looked at her knees. Was that just a theory or did Astrid know for sure why her father had been killed?

"But since he died," she continued, "there has been a shift. Without the protection of the Reach, beings with no other choice have been forced to submit to the Gloaming. And this past year, the Gloaming Lord of this province, Fahraad, was murdered, probably by the Aurora. Instead of lending aid or appointing a new Lord, though, the Gloaming hierarchy retreated like tortoises into their shells. No response to Auroran raids or purges on civilians … they just sit in their fortresses, hiding and rotting."

"If they think the Aurora're gonna give up, they haven't been paying attention the last god-fuckin'-knows-how-many years," Cal mumbled, reaching in his back pocket for a cigarette. He held one between his lips but didn't light it.

Astrid spread her hands, still looking at the fire. "I have no idea what their play is! Sitting still and quiet is not like them at all. Ten years ago, they'd have taken their revenge before Fahraad's corpse was cold, but no one has even bothered to take his *place*. I fear they're waiting for something. And whatever that is, there is no doubt it will be more destructive than anything they've done in a thousand years."

She turned and focused on Edie with those arctic eyes.

"The fact that your powers emerged *now* can be no coincidence. I believe it's already been decreed that your fate be bound up with the fate of the Gloaming and whatever is to come."

Edie suppressed a shudder. The thought that someone had already decided everything that was going to happen to her and the people around her … it wasn't a good feeling. Had her whole life—including all the bad stuff and the mistakes she had made—really been completely out of her hands?

She felt heat rise up her neck. She wanted to scream, to tell Astrid and Cal to leave her alone, that she wanted no part of this. But did she even have a choice?

"So I'm going to have to fight," she mumbled.

Astrid bowed her head grimly. "Sooner rather than later, I fear. The others are already pursuing you; the Aurora to put you down, and the Gloaming ... well, I imagine to recruit you. Unless you disobey, in which case they will kill you as well."

"I guess I'm part of the Reach, then," Edie said, half-joking, crossing her legs at the ankles and tucking her hands under her butt.

Astrid's expression cleared, and she smiled. "I was just about to say, the Reach is needed. Perhaps now more than ever. In that case, you'll need training."

Cal plucked the cigarette from his mouth and tapped it against his thigh, glowering.

Edie looked at Astrid. "Can you? Train me?"

"Not properly. My magic is very different from yours." She turned and rolled her lips between her teeth thoughtfully for a moment. "I will investigate, see who I can find that might lend some aid. There must be someone in this city who has something to teach you."

"Can't wait," Cal mumbled.

Astrid looked at him, raising a brow. "Unless you know someone who might serve us better?"

"Phff. No." He crossed his arms. "I don't hang out with necromancers. Not anymore." And then, with a glance at Edie, he added, "Okay, not till now."

"Very well, then. So, in the meantime, perhaps you can get started elsewhere. The Reach needs your help. There was a task I was about to start myself, but since I'll be occupied...."

Astrid left the fireplace, going to where the desk had been. The window, cracked where Marius had struck it, frosted over as the valkyrie approached. On the wall beside it, an ancient-looking shield and spear were mounted high on a wooden plaque. Astrid lifted them both down with ease and turned to Edie.

"My shieldmaiden, Satara, could use your aid in recruiting an old friend of mine. Someone who vowed to help the Reach many years ago. Bring these to them both, as proof that I truly sent you, and they will speak with you."

Cal eyed the spear. "How'll they know we didn't just kill you and steal your stuff?"

Astrid barked a laugh. "Satara would know if I was dead." Then she focused on Edie again. "And Edith?"

Edie looked up as she stood.

"The unattuned are oblivious to our world for a reason. They ought to stay that way, even if they are your friends." Her tone turned grimmer. "Now that you know the world for what it is, you're likely to lose things you've held dear, things that can't withstand this change. Keep your head down and tell no soul."

CHAPTER TWELVE

As she and Cal exited the shop, Edie pulled her phone out of her bag to check the time. She clicked the home button, but the screen remained black.

Right. Dead. She sighed, wondering if she'd gotten any texts from—

"Oh, shit." She froze with one hand on the passenger door as realization and dread filled her.

"What?" Cal slipped behind the wheel and started Ghost up.

Edie didn't really want to talk about it, but she'd already outed herself. Miserable, she slid into the passenger seat. "Mercy and I were supposed to perform tonight. I missed it."

He grunted, but didn't seem concerned. "Your roommate? Tell her something came up."

"My phone is dead, remember?" Edie sighed. "She's gonna kill me ... especially when she finds out about the fish."

"What fish?" Cal asked as he pulled away from the curb and made a U-turn in the middle of the empty street, heading back toward the highway.

"Mercy's. I went to feed him and he'd just sort of ... died."

Now that she thought about it, it was possible that the fish had died the same day as Hervey—she hadn't gone into Mercy's room to check. Maybe there had been some kind of accident ... like a carbon monoxide leak or something.

Cal snorted, resting one hand on the wheel's gear shift. "Fish don't breathe air, stupid."

She turned her head sharply to look at him. "You know that's fucking creepy, right? Can you read my mind?"

A nonchalant shrug. "Not exactly, but I get the general idea. It gets clearer the harder you think, usually. You were pretty excited about your theory, weren't you?"

She crossed her arms. "You've got five seconds to wipe that smirk off your face." Then, after a pause: "You know, I don't want you in my head *all* the time."

"I can't help it. But there are things you can do to keep me out. It just takes practice. You can't hear *my* thoughts, now, can you?"

She said nothing, listening hard. No, she couldn't.

They both fell silent as Cal turned onto the highway. He reached for the radio dials, but stopped just short and gripped the wheel again. Edie looked away, out the window at the trees and towns speeding past. This area was heavy with vegetation, almost completely devoid of billboards. The smell of ozone was strong in the air. It must have rained while they were inside. She glanced over her shoulder at the shield and spear resting in the back seat, both partially covered with tarp.

Finally, she sighed and peered at Cal. "So how could her fish have died? I fed him every day."

He chewed on the inside of his cheek and got that look like he'd rather be talking about anything else. But she had to push him; this was important. "Necromancy is ... a bitch to master. There are a couple ways you can bring something back from the dead—either by leeching the life from something nearby, or hurting yourself and using up a ton of your own energy to do it. Leeching is easier, and faster, and you get a stronger thrall. For example, it's the only way to make a revenant instead of a mindless husk."

Edie thought about that for a second before looking away. She remembered now. She remembered wishing Hervey was all right, wishing it so hard. She'd gotten so angry that she'd wished the fish was dead instead, hadn't she? Oh, god.... But she'd had no idea it would actually kill it!

"You didn't know," Cal grumbled. After another moment of silence, he added, "I could sense you leeching across the country, y'know. When I got to your apartment, I was surprised not to find a body. Didn't think to check the fuckin' *fish tank*. I figured you were an evil murderer."

"Not an evil murderer. Just a stupid one." Edie sighed. "If my options are either taking a life or hurting myself, seems like a pretty crummy power."

The revenant's tone grew bitter as he took a nearby exit. "Yeah, but you're not just a necromancer. You got other tricks up your sleeve besides raising shit from the dead."

Edie wrinkled her nose. What had Astrid said? Blood, death … some other stuff? She wasn't sure she even wanted to know, at this point. But if she was going to fight, she needed to be prepared.

After a second, she leaned forward and turned on the radio. She didn't want to talk about this anymore, and she was sure Cal didn't want to, either. She understood that he was bitter about everything that had happened to him, but she was still trying to process it all. Apparently, her father, whom she'd looked up to her entire life, had been not only an amoral necromancer but an asshole slaver.

She didn't like it, but it wasn't her fault. Why was Cal so intent on making her feel bad for it?

"I didn't ask for this, you know," she said, when she could no longer contain her own bitterness.

He glanced over at her, his brow furrowed, ruined mouth twisted in a grimace. "Yeah, I know that. Don't take it so personally, kid."

She crossed her arms, hugging herself. "You're the one taking it personally. Like, you're so put-upon by me, even though I never asked for your help."

"Yeah, well, I'm here now, so too late. I saved your damn life, so a thank-you might be nice."

"Great. Thanks."

Cal's grip tightened on the steering wheel, but he said nothing.

Edie dug her heels in, aggravated by his silence. She knew she shouldn't say anything, that him saying nothing was his way of saying, *Shut up now*. But still, she mumbled, "You're not being fair."

"You'll never know the things your father made me do."

The tone of Cal's voice finally shut her up. He was angry, yes, but his throat sounded … raw. His voice was close to cracking; torn knuckles turned white as he clutched the wheel even tighter.

He took a measured breath and turned up the radio.

It was nearing two in the morning when they finally reached Edie's apartment. Cal pulled around the side and parked Ghost in the alley that led to the yard, despite clear signage that he definitely should not, under any circumstances, do that.

"I can't believe you can't drive," he said as he pocketed the car keys.

Edie noticed he only had a few keys on his ring. Probably not a homeowner, then, but she could have guessed that. "Maybe you can teach me some time."

She glanced at him in time to see him pull a face. "Not likely."

Edie didn't need to show Cal the way to her apartment—he'd broken into it, after all—but he trailed behind her anyway, glancing around the austere hallway as she unlocked the door. With her hand on the knob, she looked back at him. "Mercy is probably sleeping, so just keep your voice down."

He rolled a shoulder and gestured for her to hurry up.

Edie pushed the door open, Cal following. As she took a step into the living room, she came face to face with Mercy's wide-eyed stare.

"Edie! Where the hell *were* you?" She was sitting on their couch, turned so she was facing Edie and Cal as they entered. Her concerned gaze flicked to Cal for a moment, her brows furrowing deeper, before going to Edie again. "Who's this?"

"I'm really, really sorry." Best to start with that right out of the gate, Edie figured. "Just ... something really important came up, and I lost track of time, and my phone died. I'm really sorry." She paused. "The people weren't mad, were they?"

Mercy spat out a laugh, her eyes going wide. "Are you kidding me?"

"Huh?" This conversation was already nerve-racking. Edie pocketed her house keys and quickly moved to her bedroom door, scooping up her old punk-patch-covered backpack as she passed the couch. She hadn't used it since the last time she'd gone on vacation, which hadn't been for a while.

Mercy stood and trailed behind her, leaving Cal alone in the living room. "I was *worried* about you, and you stood me up and left me to perform alone, and you're concerned what *they* thought? And then you come home with some ... some"—she gestured wildly toward the living room with a manicured hand—"stranger?"

"I know, and I'm really sorry." Edie grimaced as she wrenched open her dresser and started to throw things into her backpack—underwear, a couple pairs of pants, a flannel, socks. She wasn't sure where she and Cal were going, or how long they'd end up staying there. A couple of outfits would have to do for now.

She felt pressure—stronger than she'd have expected—on her upper arms as Mercy grabbed her, turning her so they were face to face.

Mercy's eyes narrowed as she searched Edie's gaze. She pursed her matte purple lips and asked, lowering her voice, "Are you on pills?"

Edie yanked her arms away, annoyance boiling up inside of her. She didn't need to be managed like a little kid. Why did Mercy think she was totally incompetent? "What? No, *Mom*, I'm not 'on pills.'"

"Who is that creepy guy you brought home?" Mercy laid a hand in the middle of Edie's chest, stopping her from side-stepping. "You look at him and you try and tell me he's not a drug dealer."

Edie waved a hand, scrunching up her nose. "That's just Cal." It did make her wonder just what Cal's glamour looked like. Apparently, a creepy drug dealer. She managed to bend herself enough to slip past Mercy.

"*Edith.*"

"Mercedes." Edie trotted into the living room again and threw her backpack on the couch, passing the stalwart revenant to go collect toiletries from the apartment's tiny bathroom. Mercy was right behind her, giving the stranger a wide berth.

"Edie, this, this— this *isn't* cool." She watched from the bathroom doorway as Edie threw her toothbrush, toothpaste, some hair bands, deodorant, and her makeup into a plastic bag.

"I'm sorry. I don't have time to explain. I really need to go."

Mercy didn't try to catch her as she passed, and when Edie glanced back, she thought Mercy looked … almost scared?

Her shoulders sank at the sight. "Everything's okay, I promise. My friend just has a … family emergency." That was one way to put it.

Mercy crossed her arms, popped one hip. "Okay, let me see if I understand you. You sleep until five p.m., then you blow me off and leave me to perform alone, unprepared. *Then* you don't answer my calls or texts for hours, and then when you do come home, you come with some meth-head, and suddenly you have to pack your things and flee in the middle of the night?"

There was silence. Mercy was angry, but most of all, she was scared, and that was what really upset Edie. Being uncertain and scared herself was one thing; hurting her friends was another.

"And," Mercy added, "when I came home, my fish was dead. You were supposed to feed him!"

"I did," Edie returned weakly, gripping the strap of her backpack tighter. "It's just…."

You should tell her, said her conscience. Mercy didn't deserve to deal with all this shit, and she probably wouldn't even believe it, but it wasn't right to leave her so distressed.

Edie sighed hard and turned more fully toward her. "Look … it's—"

A heavy hand fell on her arm, cutting her off. Behind her, Cal shifted so he was looking over Edie's head at Mercy. "We need to go," he said, in the same tone he'd had in the car earlier: *Shut up now.*

"But—" Edie looked at Mercy, who looked disgusted with them both. It was like a punch in the gut. Edie grimaced and pushed Cal's hand off her shoulder. She couldn't leave her only friend in the world flat like this.

But before she could blurt out the unbelievable truth, Mercy threw her hands up and let them fall loudly against her fishnetted thighs. "And I guess I'm going to have to pick Hervey up? And *pay* for the vet?"

Hervey.

She'd forgotten him. She'd forgotten her fucking zombie hamster at the vet.

Edie's stomach turned, and from Cal's shudder nearby, she knew he had felt it, too. They turned, and their eyes met.

"Fuck," he rasped after a brief second of silence.

Edie threw her backpack over her shoulder, bolting from the kitchen to the front door, Astrid's plea echoing in her mind:

Keep your head down and tell no soul.

CHAPTER THIRTEEN

Vivid Marius clutched his side as he climbed the stone steps of the Temple of the Rising Divine, his ethereal steed filtering back into sunlight as he left it behind. The valkyrie's magic had cut deep; he could feel the chill in his soul almost as keenly as he had felt the impact to his ribs when she'd thrown him.

His father had warned him not to confront her on his own—that, even alone, she was more powerful than he could currently hope to be—but Marius hadn't listened. He'd been foolish and acted too quickly, as usual. And he'd paid the price.

Father would say as much.

From where Marius was, between the Corinthian columns of the temple that had stood for over a century, the structure looked like any other municipal building: cool gray stone, with arched alcoves around the perimeter and wide front steps; above him, supported by the columns, a gable depicting an ancient battle scene. The only things that might look out of place to the unattuned were the runes carved into the frieze; the winged statues on the cornices, posing with arms outstretched; and perhaps the size of the grounds on which it stood, much more extensive than any government building. The golden dome of the building caught the light just so as the sun rose, and it shone brilliantly.

The behemoth before him was the easternmost Auroran temple in the United States, the first to see the light of the sun as day broke.

As it was doing now. Had he really been dallying for that long?

Marius let go of his side with a wince, wrenching open the door to the empty vestibule and sliding inside. The heavy wooden door closed behind him with a thud that echoed in his equally empty chest.

The marble hall before him was far grander than the outside of the building suggested, flanked with stone tableaus featuring the great triumphs and sacrifices of the gods. At the end of the hall, just before the entrance to the inner sanctum, was a large, golden statue of Tyr leaning on his greatsword, face obscured by his beard and winged helmet.

"Vivid Marius? Are you all right?"

He tore his eyes away from the statue to look at the woman addressing him, one of the two adherents stationed by the entrance of the inner sanctum. Stepping around the base of the statue, he nodded to her and forced himself to release his injured side. "I bring news of the valkyrie. Is the Radiant in?"

The woman nodded, stern as she regarded him. She was tall and wide, with a milky complexion and platinum hair braided in a halo around her head. Her eyes were lined with gold and carefully-painted streaks of white makeup—a sort of warpaint, decoration Marius rarely indulged in.

He thought he remembered that her name was Ynga. She looked older than him, but glancing down, he saw she still had both of her hands. Not a vivid, then, though he would expect a vivid to be tending to something more pressing than guarding the sanctum anyway. Despite being older, she was technically his subordinate.

"Where can I find him?" he asked as he raised his eyes again, though he knew his father must be leading first prayers. Marius had wasted hours delaying the inevitable lecture.

"Just inside, Vivid Marius." Nodding to her partner, Ynga stepped aside to make way for Marius.

Her expression gave him pause. He stopped short of opening the sanctum doors and looked at her—and she held his gaze. That was different. Usually, even the other vivids avoided looking directly into his eyes.

After a moment, he asked, "Is there something I should know?"

Ynga glanced over Marius's shoulder at the other guard, then back at him. "Radiant Eirik is ... not in a good mood."

Marius clamped his lips shut. Maybe the Radiant had already foreseen his son's failure. Or perhaps it was something else. Either way, avoiding him any longer would only make it worse. "My thanks for the warning." He opened the sanctum doors and shouldered through.

The nave was bathed in honey light pouring through enormous stained-glass windows. Auroran monks, adherents, and civilians alike had risen early for first prayers; they filled every seat in the nave, heads bowed. At the center of the transept, a little bit of light filtered in through the skylight. By the time noon arrived and the sun was directly above them, it would be as bright in the temple as it was outside.

Beyond the transept was a dais and a lavishly decorated altar covered with offerings of food and alcohol. Standing before it was the Radiant of the Rising Divine.

Eirik was a large man, his armor heavier and more intricate than Marius's. Gold and bronze plate decorated his entire body, silver chainmail filling the gaps. He wore a white and gold tabard, and a greathelm that obscured even his eyes. Bronze plates covered the length of his right arm, from shoulder to vambrace, ending in the golden maw of a wolf.

He led the crowd in prayer, his voice louder than the rest: they thanked Sól for rising another day and wished her swiftness; they asked Tyr for a blessing of bravery, glory, and righteous justice; they prayed to strengthen Fenrir's bonds; they pledged themselves to the gods once again, and asked for places in their halls.

Marius knew every word. He mouthed the prayers, but made no sound.

As the offering finally came to a close, Marius ducked to one side of the nave, starting up the aisle and toward the dais. Without pressure applied to it, his side radiated pain with every step. The worshipers relaxed and began milling, drinking, and talking amongst themselves as the ritual ended.

Marius's father met him at the transept, watching him knowingly, his air already reproachful. Without a word, he gestured for his son to follow him.

They walked side by side through an alcove and up a short flight of stairs before turning left onto a covered walkway. To their left, stone more ancient than the face of the building protected the chancel and sanctuary; to their right was a cloister garden. Women attendants wearing white tunics sat on stone benches, weaving wreaths and tending to bowers of yellow blooms. Men worked nearby, constructing new chevron trellises along a stone walkway. They would work year-round, tending to the gardens. Winter rarely touched the temple.

Instead of turning right to circle the garden, Eirik kept forward. Marius followed, dread and pain souring his stomach with every step.

Each door was older than the last as they neared the center of the temple. They passed the heavy wooden door of the chapterhouse—a ceremony room, where Marius had sacrificed his hand to become a vivid just a few years earlier. At the end of the hall, the two ascended a narrow flight of stairs and entered another passage in silence, before reaching the Radiant's private library.

It was a massive oak room with intricately decorated columns, tall bookcases, and ancient wooden benches and statues. Knotwork and the faces of the gods were carved into the crown molding and the wainscoting. On the second story of the library, the Radiant's similarly intricate desk sat on a balcony overlooking the rest of the room.

He led Marius there, but the vivid lagged behind, standing several feet away from the desk as the Radiant circled it and removed his greathelm.

His complexion was darker than Marius's, his features broader, his warm eyes the color of clay. Long black hair was done in braided twists, and as he set his helmet on the desk, he swept them up and pinned them back with a golden clip. And still, he said nothing as he removed his left gauntlet—with some effort—then loosened the straps of his right arm plates.

Finally, Marius broke the silence. "I saw the girl again. The hellerune."

"I know," his father said. He disassembled the wolf's head vambrace, detaching it from its couter and laying it on the desk next to his helmet. His right arm ended at a linen-wrapped wrist. "But she is not with you."

So Marius had been right; his father had known he'd failed before he'd even arrived. He wondered what else the Radiant knew.

Eirik's powers of foresight had always been as unpredictable and secretive as the man himself. He told Marius little of how his abilities worked—only that they had been a gift from a Norn, many years ago. The gift had served the Rising Aurorans well since Eirik had become Radiant twenty-five years ago. Their leader was strong, his devotion certain, and his conviction iron.

"Tell me what happened," Eirik said, sitting in the chair behind his desk.

Marius subconsciously reached for his side again, remembering. "I know you told me to wait, but our time is limited. So I went to Shipshaven to find the valkyrie, the one you said might know where the Holloways had gone. She said she didn't know and refused to tell me anything more."

"You went alone, despite my orders." His father nodded to his side. "And you were hurt. How?"

"I knew— I *thought* I could handle it." Marius sighed hard through his nose, looking away. "She … threw me across the room. Into a window. And a desk."

"The valkyrie Fengrave may support the Reach, but she knows better than to attack a vivid without provocation."

There was no use in hiding what had happened. Father either already knew or had guessed. He was just waiting for Marius to say it himself.

"She was giving me nothing. I knew she was lying about not knowing where the hellerune was. I was … frustrated."

Eirik was quiet for a moment before taking a measured breath, disappointment rolling off of him in waves. Marius would almost have preferred that his father shout and get angry; he had frustrated his other mentors to the point of fury before. But never his father. He'd never seen Eirik shout. It wasn't likely he was going to start now.

That didn't keep Eirik's voice from betraying his disapproval. "And so you lashed out. Do you have *any* idea what harm she could have done to you, if she'd been so inclined? Marius?"

Marius bowed his head.

Eirik watched his son for a moment, frowning tightly, before standing. "You're young, and rash as ever. Marius ... when I die, you will become Radiant. I have little foresight into my own fate; I could fall in battle at any time, son. I cannot have you acting so ... recklessly. Even the best man cannot lead like that."

It seemed hypocritical to Marius. His father made unpredictable decisions all the time, without consulting his councilors or the country's other Radiants. "But you—"

"I see outcomes and trials most are blind to. You may not always understand why I do what I do ... my child"—Eirik's expression softened, and Marius bowed his head again—"but my decisions never come easily, never come quickly or in rage." After a moment, he pulled a nearby chair up to his desk, motioning for Marius to sit. "You're hurt, Marius. Sit down."

He did so, looking up at his father. He felt like a scolded child, and it wounded his pride. Marius was a grown man, an accomplished vivid—more powerful than most, even given his age. Eirik could talk all day about how he was to become Radiant, but he still spoke to Marius like he was a boy.

Marius would never understand how his father could expect so much of him, yet still hold on so tight. If he weren't on such a short leash, he knew he could accomplish so much more.

But he said none of this as his father knelt beside his chair and searched his side. "Show me where it hurts the most."

Marius lifted an arm with a grimace, and placed a hand just below his ribs, further front than back. "I hit the desk here, and the back of my head struck the window."

"Did you not try to heal yourself?"

"I tried, but ... the chill. It's hard to work through."

He didn't admit the real reason he hadn't healed himself. A vivid's primary talents weren't healing, but Marius's skills were passable; he could have at least relieved his pain, if not healed the bruise completely. He had endured the pain because he felt he deserved it. He'd failed. The pain fed into the anger he felt at himself.

Eirik didn't utter a sound, though Marius was sure he had caught the lie. The silence only aggravated Marius's chagrin as his father prodded the spot through the leather and chainmail armor. "Keep your arm raised, if you can."

Marius did. The pain was significant, but the man before him wasn't just his father; he was his spiritual leader, and furthermore, his commander. Radiant Eirik never showed weakness. Marius doubted he even *had* a weakness. It wouldn't do to appear weak in front of him.

The Radiant took a deep breath and let it out slowly as he laid his left hand on Marius's side. His warm brown eyes flickered gold for a moment, like sun filtering through stained glass, and the power flowed outward from his palm.

The warmth was familiar. Marius had known it his whole life. At first, it was like lying in a beam of perfectly warm sunlight, but as the feeling spread up his side, it became hotter until it was a steady burn. It was painful, even for him; it took effort not to hiss or pull away, but he closed his eyes and exhaled until he felt the burn subside.

When the fire was finally gone, so, too, was the pain. The light had burned it all away, cleansed the wound.

Marius relaxed as his father stood. "Thanks." He scrubbed a hand across his face. "I'm sorry."

Eirik didn't acknowledge the thank-you or the apology. He simply rounded his desk again and sat, looking more worn than he had a minute ago. His eyes flickered once more before he closed them, resting his head on the leather of the wingback chair. "If you're prepared to try to prove yourself once more, I have a mission for you. A very important one."

Marius nodded quickly. "Yes?"

"A lightsteed won't bring you with the haste required. I'll have to order a pyre of translocation be built." The Radiant opened his eyes, then leaned forward to look into his son's face very seriously. "Have you ever been to Maine?"

CHAPTER FOURTEEN

EDIE AND CAL SAT, silently, in the parking lot of the vet clinic. Slowly, Cal lit up a cigarette and took a long drag.

Edie held Hervey's cage, empty now, in her lap. She shut her eyes tight for a moment before turning and stashing the cage in the footwell of the back seat. *Poor Hervey. Poor vets.* At least the hamster wouldn't suffer anymore.

She was pretty sure the vet was scarred for life, though.

"Let's never speak of that again," she said.

Cal grunted in agreement as he shifted Ghost into gear and peeled out of the parking lot. Hopefully, they'd be able to put this awful night out of their minds. There was no time to dwell on it, anyway—it was time to run an errand for a valkyrie.

By the time they were blazing north up I-95, the sun was starting to rise, and Edie was starting to feel the sleep deprivation hit her—not only of the past several hours but of the night before, too.

"Will you open the map?" Cal eventually asked, sounding irritated. "It's in the dash."

She opened the glove compartment and spread the map open on her lap, trying to pinpoint their location. "Where's that address Astrid gave you?"

Wordlessly, he shifted and reached into one of his back pockets, bringing out a folded piece of paper and offering it to her.

She read the address and her brows shot up in disbelief. "*Maine?* You were going to drive me all the way to Maine and you didn't think to mention that?"

Cal rolled his eyes. "It's, like, a four-hour drive. Three, the way I drive."

"Can we stop somewhere to sleep? Or eat?" She was filled with regret, thinking about that plate of fries she'd turned down a few hours ago.

"Maybe when we get there." He looked agitated at her insistence. He didn't *have* to eat or sleep, which she guessed had made driving cross-country easier, but she wasn't thrilled with the idea of napping sitting up and subsisting entirely on the mints in her bag.

But, still, it was only four hours. Edie vented her displeasure with a heavy sigh, but didn't argue. She wouldn't win an argument with him, anyway.

She looked back at the slip of paper. *Reachbarrow Inn, Bar Harbor, ME.* She remembered going to Bar Harbor maybe once or twice as a kid, mostly to go grave reading with her dad; vaguely, she remembered that everyone had seemed to know who he was, and they'd all been *very* friendly. Looking back on it, she shuddered. Could it be possible they hadn't just been polite, but scared of him?

"So, what's our exit?"

Edie glanced from the slip of paper to the map. "We have to switch onto I-295 in Portland and then back in Gardiner, then take exit 182A to, um … 395, and thennnn … 6A, later." She turned her head. "So, who's Satara? Do you know her?"

"What d'you mean?"

"You just, you know, seemed to *know* Astrid pretty well.…"

Cal grimaced at her tone. "It ain't like that. *Trust* me. Astrid is just one of the only people still around who knew Holloway almost as well as I did.

As for Satara, don't know her. Last I knew, Astrid had a different shieldmaiden."

Edie raised a brow. "What happened to her?"

"Dunno. I was gone, remember?"

"What are shieldmaidens even for?" Not really expecting a straight answer, Edie looked down and opened her bag, rifling through it. She was pleased to find a couple of loose sticks of gum.

"Sometimes they'll go into battle on behalf of the valkyrie, or with her, I guess. I never really had the chance to ask."

She glanced at him as she popped some gum in her mouth. "You were never curious?"

"I *said* I never got the chance. Your daddy didn't exactly encourage independent study."

She took the hint and changed the subject. "What's this Satara need us for, then? What exactly are we supposed to do?"

Cal sighed. "I dunno, something about a sorceress, right? Astrid didn't really prepare us a fuckin' PowerPoint. You ask a goddamn lot of questions, you know that?"

"Well, excuse me for not having read the material, Professor 28-Days-Later."

Bitterly, he gripped the steering wheel a little tighter. Under his breath, she heard him mumble, "Brendan Gleeson is excellent in that."

Edie lurched forward and choked on her gum. After a moment of struggle, she was forced to swallow it, coughing. "Oh, yeah?" she managed through incredulous laughter. "Somehow, I didn't peg you as a fan of zombie—"

"Undead."

"Fine, *undead* movies. Whatever."

"Don't *whatever* me. Can you imagine if every movie you watched starring some special white chick was called…." He gestured up and down to her, struggling for an analogy. "I dunno … Magical Cracker?"

Actually, she might appreciate the straightforwardness. "Aw, you think I'm special?" she said teasingly, nudging him.

He waved her off with a grumble of annoyance, but she swore she could see a hint of a smirk on his face.

"Hey, kid. Edie!"

Her eyes fluttered open, grainy from sleep and mascara residue. The car had come to a stop somewhere along a heavily-wooded road with the morning sun low in the sky, obscured by evergreens. There were no other cars around them. She thought she could still hear the highway nearby, but it was obscured by the tall pines lining the road.

She squeezed her eyes shut again and rubbed them. Her palms came away smudged in black, and she groaned, but someone shushed her.

She looked over quickly and jumped when she saw Cal's face inches from hers. "Oh my— *Fuck*, don't do that." He was particularly scary up close, especially since she'd awoken confused. She leaned away to squint at the woods to her right. "Where are we?"

Cal shushed her with a finger to his mouth, reaching with his other hand for the sawed-off shotgun stashed under the driver's side seat. After a moment, his head swiveled to peer down the stretch of road they'd already cleared, which disappeared around a wooded bend.

Edie was about to ask why they'd pulled off the highway and were stopped like this when she heard it, too: An engine, slowing down and then idling just out of view of their position.

"Someone's following us," Edie realized aloud, looking to Cal.

He nodded and gestured for her to get out of the car, which she did as quietly as possible. He did the same, and slowly, like Ghost was an animal he might startle, he patted the retracted soft top. On cue, it flipped open and folded itself over the car in a matter of seconds—a lot faster than Edie would have expected an old car to move. She guessed being haunted helped.

The whirring of the soft top unfolding and the idling engine of the unseen car were the only sounds filling the silence for a few seconds. Then the idling stopped, and the engine cut off.

"Get behind the car," Cal hissed.

Edie ducked, lowering herself into a crouch on the roadside gravel, back pressed up against the passenger door. "Why'd you bring the top up?" she whispered as he dropped down beside her, kicking up some loose grit with his heels.

He glanced over his shoulder, peering through the windows before turning back and starting to load his shotgun. "Less visibility. More cover if we have to make a getaway."

"A getaway? In this car?"

"You bet, sister," he scoffed. "She really moves. Now shut up so I can listen."

He readied the shotgun and pulled his knees closer to his chest, rising slightly. Edie tucked her hair behind her ears, wondering what she was supposed to be hearing.

Suddenly, Cal stood, aiming over the car and firing once before ducking back down. A canine howl greeted the gunshot, followed by a second, explosive sound that cracked the air and made Edie's ears ring.

She barely had time to recover before a blast of something rocked the car and toppled her over. Ghost groaned; Edie's head struck the gravel near the wheel well, and she felt Cal skid over to shield her.

Blearily, she looked beyond the tire, trying to see what had attacked them. She saw two pairs of human feet clad in fur-trimmed leather boots. No dogs.

Confused, she tried to raise her head, but Cal forced her back down as he staggered over her to round the bumper of the car, coming face to face with their attackers.

"Cal!" she shouted, propping herself up on one elbow. She heard a wet thud, like a blow connecting, and someone wheezing—then another booming shot.

Edie dug her fingers into the gravel and managed to find purchase, dragging herself up from the roadside. Her palms were scraped, bloody. She wiped them down her jeans quickly before easing into a crouch, using the bumper for cover.

There were more sounds of a struggle, grunts ... then Cal's shotgun skittered to a stop in front of her feet.

Automatically, she reached for it. White-hot pain raged up her arm as she touched the end of the barrel, and she let out a shriek of surprise.

Thu-dunk. Something had landed, hard, on the trunk just above her head. She didn't have to look to know it wasn't Cal; she could feel hot breath, smell the slaver of the beast, hear its ragged panting. She had no idea where it had come from, but when she raised her head, there it was. Her eyes met the wolf's blazing yellow ones.

It bared its teeth.

"Cal!" she shouted again, grabbing the shotgun by the grip and aiming it upward from her crouching position. What the hell was she doing? She didn't know how to use a gun, and there wasn't any ammo left in it, even if she did.

The wolf showed more teeth in a sort of sinister grin.

"Cal!"

She couldn't hear him. Had they killed him? Was that possible?

Terrified, she did the first thing she could think of: Staggering back to a standing position, Edie raised her arm and swung the gun down as hard as she could, aiming for the wolf's muzzle.

It connected.

The wolf whined and struggled to regain balance on the trunk of the car, its nails scratching Ghost's white paint. As soon as Edie followed through on her swing, Cal was there to snatch the gun from her and finish the job, this time with the heel of his boot.

"Witchwolves," he muttered. "Fucking shifter assholes!"

As the first wolf toppled off the trunk, Edie caught another streak of brown from the corner of her eye, heading toward Cal. "Watch out!"

The second wolf tackled him, and Edie barely dodged them. *Damn it.* She needed to find a weapon. Hoping she could find one in the car, she rounded the bumper to where the first wolf should have been lying.

Lying there instead was a pale man armored in tough brown leather, with the pelt of an enormous gray and tan wolf slung over one shoulder and across his chest. Edie's gaze fell to his shoes: fur-trimmed leather boots.

When her gaze flicked back to the man's face, his eyes were open, wild, and blazing yellow. He looked as confused as she was for a moment, then he sprang up, driving his shoulder into her stomach as he tackled her.

Edie landed on her back with the witchwolf above, crushing her against the pavement. She heard an unpleasant grinding and struggled to breathe as he straddled her. A huge hand covered her face, the palm pressed hard over her mouth, butting up against her nose threateningly. One wrong move and he could cave her whole face in; she could feel the raw strength coiled behind his grip.

One bullet, then another—these gunshots sounded different than the ones before—heated what little air there was between them. The man on top of her yelped. The round must have grazed him. Even though his hold on her remained strong, she could feel his blood dribbling into the hollow of her throat.

And it felt ... amazing.

Her skin was suddenly alive. The blood, which she knew should have been warm, stung her like freezing rain; the pain in her burnt fingers and her shoulder suddenly seemed like nothing.

Somehow, his blood was healing her.

"Hey, asshole!"

The man above her snarled and turned his head toward Cal. The revenant stood, bloodied but victorious, holding another human by the scruff of the neck: a woman, dressed similarly to the man, with the head of her pelt fashioned into a hood. She was still breathing shallowly, but showed no signs of life beyond that.

Cal shook her limp body and threw it at his feet, maintaining eye contact.

He didn't need to say anything else. The male witchwolf was already off Edie and at Cal's throat with a dangerous resurgence of energy. Cal, sandwiched between the rear window of the car and the witch, was unable to shield himself as his attacker landed two powerful jabs between the eyes.

One hand gripped the front of Cal's shirt tight; the other reeled back, tongues of primal fire licking his fist, growing into a larger blaze as he held the revenant poised.

Cal only managed a few choice words before he was struck. The sound of sizzling flesh filled the air, louder than Edie could have imagined, mingling with a groan of agony. The witchwolf snarled in delight.

"Cal!" Edie sat up quickly and felt the blood trickle from the hollow of her neck, down her clavicle, before being soaked up by her black tank top. Cal's face…. She hadn't thought it could get any worse, but there it was.

The witchwolf lined up another shot.

"Fuck … ing … kill … it!" Cal rasped, clutching at the fist knotted in his shirt. He twisted and bucked his hips forward, managing to knee the witchwolf hard enough to make him stagger back half a foot.

"Hang on!" Edie scrambled to the car and flung one of the doors open.

Behind her, she could hear the witchwolf snarl and turn on her again. She only had a few seconds to get this right.

She slid into the front seat and turned, grabbing the first thing her fingers brushed against: Astrid's shield.

The witchwolf had already abandoned a crispier Cal and was climbing into the car after her, smoldering fingers melting through the leather interior as he clawed his way in through the driver's side door. Edie scooted away, working her legs in a panic as she tried to get to the other end of the car. She could practically feel his breath on her as the passenger door flew open for her and she tumbled out.

The blood drying against her clavicle hummed, and as she glanced behind at the car, she noticed just how close the witchwolf was. With a squawk, she threw the entirety of her body weight against the door, slamming it in his face.

She heard the door lock from the inside, and Ghost honked loudly.

Right on, Ghost. But it would only buy them a second.

Edie's sneakers slid across the gravel. She was barely able to keep her balance as she hurried back around the bumper of the car, stepping over the witchwolf's unconscious mate and Cal, who was slumped against the rear wheel well. The witchwolf had given up on the passenger door and was now backing out of the car toward her, pungent white smoke following him.

Edie brought the rim of the shield down on the back of his neck before he could turn around, and he shuddered, shocked by the blow. With a loud cry, she brought the shield down again.

This time, the man collapsed for good, upper torso trapped in the footwell of Ghost's driver's side.

The sizzling of the blood didn't die, however; it hissed, almost sang to her. She could hear it in her head and feel her skin and bones siphoning energy from it. She shut her eyes tight and dropped the shield, lowering into a crouch with her head in her hands.

Behind her, she heard shuffling.

"Cal," she groaned. "I did it ... I knocked him out." At least, she thought he was knocked out. If he was dead, well ... she wouldn't know quite how to feel about that. Killing fish by accident was one thing, but this....

After a moment, Edie lifted her head and looked at the shield before her. Runes that she hadn't noticed were carved into the wooden face of it had blazed to life, glowing a strange mixture of ice blue and teal, like aurora borealis.

"Dude, are you seeing this?" she asked Cal, leaning forward to pick the shield up. She propped it against the side of the car, watching as the light passed through the runes like a lantern behind frosted glass: glimmering, shifting, then passing away.

No answer.

"Cal?"

Just as she was about to turn her head, she felt something cold and sharp against her throat.

CHAPTER FIFTEEN

"STUPID YOUNG WITCH," murmured a female voice, struggling to form each word around gasps and wheezes of pain. A pale hand with long, dirt-stained fingers reached around to grip Edie's shoulder painfully. "You'll pay for killing my mate. Your thrall is nothing but a roasted slab of meat now. I will feed him to my *dogs*."

"Feed 'em this," came a gravelly voice from behind them. Gunfire rang out.

Edie couldn't see the bullet hit home, but she could hear the wet impact of it as it buried itself in the witchwolf's arm. She shrieked, and Edie watched the stone knife she'd been holding clatter to the ground beside them.

She rolled out of the woman's grip easily and turned in time to see Cal gripping Ghost's rear tire, hoisting himself up. His eyes were squeezed tight, and he used the side of the car to feel his way over to the writhing witchwolf, nudging her with the toe of his boot.

Breathing raggedly, he waved the revolver in Edie's direction. "Get in the car."

The sooner they could leave, the better, as far as she was concerned. Edie grabbed the now-dormant wooden shield and circled around the front of the car, waiting for the passenger door to unlock before she slid in. The smell of burnt plastic and rubber greeted her. The leather of the driver's side seat was melted through to the cushion, fused to the upholstery; the dash was misshapen, too, where the male witchwolf had touched it.

Edie groaned, tucking the shield in the back again. If Cal had been pissed before, he was going to be ten times as pissed now.

She glanced over in time to see him lift his knee and stomp down hard. There was a moist crunch and a wheeze, and then nothing.

He jerked the male witchwolf out of the footwell and threw him on the pavement, then joined her in the car a moment later, slamming the door and throwing his shotgun in the back. He said nothing about the scorched interior as he dragged the car into gear and inched back onto the road, toward the highway again.

Edie was silent as she tried to catch her breath, unsure of what to say. They wobbled down the shoulder of the road at a snail's pace compared to Cal's usual speed. He was leaning forward over the steering wheel, squinting ahead. Without his help, Ghost shifted into a higher gear and sped forward.

"They really hurt you," Edie breathed finally.

"Kicked my ass, the fleabags. They were prepared for everything I threw at them. They *knew* I'd be with"—he coughed gruffly and gasped— "you. Whoever sent them ain't fucking around."

"Are you gonna be okay?" she asked as a visitors' center came up on their right.

He groaned like he'd been waiting for her to ask and cut sharply into the parking lot, pulling to a rattling stop.

Edie picked her bag up from under her seat and rummaged through it, hoping she might find something that could help. Chapstick probably wouldn't cure a fried face, but she recalled seeing some eye drops in there recently. Maybe they were still there.

"You need to heal me," Cal said, throwing the car in park and rolling up his window. He sounded miserable, and not just from the injuries to his face.

"What? How?" That was a puzzling request, to say the least. She'd been under the impression that her powers only involved bringing things *back* from the dead. How could she heal anything?

Hellerune. The word echoed in her head. Like the blood, it sang to her; she'd never heard it before Marius had said it, but it spoke of an ancient time and place of great power, something so profound that the lines of her hands and the roots of her teeth and the marrow of her bones remembered it.

"I thought I could only bring things back to life," she said, watching him as he checked his face in the rearview mirror.

"How many times does someone have to say it before you get it through your thick fucking skull: *you're not just a necromancer.*"

"I know, I get that, but I don't know how to do any of that other stuff." She spread her hands, frowning at him. She barely knew how to *do* the necromancy, if she was being honest. "What can I even do that would help you? I'm not a healer."

"What d'you want, a pamphlet? You can use death magic to manipulate dead flesh, make it regenerate. Your dad could, anyway. It's called necrohealing, and I'd, uh, *really appreciate some,*" he rasped, laughing with frustration.

"Okay." She spat out a breath. "But you'll have to show me how."

Cal grimaced and took her hands.

She'd assumed that touching his skin would be unpleasant—that he would feel sticky and broken and wrong—but she found, instead, that it wasn't much different than touching another human. Just leathery and pitted.

"What?" he asked, his watery eyes gauging her expression.

"You just … don't feel very rotten."

"That's 'cause I'm not," he grumbled. "Not any more than I was when I came outta the ground, anyway."

"How?"

"It's a charm. *He* cast it. I wouldn't be any good to him if I kept rotting, would I?" He snorted. "Can we get on with the healing? I'm feelin' like

Canadian bacon over here."

Edie took a deep breath and moved her hands to his face, already certain she wouldn't be able to do anything. But the second she touched the burnt skin, something changed. She felt strangely like she was touching some sort of invisible membrane. Rubbery threads stuck to her fingertips, and if she moved her fingers in the right way, she could guide them away from their current alignment in frayed, ashy paths.

Somehow, suddenly, it made sense.

She concentrated, zoning out as she gently worked each sinewy strand into different avenues—the right ones. She could feel a bit of elasticity return to the membrane as she coaxed it into place, and was able to move the threads a little more quickly.

Cal grunted in pain, drawing her attention. The exposed tissue and muscle on his face was turning; charred skin renewed, not exactly *lifelike* but not burnt either. The blackened veins branching across the planes of his face faded, rid of irritation. His ruddy, grayish-yellow hue returned.

Spots of darkness closed in on her vision.

"Kid? You all right?" Cal took her hands and carefully unstuck them from the invisible membrane of his aura, then forced them down into her lap. He reached up and flipped the rearview mirror toward her.

She hadn't looked on top of the world before, but now she looked ... demonstrably worse. Worse in a way she hadn't thought was possible, given that she'd looked normal mere hours ago. Now her complexion looked like a melted candle, waxy and pale. Her eyelids were bruised, ringed in deep purple, and her lips matched.

"Just take it easy," Cal said, rolling his window down.

Edie's head lolled in his direction as she gave him a once-over. He looked much better, albeit a little the worse for wear—but wasn't he always? His eyes were no longer smoky, his face wasn't burnt, and he looked aware of his surroundings.

He glanced back at her, lips tight, killing the engine entirely. "Didn't realize it would take so much outta you."

"I'll be fiiiii…. Just need … rest," she managed, raising her shaking hands to rub her own face. Suddenly, she could barely think, drained by something that had seemed so simple a moment ago.

Cal opened his door. "There's probably vending machines in there. I'm gonna grab you something." He slammed it as he left.

The blood drying on her clavicle sang to her again. Without even meaning to, she drank in its song. The hot, fuzzy darkness clouding her mind abated, but only barely.

She turned, curled herself tight against the leather seat, and fell asleep.

Zaedicus growled in frustration, striking the surface of the cool water in the scrying basin. Droplets hit his armed guards, who were packed tightly into the small, dark room; the water sloshed gently over the side, staining the basin a darker black.

This was not acceptable.

The high-wight leaned forward, gripping the sides of the scrying basin and looking into its now-dark waters. With only a candle lighting the room, he could barely see his reflection staring back. Across the basin, the vampire woman from the previous night—Scarlet—stood. She had downgraded from her dress to a leather bustier and trousers, and she chewed on her bottom lip as she watched him.

For a long time, the only sound between them was Zaedicus's frustrated breathing. Finally, he said, "Is this all you can show me?"

Scarlet knit her brows, eyes narrowed. "The connection was severed when she passed out. I could try to connect to the revenant—"

"No. It is no matter. I've seen enough."

Scarlet was tedious, but she had proven herself useful, and a loyal member of the Gloaming. She was a talented scryer, and a memory leech. He had plans for her. If she followed orders, the Wounded would surely reward her.

The same could not be said for Zaedicus. If he didn't pin the hellerune down soon, he would be punished.

He raised a hand and shooed the vampire away. There was no sense in prolonging the inevitable. His lord had to be told what was going on, if he hadn't already been enlightened.

Scarlet looked him over with those unreadable black eyes of hers, then left without another word. Zaedicus waved his guards after her as well. Whatever punishment would be dealt, he couldn't abide the embarrassment of having them witness it. The harder, the more untouchable he seemed to them, the greater their fear and the easier they were to control.

The high-wight felt his injured pride whimper in pain. The Wounded was powerful, influential, but he was still a human—and a *young* human, at that, no older than five-and-twenty years. Zaedicus was practically serving an infant, yet he trembled at the thought of holding an audience with him.

Once he was alone, Zaedicus raised the lit candle from its notch on the rim of the scrying basin and held it above his head, surveying the room. It was no bigger than a maintenance closet, with no windows, the walls and door obscured by thick, claret drapes.

He faced the back wall and, on his knees, placed the candle on the oak floor, illuminating the invocation stave and runes that were carved there. The candle cast the barest yellow glow as the high-wight drew a knife from within the luxurious folds of his robe.

"*Nøkkviðr minn sár, rjóða minn knífr.*" He drew the knife across his forearm, wetting the blade with the sluggish flow of dark blood. As he whispered the rest of the incantation, he held the cut over the invocation spell and squeezed it.

Only a moment after the first drop of blood touched the stave, the spell leapt to life; fire roared up from the ground, though he could not feel the heat of it. Slowly, a figure appeared, orange flames licking its calves and knees.

It was the figure of a man, perhaps a couple inches taller than six feet, built like a fighter, with the shadow of a great claymore strapped to his back. Zaedicus dared not look at his face, but remained kneeling instead, studying the strange red markings climbing the man's arms—the wounds for which he was named.

When they had first met, Zaedicus had assumed they were tattoos. Now, he knew better.

The markings flared red, the magic that moved in the man's veins flowing too fast and stumbling over itself, weaving angrily like a swarm of beetles. With a measured but crushing movement, the Wounded seized Zaedicus by the front of his robes and drew him up so their faces were level. His face was still cast in shadow, but Zaedicus could see the bridge of his nose furrow in unspeakable fury, like a wolf about to strike.

He said nothing, and after a moment, he released Zaedicus. The frenzied magic pooling in his scars faded slightly. *"You failed."*

"My lord, forgive me. I never expected such resistance."

"You had every chance to prepare yourself. There is no excuse for such careless planning. Where. Is the girl. Now?"

"Forgive me, my lord," the high wight mumbled again.

"Enough groveling. Tell me where she is, if not with you."

"In a province called Maine, my lord. The Holloway thrall found her, brought her to the valkyrie Fengrave. She's sent her to fetch someone from the coast."

The figure folded his hands behind his back and began to pace in a tight circle. *"Who is this someone she and her thrall are to fetch?"*

"I ... am unsure. My scryer was not able to determine." Zaedicus braced himself for the Wounded's fit of rage.

But it didn't come. The Wounded paused, thought for a moment, then turned fully toward Zaedicus. *Laughing.*

He almost would have preferred the fit of rage.

"Take heart, elf. She will come back, and you will engage her here, where you have an advantage. And this time, you will *be prepared."*

CHAPTER SIXTEEN

By the time Edie woke, the highway was long gone. They were coasting along a winding road lined with trees, with the occasional vacation home or random antique shop along the way. Ghost's top was down, and the wind whipped Edie's face pleasantly. As she lifted her head, they passed a little white church with a sign out front that read RECREATION NOT WRECK CREATION.

Her puzzled laughter drew Cal's attention, and she saw him grin. A few seconds down the road, they passed something called Three Chicks Farm. "Sounds like my kinda farm," he said, drumming the steering wheel with his fingers.

Edie sat up a little straighter and reached for her phone to check the time. It'd had time to charge off the external battery she'd packed, but when she turned it on, all the notifications from last night came bombarding her at once, throwing her phone into a vibrating fit for almost a full thirty seconds.

She sighed. It was noonish. "Where are we?"

"A couple minutes from Bar Harbor. Guess we'll see about where the inn is when we come up. Might have to ask someone."

Edie snorted and pulled down the system tray of her phone, turning on her location services. "It's fine, I can just look it up on my phone." She shook it at him as the app loaded. "You should get yourself one of these."

He didn't respond, but he raised his brows like he was considering it. "Don't know where in the Reachbarrow Inn we're supposed to be meeting this Satara broad."

Broad! Edie thought, biting back a howl of laughter.

"Can your phone tell us that?"

"It's a Samsung, Cal, not Saruman." She pointed as they approached an intersection. "Take a right."

The town was a lot busier than she had envisioned or remembered. All along the main road were shops and cafes and inns, ending in a park and pier where some of the bigger houses and fancier restaurants stood overlooking the harbor. The town was definitely in season; pedestrians swarmed the sidewalk, and every place with outdoor seating seemed to be full. She and Cal were stuck at a crosswalk for almost a full five minutes as people crossed from both directions, relentlessly.

"I remember it being a lot quieter," Edie said when they were finally able to turn. She watched as they passed a giant wooden statue of a lobster holding an ice cream cone—a terrifying effigy if ever she'd seen one.

"That was over ten years ago, kid. The whole world was a lot quieter."

The Reachbarrow Inn was farther from the busy storefronts—south, according to Edie's phone. It was only a matter of minutes before they pulled up to an old Tudor-style cottage with peaked roofs and an old wooden door that reminded Edie of the one in Astrid's shop, with an iron knocker shaped like a bear's head. Two chimneys rose from the scallop-tiled roof, fat at the bottoms and thinner at the tops. The windows were arched, and as she and Cal stepped out onto the newly-paved sidewalk, Edie noticed some sort of pattern frosted into the trim of each crystal pane. A worn brass placard next to the door read *Reachbarrow Inn*.

She tipped her head up, shielding her eyes from the sun as she studied the building. For a second, she swore she saw someone watching them from one of the second-floor windows. Cal must have noticed, too; he seemed tense. With a reluctant grumble, he motioned for Edie to lead the way.

Okay. No problem. You can do this, she thought. *You're just walking into a strange house in the middle of a strange state with a dead person you barely know*. She had to admit it would be nice to get inside, though. It was pretty hot for a spring day, and she was sweltering in her leather jacket, black tank, and dark jeans.

She climbed the cement steps up to the walkway and stopped in front of the door. The inn looked so much like a private residence that she wondered if she should knock first—there was a knocker, after all. Ultimately, she tried the doorknob, and was happy to find it unlocked.

The inn was just as quaint inside as it was outside, filled with antique furniture and kitschy wall decorations. The floor was slanted, rough-cut cedar covered with heavy Victorian carpets here and there. A wreath of summer flowers with a crucifix in the center hung above a small check-in desk.

Cal swiped a few root beer candies from a bowl on the edge of the concierge desk as Edie leaned over it, looking for any sign of life.

"Hello? We're here to, um ... check in?" She wasn't sure if they would actually be staying there, but it was sure to get the innkeeper's attention.

There was a rattling from somewhere deeper in the cottage, and eventually, a man emerged from a door Edie hadn't even noticed was there, wedged in between a bookcase and a taxidermy elk. He was old but stood straight, and looked built and confident despite his ridiculous coke-bottle glasses—which made his eyes appear cartoonishly large—and mustard-yellow sweater vest. Three deep, angry scars marked his face from brow to chin, interrupting his well-trimmed gray beard at intervals.

He smiled warmly at Edie and adjusted his glasses. "Hello, ma'am. You checking in?"

"Yes ... kind of." Edie shoved her hands in her jacket pockets. "A friend of ours is expecting us. Her name is Satara?"

The old man nodded and retrieved a spiral-bound ledger from under the desk somewhere. Edie thought he must not see much business if he didn't even bother to keep digital records. Or maybe a literal paper trail was just easier to get rid of for good. She shuddered.

"I don't know why I got this out," the man said with a good-natured snort. "I only have three rooms occupied. Not that hard to keep track of, even for an old dog like me."

Cal grumbled behind Edie. After their encounter on the road, she wondered just how literally he meant *dog*.

"May as well take your name down anyway." He bent over the ledger, then looked up, glancing over Edie's shoulder to one of the windows. He still hadn't even acknowledged Cal's existence. "Is it nice out?"

"It's pretty nice, but I'm not big on the heat." She pointed to the ledger. "Edith Holloway."

The old man tensed up when she said her name, then his gaze went to Cal. "Oh...."

"Something the matter, Rin Tin Tin?" Cal asked, stepping forward and jabbing at the ledger with one discolored finger. "You gonna put the name down or what?" It almost sounded like a challenge.

"That's ... okay. Your friend is in the Acadia Room ... up the stairs, last on the left." The old man—though after Cal's remark, she was sure he was some sort of wolf-person—addressed Edie. Weird. He seemed less concerned about the armed dead guy and almost scared of *her*.

Just what had her father done to make all these people so frightened of him?

She didn't feel great about it. But for now, it seemed convenient—as horrible as that was.

"Thanks," she said as politely as she could, before trotting over to the staircase. It was cozied up to a small sitting area comprised of two wooden chairs and a breakfast table stacked with books about birds. The stairs led to a dark hallway with the same rough-cut cedar floor and matching beams in the ceiling. It was a cozy, slanted hallway, with only one high window at the end of the hall to illuminate it. Edie got the distinct feeling of being transported to another place and time, somewhere so far away from present-day Maine, yet strangely familiar.

"There it is," Cal mumbled as they approached the end of the hall. The last door on the left had a brass plaque on it that read *Acadia Room*. On the matching doorknob hung a DO NOT DISTURB sign.

Edie swallowed, glanced at Cal, and knocked.

"Who is it?" came a voice. It was a rich, feminine voice, but quiet, muffled by the thick walls.

"Edith Holloway and, um, Cal. Astrid sent us."

There was a moment's pause, then: "Come in."

Okay, you can do this.

Edie got anxious even meeting new *human* people. This not knowing who or what she'd find on the other side of the door, and whether or not they would want to kill her, was about ten times more stressful. She flexed her hand a moment before opening the door and stepping through.

The woman was standing on the far side of the bedroom, where the cedar walls slanted on either side of an intimate window seat. The bed to their right was nondescript save for the bear pelt sprawled across the foot of it, and besides a few rustic pieces of furniture, there wasn't much else. The woman herself had her back turned to them, framed by a golden corona such that Edie couldn't make out much about her besides her height and lean, athletic build.

"I admit, I expected someone older," the woman said, her tone tense. "And taller."

Taller? She must have been the one watching them from the window. Edie wasn't sure what to say. She shrugged a shoulder. "Uh ... sorry to disappoint?"

The woman finally turned, her dark eyes fixing Edie with an unreadable stare. Her umber skin was the same shade as the smoky quartz bracelet she wore; the sun pouring in from the window highlighted her high cheekbones, round nose, and smooth brow. Her thick black hair was done in two elevated goddess braids, with the sides of her head close-shaven.

But what struck Edie most about her appearance was what she was wearing: smooth leather leggings, a maroon tunic; a thin, worn cream gambeson and a distressed copper breastplate and gorget. Leather pauldrons lined with raven feathers were secured by straps across her chest, and she wore long vambraces to match. At the moment, she was barefoot, but Edie spotted a pair of steel-plated, knee-high boots by the door.

"You Satara?" Cal asked as he slowly shut the door behind them.

The woman nodded, looking him over. "You must be the revenant. Calcifer."

"Cal's fine," he said, taking a pack of cigarettes and lighting one up without pretense.

Edie felt a strange shimmer of energy next to her, and glanced in his direction. To her eyes, nothing seemed to have changed, but now Satara was staring at him. Edie realized he must have deactivated his glamour. The shieldmaiden's expression was curious—and a little irritated, probably at his manners—but she said nothing.

Edie wasn't sure what kind of pleasantries Norse warriors expected, but Satara didn't seem overjoyed to meet them. She decided to get right to business. "Astrid said that you needed us, or had info or something."

Satara considered her for a moment, brows drawn, before nodding. She sat in the window seat, hands on her knees. She offered neither Edie nor Cal a seat, so they both stood awkwardly. "Yes, she sent me a note by bird early this morning, saying you'd be coming. I must admit it came as a surprise, hearing that Richard Holloway's daughter had shown up."

Her tone wasn't angry or anything, but her expression was far from impressed. Edie got the feeling Satara was wary of her, but that wasn't new at this point. Maybe Satara hated her father. Everyone but Astrid seemed to have some kind of beef with Richard Holloway, and even Astrid hadn't been singing his praises.

"The Aurora and Gloaming have been making defensive moves in the past couple of months, gathering up allies." Satara fingered one of the frayed pillows beside her. "Astrid believes that this means some sort of conflict is on its way. It probably won't result in anything more than a simple skirmish for now, but no doubt it's part of something bigger. The Reach should be involved before we find ourselves even fewer in numbers."

Edie shifted feet anxiously. "So, the Reach is in some kind of danger of disappearing completely."

Satara drummed her fingers on her knees. "It *has* disappeared. The Reach used to be significant, a yawning expanse between two extremes. Leadership began to dwindle hundreds of years ago." She looked between them. "If we could harbor civilians, *protect* people? It would mean a solution to the strife and death that the Aurora-Gloaming conflict has caused. But we're not powerful enough anymore."

"That's what Astrid and your dad were trying to do all those years ago," Cal mumbled around his cigarette. "Supposedly."

Edie looked at him. "You'd think you'd be able to tell me more, then."

"Who, me? He had me bashing heads, not printing out brochures."

Satara waved a hand as if to dispel their tangent, though her gaze lingered on Cal as she spoke. "We need to bring our own allies together. I only have so much time to do what needs to be done. For some reason"—she looked to Edie again—"Astrid trusts you, and thinks you can help me. Apparently, if I present you, the sorceress I'm after will take my proposal a bit more seriously."

Oh. Edie's face burned with embarrassment. She was starting to see the problem. Satara wasn't happy she was being undercut by someone who didn't even know what was what, let alone how to handle it.

Satara sighed and looked away. "I've been tracking her for over a week, preparing to make contact."

Cal ashed his cigarette into one of the pockets of his cargo pants. "Hit us, jack."

Satara seemed confused by the expression, and glanced at Edie.

"He means tell us."

The shieldmaiden stood and picked up a small duffel bag on the floor next to her. "First, I need to know you are who you say you are. Show me the shield."

CHAPTER SEVENTEEN

SATARA TESTED the weight of Astrid's spear in her hand, then turned to Cal and Edie, who were waiting on the sidewalk behind her. She smiled tightly. "Now there can be no doubt my battlemother sent you. It should be proof enough for the sorceress, too. And it will be good to have weapons in case we run into trouble." After a pause, she continued, "So, you truly are who you say you are. I'm not sure if that should worry me."

Cal crossed his arms and snorted. "What's that supposed to mean?"

"You two aren't exactly experienced. I can already tell you lack discipline." She twirled the spear like a baton, testing the balance.

"And I guess you're a paragon of grace." Edie tried to keep her tone light, but she still didn't take kindly to being insulted. Even if those insults happened to be true.

"Excuse my arrogance," Satara said flatly, then added, "I'm not too proud to admit I still have things to learn. But at the very least, I *have* training. You're just ... not what I expected."

Edie frowned deeply at the pavement. It was true that she was new to all this, but she was doing her best. And she hadn't meant to overstep her boundaries. All this had been Astrid's idea, anyway.

Cal seemed to sense her discomfort. He lit another cigarette as he climbed behind Ghost's wheel. "Let's get a move on, yeah? Tell us about this *ally* we're supposed to be recruiting."

With a mumble, Edie offered Satara the passenger seat, but she declined, saying she preferred to stay in the back where she could keep Astrid's spear and shield close.

Once Satara put her overnight bag in the trunk and they were all settled in, the two turned to watch the shieldmaiden expectantly. She seemed preoccupied with the car itself. "This is quite old, isn't it?" she remarked, then looked to Cal. "Where in the world did you get something that looks like this?"

"I inherited it," he said without missing a beat. "It's a '63."

She raised a brow at the melted upholstery and dash. "Is that an original feature?"

Cal followed her gaze and cleared his throat. "There was a, uh, problem on our way here. How old are you, anyway?"

"Twenty-six."

God, she was only a few years older than Edie and she already had her life figured out. Not that *shieldmaiden* had really had a table at Senior Career Night. Still, it must be nice to have a path laid out for you.

"Ready?" Satara asked, looking between them.

Cal turned back to the wheel and started the engine. "Yeah, just tell me where I'm going, so I can head there while you fill us in."

"She lives on a rock formation by the sea, on a beach called Thor's Landing. Head toward Acadia National Park and you can follow signs from there."

Cal pulled away from the curb while Edie spoke: "A national park seems like kind of a shitty place for a hermit to live. Wouldn't tourists come bothering you all the time?"

"Her home is concealed most of the time. That's why we have to get the timing right. Otherwise, it won't appear to us, and we can't find her until tomorrow."

"So tell me about this chick," Cal said, adjusting the rearview mirror so he could see Satara.

She didn't look like she was a huge fan of his indelicate wording, but she obliged nonetheless. "Her name is Tiralda. She was once a priestess of Freyja. Now, she's just a hermit sorceress—a *seiðkona*. Seidr-woman."

"Ooh," Cal said, grinning wickedly as he headed back toward the center of town.

Edie looked over. "What's a seidr-woman?"

"A sex witch," he replied in a low tone, drumming his fingers excitedly on the steering wheel.

Satara spat out a half-breath, half-laugh from the back seat. "That's ... a sickening oversimplification of a complex system of magic."

"He's sickening," Edie said. "You'll get used to it."

Satara rubbed her forehead. "Seidr *sometimes* involves sex rituals, but Tiralda is not a *sex witch*. She's a spell-weaver—and a seer, to a lesser extent. And she's apparently still very powerful."

Edie looked at Cal to gauge his reaction, but he'd become distracted at an intersection by a busty blonde in a bikini top, innocently enjoying an ice cream. It was melting faster than she could lick it, and vanilla dripped on her cleavage. He looked bewitched.

A Chrysler behind them honked, which seemed to shake Cal out of his trance. He roared around the turn ahead of them at a borderline-dangerous pace.

Edie looked back at Satara. "I don't think he appreciates the nuance." To Cal, she said, "Cal. No ice cream bikini babes while driving."

He seemed embarrassed, taking a pair of wrap-around sunglasses from the seat between them and putting them on quickly. Edie bit back a cackle and decided not to push it. This probably wasn't a good time to poke the bear.

"Anyway," the shieldmaiden said, eyeing the back of Cal's head, "Astrid knew her a long time ago, and thinks she'd make a good ally. She made it seem rather urgent ... so I have a feeling someone else is trying to contact Tiralda as well."

Edie had to admit that she still wasn't completely on board with being conscripted to run errands for people she barely knew, but this whole Reach thing—protecting helpless people—*sounded* like a good cause. Cal seemed to like Astrid, anyway, and he wasn't all gung-ho about factions or whatever, so it couldn't be all bad.

Edie would go along with the ride for now; she could hardly sit at home and go about her business while there were people out there trying to kill her.

Ugh.

She saw the first sign for Thor's Landing and felt butterflies in her stomach. Sure, she'd go along for the ride, but it was still totally weird to be meeting a lord-only-knew-how-old priestess for a goddess Edie was starting to doubt was just a myth.

And that was another thing: Astrid and Satara talked about "the gods" a lot. Edie had never been religious, and she guessed that everyone wanted to believe in something bigger than them. But the way they talked about it so matter-of-factly, like it was a given that all-powerful beings ruled over the universe and watched everyone's every move, was still unsettling.

Though, at this point, the vampires and valkyir were bigger shocks to her system than anything about a god.

Satara had fallen silent in the back; apparently, she didn't have much to say to an infant and a dead pervert.

"Sooo, where does Astrid know this lady from?" Edie asked, finally breaking the silence.

"They've both served Mother Valkyrie, of course. They probably met at one of her temples. Or perhaps even Fólkvangr, Freyja's domain in Asgard."

Right, Edie thought. *They were just hanging out in Asgard and happened to meet each other*. In any case, Edie vaguely knew who Freyja was just from general knowledge, and recalled Astrid mentioning something about a Mother Valkyrie. "Mother Valkyrie is Freyja?"

"She is, yes. Among other things. Tiralda is not a valkyrie like my battlemother. Not all followers of Freyja are, and I don't know of any valkyrie priestesses, though there may be some. Freyja was the first to practice seidr, and she taught Odin and the other Aesir...."

"So it's kind of her thing," Edie concluded. "So why quit being a priestess to hang out in Maine, of all places?"

Satara looked at their surroundings as they drove along the more isolated, winding roads, down the mountain toward the entrance to Acadia National Park. "I'm not sure why she left Freyja's service. She's over a thousand years old. Perhaps she got bored. As for Maine, you have to admit the scenery is unmatched. And she ... likes water. You'll see when we get to Thor's Landing."

Edie thought she saw the barest smile pull at the corners of Satara's mouth.

At around 7:30, a couple of men exited the ranger station adjacent to the Thor's Landing Campground. One of them headed to his car to leave; the other secured the outer door of the ranger station, locking it for the night. Edie, Cal, and Satara waited just inside the nearby campground, concealed by thick evergreens and mossy boulders.

Edie swatted yet another mosquito away from her neck and groaned, popping her leather collar. "How much longer do we have to wait here?"

"Until they leave. No one is allowed on the rocks at night. We'll have to walk the rest of the way." Satara pointed at a break in the trees, where the ocean and a distant rock formation could be seen. "Tiralda lives there, atop Thor's Hole."

"*Thor's Hole?*" Edie looked at Cal. The fact that he was already smirking made it even harder for her to suppress her giggles. "Damn, what an honor."

Cal choked on his cigarette and finally snickered.

Satara rolled her eyes at them both, nostrils flaring. "Very original."

Sounds of the park rangers calling back and forth drew her attention again, and they all watched as the first drove out of the parking lot. The second followed soon after in his SUV. Now, the only sounds were the distant waves and sea birds, the ambiance of the forest, and the far-off sounds of children and families behind them, deeper into the campground.

"Come." Satara motioned for Edie and Cal to follow her as she slunk out of their hiding place, heading toward Ghost. She retrieved the spear and shield, strapping the latter across her back. Cal grabbed his shotgun and revolver from under the driver's seat, his milky blue eyes sad as his gaze fell on the melted leather interior.

Edie looked between them. "I feel kinda useless without a weapon."

"You got weapons." Cal gestured to her hands with the barrel of his shotgun.

Yeah, as if I'm ever going to learn how to properly use these, she thought as she looked at them.

"We don't have much time," Satara said as they continued up the unpaved road. "Her home reveals itself at twilight, for one hour. Follow me, quickly."

It was just a short walk down a paved road, but the shieldmaiden darted down it, her braids swinging as she did. Cal followed close on her heels, but Edie had to struggle to keep up with them in her high tops. If this wasn't all some crazy dream—if this was really her life now—she was going to have to get in better shape. Jogging a couple miles every few days wasn't going to cut it.

Just as she was considering yelling ahead for them to slow down, they reached a long, newly-paved parking lot, empty at this time of night. The trees had obscured the ocean as they were running down the road, but now that Edie could see, the rock formation was much closer than she'd expected. Only a flight of stone steps and a footpath separated them from Thor's Hole now.

It was a natural formation, but more or less rectangular. It extended across the beach like a shelf, with many uneven layers of stone making up its rough surface. Running adjacent to it was another stone outcropping that was much closer to the water and jutted seaward. It had been paved, turned into a sort of viewing platform complete with steel railings, and was low enough to the water that every time a particularly large wave came in, it washed over the walkway. To the left of that, further down the footpath, were some flat rock shelves and what looked like the beginning of an ocean trail.

It was high tide, and the weather was gloomy. Great walls of sea foam splashed up every time the waves came in. Edie watched as it happened; every splash was accompanied by the incredibly loud noise of thunder rumbling.

"What was that?" she asked, looking to Satara. If it was about to storm, she didn't want *anything* to do with this place. Everything about it looked sharp and dangerous.

"Come, and I'll show you." Satara was smiling as she stepped down the uneven stone steps, onto the tourists' footpath. She motioned for Edie and Cal to follow.

"I'm ... not sure that's such a good idea." The waves came in again, hard, and the thunder growled fiercely.

Satara sighed. "It's not real thunder. You're not scared, are you?"

Cal prodded at Edie's shoulder, encouraging her forward. She groaned and shuffled, but took a couple cautious steps down before reaching Satara. She'd lived in the city all her life, could count the number of times she'd seen the ocean on one hand—and she'd hated it every time. Something about it was just ... squicky. It was way too big, and the water was too dark and too strong, and you never knew what was just under the surface.

Satara must have noticed her shaking. Her shoulders relaxed, her expression softening slightly as Edie stepped down to her level. "The most that will happen is you'll get wet," she promised as they started down the footpath, toward the outcropping with the railings.

Now that they were closer, Edie could see an informational board set up near the end of the catwalk. A triangular gate blocked the paved outcropping, but Satara simply stepped over it and waited for Edie to follow suit. The walkway was narrow, divided into three tiers, with each subsequent step lower to the water.

The pavement was also damn wet.

Edie's heart practically pounded out of her chest as she moved to look over the railing. The rock formation, dark in the twilight, was snuggled up close to the outcropping on which they stood, forming a small inlet. She watched as another wave crashed in, deafening. The water launched into the air like a geyser, spraying the two women with foam and raining salt water down on their heads.

Edie shrieked. "I hate this!" she managed, trying to guard her face. "And what's that *sound*?"

Satara grabbed her attention with a tap to her shoulder and led her over to the informational board, which Edie gripped for dear life as she read it.

Welcome to Thor's Hole!

For centuries, the people of Maine have come to enjoy the natural magic of this formation, as there are few like it in the entire world! At the bottom of the Thor's Hole inlet, there is a small cavern filled with rocks. As the waves pull out, the water level drops just below the ceiling of this cavern, causing air to become trapped. When the waves roll back in, the force of it collides with the air and creates tremendous pressure which causes a booming sound to erupt! At high tide, these waves can reach up to 40 feet high!

A diagram accompanied the explanation. Edie peered over the top of the information board, trying to catch a glimpse of the hole. The waves pulled out at a tear, leaving the face of the formation as black and shiny as pitch, covered in green algae and god only knew what else. For just a moment, she caught a glimpse of a dark fissure toward the bottom of the inlet. The thought of it made her shiver. Who knew what could be down there?

"Let's get back to the path," she mumbled, looking at Satara, who seemed delighted with the waves. *At least one of us is enjoying themselves.*

"Why? We have time before twilight," Satara replied. "And besides, Tiralda's home is atop the formation. We'll see it as soon as it appears."

"I don't want to get any wetter than I already am." *Never thought seeing Thor's hole would make me so wet,* she thought. The joke was so stupid that even if she hadn't been half-paralyzed with fear, she probably wouldn't have laughed at it.

From the footpath, Cal called to them, but he was barely audible over the sound of the waves tearing in and out.

Edie looked at him and raised a brow, spitting out strands of hair the wind had whipped into her mouth. "What?"

Cal cupped his hands around his mouth. "I said *look—*" The false thunder cut him off again.

She waited until the sound faded, then called back, "You really should give up smoking, Cal, it's not good for your vocals!"

He was waving both arms hard, looking like a total dork as he did. This time, though, he shouted loud enough for her to hear: "*I said look out!*"

Before she could ask what she was supposed to be looking out for, her feet were swept from under her. She fell to her knees, and sea foam raged past her shoulders and rushed into her nose and mouth.

A monster wave had blasted the outcropping and surged straight over the railings.

For a moment, she was so shocked by the soul-chillingly cold water that she only felt mild annoyance at the situation. Then a heavy sheet of water fell over her head and shoulders and the tide pulled out again, hard, snaring her in its clutches and dragging her to the end of the outcropping. Her jacket rode up as she rolled, and the skin of her back and side screamed as it was stung by the rough cement of the walkway and the cold water.

She turned her head in time to see Satara fall through the railings and into the water. Her braided head disappeared beneath the waves in a second, pulled in by the undertow.

Edie tried to call out for Cal, for anyone, as her body collided with the same railings with a dull *pang*. One leg swung under and she slipped, her bottom half practically hanging over the open sea, which was now reeling back for another punch. She held the railing until her joints burned with effort, trying to pull herself back fully onto the walkway.

She might have been able to, too, if another huge wave hadn't come in. Her butt slipped off the walkway, and in another moment, her arms were washed from the railing. In less than a second, she tumbled, fell, then felt the sting of the water hit her back like cement.

The wave pulled out; the undertow tugged. She was swallowed up.

CHAPTER EIGHTEEN

THE DEAFENING CRASH of the waves disappeared the instant her head ducked under the water, replaced by the loud ambient hum only something as huge and silent as the Atlantic Ocean could have. The water was frigid, zapping every nerve in her body and paralyzing her as she sank.

Vaguely, she thought she should try to swim. She managed to begin kicking her legs, but just as she was about to breach the briny green surface, another wave rolled over and she somersaulted head-over-foot, her body twisting painfully as she hit something solid.

She opened her mouth and let out a choked gurgle of pain. Salt water filled her eyes, her nose, her mouth. The pain of just breathing the water in was shocking.

She'd always imagined drowning would be a peaceful way to die. Apparently not. She could feel her throat spasming, trying to keep the sea water from entering her lungs; she could feel herself losing focus as panic set in.

The undertow yanked her like she was a dog on a chain, and she was pulled farther, deeper ... she thought. It was impossible to tell which way she was going, and now that she was far away from the twilit evening, the sickly green of the ocean had turned entirely black—as inky and impenetrable as if someone had pulled a hood over her head.

That same blackness began to enter her head. In a desperate attempt, she kicked her legs again and pushed up from the rocky seabed. The slime on the rocks made it a devastatingly ineffectual push, but she felt which way was up and shimmied as best she could in that direction. Her strength was almost completely depleted. She could feel her body becoming weaker, knew this was her last chance to regain the surface.

It was no use. Just when the blackness seemed to thin to gray, the undertow tugged again and pulled her farther and deeper.

Then something else tugged—at her waist. In fact, she was pretty sure she felt two muscular arms wrap around her.

In an instant, her head and shoulders shot to the surface like a torpedo launched. Her tongue finally tasted oxygen—then bile, then warmish seawater as she regurgitated it.

Someone was dragging her along the surface of the water, holding her tightly, their pace adjusted perfectly to the swell of the waves. She could feel the pull of the undertow, but her rescuer was undaunted, never giving an inch.

The trip back to shore was a blur. Consumed by the pain and the discomfort as her stomach and lungs rejected the salt water, she could barely remember who she was or how she'd gotten in this situation.

The next thing she felt was warm, uneven ground at her back.

Rocks. Rocks and sand.

She was lying on a rocky beach, her shirt and jacket pulled up to her ribs. The ground beneath her wasn't warm at all, she realized; it was just warmer than her skin.

"Edie, Satara!" It was Cal's voice, somewhere far behind her. She turned her head in the direction of the sound and opened her eyes long enough to see him and two other figures booking it down the beach toward her. She squinted, turning her head in the other direction to see Satara lying near her, in a similar condition. She didn't seem to be awake.

Edie closed her eyes fully. It stung to keep them open.

But wait. If Cal was running toward her, and Satara was passed out beside her....

Who had grabbed her?

Edie shifted and tried to prop herself up on her elbows. Her arms trembled and failed, and she fell on her back again.

It was then that she felt a cold, slimy hand on her chest, pressing her firmly down.

"Stay still, mortal." It was a male voice, deep and flanging; each fried syllable ended in a sort of gurgle, as if forming these words was unnatural for the speaker.

The sound of it set her hairs on end. Despite the aches in her shoulders and neck, Edie raised her head to look at her rescuer.

She wasn't sure what to call what was staring back at her. He was almost a sea creature, almost a man. His murky turquoise body was completely exposed and slimy-looking in the twilight, muscular and lean with long arms and a broad chest. The coloring there faded from a dark blue-green to white, like the underbelly of a fish, and black, maze-like markings covered his iridescent scales.

He had no hair, just a barbed crest that followed his backbone. Spiny little ears and prominent, pale gills fanned out just behind his jaw and along his throat, and his eyes were enormous, almond-shaped, and pure black.

Edie tried to sit up again, but the creature kept a firm hold on her. When she looked at his hand, she saw thick, fatty webbing between each of his fingers and—her puzzled and horrified gaze darted upward—almost the entire way up his arm.

The flanging of the creature's voice intensified, and his slitted nostrils flared. "Stay still, before I change my mind and break you upon these rocks."

Edie glanced at the rocks under her. The biggest one was barely the size of her fist. Was this guy for real?

"Oh, by the Blessed Mare, you again!" cried a woman. Both Edie and the strange creature turned their heads to look in her direction.

She was at least five foot eleven, with skin the color of the sand beneath them. Her hair was longer than Edie had ever seen on a person, reaching to her knees even when swept up over one shoulder, and she wore a sheer white dress and held a tall staff. Long, webbed ears peeked out from her curls and reached toward the half-lit sky. As she came closer, Edie noticed the skin on her bare arms and legs shimmering like scales.

But the scales, the fish guy, the fact that she'd almost just drowned ... all were dwarfed by the biggest surprise of all, coming up from behind the woman.

Marius, in full armor and burning a hole in Edie with those golden eyes.

The scaly woman waved her wooden staff at the sea creature still kneeling over Edie. "Shoo! Shoo!"

Edie thought it seemed pretty silly to be waving a stick at such a big creature, but miraculously, it worked. The fish guy hissed and recoiled, retreating from the shore at once. Before Edie could even sit up fully, he was just a streak in the water.

The woman snarled and planted the end of her staff in the sand, her other hand on her hip. "Good riddance. And my apologies. That disgusting thing has been haunting my shore for ages now."

Cal rushed to Edie's side and helped her sit up more fully. Behind her, she could hear Satara coughing up seawater. The sound of Satara gagging and the way Cal was jostling her caused another surge up her throat, too; she rolled to the side and hacked out what felt like a gallon of hot bile.

Great, just what she needed: Marius seeing her in another humiliating situation. That guy did *not* need more ammunition to use against her.

"Jesus Christ," Cal said, looking between her and Satara. "You're both cut to shit."

Edie followed his gaze as it dropped to her bruised and scraped torso, then glanced over at Satara. Her tunic and leggings were torn, the feathers decorating her armor soaked. Her skin was smeared with blood from cuts on her hands and forehead.

Edie raised a hand to her own face, not surprised when it came away pink with blood and black from her ruined makeup.

"You all right?" Cal asked over Edie's shoulder. "Nothing broken?"

"Just a few scrapes and bruises," Satara managed between coughs. "I'll be fine." She looked up after a moment of gathering herself, though she still shivered from the cold. "I see you've found Tiralda."

"You're lucky to be alive, little darlings," the strange woman said, leaning against her staff and watching them both with concerned eyes and drooping ears. "The sea here can be unforgiving, and so can her inhabitants."

Edie looked up at Tiralda, trying to ignore Marius only a few paces behind her. "Why did you chase that fish guy off? We'd both be dead if it wasn't for him."

"Yeah," Cal said, sounding indignant and oddly protective of Fish Guy now that the point had been made. "I didn't see you or Sparky over there"— he tossed his head in Marius's direction—"diving in to save anyone."

"Neither did you, rotter," Marius returned under his breath.

Cal's grip on Edie's arm tightened so hard she thought he might snap it in half, but she was still too dazed to smack him away. "*Undead* and water don't mix … if we can help it."

Tiralda didn't get the chance to answer Edie's question. From behind them, there was a cry of frustration.

It was Satara, and when Edie turned to look at her, she was sitting with her shoulders tense and her forehead resting in her palms. "May this beach dry up into a desert," she spat.

"Whatever is the matter, dear one?" Tiralda asked, yanking her staff from the sand and crouching near the human woman. The sorceress's white dress billowed out around her and rode up her thighs, where the pearly scales Edie had noticed earlier were speckled a much lighter color.

Tiralda laid a hand on Satara's shoulder, whispering something. Tiny white lights appeared at the tips of her fingers and skimmed over Satara's skin, slowly closing the shieldmaiden's cuts and healing her bruises. A sheen of watery magic washed away the blood coating her face and hands.

When it was done, Satara looked livelier but no less devastated as she spoke: "I was holding Astrid's spear when I fell. I … dropped it. The shield at my back was washed away, too."

Damn, Edie thought. She didn't know much about the provenance of the weapons, but they had to be pretty old. They'd definitely looked it.

"I see," Tiralda said, frowning. "Astrid will not be happy to hear that...."

"No, she won't." After a moment, Satara raised her head, looking at the seidr-woman hopefully. Her building panic was evident. "I may need your help retrieving them."

"I'm afraid there's nothing I can do." The sorceress spread her hands apologetically. "Under normal circumstances, I'd be happy to dive and search for it, but I must leave my home as soon as possible. There is no time for such things."

"Leaving?" Edie piped in. Wasn't she supposed to be a hermit or something? "Why?"

Marius crossed his arms, chainmail glimmering in the quickly darkening twilight. "Because she's coming with me."

"What?" Satara, Cal, and Edie said it at almost the exact same time.

Their confusion seemed to amuse the vivid. He smirked. "She's agreed to help the Aurora move against the Gloaming ... and anyone *else* who might stand in our way."

"The Aurora?" Satara whipped around to face Tiralda properly. "You swore years ago that you would help the Reach, should we ever need you."

Tiralda shook her head. "Exactly. Years ago. My oath is old and severed. Things have changed. The threads of fate skew troublingly. I've seen it, as others have. I see the Gloaming rising like the tides of this sea, clamoring for power and washing away innocent people in the process." She glanced at Edie. "The Reach is simply not equipped to stop it."

"Oh, shut up," Cal snapped, gesturing from Tiralda to Marius. "You think the Aurora ain't gonna do the exact same thing? You think they won't hurt innocent people?"

Tiralda rose from where she was crouched near Satara. When she looked at Cal now, her face looked ... different. The ridge of her brow was more prominent, cheekbones sharp. Her pupils dilated, webbed ears flaring. "Hold your tongue, *zombie*."

Cal stood as well, hazy eyes narrowing. "You don't care about innocent people. You just care about bein' all self-righteous. You just wanna *win*."

The sorceress glared at Cal but addressed Edie: "At least your father knew how to keep his thrall quiet. And this is who Astrid grooms as the new Reacher?" Her gaze slid over Edie and landed on Satara. "A clueless, powerless child? Was this supposed to impress me?"

Edie had no idea what Tiralda was talking about—besides insulting her, and she was getting used to that by now—but her questions could wait till later. Edie's blood heated, flushing her cheeks. "Don't talk about Cal like that." She tried to sound as authoritative as she could while also using a nearby boulder to stand up fully.

She almost immediately regretted trying. Her lungs felt completely burnt out, and her entire body ached from the beating it had taken. With a yelp, she faltered, stumbling down onto one knee. *Oh, god.*

More vomit and water came, pinkish this time; and there was a new pain, blossoming in her stomach. Someone reached out and held her shoulder.

"Edie?" Cal's voice was soft—but it wasn't his hand she felt. It was way too warm.

She raised her head and realized Marius had come up from behind to help steady her. He was looking at her with his usual tight-lipped disapproval.

"Stay still," he said. After a moment, she felt warmth spreading from her shoulders, all through her body. The warmth soothed the ache in her lungs and numbed the pain of her bruises and cuts.

Then she felt it flow gently into the tangle of pain in her middle. It felt like taking the first sip of a hot drink, hot enough that you can feel it change the temperature of your body as it slides down your throat and relaxes into your belly. The heat was intense, and painful on its own for a few moments before it eased and disappeared, burning the ache away with it.

Marius had already pulled away by the time Edie realized what he'd done. "You healed me," she murmured, brow furrowing. She followed him with her gaze, confused.

Marius's disapproval never faltered. "You had minor internal bleeding."

"I thought you wanted me dead."

"I'd settle for a thank-you."

She didn't miss the fact that he hadn't countered her assumption. After a second, she obliged, albeit quietly. "Thank you."

He didn't even nod, simply looking past her and Cal and motioning for Tiralda. "My lady, we should leave as soon as possible. Radiant Eirik was very clear that I should deliver you as soon as I found you."

Tiralda shifted, her wooden bangles clanking against her staff as she did. "Yes, very well, Vivid. Let me pack my spinning wheel and a few other things, and I will be ready to go with you."

Marius gave them all one last look of warning—a look that said *don't even think of following us*—before he turned and followed Tiralda down the beach.

CHAPTER NINETEEN

So, that was it. The seidr-woman had slipped through their fingers.

"She was a jackass anyway," Cal murmured, more to Edie than to Satara, who was trudging ahead as the dejected group made their way back toward the campground.

"Yeah." Edie glanced over, fingering a bruise on her brow. "Sorry," she added.

Cal shrugged. He didn't need to say anything. Maybe whatever bond they shared let her see it more clearly, but Edie knew that what the sorceress had said was bothering him. She couldn't imagine what it was like to move through the world known only as Richard Holloway's property. It was exhausting enough being recognized as his daughter.

"What was her deal, anyway? Like, what is she?" She looked at the back of Satara's head, where her wet baby hairs clung to her neck.

"She's a vættr, a nature spirit. But that's a broad term. Specifically, Tiralda is a sjóvættr—sea spirit," Satara said. "In the beginning times, vættr were physical manifestations of their respective elements, but ... as you can see, they've developed beyond that." She sighed hard. "I couldn't tell you much more, myself. They're very secretive."

"And did you get a load of that fish guy?" Edie could still remember the feeling of his weird, cold hand on her chest, holding her down.

"I'm not sure what that was," Satara admitted softly. "But we do owe it our lives."

Cal rolled his eyes. "We coulda thanked him if Ursula there hadn't scared him off."

"I dunno why he was scared of her," Edie said. "He was, like, what, seven feet tall?"

"Vættr are more dangerous than they look. If she had wanted to, she could have washed us away and impaled us on the rocks. Or eaten us. They tend to have a taste for human flesh." Satara stopped at the entrance to the campground and looked over her shoulder at them. "She was only polite because she once cared for Astrid."

"Why didn't she help us grab the spear and shield, then?"

The shieldmaiden grimaced at being reminded of the lost artifacts. "I might have convinced her," she said, looking at Cal, "if you hadn't started *arguing* with her. Now the shield and spear are gone."

"Hmph. Sorry."

"It's ... okay." She sighed. "She might have refused anyway. Just because she didn't kill us doesn't mean she didn't take pleasure in seeing us miserable."

Edie shivered and tightened her jacket around her middle as an ocean breeze whipped through. "I thought mermaids would be a lot nicer."

Satara shook her head. "Not a mermaid. If you ever met a mermaid, you would know."

Ominous. Edie looked over at Cal, and his expression was solemn. Damn, if even he couldn't make some crude joke about screwing fish women, mermaids must be serious business.

Satara stepped into the campground parking lot, followed by the others.

"Go ahead and let yourselves in," Cal said, tossing his keys to Edie. "I need to piss."

Edie pulled a face as he diverged from the path. "Charming."

As she and Satara reached the car, Satara turned to her. "Do undead...?"

"Pee? This one does, only 'cause he goes through Jack Daniels like mineral water, apparently." The floor of his back seat, littered with all sorts of bottles, was proof positive of that. She unlocked the door, and without Edie's interference, it flew open so Satara could slide in the back.

"Thank you," Satara said to Ghost, as though she met haunted cars every day. Then, to Edie: "If he ... *pees*, does he also—"

"Listen, I didn't ask, and I don't wanna know." Edie paused. "He did mention he doesn't eat, though."

Speaking of eating, she hadn't in something like thirty-six hours. She definitely regretted not eating those fries at the diner the previous night. Hadn't Cal mentioned something about grabbing her snacks at a service station? She thought she remembered something like that before passing out.

"Let's talk about something else," Satara suggested, relaxing back against the leather seat.

Edie unwrapped a granola bar she found in the dash and turned in her seat to face Satara. "What are you gonna do about the shield and spear?"

Satara looked away, blinking. She looked overwhelmed and frustrated, and like she was trying hard not to cry. Though Edie hadn't known her for more than a few hours, she could already tell that the current situation wasn't just stressful; it was devastating.

Besides worrying for Satara, it made Edie more curious about the weapons.

"I'll have to tell her the truth," the shieldmaiden said. "She ... won't be pleased. She may punish me."

"Punish you how?" Edie raised a brow. "Take away your birthday?"

Satara took a deep breath, her voice quiet. "She may revoke my investitural rights. That shield and spear were a gift to Astrid's old battlemother from Skuld herself. They're irreplaceable."

Edie pretended to know who Skuld was, opting instead to ask the more pressing question: "Investitural rights? What do you mean?"

There was a silence. Satara avoided Edie's questioning gaze.

The wheels in Edie's head spun. Quietly, she said, "Astrid never told me how someone becomes a valkyrie."

Satara raised her head, picking Edie apart with her gaze as if trying to find her ulterior motive for asking. The shieldmaiden's expression had shifted; now, she looked scared and vulnerable.

Suddenly, a rough yelp rang out from the forest—unmistakably Cal. Edie started and exchanged a look with Satara. In a few moments, they had both rushed out of the convertible and were jogging in the direction of the sound.

Fifteen yards away stood the boulder they'd hidden behind while waiting for the park rangers to leave, and as they approached it, the sound of heavy boots came closer. Edie, running in front, collided with Cal as he rounded the corner at top speed. He grunted as she bounced off his body like he was made of rubber, and she was barely able to keep herself from falling on her ass.

"What happened?" Satara asked. "Why did you call out?"

Cal was either unable or unwilling to respond with a coherent answer. After clumsily zipping up his fly, he could only say, "Jesus Christing shit-bastard scared the fuck out of..." and gesture past the boulder with both hands.

Edie steadied herself and glanced behind the boulder, at the little canopy that led into the forest proper. "What? I don't see anything."

He growled, waved her closer, and took off at a trot back under the canopy. Edie and Satara exchanged another glance before following.

Soon, the three found themselves in a thick wooded area, dark now that dusk had fallen; only a little gray light filtered through the trees, enough for them to see the path and one another. Edie hugged herself tight, starting to shiver uncontrollably now. She was still wet and freezing, her pants were stiff with salt, and she just wanted to go home.

"What was it, Cal?" she asked, tiptoeing after him as he elbowed through the foliage.

"I swear to god, he's just lucky my shotgun wasn't loaded," he grumbled in reply, pulling her along by the back of her jacket for a moment before slowing and squinting through the trees. "It was around here somewhere, unless it got up and ran off."

He didn't have to look for very long.

"There." Satara pointed at a nearby bush, which was shivering curiously. She perked up as the thin light caught the metal tip of a spear. "It's Astrid's!"

Edie looked between her and Cal and motioned for them to stay quiet as they approached the totally inconspicuous spear-wielding bush. Who was in there, anyway? Who could possibly have gotten the spear and shield from the bottom of the ocean?

There was really only one answer that made sense.

"You can come out," Edie promised, trying to keep her tone friendly. "We won't hurt you. You just ... startled my friend."

After a moment, the spear dropped to the ground, though the shield was still out of sight—if he had it. Satara bent and picked it up, looking pleased at the show of good faith. But her expression quickly turned from pleased to disgusted when, as she pulled her hand from the shaft of the spear, it came away slimy.

Finally, the creature crept from the bush. Edie recognized him just from his shape, even though he was crouched: large, with broad shoulders and eyes blacker than the night around them. When he stepped into the gloomy light, she could see that he was clutching the shield to his middle, webbed fingers drumming anxiously against the ancient wood.

Fish Guy offered a sharp-toothed, almost sheepish grin.

Edie's shoulders relaxed. She saw it, but she could barely believe it. "Uh ... hello again."

Cal stepped forward. "What's your deal, sneaking up on a guy while he's ... *vulnerable?*" he demanded.

In turn, Fish Guy straightened to his full height, towering over all three of them; just when Edie was sure he was tall enough, there seemed to be more of him. He puffed up his chest and jabbed a clawed finger at Cal, looking down at him like a god about to smite a disobedient acolyte. It probably would have been more threatening had he not been naked and dripping sea water. "Again-walker, I am centuries your elder. I will not hesitate to tear your impudent flesh from the bone!"

Cal sneered. "You're welcome to try, if you want new lead fillings."

"Guys! Come on." Edie gave Cal a reproachful look before turning her attention back to the fish guy. "Who ... what ... are you? Why did you bring us the shield and spear?"

He could have easily just left the weapons sitting at the bottom of the ocean to be swallowed up by silt, or brought them to whatever hovel he called home and kept them as souvenirs. He'd had to go out of his way to find them, emerge from the ocean, and deliver them to a group of people who had already inconvenienced him once—or, at least, gotten him in trouble with a sea spirit sorceress.

The fish creature lowered his arm and hunched again, clutching the shield tight. He looked at Edie. "I am sjóvættr, of course." His tone was much too dignified for someone whose breath smelled like low tide.

"A sea spirit?" He didn't look like much of a sea spirit to her; he was sort of slimy and gross. Tiralda had been different, ethereal with the power and energy coming off her. "What's your name?"

The spines running up his back bristled, and he opened his mouth to answer her—but what came out was a series of ugly, guttural sounds and hisses that sounded more like someone choking than an actual language. It went on for a while, too; long enough that Edie could have introduced not only herself but also Cal and Satara.

When he was done, he asked politely, "And what are you called?"

She shared a glance with Cal and Satara, then looked back at Fish Guy. "Wait, back up one second. What was that?"

He began to repeat the sound, but Cal cut him off: "We don't speak fish, Jabberjaw!"

"Do you perhaps have a ... shorter name, one we mortals can pronounce, scale-friend?" Satara asked carefully, peering up at him.

The fish man seemed to respond favorably. At least one of them knew how to talk to mythical beings. He perked up and smiled at Satara. "Hm. Well ... in times past, mortals have called me Fiskbein."

"Fiskbein? Very well."

"Fiskbein it is," Edie said, looking him over. He was totally naked, but also totally flat *down there*—a small mercy. "I never got to thank you for saving me."

"Yes ... *she* chased me away." Fiskbein bared sharp teeth. "The sea witch will tell you I'm a *creature*. She lies! I am vættr, like her."

Edie had the feeling she wasn't getting the whole picture. After meeting her, Edie wasn't Tiralda's biggest fan, but surely there must be a good reason she hated the other sea spirit so much. Was he dangerous? "Why does she treat you like a creature, then?"

"Her kind deny spirits like me, their own brethren, the right to reach our full potential. They are wicked, wicked, vain beings!" His voice became deeper in anger; the flanging intensified, vocals frying. "They fear our ugly bodies and the magnitude of our power. That's why you must let me come with you! Their selfishness must be punished. If I could only develop my magic..."

Satara dug the base of her spear into the dirt and leaned on it, brows knit. "You expect us to take you on so you can, what, have your revenge? We have a mission of our own, Fiskbein. It has nothing to do with dismantling vættr hierarchy."

"But I could do whatever you wanted!" insisted the spirit.

Edie snorted. And here she had been thinking he was some sort of all-powerful lord of the ocean based on the way he'd spoken to them, calling them "mortals" and threatening them. She shook her head.

Cal cut in. "So, basically, you're a sea spirit just like Tiralda, but shittier? Listen, buddy, we were sent to pick up a witch, not some bottom-feeder." He pulled out a cigarette and lit it. Edie thought about scolding him, seeing as how they were in the middle of the forest, but she didn't want to derail the conversation.

Smokey the Bear would be so disgusted with me.

Fiskbein's fingers tightened on the dented iron rim of Astrid's shield. "You owe me a life debt, twice-fold, and I've brought you the weapons you foolishly lost," he said, voice rising in volume. "Will you truly insult me and then turn me away?"

Edie had to admit, she felt bad about it. She was absolutely certain she would have died without his help. She looked at Satara and noticed that she, too, looked conflicted; her shoulders were limp, her eyes roving over Fiskbein in thought.

The spirit tucked Astrid's shield under one arm, baring his teeth again. "If you leave without me, you leave without the shield."

He didn't look as intimidating as his words sounded, though. His gills drooped, his back hunched. He looked starved and unkempt and desperate. Edie had a feeling that if one of them pressed him hard enough, he'd give the shield up anyway and high-tail it back to the ocean. So much for tearing the flesh from their bones.

Edie looked to the others. Cal stood with his arms crossed, a disapproving glare stuck on his face.

Satara looked concerned, but considerably more open. She sighed. "I ... suppose you can come back with us. But," she added before he could start celebrating, "if Astrid says you have to return, you *must* do what she says."

Fiskbein's gills flared, this time in delight, and he flashed them all a frightening grin. "You won't regret this, mortals. Tiralda, tear her scales, will be sorry she broke her oath to you. I am twice the sorcerer she is."

Edie sighed and followed Satara as she started back to the car. "Oh, yeah? Do you do seidr, too?"

The hulking spirit—it felt strange to think of him as a spirit, since he was very clearly corporeal—trudged along beside her, gait uneven and galumphing on land. "No, no. Freyja's Craft is of no use to most water elementals. We favor her father."

"Her father?" Edie looked to Satara for help.

"Njord," Satara said. "God of the sea."

Fiskbein perked up a bit. He seemed surprised Edie had to ask, but said nothing.

"So, you can control waves and water and stuff like that?"

He paused before clearing his throat. "Potentially."

Okay, she got the feeling he wasn't as powerful as he'd advertised. "Right. Potentially."

He grinned sheepishly and changed the subject. "You never told me what you call yourselves."

"I'm Edie Holloway"—she was relieved to see he didn't recognize the name—"and that's Cal, and Satara."

Satara glanced back as they reached Ghost and nodded.

Cal wasn't as cordial. "Fuckin' terrific, someone else I gotta babysit," he muttered around his cigarette, sliding into the front seat and jerking a thumb back. "Edie, since it was your brilliant idea to go fishin', you get to sit in the back with him."

Edie groaned, but she didn't have the energy to fight. She was exhausted from a near-death experience, she was shivering cold in her still-wet clothing, and she was voraciously hungry. "Fine," she mumbled, moving to climb into the back seat.

With great force, the trunk popped, and the headlights flickered on and off.

"Oh, yeah," Cal added, reaching out the window and ashing his cigarette on the gravel. "Lay the tarp down before you get in. I got a blanket in the back, too. I don't wanna have to reupholster the *entire* goddamn interior 'cause of your wet asses."

Edie rolled her eyes and slid out of the car again, going to retrieve the stuff from the trunk. The tarp smelled suspiciously tangy and had some stains on it that she tried not to think about as she tossed it in the back seat. She handed the blanket to Satara, who covered her own seat with it before moving so Edie could squeeze in.

Once Ghost's protective barrier was laid out, Fiskbein climbed in, too. He had to hunch over just to fit, and even then, his head and back were pressed up against the soft top.

Cal kept the top up as they pulled out of the campground. Probably a good idea if they wanted to keep a low profile. The group called enough attention to themselves as it was. Unfortunately, the enclosed space also trapped the briny odor of their new companion. Edie's stomach stopped growling and started turning instead.

Despite Cal's protestations, Fiskbein stroked the interior of the car. "This is peculiar. Do you live in here?" He turned to look at Edie, blinking.

"Uh, no. I live in an apartment."

"How far is it?" Fiskbein asked, craning his neck downward to gaze out the window.

"Three or four hours from here."

Everyone in the car was silent for a while; Cal played the radio quietly, and every so often, one of the humans would cough from the intense stench in the cab.

They were probably about fifteen minutes into the drive when Fiskbein asked, "How far is it now?"

Edie and Cal exchanged a look in the rearview mirror. It was going to be another long night.

CHAPTER TWENTY

EDIE BIT into her second Big Mac and watched Fiskbein levitate the ice out of her soda. With the windows down, the smell in the car had finally dissipated enough for her appetite to come back in full force, so they'd stopped by a McDonald's and ordered two Big Mac meals, a Filet-O-Fish for Fiskbein, and water for Satara. She and Edie had been sharing fries and watching the sea spirit's tricks ever since they'd pulled back onto the highway.

They were on the last leg of their trip, with nothing better to do. It seemed like they had already exhausted possible topics of conversation, and Cal had put a ban on road games after a round of I Went on a Picnic ended with Fiskbein using the runic alphabet instead of the English one.

"So," Edie said, "you can only manipulate liquid that already exists? You can't just poof water out of thin air?" She glanced down as a rogue ice cube bounced out of the floating collection Fiskbein had amassed and hit her thigh, then took another bite of her burger.

"Mmm … well…."

"Let me guess," said Cal, "you *can* do it, you just don't wanna."

Edie couldn't help but snort a little. Whenever they questioned him about his magic, he'd change the subject, or make excuses as to why he couldn't show off his all-powerful abilities.

He bared his pointy teeth at Cal. "My powers are not a toy that I can simply summon for mortals' amusement."

Edie whacked his arm lightly. He was drier now than he had been—almost like a snake. "You know, you don't have to act like a dick and lie about your powers. I'm still learning, too." She took another bite of her burger, then said around it, "I've never even cast a real offensive spell before."

Fiskbein looked at her quizzically as he compacted his collection of ice cubes into one big, misshapen ball of watery ice. "How can that be?"

"How can what be?"

"The sea witch talked about you like you were someone important. I was listening. And your companions answer to you with deference."

Edie squirmed uncomfortably, but before she could protest, Cal piped up: "Hell no we don't."

Satara looked like she had tasted something bad, but she mumbled, "Edie's father was a leader in our community, once."

Dammit. As soon as Satara mentioned Dad, Edie became almost as tense as Cal did.

"Our faction is called the Reach," she continued as she unwrapped a granola bar. "Perhaps you've never heard of it, but it used to be huge."

"We tend to keep to the waters. We have no business on land. But...." Fiskbein squinted. "I think I remember something of that nature, back when we *baseborn*"—he spat the word—"were still allowed in the E'ularu and the cities. I think I remember some of the wellborn in disputes about something like that. Feuding on land."

There would be time to ask him about the ins and outs of sjóvættir society later; for now, Satara just nodded as though she understood what he was talking about. Edie supposed they had enough information to at least get a vague picture. "Richard Holloway studied the old Reach for years, then sought out others who wanted to restore it. Like Astrid Fengrave, my battlemother. It's a noble cause. The Gloaming and Aurora have gone unchecked for too long."

"Yeah, so noble. Dick Holloway, what an upstanding fuckin' citizen," Cal said, his voice dripping with venom. "What would we all have done without him?"

Edie felt an almost painful surge of anger coming down the line of their mental connection. The comment effectively ended Fiskbein's brief history lesson. Satara studied Cal but said nothing. Edie looked away, out the window.

There was a period of silence before she remembered something—something Tiralda had said. At the time, it hadn't seemed important, considering Edie had almost just drowned.

"Tiralda said something about Astrid 'grooming' me to be *the* Reacher." She looked back at the others. "It doesn't feel like Astrid is *grooming* me to be anything. So far, all I've done is run an errand for her." *And nearly get killed in the process*, she added mentally. "What is *the* Reacher?"

Satara's gaze was mostly impassive as she turned it on Edie, but bewilderment shone just under the surface. "Astrid ... didn't tell you?"

"No?"

Satara glanced at Cal before taking a breath. "The leader of the Reach."

Holding a beer, Cal watched from the couch as Edie wrote *SALT!!!* on the grocery list stuck to her fridge. With her hair down from its usual spiky bun, with her exhausted face, piercing eyes, and pasty skin, she looked so much like her father.

Too much.

Whenever she looked at him, he had to remind himself that this was different. Had to be. There was too much at stake for him to run away again.

But he would if it came down to it. He was sure of that.

He exhaled hard through his nose—such as it was—as she padded through the kitchen to sit down next to him. Relaxing a little, he sat back and gestured to the empty hamster cage on the coffee table. "So, you gonna get rid of that, or is it a piece of modern art now?"

Edie sighed, sweeping her hair over one shoulder. She looked a lot more comfortable now that she was in dry clothes. "I'll take care of it eventually. If you haven't noticed, I have a lot on my plate at the moment." She leaned forward to peep beyond the kitchen, toward the bathroom door. "Is everything okay in there?"

There was a soft trilling, then Fiskbein called, "Thank you for the salt, human!"

"You know table salt isn't the same thing as sea salt, right?" Cal asked under his breath, raising a brow in her direction before taking a long swig of beer.

"Yeah, I know. It'll have to do for now, though. Maybe Astrid can afford to buy buckets of aquarium salt, but I can't."

Satara had wanted to skip Edie's place altogether, but the kid looked like she might fall over dead if she went another night without sleep. And Fiskbein had complained the whole last half hour of the trip that he felt sick and needed water.

The shieldmaiden hadn't been too pleased with their change of plans, but she'd conceded and gone to find somewhere in town she could rest and freshen up. Poor gal. Edie seemed totally oblivious to why Satara wasn't fond of her, of course, and had been wondering aloud about it for a while now.

It seemed obvious to Cal. But he'd let her figure it out.

Edie dragged her hands down her face, sighing hard. "I'm going to crash soon. I'm so freaking exhausted."

"What're you gonna do with Barnacle Boy?" Cal jerked his chin in the direction of the bathroom.

He could tell it was a good question because of how miserable she looked when he asked it. "Well ... Mercy is probably at Drake's house or working, but she'll have to come home eventually, and Fisk"—she'd given the thing a nickname?—"definitely has to clear out of the tub by then." Edie's face crinkled in deep thought for a few seconds, then went slack with exhaustion as she gave up. "Astrid will have a better idea of what to do. But for tonight, I guess he can just hide in my room if Mercy comes home."

Cal curled his lip. "Slimy."

"At least he's taking a bath in water that's clean, even if it's filled with table salt. He won't be, uh, briny. You don't think he'll try to climb in bed with me, right?"

The revenant shook his head. "I'll take care of it," he replied shortly, and nudged her shoulder with the butt of his beer bottle. "Go to bed. You almost died twice today."

"Surprisingly, not a new record." She sighed as she pushed off the couch and retreated to her room with more life in her movements—probably genuinely excited to finally sleep in her bed. Even from the other room, behind a closed door, Cal could feel her relax and eventually drift off.

Yeah, he'd run. If he had to—if she turned out to be just as bad as her father—he'd leave her behind in a heartbeat. Before she could stop him.

He was surer of that than of anything else.

When Edie woke up, it was light out, and there was shouting coming from somewhere in the apartment. It sounded like—

Shit. Shit, shit, shit, shit!

She tossed her comforter off and bolted out of bed, almost tripping over her guitar case on her way out of her room. With a groan, she kicked it under her bed and flung open the door, looking down the hall.

Sure enough, there was Mercy—in her patterned shorts and fishnets, a crop top, and her black sun hat—cussing Cal out. He stood in front of the bathroom door with his arms crossed tightly, mouth pressed into a harsh line.

"Who the hell do you think you are?" Mercy was demanding. "This is *my* apartment! If you don't leave right now, I'm calling the fucking— the police!"

Oh, god. This was bad news. Mercy would never make a scene like this unless she was *really* pissed off.

"Call the cops, see if I care," Cal growled, taking his lighter from his back pocket and starting to light a cigarette.

Mercy straight-up smacked it out of his hand. "That is *it*! You— you asshole! I'm getting Edie."

She spun on her heel, probably barely refraining from trying to physically *throw* Cal out of the apartment, and came face to face with Edie. Her round sunset glasses slipped down her nose as she looked Edie over, brows drawing inward and lips pursing

"You look awful," she said, her voice filled with anger but also sincere concern. No doubt she was wondering what sort of drugs Edie had been getting into, if their last conversation was any indication.

Edie sighed and smoothed back her hair. "I know. What's going on here?"

"Your new friend"—Mercy flung an arm in Cal's direction—"says I can't go into the bathroom. What the heck are you doing in there? Edie...." Her voice became strained, and she reached forward and took Edie's hand. Her grip was tight. "Edie, what's going on? What's happening? Did something *happen*?"

Edie tried to laugh it off, smiling. "I'm fine, Mercy. Seriously. How was your night? You weren't around when I came home."

"I was at Drake's." She shook her head. "What's going on? Why can't I, y'know, *go in my bathroom*?"

There was a slippy squeaking sound from the tub, *very* audible from the hall. Both Edie and Mercy turned to look in that direction. Cal sighed in frustration.

"What— Is there someone in there?" Mercy let go of Edie's hands and tried, once again, to push past Cal.

It was about as effective as trying to shove a brick wall. He hip-checked her and managed to get her at arms' length, though he didn't touch her. "Take a walk, sweetheart."

Mercy's mouth hung open. She turned back to Edie and took off her glasses. "Aren't you going to tell him to stop?"

Silence fell between them.

When Edie didn't answer, Mercy continued, "Or is this just you now? You meet a new guy and two days later you're letting him cook meth or whatever in our bathtub?"

Edie tried not to gag at the "new guy" part—*ew*—and shook her head. "Mercy, it's just ... complicated."

It wasn't all that complicated, just weird, really. Unbelievable. Not something a sane person could or should tell their sane friends. But her heart was aching, lying like this. Mercy didn't deserve to be so worried about her all the time.

Astrid had mentioned that Edie might lose things now that she knew about the truth all around her. She had never guessed one of those things would be a long-standing friendship.

Mercy looked at her for a long time before putting her glasses back on and grabbing her purse from the couch. "Fine. Whatever. It's none of my business, anyway."

As she started for the door, it took everything in Edie's power not to go after her.

"I'll see you whenever," Mercy said, and slammed the door.

Edie stood still for a while after Mercy left. The apartment was silent. Her face felt numb all over; she didn't realize she was crying until she heard the tears pattering on the carpet below her.

When she started sniffling, Cal uncrossed his arms and came to her.

"Hey ... kid. It's all right." He laid a heavy hand on her shoulder and steered her to the couch, sitting her down. "She'll come back."

"You have to go after her," Edie said, taking his shoulders and squeezing hard.

He looked uncomfortable—probably both from being touched and her vulnerable state. "Don't think she'll come back if *I* ask her."

"No, I mean follow her. Please? What if she goes to the police? What if, I don't know, one of the Gloaming find her?"

Cal snorted. "They'd probably just think she was one of them. The Gloaming is full of goth chicks."

"Cal! Please, god, just stop and be serious for, like, two seconds, okay?" Edie threw her hands up. "*Please*, just do what I say."

He threw up his hands right back, standing straight and glaring at her. "Fine! Jesus, no one can do anything for themselves around here." He turned and picked up the cigarette Mercy had smacked out of his hand, then lit it as he stomped toward the door. "Fine. Just send Cal to do your errands. That's what he's for, anyway."

Edie sighed, holding her head as he, too, slammed the door behind him.

Great. Now everyone was mad at her.

She sat there for a while, trying to calm herself down, until the bathroom door creaked open. Fisk crept out, wrapped in Mercy's fluffy purple bathrobe—though, honestly, it was more of a tight jacket on him than a robe. He looked almost as exhausted as she did.

Edie raised her head. "Hi."

"I heard someone bellowing at Cal. I wanted to come express my appreciation, but they left." He smirked, and promptly *slammed* the bathroom door behind him.

"Yeah, that was Mercy. My human friend. Can you not slam the door? I've had enough of that for one day." She watched as he moved to sit in the armchair across from her.

"My apologies. I'm still getting used to … what is this word? *Door*."

He said the word with such distaste that Edie managed a little laugh. To be fair, the last two people who had used a door in this house had slammed it shut; he probably just thought that was how normal, rational people shut them.

Fisk leaned forward in his seat. "Cal made me spend a couple of hours in your bedchamber last night. There was a strange item. When I inspected it, I realized it was a stringed instrument."

She smiled a little. "It's called a guitar."

Fisk sat up straighter, his spines bristling. "All my kind delight in music. You're very accomplished … for a mortal."

Edie snorted. "Thanks, I guess. I mean, I want to do it for a career, but I know better bassists—"

"A career? You're a skald, then?"

Skald was kind of a ridiculous word to use to describe what she did; it brought to mind images of a traveling bard covered in animal skins and colorful beads, someone revered as a person who knew all the lore of the land and sang about it. Really, she was just in a band—but she supposed it was close enough. Amused and a bit puzzled, she answered, "Uh, yeah, I guess."

Fisk looked like he was wrestling with something, wringing his hands so his markings shimmered in the late morning light filtering through the window. Finally, he took a deep breath—kind of a creepy, shuddering sound—and gave a sharp smile. "Will you play something for me?"

Edie raised her brows, pleasantly surprised. If Astrid decided Fisk had to go back to Thor's Hole, she might actually miss the big fish stick. If nothing else, his attitude was good for a laugh.

"All right," she said. "I hope you like The Cure."

CHAPTER TWENTY-ONE

MARIUS LET the heavy door of his father's library slam behind him.

Disappointing. Despite having delivered the sorceress on time, unharmed, and in good spirits, his work had been "disappointing." He'd been "indiscreet."

Were you hoping for glory? the Radiant had asked.

The Radiant—no, his *father*—was infuriating as ever.

Marius had always excelled in his skills, mastering light magic early and always following Auroran laws and observing formalities. Still, for as long as he could remember, there had been whispers of nepotism among the ranks of the Rising Aurora. From the beginning, his father had tried to quash them immediately ... by adding to Marius's workload, by inhibiting him and handing him busywork the other apprentices didn't want.

And still, Marius had answered the call of duty. He'd done his best to make his gods and his people proud.

Yet it wasn't enough.

This life, these people, were all he had ever known; their approval, and the approval of his father, was what he lived for. His father *knew* that, and as Marius got older, it was almost as if he used it as a weapon against him— as a short blade, concealed, dressed in fatherly concern and impossible standards. His jabs were short and casual: "I don't have the time if I'm going behind you to check your work," or, "This apprentice would benefit more from a teacher with more patience than you." "You would already have advanced if you followed direction," or, "I need you to really *try* this time...."

How could he not know how deep his words cut?

His father had become Radiant years ago because, frankly, he'd neglected all else; he barely slept, he often forgot to eat, he did nothing but work. It was a wonder he hadn't dropped down dead from exhaustion. Was that what he expected from Marius? If that was the case, Marius would *never* be good enough.

He descended the circular staircase of the tower until he came to a corridor that ran behind the temple, leading to the annexed monastery where his and the other warriors' dormitories were. Across a field, behind the temple and monastery, was another, plainer building that housed other Aurorans. Though most lived elsewhere within the city, some acolytes, scholars, even some civilians kept close to the hub of their order.

Marius descended another flight of stone steps, which led out to the monastery courtyard. Many adherents, most of junior rank, sat at the stone tables and benches or walked the gravel paths which ran through the courtyard in a uniform grid. At one of the far corners, a few circled each other within a dirt sparring ring flanked by racks of training weapons and burlap-sack dummies marked with red paint. Old limestone walls, covered in lattices of vines and white flowers, encircled the yard like a parent with a child. The ancient stone cradled the monastery and overshadowed it.

One familiar face caught his eye: Ynga. The adherent was sitting at one of the round stone tables, wearing her armor but relaxing. She was eating lunch—a sandwich and soup in a cup—from a wooden tray, a book in her other hand. Marius glanced around to see if anyone had noticed him, but they all seemed to be going about their business.

As if sensing his arrival, Ynga looked up and spotted him, then nodded. He went to her after a moment, hesitating before sitting at the other end of the curved bench.

"Afternoon, Vivid Marius," she said, not putting her book or her sandwich down.

"Good afternoon."

"I see you're back from your secret mission of glory."

Marius grimaced. And though he knew he shouldn't be talking to her about it without clearance, he couldn't stop himself: "It was hardly a glory mission. I had to deliver some hermit from the coast."

She took a bite of her sandwich. "A hermit? For judgment?"

"No, to aid us." He paused, considering before divulging more information. Ynga looked so uninterested that he supposed there was no harm in it. "Some vættr. A seidr-woman."

Finally, she lowered her book. "What on earth would we need an outsider sorceress for? We have plenty of people here for whatever it is the Radiant needs."

Marius shrugged, though he knew full well why they needed her. Though his father wouldn't say it outright, something was coming. Marius didn't have the gift of sight, but he could feel it, too. True, the Aurora and their allies had increased in number in the past decade ... but so had the Gloaming. And since the Aurora's triumph over Lord Fahraad, things had been heating up. He knew that his father wanted to move against the Gloaming again, before they could strike first. Whatever the Radiant had seen, he wanted to stop it before it started. That was the only reason Marius could figure he now wanted outside help, and from such powerful strangers.

And Tiralda *was* powerful. Edith Holloway and her friends had stumbled their way to her home so unceremoniously that he doubted they even grasped just how ancient and important the sorceress was. That was why the Reach would never rebuild, at least not without proper leadership: the younger members had no idea what they were doing, and the older ones were stuck in the past.

Ynga looked Marius over before tilting her head back and finishing the soup in her cup in one long gulp. Then she closed her book and scooted it and her tray away from her, folding her thick arms on the stone table in front of her. She smiled at him and asked, abruptly, "You want to spar?"

Did he? He looked from her to the sparring ring across the yard. He hadn't gotten any practice in yesterday, busy with having to fetch the sorceress, nor had he had time today. And he needed the workout. Perhaps it would help blow off steam.

He couldn't think of anyone better to spar with. Ynga seemed ... different from the others. She didn't seem to care either way who his father was. She wanted nothing from him, asked nothing of him; she wasn't frightened of him and didn't look on him with disdain.

Marius peered at her. She was easily a decade older than him, but he could see himself calling her a friend ... the only friend he'd had in years.

Eventually, he answered with a shrug and swung a leg over the stone bench, standing.

Ynga smiled and left her things behind, keeping pace with him as they crossed the courtyard. Heads turned as they did, and once they reached the hard-packed dirt of the training area, the two adherents sparring there turned. The one closest to them—a huge, leather-clad man with a carefully-plaited red beard—regarded Marius for a moment before looking to Ynga with a nod.

"You might want to clear out, brother," she said, hands on her hips. "I need enough space to kick the vivid around a bit."

Marius kept his mouth clamped shut.

The man glanced at Marius again before grunting and pacing over to the nearest weapon rack. He returned his training axe before gesturing for his partner to follow him, and they made their way across the green, joining a couple other Auroran adherents.

Ynga smiled. "After you."

Marius paused for a moment before moving to inspect the available weapons: swords, axes, spears. An adjacent rack held shields of varying sizes. He was silent as he looked them over, trying to ignore the stares on him.

He was silent for long enough that Ynga broke her respectful distance and came to him, picking up an axe and testing the weight. She glanced at him. "Having trouble deciding?"

"I don't usually do combat with corporeal weapons."

"No, but you train with them, don't you?" She quirked a brow.

"I try to hone my abilities as a vivid, not just combat skill."

"Without meaning to offend, Vivid, I don't really want to get hit with pure plasma." She smirked, discarded the axe, and instead went for a spear, holding it confidently in both hands. "If you remember how to hold a sword and shield, pick them up and let's do this."

Her challenge held just enough edge to heat his blood—enough that he picked up the nearest shield with renewed certainty and turned to her. Her mail glinted just so in the sunlight as she backed up and took position, facing him and planting her feet in the dirt.

Marius took a breath, strapped the shield to his right arm, and selected a sword, focusing. He could see her do the same. Stares burned into the back of his neck, but he ignored them, adjusting his stance.

Without warning, she lunged forward, jabbing at him with the dull spear. He had just enough time to react, deflecting the blow and whipping the spear to one side with his shield. She hadn't asked if he was ready, or bowed to him. She grinned wickedly at him and lunged again.

He parried with the sword, brows drawn. "Rather opportunistic of you."

"Forgive me for saying, Vivid"—she lined herself up again—"but the enemy isn't going to wait politely for us. And they certainly aren't going to fight fair."

She was right, but sparring, especially with a superior, was different. "Wouldn't you rather fight *me* fairly?"

"Where's the fun in that?" she asked, and feinted to the right before striking his left side. Their weapons were so dull that there was no worry of her ever piercing his chainmail, but he staggered back a step, and she tipped her chin up. "You're getting so wrapped up in what you *must* do that you've forgotten what you *should* do."

Marius wrinkled his nose and adjusted himself so he held his shield fully in front of him, peering over the top at her. "Where are you from?" he asked through a huff as he deflected another blow.

Her grin turned to a smile. She struck again, this time seemingly hitting the shield intentionally, though still hard enough for him to dig his heels into the dirt. "My family were servants in the Temple of the Setting Divine in Sandgerði."

Marius's brows rose. "Iceland?"

"I was born there." Her lips went tight, the smile fading from her eyes as she struck the shield again, jabbed, then recovered and jabbed again before he could prepare himself, striking his side once more. "Are you going to fight me or just stand there while I hit you?"

He ignored her. "What happened to them? Your family."

She swung the spear over her head and lunged, giving him less than a second to save his own throat. He parried with his sword and followed through, twisting downward as he pressed her, leaving a long scrape on the spear's shaft. With only another second before she inevitably recovered, he side-stepped her and lashed out with his shield, bashing her shoulder blade.

Ynga staggered forward a step before pivoting and jabbing. "They were killed."

He parried again and riposted, the dull end of his sword making light contact with her ribs. If he'd hit her a little harder, he might have knocked her off balance and won the duel, but he wanted to hear the rest of her story. "I'm sorry." What else was there to say?

"I was only a child. The temple was sacked, and I was taken for a prize," she said, lining herself up again and looking him directly in the eyes. Hers were arctic. "I was brought here as a thrall."

Marius looked between her stare and the tip of her spear. It was no wonder she wanted to kill the Gloaming. He paused, lining his shield up and retreating half a step. "What did you do?"

"I killed the patriarch"—she aimed the spear downward, going for his kneecaps—"and murdered his wife and children in their beds."

Thrown off by her frankness, he could do nothing but retreat. The tip of her spear hit the dirt, and there was silence between them as she lined herself up again.

Marius considered her for a moment before asking, "Was that fair?" Killing the man who'd kept her, certainly—no one could argue against that. But the children? He didn't know the answer, himself; he wondered what she thought.

Ynga studied him right back. Her expression cleared; her shoulders relaxed. She straightened her posture. "Was it fair? Was it honest, or honorable? No." She tipped her chin up. "But it was justice."

Marius straightened up, too, and lowered his shield.

"Why don't we switch?" she suggested, passing him to grab a shield of her own. The courtyard was silent. Their spectators had gone away.

With a nod, he switched positions with her. They sparred like that for a while, Ynga keeping him on his toes with capable ripostes, showing him no mercy. He'd have to see her in an actual battle, he thought, but if his father ever asked her to become a vivid, Marius would be honored to fight beside her.

But he was having to work twice as hard against her attacks with only one sword arm; for every thrust he dodged, she landed two. It took all his will not to summon his shield of light. His strikes became harder, less focused. She parried one, pressed the blade, and the frustration within him burned.

He lunged forward with his right arm. With a hard *clang*, the wolf's head at the end of his wrist connected with the iron banding of Ynga's shield.

The wood splintered as the wolf's steel teeth and snout dug into it; the punch reverberated through the shield and left Ynga's body shaking. She retreated.

Marius breathed hard, realigning himself.

At length, he said, "The Gloaming killed my mother, too."

Ynga raised her shield and peered at him in response.

"There was a battle in the wilderness surrounding a runepriest monastery. The Gloaming outnumbered our forces ten to one at least, and my father called for a retreat into the monastery, where they would at least have the high ground." Marius feinted upward and slashed at her knees when he saw his opening, the blade panging dully against her armor. "They stayed like that for a day and a half, firing on any Gloaming troops that approached. They anticipated a stalemate, that the Gloaming would eventually retreat."

Ynga blocked another strike with her shield, and used the momentum to follow through, pressing the blade and bashing the shield into Marius's wrist.

He faltered and nearly dropped his sword, but recovered quickly. "The Gloaming found a way in to the monastery keep through an abandoned drainage tunnel, and they sent an assassin. My mother was guarding the runepriests' relic room, keeping the hidden apprentices calm." His lip curled. "They murdered her before she even had the chance to summon her bow."

His blood heated, and he reared back before thrusting forward. Ynga barely held her shield up in time to block his onslaught. He couldn't remember his mother—he'd been so young when she died—but they had murdered her. The assassin hadn't even granted her the dignity of one last battle, had probably not even looked her in the face when they'd done it.

Another furious onslaught, both with sword and fist, and he grumbled, "They killed all the apprentices and priests. Nearly killed my father."

He could see it in his mind's eye: a shadowy revenant driving its poisoned blade into his mother's back, grabbing her by the nape of the neck and holding her close, then tossing her to the side.

The sword in Marius's hand spat yellow embers. He snarled, reeling back before slashing with all his might at the shield in front of him. Sparks flew, scorching the surface. The blade glowed as it dug into the wood. He wrenched it out, spun it easily in his hand, and turned; gripping the sword in reverse, he brought it down.

It whistled with power as it thrust through the air, then screeched as it found its home deep in the wood of the shield.

"Marius!"

Oh. He let go of the sword and staggered back, dazed. The sword stayed in the shield, still sizzling. Behind it, Ynga's terrified face.

There was only the high-pitched hissing of the blade as Ynga gripped it and yanked it out. He had broken the shield—torn a huge, splintered hole through it. And almost through her as well.

She glared at him. Then she dropped the sword and shield at his feet. A last breath of ember and smoke rose from it and died. Between her teeth, she ground out, "I didn't kill your mother."

Marius took a few steps back.

Then he turned and ran from the courtyard.

CHAPTER TWENTY-TWO

EDIE CAME out the other side of the portal shaking like a leaf, her fingers knotted so tightly in the spectral wolf's bloodied fur that her knuckles had gone white. She hadn't thought to ask, before, how Satara had managed to get from Shipshaven to Maine. The answer was Astrid's spectral, portal-hopping wolf, a thing every valkyrie apparently had. Satara had only to blow a tiny glass whistle to call it and go wherever she wanted.

Satara, sitting in front of Edie and armed with Astrid's shield and spear, slid from the creature's back and landed securely on both feet. Tossing her braids over one shoulder, she looked back and opened her mouth to say something, but the sight of Edie's face seemed to give her pause. She stared, bemused. "Are you all right? You're so pale."

Edie tried to mumble something in the affirmative. She wanted to get off the wolf, but she felt frozen in place.

Satara raised a brow. "It takes getting used to, but it's the fastest way to travel." After a moment, she offered Edie a hand.

It took Edie a few moments to pry herself from the wolf and hop down, shuddering the whole way. Her legs felt like Jell-O. From behind her, there was a mighty surge of wind—it smelled horrible, like blood and gore—and when she glanced back, the wolf was gone, teleported away in the red haze from which it had come.

Still shaking, she reached into her shoulder bag and checked her phone for the time. Mercy wouldn't be home until late that night, and Satara had been adamant that they visit Astrid as soon as possible. They had a lot to tell her, not the least of which was that they'd totally failed to secure an alliance with Tiralda—an alliance that had, according to Satara, been pretty much assured.

Leave it to me to fuck up an ancient contract, Edie thought as they walked out of the alleyway in which they'd appeared and up to Astrid's shop.

It was only early afternoon by now, barely 1:30, and Shipshaven's shopping district was relatively busy. The establishments surrounding the valkyrie's corner shop were folksy—an ice cream shop, an independent shoe store, a comic book place, some cafes—but they all had a modern quality about them. They all looked relatively new, well-cared for, nicely-appointed. Among them, Astrid's loomed like a dark, ancient oak in a forest of saplings. In the daylight, Edie could finally make out the sign: *Harbinger Trinket & Tome*. There was a little carving of a raven holding a key, and under that: *books, gifts, magic.*

She looked over at Satara, who had stopped to wait by the door while she took the place in. Her gorget and breastplate shone like liquid in the mid-day sun, and her dark eyes were curious, watching Edie. If any of the passersby thought she looked strange, with her shield and spear and feather-trimmed leathers, they didn't show it. Edie gripped the strap of her bag and glanced around.

As if reading her mind, Satara said, "Most of the people here know me. Shipshaven doesn't get many unattuned tourists."

Edie looked back. "You live here, too?" For some reason, the thought had never occurred to her—that Satara would live with Astrid.

She smiled slightly, though it didn't quite reach her inquisitive gaze. "I've lived here for a while." She looked up at the shop's sign. "I came to Astrid when I was sixteen, to follow the path my family laid out for me."

"Path?"

"I am human," she said quietly, "but those of us who still follow the gods, who have knowledge of the truth around us or have powers, rarely bother with human laws and governments—mostly by keeping isolated and secret. I was born within a sect of Freyja's followers. My ancestors are nearly all great warriors and scholars. But the elders there convinced my parents that I was meant to serve the goddess more directly, perhaps become one of her daughters one day. So, I became a shieldmaiden. I've been training for years." After a moment, she added, "It meant honor for all of us."

Yikes. It didn't sound like Satara was very honored to Edie. Resigned, more like. It seemed like she hadn't had a lot of say in the matter. And, finally, it explained why she hadn't exactly been gung-ho about bringing Edie on board: she'd been sitting right there, for years, yet Astrid had chosen someone as clueless as *Edie* to become the Reacher instead of her.

Speaking of which, Edie was going to have to talk to Astrid about that. She hadn't agreed to *lead* anything. She looked at Satara, brows drawn tight. No freaking wonder things had been so tense between them.

"You have questions," Satara observed with a sigh, "but they can wait. Come on." She adjusted the shield over her shoulder and opened the shop's front door. Chimes tinkled softly as she passed through.

Edie followed close behind, but took one last look behind her, out at the cobbled streets of the shopping lane. How many of the humans milling around were like Satara, revering the Norse gods like it was the most natural thing in the world, like their existence was indisputable fact? How many of them followed laws of blood and honor or whatever instead of the ones Edie had known all her life?

Why hadn't Dad prepared her for any of this?

She stepped through the shop's old door and shut it softly behind her.

Satara was already on her way toward the back of the shop, but Edie was struck by how different it looked in the daytime, when it was open. It was still cramped, the air still heavy with incense, but it was bright now. A blond girl about Edie's age was rearranging the display of iron jewelry she'd noticed the other night, an orange tabby slept on the worn sales counter, and a smaller gray cat lorded over a nearby stack of large, cracked tomes.

It was weird to see the shop like this, so full of life. It had seemed so ancient and forbidden the first time she'd visited it. Now, it was just a cute little bookshop.

Edie passed a display case full of crystals, briolette pendants, geodes, and jewelry made of animal bones (or what she hoped were animal bones) before something stopped her. The feeling of being watched suddenly crept up, raising the hairs at the back of her neck, and she turned to confront whoever was staring at her.

Between two bookcases stood a tall, thin cabinet. Within were rows of small statues, each unique—some carved from wood or marble, others cast in iron or steel. Edie watched them warily for a moment before glancing around. There wasn't a soul still in the room besides the salesgirl, who now had her back to Edie.

Her gaze slowly shifted back to the cabinet.

One wooden statue in particular drew her eye: a tall, faceless woman in robes, carrying a spear and shield similar to Astrid's, if more intricate. Edie crossed to the cabinet, hesitating before picking the figurine up. It was carved in detail, right down to the rivets in the shield, on which was etched a tree with ample boughs and roots flowing downward, twisting in a never-ending knot that fed into itself. She could make out the smallest detail in the trim of the figure's robe—but still no face.

Somehow, it was like the statue was ... watching her.

It was only about the length of her hand, and she turned it over, examining it from all angles. When she tipped it and looked at the bottom, she found runes circling a geometric pattern: three vertical lines with several diagonal ones latticing them from the left and right.

Wonder what it means. She'd have to ask Satara later.

Another wave of apprehension hit her, and she shivered. She'd had enough of *waves* for a lifetime, and there was something so familiar about the grip of this feeling—like undertow.

Someone was watching her, and not only that, but she was sure they'd been trying to grab her attention. Righting the figurine, Edie glared at where its face should have been.

The feeling faded. Now she was just a weirdo glaring at a statue.

"Edith?" It was Astrid's voice, calling her from the back room, and it almost made her jump out of her skin.

"Coming," she called back, and hesitated at returning the figurine to the shelf. She stopped, gripped it in her fist instead, and brought it with her to the back of the shop.

When Edie entered, Satara was already sitting on the coarse carpet in front of the fireplace, sipping something from a cup. Astrid's back was to them, and Edie noticed her hands shaking slightly as she mounted the shield and spear back on the wall.

The two younger women exchanged glances; Satara gave Edie a warning look, and Edie blinked.

Astrid didn't say anything; she didn't need to. She turned away from the weapons and moved to the nearby range, clearly seething. Edie had never heard such an aggressive silence.

Astrid banged a wooden spoon on the rim of the water pot a little too loud. Edie grimaced, but Satara sat still, looking into the fire. Her face was hard; she looked frustrated—and *bored*, like she was tired of this old drama. With dread, Edie realized Astrid must be angry more often than not. And an angry valkyrie didn't sound particularly fun to hang out with.

Maybe Edie couldn't blame Astrid. She'd be pissed off, too, if one of her oldest friends had broken a promise to stick by her side.

Or maybe, Edie thought with a sigh, she'd understand. Mercy already knew she was lying to her about something. How long would it be before they had another, bigger fight? How long could their friendship continue if Edie was forced to constantly gaslight her best friend?

Their friendship wasn't perfect, of course. That was a given. Mercy had always been cooler, more independent, more successful. She had always carried herself with the sort of confidence that made Edie wonder if she even deserved to be in her presence. It wasn't a good feeling.

But there were good things, too—great things that outweighed those feelings a thousand times over. Mercy had always looked out for her and had her back, and Edie had done the same in return. They'd made each other laugh, lightened each other's spirits, knew things about one another that no one else did. Edie couldn't count how many times her best friend had held her while she cried, had stroked her hair when she was tired, or held it back for her when she was sick; she couldn't count the number of times she'd done the same in return.

Mercy deserved to know. About all of this. The alternative was cutting Mercy out of her life completely. Could Edie even do that after everything they'd been through? Could she hurt her like that, without explanation?

Mercy had to know. And not just for her sake, either. The lies, the worry.... The thought of never telling her was killing Edie.

Either way, she might lose her.

She looked at Astrid, watching the valkyrie as she roughly chopped more herbs for tea. Astrid was old—probably really old. How many friends did she have left? Edie was willing to bet it wasn't many, stuck in a dead faction that seemed to contain only her and her shieldmaiden.

Astrid's back was still to the room, but the silence was becoming oppressive. Finally, Edie cleared her throat and said, "I'm ... really sorry."

Astrid stopped in the middle of chopping, one strong hand tightening on the wooden handle of the knife. Maybe it hadn't been the best idea to speak when the centuries-old ghostly spirit of death was holding a sharp implement. Edie shifted from foot to foot, hugging her leather jacket closer. Was it just her imagination or had the room gotten colder despite the fire?

"What did she say," Astrid finally replied, her voice terse as she scooped herbs from her cutting board and dumped them in the pot on the range.

Edie glanced to Satara, but she was just looking at the fire and nursing her tea. All right. So Edie would have to explain this one without backup. She probably deserved that. "She said that, uh.... Well, she kind of said things had changed, I guess, and she'd already agreed to go with Marius—"

"Marius!" the valkyrie hissed.

Edie tried not to gulp audibly. "She pretty much said that something was happening with the Gloaming and she wanted to be on the winning side." Total dick move, but understandable.

Astrid slammed her palm against the range. If it burned her, she didn't seem to notice or care. "Oath-breaker!" she snarled.

She turned sharply toward Edie, who caught a glimpse of the strange blue power that sometimes revealed itself behind the eyes of the dead. When they had first met, Edie had been intimidated by Astrid. Who wouldn't be? But now, with her gaze pinning her where she stood, with the chill in the air, she felt ... frightened. The being standing before her was older and probably more powerful than she could possibly imagine, and she'd just pissed it off.

"She will fail," the valkyrie said icily. "She and the order she's now pledged herself to will fail and die where they lay, like animals, on their battlefield."

Okay, then. Edie took a breath and finally dared to glance away once Astrid turned back to her boiling water. "What do we do now?"

"Nothing." Astrid slammed a cup against the sideboard and poured her mixture in. Boiling water sloshed out of the cup and over her fingers, and though her skin turned red under the scalding water, she didn't so much as flinch.

"What do you mean, 'nothing?' " Edie asked.

"If the Aurora think they can win this war, so be it. If they do, they will conquer everything just as surely as the Gloaming, and eradicate every being they deem unfit to live. If that is of no concern to my *friends* or my gods, then let it be. When they are crying for help, when the Aurora comes for them, they will finally understand."

Edie was stunned for a moment. Words passed her lips without consulting her brain: "You can't be serious?"

"Why should I help those who don't help themselves?"

She looked to Satara. The shieldmaiden had turned her head, too, and was watching Astrid with an expression like she had just cut her: raw hurt and confusion. For once, her expression held back nothing; she looked truly speechless.

Even though she'd only met Satara twenty-four hours ago, Edie felt her hurt keenly. If there was one thing she could understand—pretty well, lately —it was what it felt like to be disappointed by a parental figure.

Edie looked back, a new flame sparking in her chest. What the hell was Astrid thinking, just giving up after all these years? After pulling others into it and putting them in danger? "No. That's ... that's dumb."

Astrid growled.

"You can't just say to hell with it and give up after everything— after everything you've put me through. After everything you've put *Satara* through!" she added, exasperated, thinking about what the shieldmaiden had told her as they stood outside the shop.

"I'm *tired*," Astrid said, turning with a cold warning in her eyes.

The flames in Edie's chest jumped higher, licking her heart. That wasn't fair. That wasn't fair *at all*. "Sure! Who wouldn't be? You've probably been doing this for decades now, limping along with only a couple people in the stupid Reach. But then what was the point of all this? Of getting a new shieldmaiden after my dad died? What, did you just want someone to yell at and boss around?"

From the corner of her eye, Edie saw Satara look up at her sharply. She rose and focused Edie with a look that said *That's between me and Astrid, so drop it.*

Edie gritted her teeth. "And if you're going to give up, what was the point of dragging me into this and trying to make me the leader of something I'm totally clueless about? My life can *never* go back to the way it was. You're just going to make my whole world a smoking pile of garbage and then leave? And what about Cal?"

"What *about* him?" Astrid snapped in return.

"He ran all the way across the freaking country, and you know why he stayed? You know why he even bothered to bring me here in the first place?"

Her voice was growing louder, and she could see that Astrid was growing angrier, but Edie stood her ground.

"Because of you! And when it turned out you needed our help, he stuck around, because he was your friend and he cares about how all of this ends up. Whatever the fuck *this* is."

Satara fixed Astrid with her stare this time. "You're not the only one who's tired."

Edie gestured in her direction with an open palm. "Yeah! Cal was basically a slave, and you *never* did anything to help him, and he *still* decided to help, and he *still* likes you because he believes in you. And I haven't seen you do anything to deserve it!"

She was probably making up half of this. Who knew why Cal did anything he did? Edie had gotten to know him okay in the past few days, and she'd grown to like him, but he was still pretty much a mystery.

But if it was all made up, it didn't matter. What she'd said seemed to resonate with Astrid. With her own cup held in both hands, the valkyrie sank down on a nearby chair, staring at the steam as it rose from her tea. Her eyes were glassy, nothing angry slithering behind them now. She really did look tired.

For a second, Edie felt kind of bad for yelling at her. But only for a second.

"It's just been so long," the valkyrie finally said, brows knit tightly as her gaze traced the serpent-shaped incense holder on the table next to her. "And I am so old. There are times when every day feels like the last day of the Reach, and I wonder why I ever bothered."

That didn't make sense to Edie. Why would helping people, keeping them safe, be a waste of time? Maybe she'd feel the same way if she were immortal. Maybe Astrid didn't even see humans as ... well, human ... anymore.

"You're still here," Edie said, her voice still shaking with anger,

Astrid exhaled hard through her nose and met her gaze. "And so are you. And you are so much like your father."

Compulsive pride clashed with embarrassment, anger, unease. A couple of days ago, Edie would have taken that as high praise. Now, she wasn't sure what to say. Physical discomfort lanced through her gut like nausea. She looked away, mouth in a tight line.

"You're right," Astrid finally said. "The loss of Tiralda is painful and unforeseen. But we are still here." She paused for a moment, thinking, before she set her cup aside and crossed to where her desk had been a couple days previous. Now everything that had sat on top of it was stacked haphazardly: books resting on the windowsill, loose papers and trinkets thrown into ratty cardboard boxes, a pen or sticky note or sheet of paper on the floor here and there.

The two younger women watched the valkyrie as she took a small, leather-bound book from the windowsill and began to flip through it.

"You're thinking of someone else?" Satara asked, brows drawn together. Edie looked between them. It must be some sort of address book.

"I'll have to consider. Tiralda has a very specific set of powers that I was hoping we could utilize. I will have to find someone who would do just as well."

"We could try scrying for someone now," the shieldmaiden suggested with bright eyes, energy renewed now that there was some chance of making things right.

"Or we could just call them on the phone," Edie mumbled, pointing to the little leather book.

Astrid looked vaguely puzzled for a second before she smirked and shook her head. "I doubt most of the beings in these pages have much use for phones. It's less a phone book and more like a ... roster."

So, she kept documentation on all the supernatural things she came in contact with. Edie supposed that was probably smart, if she wanted to keep track of who was willing to work with the Reach and who wasn't, but keeping it in a journal seemed dangerous. Maybe they should go digital.

Astrid laid the book out on the table by the window and continued to flip through it, eventually slowing as she came to a page toward the back.

As she lingered over the names on the page, Edie asked, "So, how are we supposed to scry ... *on* them? Is that the right preposition?" In any case, she now had an image of Astrid rubbing a crystal ball.

"I will need time to work through the journal to find someone suitable. But ... scrying *may* turn someone up quicker. Simply seeing if we can divine who our next ally is or where we can find them."

Satara rose from where she sat and spread ashes over the fire, smothering it. "I'll go fetch the basin."

"Thank you, dear." Her battlemother didn't look up from her book, scanning the names with a finger.

Once Satara was gone, Edie was suddenly reminded of how angry she'd made Astrid earlier. The valkyrie seemed calm and focused now, but who knew? Maybe she was just waiting for them to be alone so she could throw her across the room like she'd done to Marius.

Make some conversation before you die of awkward silence first. Edie took a breath and held it before asking, "Did Satara tell you about the, um, fish ... uh, vættr we met up with?"

Astrid barely glanced up. "She did. If he wants to help our cause, so be it; he may stay, as long as he keeps out of sight."

"Right. But I don't really have anywhere to put—" Edie cut herself off and sighed. She got the feeling Astrid didn't really care what she did with him, as long as she didn't have to deal with it. They'd figure something out.

In the meantime, there was something more pressing she needed to ask Astrid about: the Reacher.

She came to sit in the chair across from Astrid. Considering her wording carefully, she began, "Why didn't you tell me you were looking at me to be the Reacher?"

The valkyrie finally looked up, lowering her book for a moment. She tilted her head. "You are your father's daughter. I was always sure you would have his spirit, and that you would be ready to lead when you came to me."

"Yeah, well, I'm not." Edie clenched her jaw. "You didn't even ask me.

There's no one in the world better suited to this than me? What about you? Or Satara?"

Astrid paused a moment, like she had never considered the possibility, but she brushed it off quickly. "I have no desire to lead the Reach. I've done so in an unofficial capacity for years, but I am a warrior, and so is Satara. We have other obligations."

"I—" Edie wiped the air in front of her with her hand. "So what I want doesn't factor in *at* all?"

With a heavy sigh, Astrid said, "We'll see."

Edie clenched her fist. The unyielding angles of the wooden statue she still held bit into her palm, and she remembered she'd brought it with her. Deciding to drop the subject for now—the next shouting match might get her killed—she set the little figurine on the table in front of them. "What's this?"

The valkyrie went back to her journal. "A statue."

"Is there anything special about this one?"

Clearly annoyed by Edie's persistence, she raised her head. But this time, she considered the figurine a little more carefully. "I doubt she's anyone in particular. A representation of a lesser Norn, I think."

"There's this design on the bottom...."

Astrid went back to her journal again. "A matrix of criss-crossing lines?"

"Yeah."

"It's called the Web of Wyrd. The nine-staved net of fate as woven by the Norns. It symbolizes the interweaving of timelines; all our past, present, and future actions are connected, and they determine the color and shape of the tapestry we keep." Her frown deepened thoughtfully, and she looked up at Edie. "What made you pick that up?"

"She was, uh ... watching me." She felt like an idiot saying it out loud, so she followed up quickly with, "Why doesn't she have a face?"

Astrid's brow creased. She opened her mouth to say something but was interrupted by Satara, who reentered with an armful of things: a large stone bowl, a bunch of candles, and silver jug all stacked together. The valkyrie stood to go help her, leaving Edie alone with the little wooden Norn.

With a sigh, Edie reached out and turned the Norn over, still wondering why she didn't have a—

Holy shit, she has a face. A pretty woman's visage stared back at her now, just as detailed as the rest of the statue. Her expression was neutral, calm; nothing scary, but Edie felt fear stab her heart.

Someone *had* been watching her, hadn't they?

CHAPTER TWENTY-THREE

CAL'S FIST tightened around his glass of Scotch as the mellow tune from the stage filled the dark bar. The bass flowed through the building like a heartbeat, with Mercy's soft, low voice accompanying it like the hiss of blood through veins.

For the first time in a while, he felt like he was in the gullet of a beast waiting to swallow him whole.

Leave it to Edie to work in a vampire's den without even knowing it. At least it didn't seem to be Gloaming-owned. Too many uneaten humans, not enough blood-fueled orgies, not a thrall in sight. But vampire-friendly, for sure. The pretty, platinum-haired one—a guy or a lady? Eh, it didn't matter to Cal—at the bar had been flashing him nervous looks ever since he'd set foot inside.

Tracking Edie's friend through the city had been one thing. She'd gone all over, furiously trying to blow off steam, and had led him on a winding chase through the shopping district and some hippie outdoor market before finally heading to Nocturnem with the setting sun.

This was much easier. She was mostly just in one place: on stage. And when she wasn't, he had a view of the exit. And a glass of fancy Scotch, which was a bonus.

Mercy didn't seem aware that a good two-thirds of her coworkers were vampires, either. He wondered if it was a human thing or a stupid thing, though more often than not, the two went hand-in-hand. They could create the fucking internet out of air and glass, strap flimsy metal together with a lick and a promise and send it into space, but no way vampires could exist, right?

A particularly bassy note from a nearby speaker sent ripples through his Scotch, and he raised the glass to his ruined lips, throwing it back in one go. He had to admit ... as ridiculous as Mercy had looked trying to manhandle him a few hours ago, she was in her element here. Maybe could be mistaken for a vampire, too, if her scent didn't scream human. Under the hazy red and blue lights, her velvety black dress glittered like rainwater over fresh tarmac.

She was singing a particularly overwrought cover of U2's "Wake Up Dead Man," cradling the mic in both hands as her breathy voice entwined with the music. That sound, combined with the song itself, made Cal's jaw clench. If things were different, maybe...

Maybe what? He wasn't in Vegas anymore. He wasn't free. Probably, he never had been.

The revenant glanced around the room for a *No Smoking* sign. There were hookahs on some of the tables, so one cigarette wouldn't do much harm, would it? Besides, he doubted anyone could see him, tucked away in an alcove booth, sandwiched between two ugly-ass wicker mannequins. Maybe he'd do the owners a favor and catch one on fire.

He took out a nearly-empty pack and lit one up. Jesus, this past week he'd been smoking like it was going out of style; he'd only bought this one a couple hours ago. As soon as the smoke curled around his face, a wave of calm came rolling in.

Oh, well. Wasn't like he couldn't afford it. He'd been scraping off the top of Holloway's stashed fortune for ten years and had barely made a dent. Guess it helped when you didn't have to eat and didn't need a place to sleep. Maybe the right thing to do would have been to tell Edie she was filthy rich as soon as he'd met her. Maybe there were a lot of things he should tell her.

For now, he'd play it close to the vest.

God, this was a fucking wreck. How had he let himself get pulled into this again? What the hell had he done for himself, if he still came running to a Holloway at the drop of a hat?

No. He hadn't fucking done that. He had to keep reminding himself of that. Sure, he'd dropped everything to go clear across the country—but only to put her down.

And then ... turned out she needed him. She'd definitely be dead if it wasn't for him.

But that shit was in Astrid's hands now. He could leave now, get away with Ghost and the cash and forget about all this again. Whatever was coming—whatever fuckin' beef the Aurora and Gloaming had with each other—none of it was Cal's responsibility. *None* of it.

He hadn't asked for any of this bullshit.

Neither did the girl. The thought crossed his mind like a snake weaving through tall grass, darting between patches to avoid being seen. It was all he could do not to smash his glass down on the glossy black table. *Fuck the girl!*

"You okay, darling?"

The sound of liquid being poured and the feel of someone nearby registered. Someone was refilling his Scotch.

Cal's eyes darted upward, and his shoulders hunched—a reflex he thought he'd gotten rid of in Vegas. No one had made him feel small in ten goddamn years. Being back here, unearthing all that shit, had changed things. It wasn't even the girl's fault; there was nothing she could do to stop it. But that didn't make him feel any less fucked up.

When he looked up to tell the stranger to go away, his eyes met with a pair of perfectly round tits squeezed into a red leather sweetheart top. Whoa. So his Scotch-fairy was taller than he'd assumed. He met her eyes this time, and her easy smirk. Her full lips were painted in a purple to red ombre, and her pin-straight hair hung around her shoulders, sleek like the hood of a black Trans Am.

Vampire. And not a fucking subtle one, either.

"What?" he grunted, pulling his Scotch glass closer.

The woman seemed unperturbed by his harsh tone, and set down the crystal decanter she'd been holding. She leaned in, inky locks slithering over her moon-white shoulders. "You just look troubled. May I sit with you?"

When it came to knocking boots, vampires and zombies went together like peanut butter and jelly. He'd had plenty of time to figure this stuff out. Revenants needed fresh blood in their system to get the "plumbing" working, and vampires usually had plenty on hand. The human ones, anyway—Cal knew next to nothing about the elves. In Vegas, he'd dated vampires pretty much exclusively. No way he was going to lie to a clueless human about what he was—both because it was a pain in the ass and because it was a fucking scumbag thing to do.

Maybe this vamp could smell it on him.

"Do what you want," he mumbled at the rim of his glass, knocking back another mouthful. Best to be cautious. He was supposed to be watching out for Mercy, anyway.

The vampire's black eyes followed the motion. A pleased smile graced her face as she slid into the booth next to him, her leather dress whispering softly against the booth's upholstery. As she came close, her thigh touching his, Cal tensed.

On another night, in another place, she'd have his attention; they'd chat, maybe he'd buy her a drink, see where it went from there. But now, here, in this godforsaken fucking city, his brain was so far from that place.

Maybe his balls had fallen off somewhere between Nevada and Massachusetts.

He kept his eyes fixed on the stage, trying not to notice that the vampire was seriously starting to snuggle up to him.

"My name is Scarlet," she said.

Of course it was. "Yeah?"

"What's yours?"

It had been ten years, and this was a decent-sized city. She probably wouldn't recognize his name. "Cal," he replied around the filter of his cigarette, glancing at her from the corner of his eye.

She just smiled. Okay, good—so she didn't know who he was. Or, if she did, she was a great actress.

"You're new in town," she observed, and leaned on him more heavily, nestling her arm up against his and putting a hand on his shoulder.

"Am I?"

"I don't know your scent. And there aren't many handsome revenants around here, you know...."

"Right." He ashed his cigarette into his now-empty glass. If she worked here, she clearly didn't give a shit that he was smoking, so there was that, at least.

They sat in blessed silence for a while. Mercy finished her set and mumbled her thanks into the microphone. Who knew how long it would take her to chat and change, but Cal fixed his eyes on the curtains to the employees-only area. As tedious as tailing her was, he didn't want her coming face to face with Fiskbein. Talk about a disaster waiting to happen. The fucking guppy needed to go, shouldn't have been there in the first place, but until Astrid told Edie as much—

"Can I see?" Scarlet asked suddenly, raising a hand to his hair. She stroked her fingers through what, to her, must look like dark locks; in reality, she was barely brushing the few patchy bits of hair he still had left on his scalp.

Cal shot her a look of warning at the touch. When she pulled back—slightly—he asked, "What?"

"You." She wrinkled her nose, still grinning. "I want to see the real you, darling."

So she was one of those freaks. The only way to scare those types off was to give them what they wanted until they realized they didn't really want it at all. Without dropping the glamour completely, Cal weakened it. Any humans watching probably wouldn't notice anything.

She certainly did, though. Although her expression was closed, he could see her gaze shift in the low light, her smile fade slightly.

In response, he flashed a terrible grin back at her, leathery skin protesting against the sudden strain. "Careful what you wish for, sister."

But beyond her flinch, Scarlet seemed undaunted. She leaned more heavily into him, sliding a cold hand under his arm, over his chest; with her free arm, she linked their elbows and squeezed. It felt like a snake tightening around its prey.

Strangely, the feeling spread to his chest. As he glanced at the stage, he noticed that the lights seemed overblown and foggy. Eyes watering....

Something was wrong. Vampire mojo usually didn't work on him. He only had one master, after all, he thought bitterly.

"I gotta go," he slurred, feeling genuinely drunk for the first time in ... as long as he could remember, actually. He could wait for Mercy outside.

In vain, he strained against Scarlet's grip, but he felt weak; his brain started to feel heavy, and a wave of intense heat and nausea hit him a second later, causing him to shudder.

He glanced at the empty glass of Scotch.

Scarlet was saying something to him—pleading with him to stay, he thought, though he barely listened as he thrust his way out of the booth, practically dragging her along. She finally relented and let him go.

"I gotta go," he repeated. He hadn't been watching when she poured his drink. And after that, he'd been looking at the stage.... *What the fuck?* "I gotta go, babe."

"Of course." Her voice came through with startling clarity, but her tone was so cold.

The floor seemed a lot closer now. Pressure on his wrists, the ridges of carpet under his fingers. A gray haze seemed to replace most conscious thought. *Gotta lay my head down. Just for a second. Gotta make it stop spinning.*

The fucking bitch....

All breath left Cal's lungs as he saw, across the room, Mercy heading toward the exit. Then everything was gray.

CHAPTER TWENTY-FOUR

"So, what do we do first?"

Astrid, Satara, and Edie sat in a circle around the stone basin they would apparently be using to scry, though Edie still wasn't completely clear on what that entailed. The curtains had been drawn, and now most of the light in the room was blotted out, replaced only by weak, flickering candlelight. Satara held the silver jug between her knees, watching her battlemother.

"Now, we pour the ewer, and then we can begin scrying."

With a nod, Satara shifted and slowly poured the water into the basin. Astrid closed her eyes and began to whisper something under her breath.

Slowly, it began to feel like their little circle of candlelight was the only safe thing in the room—like if Edie stepped out of its bounds, she'd fall off the edge of the world and into ... something else. Whatever was waiting for them beyond the veil of reality. *Veil* was a good word for it; like a thin curtain not only dividing two sides of a room but also protecting one side from seeing what lay on the other. And Astrid had just waved it away like it was a pesky spider web.

The way the basin's contents glittered in the low light made Edie shiver. Sitting together in a dark room and staring at a bowl of water hadn't sounded this creepy when Astrid had explained it, but now she could feel a strange energy filling the room almost like a living thing. Like the darkness was the body of a giant snake, coiled around them and slowly, slowly tightening around their little circle.

"Just look into the water," Satara whispered, nudging Edie. "Look for a vision of someone who might help us."

Edie took a deep breath and nodded, trying to ignore everything around her and just focus on the way the flames danced in the water.

Astrid's chanting slowly died off. Now, the three of them simply stared in silence.

The silence had stretched for a few minutes, long enough that Edie was about to ask what was supposed to happen, when she finally saw something. She thought she caught something in the water, no more than a flash of movement.

It could have been the flames, a trick of the eyes. But when she closed her mouth and watched more closely, it happened again—and again, until it was no longer just flashes riding the water's tremulous surface but a full picture. She was looking into another place: a room, dark but not as dark as this one, with shadows moving back and forth.

Her human instinct told her to call out and tell the other two she had seen something, but another, stronger instinct—belonging to some faraway experience only her DNA remembered—told her to keep quiet and watch and listen if she wanted to learn more.

But ... *ugh*. Her head was killing her. That nausea she had felt before seemed to resurge, a tickle threatening the back of her throat. Her cheeks felt warm—

Edie pulled back from the basin, resting her forehead in one hand. Her fingers were hot, too. *Am I having a panic attack?* Was it possible that scrying had triggered this? Sure, the experience was uncomfortable, even anxiety-inducing, but this—

Another, more intense wave of nausea washed over her, and she stood up, desperate to find the door. The room instantly felt brighter, the coil of darkness gone.

Astrid and Satara were ... speaking, she thought, asking her why she'd broken the circle, but their voices seemed so far away. Another noise, unrecognizable at first but quickly becoming clearer, was drowning them out. It wasn't even a noise, really. More like thoughts. Loud, intrusive thoughts, too jumbled to pick any one message out.

Thoughts that weren't her own.

She took a couple steps back and sat in one of the chairs near the window, trying to cool her forehead with the back of her hand.

"Was it too much?" someone was asking. "Did you see something?"

No. No, she'd just seen ... she'd just seen a room. This was ... something else. This wasn't because of the scrying; it had only interrupted the scrying. This was—

Cal.

She stood up so quickly that the chair scraped across the rough-cut floor and hit the radiator behind it.

"Are you all right?" Satara gave her a once-over. "You're pale. Well ... paler than usual."

Edie whipped off her leather jacket and unzipped the hoodie layered underneath it. The room was suddenly boiling hot. "I—"

Words didn't come easy. The thoughts were so loud and so panicked, like a pack of animals straining against their leashes, biting and bumping into one another.

Astrid's expression turned to one of distress, blue eyes bright. "It's Calcifer, isn't it?"

For a second, Edie thought she'd just have to nod silently. But she surprised herself, croaking, "Yeah."

Cal had told her they had a link, but until now, it had been mostly one-sided. Just like he'd said, he was practiced at nailing his brain shut in such a way that she probably couldn't breach it even if she tried.

But something had got his guard down. Fear and confusion railroaded down their connection and into her brain.

There was no doubt about it: wherever Cal was, he was in deep trouble.

. . .

The first thing Edie noticed when they stepped out of Harbinger Trinket & Tome was that the sky was black; no sign of a sunset, not even dusky twilit clouds. She turned when Satara exited the shop after her, her voice on the edge of panic as she asked, "What happened? What time is it?"

The shieldmaiden sighed and glanced up at the sky. "It must have been the scrying. Sometimes it distorts time. What feels like minutes might be … hours."

Shit. Edie whipped her phone out of her jacket pocket and gaped at the time: nearly 11 p.m. Now they were dealing with a supernatural timecrunch in addition to the urgent pinging she was feeling off Cal.

"Let's check the club first. If he's still there and there's trouble…." She trailed off and looked to Satara, who had already blown her little dog whistle.

The creepy, pungent red haze appeared again and birthed a bloodied gray wolf, and Edie groaned at the prospect of having to ride it after last time. She was starting to regret separating herself from Cal. At least he knew how to drive, which was more than she could say for herself or Satara —she assumed.

How the hell was she supposed to become a leader if she almost barfed every time she had to ride this furry Tilt-A-Whirl?

At Nocturnem, Ghost was nowhere to be seen.

Edie steadied herself against the wolf's flank as she looked up and down the street, peered into the nearby alley, but there was no sign of the muscle car. Had Cal left in the middle of watching Mercy? It wasn't like watching her involved anything beyond sitting there and drinking, which sounded like it suited his talents just fine.

"Where the fuck is he?" Her voice was raw and sounded foreign to her ears.

Satara stood closer to the curb, still dressed like she'd just walked off the set of *Spartacus*. It wasn't quite Nocturnem's aesthetic, and Edie wasn't sure how people would react, but it wasn't like there had been any time for her to change. Edie waved her closer anyway.

"I work here. I'll be able to ask people if they saw where he went."

"You *work* here?" The shieldmaiden looked at her, skeptical. She peered down the dark stairwell, and the multicolored lights highlighting the doorway glinted off her armor.

Edie started down the stairs, mouth dry, breath already coming shallowly. *Please, god, don't have a panic attack. He's going to be there, he's going to be fine.* The thumping bass emanating from the club calmed her somewhat, at least; it was familiar, grounding. At least she knew how to move through *this* place, and Satara didn't. For the past couple days, it had been the opposite.

"Come on," she urged Satara, her voice gentler now, already on the first landing of the switchback staircase.

Her companion lingered. For a moment, Edie thought she might turn around and run all the way back to Shipshaven. But then she drew herself up and began to creep down the stairs.

Edie usually had to put all her weight behind opening the heavy metal door that led to the club's vestibule, but with adrenaline thundering through her veins, she wrenched it open like it was plywood.

The club was full of people, crowding around the bar, sitting at or milling between tables, sandwiched together on the dance floor. The lights were low, and spotlights of red and blue swung around the room, coruscating and clashing with twinkling bottles and glasses. There was a girl on stage with a full head of cyberlox and a gasmask, working an LED-covered DJ booth.

"Where's Mercy?" Edie mumbled to herself. She was still supposed to be working, and unlike Edie, Mercy only performed here—no waitressing or bartending.

As Satara came up to Edie, she flinched like she was bracing against a forceful wind. "What! Is it always so loud? I can't hear you!"

Edie pulled the shieldmaiden closer and spoke right in her ear. "Mercy is supposed to still be performing!"

Satara pulled back and looked at her with worried eyes. "Is she taking a break?"

That was probably it. That *had* to be it. The only other alternative was that she had left, and if she'd gone and Cal had followed, they might *both* be in trouble. Edie tried not to entertain that possibility. Best to take things one life-shattering meltdown at a time.

"Okay." Edie loosed a puff of breath, eyes flying around the darkened room. "Okay, okay. I just need to find someone who saw where they went." Scarlet, maybe? *Someone* she knew had to be around.

"Edie!" came a voice from the bar. It sounded kind of surprised, kind of relieved, and kind of nervous.

"Klein?" She found the edge of the bar and gripped it as the bartender made their way over to her.

Klein was practically bouncing on their feet, looking full to the brim with anxiety, but they still showed an easy smile. "Didn't expect to see you here tonight. Business or pleasure?"

"Neither," Edie mumbled, taking another glance around the bar. Could Cal or Mercy, by some total miracle, be in one of these alcoves? Empty-handed, she turned back to Klein and asked, "How's it going?"

"Well … not slow, as you can see, but not too crazy either." They tilted their head, looking Satara over slowly before returning their gaze to Edie. "Why?"

"It's just— you haven't seen anything weird? No fights, or...?" She couldn't imagine Cal picking a fight and losing, but she could still feel the dull throb of panic coming down their connection.

Klein frowned, dark brows furrowed, and shook their head.

"I'm gonna go backstage and find Mercy." Edie pushed off the bar and started toward the employees-only area. The main priority had to be making sure her best friend *didn't* go home and discover the fish man in their bathtub.

"Edie! Where are you going?" Klein had trotted to the end of the bar, meeting her as she rounded it. "Mercy isn't here."

"Wh— I thought she was working?"

"She had to run early."

"Great," Edie mumbled. "Did she say where she was going?"

Again, Klein looked from Edie to Satara, whose expression twisted as she braved every new inch of the club. The bartender looked nervous, suddenly, wringing their half-apron between their pale hands. "Um, she said she felt sick. She was going home."

"What?" A swell of dread raced up the back of Edie's neck. Cal was supposed to be watching her, making sure this exact thing didn't happen. Had he followed her back to the house? Was that why Edie could feel him panicking?

"Maybe it's not too late to stop her," Satara called over the music.

Edie looked Klein dead in the eye. "When did she leave?"

"Um ... I don't know, like, maybe a half hour ago?"

Shit. Shit, shit, shit, shit, shit.

Satara was flying out the door and up the stairs in a matter of seconds, Edie close at her heels. Aside from the fact that Mercy was about to find the Creature from the Black Lagoon in their bathtub, she and Cal might both be in serious danger.

The cold night wind cut her face, and Astrid's words chased her: *Don't tell a soul.*

CHAPTER TWENTY-FIVE

THE SOUND of police sirens in the distance drifted through the night with the early summer breeze, their wails making Mercy shiver. The world had been too silent for the past week, like a heavy cloud of gloom hung over her and Edie's apartment. The sounds of the city were welcome, comforting in a way she had never fully appreciated until recently.

She supposed anything familiar would be. Her whole world had been turned upside down since Edie had started acting weird. *Beyond* weird. Out at all hours, bringing strangers home, mysteriously killing *both* of their pets…. She was obviously hiding something huge, and it was scary. Maybe losing her job at the garage had really affected her somehow, although Mercy couldn't imagine why. She could find another one easy enough.

Mercy just wished things would go back to how they had been last week, when everything had been normal. She wanted to go back to a time when she could trust her best friend.

In the hallway outside their apartment, Mercy rummaged in her purse for her keys. Since she and Edie had met in high school, they'd been inseparable. They took care of each other. The thought that all that might end soon made Mercy's chest physically ache. There had to be something she could do, if only Edie would just let her in. She'd always shared her problems before. What made this time so different?

Mercy took a deep breath, ready to face whatever her friend had waiting for her this time, and entered the apartment.

The moment she did, she could tell something was wrong.

For one, there was a strange smell. Not easily identifiable, just … off. Something familiar, yet she couldn't put a name to it. She took a step further into the apartment, and the briny scent tickled her nostrils. Her mouth went dry, her tongue salty. Her heart began to pump harder.

She was almost certain, now, that someone had been in the apartment recently.

Never mind what Edie was getting herself into; what had she gotten *Mercy* into? What if the intruder was still here? What if they were waiting just beyond the shadows in the hall, ready to strangle her or something?

Muscles tense, Mercy swept the living room with her gaze. Everything seemed to be in place—nothing stolen or even moved. Except….

Down the darkened hall, she heard the squeal of wet skin sliding against the sides of the bathtub.

"Edie?" Mercy said, barely above speaking volume. She slowly turned toward the bathroom. From where she stood, she could see that the door was closed, but light was pouring out from the crack under the door. There was no doubt that someone was in there.

She took a hesitant step forward.

Squlch.

The disgusting sound was enough to stop her in her tracks, but in the darkness, she couldn't see what she had stepped on. Slowly, she raised a shaking hand to take off her sunglasses.

At first, it appeared she'd just stepped in a black blob, a darker piece of carpet with no discernible shape. But as her eyes adjusted to the light, horror mounted.

It wasn't just some spilled drink or tracked mud. It was a wet footprint, somehow wet enough to have saturated the carpet deeply. And it was enormous.

If anyone was prepared to handle a home intruder, it was Mercy. But her self-defense training, her collection of knives, even her instinct to flee ... it was as though it had all dropped out from under her. Her survival hind-brain had suddenly been liquidated, and with the way her head pounded, she thought it might start to melt out her ears at any second. She stood, frozen in fear, for what felt like hours but was probably more like a minute.

Another squeak from the bathtub and a soft, strange trill—oddly melodious—prompted her forward despite terror batting its wings in her gut.

She stepped into the hallway, and the darkness seemed to close behind her, shutting her in as if in a vault—and though her breathing was shallow, she could no longer hear the sounds of traffic. It was like her fear had transported her to another place, somewhere unbearably private. Just her and whatever was behind the bathroom door.

The doorknob was cool to the touch, slick with a layer of water and ... strange, gritty slime. This close, she could hear water dripping from the faucet into the tub, a slow tick, and something shifting in the bath.

Mercy stood as still as possible. She knocked, just to be sure it wasn't Edie or her weird friend in there.

Nothing.

"I'm coming in!" she warned.

Still nothing. Just more melodious gargling.

She turned the knob and opened the door.

The air inside the bathroom was thick with the briny smell. Mercy's gaze touched every familiar thing in the room as she tried to ground herself. Toilet. Sink. Mirror. Cabinet. Towel. Perfume. She lowered her eyes, breath hitching.

Three canisters of table salt lay discarded on the bathroom floor, their labels peeling and saturated with water.

The tub was adjacent to where she was standing now, nestled into a corner, behind a wall. She felt as though her lungs were filling up with dread. It would drag her down and she would drown in her own panic.

There was only one logical way to do this: quickly.

Fear and anger mingled. Mercy was a patient person. But Edie had brought someone into her house, had denied her access to her own bathroom all day, had lied and brushed her off and abandoned her and left her to worry. No more. Whoever lay in the bathtub now was vulnerable— and they *should* feel vulnerable.

My home. My life. No more bullshit.

With renewed courage, she stomped around the corner to confront the intruder.

There were no words.

Her mind could hardly make sense of what she was seeing: a man, but not a man at all. Shimmering, iridescent teal skin with a labyrinth of onyx markings; long, sharp teeth and flared gills; enormous, blinking eyes the color and luster of obsidian.

It was impossible, yet there it was.

Her heart still thundered, but after a moment of silence between them, her fear subsided and gave way to a fluttering anxiety—a bone-deep understanding that she could never come back from this moment. There was her life before the fish man, and her life after. They were two very different lives, and one of them had just ended.

The creature rose up, all seven feet of him, the webbed spines down his neck and back bristling. His expression showed no fear, but no aggression either. Actually, he seemed rather ... transfixed. By Mercy.

When she finally regained her ability to speak, she managed to creak out, "Are ... you ... one of Edie's friends?"

Ever since the wraiths had attacked her, Edie had avoided cutting through the playground to get to her apartment. Even looking at it gave her the shivers, but there was no time to be squeamish. Hoofing it around the corner, she immediately skirted past the line of sparse bushes and trees through which Marius and those creatures had torn only days ago.

She looked up and down the street as she and Satara reached the other end of the playground safely, then headed toward the yard entrance. No Ghost parked on either side of the street or in the alley.

Cal hadn't followed Mercy home.

What the hell had happened to him?

Where are you? Could he hear her? His emotions had quieted considerably on the other end of the connection, like someone trying to speak underwater, but she could still feel the dull throb of panic and confusion.

"He's not here," Satara murmured before Edie could. Her fists were clenched, her shoulders stiff; she looked uncomfortable.

"You okay?" Edie asked, only half-listening as she fished in her jacket pocket for her keys.

"I didn't think to grab a weapon from Astrid's before we left. I should have."

She looked back as they reached the stoop that led to her back-hall apartment. "Don't ... don't hurt Mercy. Whatever happens. Please."

Satara frowned. "Why would I do that?"

Though there was no time to stop and apologize, Edie at least had the sense to be embarrassed at what she'd said. She'd been thinking mostly of Astrid when she'd said it, but of course, Satara and the valkyrie had already proven to have vastly different approaches to things.

Edie loosed a puff of air as she pushed through the front door, rushing to the end of the hallway. From where she stood with the door closed, she could hear nothing but unintelligible, muffled noise. But when she opened it—

Laughter. A light laugh that she immediately recognized as Mercy's, and a lower, wheezy one accompanying it. Light spilled from the living room into the hall, and the smell of something warm and savory wafted from the kitchen. Panicked still, Edie hurried into the living room and locked eyes on the couch.

Mercy sat there with her knees pulled up to her chest, her face flushed and her hair and clothes damp in places. Fisk was next to her, sitting on a towel and facing her with one leg tucked under himself. They both held mugs, though Fisk's looked comically small in his large, webbed hands. Neither looked completely at ease with the other, but there they were: smiling, laughing, sharing a drink in the living room like he was a high school friend who had awkwardly dropped by.

The two turned their attention to Edie, and Fisk was the first to greet her: "Hail, Skald Edie!"

"I ... hi," Edie mumbled, glancing between them. Oh, god, what was she supposed to say? *It's not what it looks like? I can explain?* Whatever she said, what were the chances that Mercy would even believe her? Thanks to Cal—who they *really* needed to find next, if she managed to smooth this catastrophe over—everything was starting to fall apart. Including a friendship Edie had wanted so desperately to save.

Mercy watched her with wide eyes. Her brows were knit, but she didn't look ... angry. Perplexed and overwhelmed, but not angry. When she spoke, her voice was raspy, her tone hesitant. "Hi...."

"Hi." Edie spat out a breath. "Looks like you've ... made friends."

Satara stepped more fully into the room and peered at Mercy and Fisk.

"Great," Mercy said, struggling to smile. "More ... people?"

The shieldmaiden glanced around anxiously. "Yes. People."

"What's going on?" Mercy prompted, expression beginning to sour.

"I...."

Her friend wasn't stupid; there was no lie Edie could tell her that would fool her into thinking Fisk was human and this was all some sort of misunderstanding. But Mercy also wasn't fucking insane, so what were the chances that she would completely accept the truth?

Hopelessly, Edie said, "You'll never believe me."

Slowly, Mercy leaned forward and set her mug on the coffee table, and Fisk mirrored her action.

She flashed him a nervous half-smile before looking back to Edie. "I, um ... don't know what to believe anymore. I didn't *want* to believe that my best friend was ... addicted to drugs or something—"

"But—"

"I didn't *want* to believe that you would let someone kick me out of my own house. I just...." Mercy spread her hands. "I don't *want* to believe that this—" A pause. "If this is what you were hiding from me, then I guess I—" She blinked and looked away. "Listen ... I just want whatever you tell me to be the truth."

Edie's vision blurred as her eyes welled, her body beginning to shake.

With a sigh, Mercy moved her mug and held her hands out for her. Edie took them, slowly easing herself down onto the coffee table across from her friend.

"I wanted to tell you right away. God, I was so stupid. I should have told you."

"What happened?" Mercy wiped at her own eyes with the heel of her palm.

"Hervey. He wasn't sick. He died while you were away. I touched him, and it ... brought him back to life. He was dead, and then I touched him, and he wasn't dead anymore. Like a zombie."

She watched for Mercy's reaction, but her friend's expression of deep concern didn't change, so she continued.

She told Mercy everything: about the fish, the wraiths and Marius, how Cal had found her, her dad. She told her about the diner, and Astrid, going to Maine and meeting Satara. She told her about how she could feel the power in the roots of her teeth when she drew it in, and how she'd absorbed energy from the witchwolf's blood, and about meeting vættir for the first time. She told her how Cal was missing and in danger, she was sure of it, and she had no idea what to do or where to start looking.

She talked and talked until it hurt, completely forgetting that Fisk and Satara were there. Every doubt, every fear and raw nerve and injustice—she opened it and showed Mercy.

When she finally stopped, her cheeks were clammy with residual tears. At some point, someone must have gone to the kitchen and turned off the oven, because she couldn't smell the cooking food anymore.

Edie rested her head in her hands, barely treading water as wave after wave of anxiety washed over her. Should she have told? What would happen now? She had this horrible vision of Mercy saying she was completely crazy and leaving and never coming back.

But when Mercy finally spoke, her voice was sure: "How can I help?"

The revenant's will would break soon. Everyone in the room could feel it.

Though he slept, his memories still resisted Scarlet's prodding, and it was becoming tiresome. Zaedicus almost wanted to shove her aside and try to open him up himself, though he'd loathe to have his mind touch the disgusting creature's.

But the revenant wouldn't resist for very much longer. Scarlet assured him as much, her voice low as she concentrated: "The rotter's mind is not easily opened. If I move too fast, I might leave behind a traceable scar. But once I ease a hole big enough…."

Zaedicus looked on as his new protégée carefully manipulated the web of the zombie's memories, stripping each neuron and pinning it open like an animal dissected. Everything would go back to its place seamlessly once the vampire found what she wanted.

Thralls were wonderful subjects when it came to extracting memories— they saw nearly everything their masters did, and it would be a small thing if Scarlet made a mistake and tore a hole in Calcifer's mind. As long as he remembered how to load that obnoxious shotgun of his, no one would notice.

"Have you been able to extract anything intriguing yet?"

Scarlet hummed, her fingers twitching as she held them over the revenant's unconscious face. For a moment, she opened her eyes to glance in Zaedicus's direction, shrugging one shoulder. "Nothing of consequence." She smirked slightly as she said it.

He sighed from his high wingback chair and reached for his goblet. "Make haste, then. I'd like the information I'm looking for in my possession before the end of this decade, if you please."

The vampire's smirk faded completely, her sickly-pale cheeks and forehead flushing weakly as she snapped her gaze back to Calcifer's limp body.

The more Zaedicus thought about his plan, the more he liked it. If only there was someone who could appreciate what he'd done. He planned to have Scarlet dig until she could tell him, second by second, exactly what the Reach had been doing these past few days. And, most importantly, where the hellerune was and what she was doing *now*, who she spoke to. If they were lucky, she would notice her revenant gone and come after him, right into their hands.

The Reach was tedious, it was true—the Aurora, even more so. But the Wounded had made it well clear that securing the girl was to be Zaedicus's primary objective.

The thought of the angry red markings crawling up the man's flesh, teeming across his skin like living things, made Zaedicus shiver. If he didn't complete his task soon, the Wounded might decide to do it himself. He might decide that Zaedicus's counsel and information were superfluous.

Gods help whoever was superfluous when that boy set his final plans in motion.

"Lord Oldine."

The high-wight lifted his head, directing his focus back to Scarlet. "What is it?"

"I've found a cluster of memories. Very recent, throbbing with anger. They must be what we're looking for."

He sat straighter in his chair. "Good." She would need time to drink of the memories and put them back where she had found them; even someone with her skill at memory leeching needed time. "I will leave you to your work."

The vampire was already extracting them. Her fingers worked carefully and delicately as she pulled the metaphysical string from the rotter's skull: a thin, translucent purple thread, crimped and curled slightly as though it had been pulled from the edge of a thinning rug. Not at all the strong, ropy, bright blue strings he'd recently observed her extracting on other subjects.

He frowned, pausing his exit. "What is that?"

"Something of interest ... I think."

"Is that so?"

"To me, at least," Scarlet conceded, never looking him in the eye but still smirking. "If you'd permit me, I'd like to dig a little deeper. I *will* bring you the memories you need."

Zaedicus could not keep the look of disgust from his face. She wanted to rifle through the mind of this maggot-filled behemoth ... for fun? Put in her position, he would only expose his mind to such filth for as long as he had to, and not a second longer. In the low light of the richly-furnished VIP room, he could see her black eyes glinting with excitement and pleasure.

She was ... *mad*, he realized suddenly. A freak.

But, for now, useful.

"Do as you will. But only *after* you've found what I asked for, and do not delay. You will regret it."

Clutching his goblet close to his chest, Zaedicus exited the room.

CHAPTER TWENTY-SIX

EDIE, Satara, and Mercy had arrived at Nocturnem to look for Cal again and maybe retrace their steps, but they hadn't actually had the chance to ask anything. The second they had walked in, Klein had sat them down to talk: rumor had it that Edie was related to Richard Holloway, and since it looked like she was hanging out with Norse warriors now, she ought to know they were a vampire.

If Edie was honest, this revelation wasn't all that surprising. Even before she had known this stuff existed, she'd always suspected something was up.

"I'm sorry I didn't tell you earlier," Klein said as they poured Edie another glass of water from a large jug. "I can't just go around telling my human friends, 'Hey, I'm a vampire!' " With a sigh, they added, "That goes over about as well as you'd expect. Talk about coming out, am I right?"

"It's ... fine."

"But, hey"—they slipped her a sly smile—"I didn't know that you were Richard Holloway's daughter, so I guess I wasn't the only one keeping secrets."

"It wasn't me being clever," Edie mumbled, taking a long sip of water.

Her throat still burned from her confession to Mercy an hour earlier. "I didn't know my dad was ... you know."

"The Reacher," Mercy finished, sipping her own martini.

Edie looked over and nodded, and her best friend smiled proudly in response. *Should have been her*, she thought. In her position, Mercy would have learned everything with ease and remembered it all. And would probably look a lot better punching werewolves or whatever.

Beside her stood Satara. She looked less likely to flee now that the DJ was gone and the club was quieter—and good thing, too. Social situations clearly weren't her favorite, but when it came to diplomacy and steering conversations in the right direction, the shieldmaiden was ace.

"What else didn't you tell her?" she asked Klein pointedly.

Klein looked nervously between her and Edie. It was an unfamiliar look for sure. Edie was used to them being just as confident and chipper as could be, no matter how absurd or long the shift. She guessed that probably came with never having to sleep. Still, Klein had never faltered or hesitated or seemed afraid like they did now.

"Did you see an undead, um, revenant come in here earlier tonight?" Edie asked.

Mercy added, "It would have been right after I arrived."

Klein's brows furrowed, and they sighed. They were quiet for a while, idly checking already-clean glasses; then, at length, they mumbled, "When you said you were looking for someone, I was reeeally hoping he wasn't who you meant...."

"So, you did see him?" Satara laid a hand on the bar—a subtle gesture, but it commanded attention.

Klein addressed her directly next. "Yeah. He came in right after Mercy. He ordered a drink and went and sat over there." They gestured toward a round booth near the back wall, tucked into an alcove in such a way that it granted more privacy than most. "It didn't seem like he wanted to be bothered, so I didn't send anyone over for refills or anything, but...."

"But what?"

Klein looked over to Edie and Mercy and said simply, tone flat, "Scarlet."

"Oh, god," Mercy mumbled.

Satara looked at Edie with one brow raised expectantly.

"Our boss," she explained. "She's ... a pain in the ass."

"She could make the Wicked Witch of the West cry," Klein retorted, leaning against the bar. "Of course, she's not as hard on you humans as she is on other vampires."

Edie snorted. She couldn't say she was at all surprised to find out Scarlet was a vampire, too. "I haven't found that to be true. But why?"

"Because she feeds on you."

She and Mercy exchanged glances. "I haven't noticed any bite marks on me."

"Bite marks? Oh, *phff.*" Klein waved their hand and reached for a glass to clean, probably trying to keep their hands busy. "Not Scarlet."

"But vampires ... drink blood, don't they?" Mercy frowned and looked over Edie's head to Satara.

"Some do," Satara replied simply, her expression still closed.

"Most do," Klein said. "I do, most of the vampires you've probably ever met do. But it's like ... you know how some people are more in tune with people's brains and emotions than they are with anything physical? Whether they're manipulative assholes or empaths. When people like that become wights, they get more out of eating people's emotions than their blood."

"Oh!" Mercy leaned forward, flapping her hand. "Oh, I've heard of this! Psychic vampires! They feed off energy and memories and stuff instead of blood."

Edie and Satara both looked at her in astonishment.

"What?" She cradled her martini close to her chest, shrugging defensively. "I mean, I always just thought it was a spiritualism thing. I didn't think anyone was actually, you know ... magical. Or dead."

Klein smirked. "Well, you were right, so you get your junior vampire hunter's badge. Turns out it's just easier to feed off human emotions than vampire ones. You guys just throw your energy all over the place, willy-nilly."

Satara rubbed the bridge of her nose. "This Scarlet. What did she do to the revenant?"

"Oh. Right." They looked a little embarrassed, and the apprehension in their expression and tone reappeared right away. "She comes up to me and is like, 'Who's that guy over there,' so I told her I didn't know, just some zom— uh, revenant," they quickly corrected themself. "But then she looked at him and said, 'I think I know him,' so I'm like, 'Great.' So she grabs a decanter of something— I dunno what it was, whiskey or something. Anyway, she goes over there."

Klein set down the glass they were cleaning and topped off Edie's water. It overflowed a bit, ice clinking over the rim and onto the sleek bar, reminding her of Fisk's ice trick. Poor Fisk—he was mostly stuck inside for now, on Astrid's orders, and mostly confined to the bathtub. At least Mercy hadn't filleted him.

"And?" Satara urged.

"Well," Klein said with a sigh, "they talked for a while. He didn't seem to recognize her. He looked kinda pissed that she was bothering him, anyway." After a pause, they added, "And you know what was *really* weird?"

"What?" Mercy asked the rim of her glass, chestnut eyes wide. Satara shifted where she stood, drumming her fingers impatiently, which was understandable. It seemed like Klein was trying to divert the conversation at every corner.

"She was all over him. Like *all over him*. I mean, his glamour wasn't bad, but you know how she feels about—" Klein cut themself off and waffled for a second. "I guess you don't. Let's just say she doesn't believe vampires and undead should mingle."

"But vampires *are* undead," Mercy said.

Klein shrugged. "Bigoted logic doesn't usually make sense, does it? But anyway, so it was just *weird* that she was so into him. I mean, even if he wasn't a revenant, she's not really the type to fall all over guys in general. She's, like, an ice queen."

"Yeah," Edie mumbled. "And then what happened?"

Their face fell again. Apparently, they were more comfortable dishing out gossip than information on whatever it was they saw. "He was … watching Mercy pretty closely."

"Probably trying not to look at Scarlet," Edie said, managing a teasing smile at Mercy.

"Wait," Mercy said. "What did you mean by *glamour*? That's not what he looks like?"

Klein continued before anyone could answer: "He was watching Mercy pretty closely, and I … saw Scarlet slip something into his drink," they finally admitted, clearly ashamed. "And the Worst Bartender Ever Award goes to…."

Edie set her glass down a little too hard, snorting some water up her nose in the process. Through a fit of short coughs, she managed, "Scarlet *roofied* him?!"

"Yeah. Right in front of me. And then looked at me like, 'What are you gonna do about it?' and the answer was nothing." Klein looked away, wringing their hands. "I think he realized it, though. Mercy, that was around your last song, actually. He shook her off and got up pretty quick, I guess to follow you." They glanced to Edie for confirmation.

"Yeah," she said, lowering her gaze. "I sent him out to look after you. And make sure you didn't come home and find Fiskbein in the tub."

"Fiskbein?" Klein wrinkled their nose, then held up a hand. "On second thought, don't tell me. I don't want to know."

Satara took a breath, brow creasing in concern. "We need to know what happened to him as soon as possible."

Klein looked uncomfortable again. "He … passed out, and she moved him out back. I didn't see what happened after that. You don't think she's going to hurt him, do you?" They frowned deeply. "I can't imagine what she'd want with him."

"Wait." Edie shook her head. "You saw her drug a guy and drag him off and you didn't … I dunno … think to tell anyone? Report it?"

They shrugged helplessly. "To who, the police? It's a free-for-all out here, Edie."

This wasn't like Klein at all. They were usually absolute death on people who even so much as looked at patrons funny, much less drugged them. Edie tried to hide the betrayal she was feeling. If she'd learned anything this past week, it was that you never really knew someone, and people you loved could turn out to be ... awful. But *Klein*? She turned to exchange a look with Mercy.

"Look," Klein said, probably sensing their distaste. "I *know* it's fucked up, okay? No one knows that better than me. But you don't know the kind of people she hangs out with."

"Gloaming?" Satara asked.

The bartender looked less than thrilled that she'd even said the word. "Yes. I'm totally against those assholes. I take my chances with being neutral —in more ways than one," they added wryly. "But who else could she be working with if she's kidnapping dudes and spending all her free time at The Ash Wyrm Club?"

"Ash Wyrm Club?" Edie looked to Satara. "Is that somewhere important?"

"I've heard the name," she replied with a frown. "It's a Gloaming meeting place. Astrid would know more."

What little color there was in Klein's face drained away. "Not Astrid Fengrave?" They looked at Edie. "What the hell have you gotten yourself into?"

"I don't know," she answered honestly. She glanced at her drink and thought about finishing it, but the nausea from before was starting to come back. "Do you think that's where she brought him? The club?"

"Maybe. I don't have any other guesses. He isn't here."

"I know," Edie replied. She wasn't sure how she knew; she just had this feeling that if he was in the same building as her, she'd just ... *know*. "Where's The Ash Wyrm?"

"On the corner of Duke and St. Michael's, I think."

Edie slipped off the black vinyl barstool as Satara drew back from the bar. Mercy downed her martini quickly before following suit.

"Edie?" Klein said, their voice timid again. "I'm really, really sorry." After another pause, they added, "I thought she would kill me if I told."

Edie looked back at them, shoulders sinking. They weren't a bad person. Plenty of people would have done the same. Cal was nothing more than a stranger to Klein, and she had a feeling Klein's fear of Scarlet killing them was founded. How many people had Klein seen her murder?

Remembering just how little she knew about the dangers of this new world made her stomach churn. If she thought about it too hard, she was likely headed for another breakdown. Best to just shove it down and take things as they came.

"I hope you find him," the bartender called after the three women as they exited onto the midnight streets.

CHAPTER TWENTY-SEVEN

"This is it," Satara said as the three of them turned the corner, only a four-lane road away from The Ash Wyrm Club.

They had collectively decided to leave Astrid out of the situation for now. Besides the fact that they'd have to tell the valkyrie about Mercy, Satara pointed out that they didn't have the *time* to be running back and forth from Shipshaven. Edie agreed; Cal's emotions were getting even more harried.

After not being able to find the club on Edie's or Mercy's GPS app, they'd had to settle for asking a real person for directions, and it had taken a few tries before they found anyone who was willing or able to help. It was around a quarter past midnight, now.

"Why do I get the feeling this is a really bad idea?" Edie murmured, aggressively zipping up the sweatshirt layered under her leather jacket.

"Like walking into a lion's den, unarmed." Satara looked down at her, only mostly succeeding in hiding her own fear. "It's not a good idea."

She was right. Edie was considering turning around when another stab of pain sank through her gut, and she swallowed hard, shaking her head. "I think he's nearby. We gotta find him before she does something to him."

Just *what* Scarlet would even want with Cal—let alone what she was capable of doing to him—wasn't clear to Edie, but he'd gone out of his way to save her before, hadn't he? A couple times, in fact. She couldn't just leave him.

If Edie was terrified, Mercy looked terrified times ten. She was hugging herself around the middle, eyeing the building owlishly. For a human who had no powers and had never been in a battle, it really *was* like walking into a lion's den. It was practically slathering yourself in antelope guts and then *dancing* into a lion's den.

Satara followed Edie's gaze, and her shoulders relaxed a bit. "You can wait over here if you want," she told Mercy gently.

But Mercy shook her head. "I said I would help."

Edie frowned. "If anything goes wrong—"

"Just run," Satara finished.

Edie hadn't expected that coming from a Norse shieldmaiden, but she agreed wholeheartedly. If Satara wanted to protect Mercy, she had no problem with it. She looked back at her friend and nodded.

"Okay," Mercy said, apprehensive.

The Ash Wyrm Club was nothing like Nocturnem. Nocturnem had a sort of hidden, homely, hole-in-the-wall vibe. The Ash Wyrm was an unfeeling block of black steel and tinted glass, with a slate marble walkway separating it from the sidewalk. A lush, wine-colored carpet lined with matching rope barriers led to an entryway of column lights, which danced with a gossamer purple aurora. Just beyond it, set into the building, were huge double doors.

Above the doors was emblazoned a strange symbol: a circle with another circle in the center and lines ending in hatches, half-moons, and forks reaching outward—a sort of wagon wheel with bizarre spokes. Edie had seen similar-looking symbols in Astrid's shop, but never this one.

"One of the Gloaming's symbols," Satara answered before she could ask. "A bastardization of an Icelandic stave."

Standing outside the door was a stocky but well-muscled guy in a black T-shirt and jacket, mid-30s, with a wide jaw and dark red hair. He looked like any bouncer at any fancy nightclub, but he reminded Edie of Cal in a weird way. Maybe it was the way he stood stone still with his eyes straight ahead, or the sour expression on his face. Or maybe it was the bulge under his jacket that was almost certainly some kind of firearm.

He'd no doubt clocked them a while ago, and didn't seem surprised when the three of them finally crossed the road and approached the club. He had just unhitched one of the velvet ropes to let a couple through when Satara, Edie, and Mercy started up the claret carpet. By the time he had hitched his rope back in place and turned, they were waiting in front of him.

He grunted, and his voice was low and gravelly like grating stone as he said, "Names?"

Oh. Edie straightened up a little, peering closer. As his eyes traveled from one face to the other, she recognized the little points of blue light deep inside his skull. *A revenant?*

"We're not on the list," Satara replied, every muscle in her body wound tight. "Someone is expecting us."

"If you're not on the list, no one's expecting you." His eyes lingered on Edie for a moment before he turned his attention to Mercy, who was standing there with a large wool jacket over her shoulders, shuddering.

"There's a vampire in there who invited me," Edie said. "Scarlet. She's a friend of mine." She tried to reach out with her powers and prod at the bouncer's mind, wondering if she could force him to let them in like the time she'd forced Cal to leave her apartment, but she honestly had no idea how she'd done it the first time. Just thinking it at him was only giving her a headache.

The bouncer scratched the back of his head like he'd felt a gnat bite him there or something, and Edie felt her heart race. Could he feel her trying to use her powers on him? Hoping that meant it was working, she continued prodding.

"Scarlet?" the bouncer grumbled. "Scarlet invited three humans, here?"

Satara clenched her jaw and muttered, "Yes."

Edie felt her tendrils of power hit a hard wall; more than that, it felt like something had caught her tendrils and given them a good slap. A shard of pain cut into the base of her skull and the coils retreated, snapping back into her body like rubber bands. It stung, and she had to turn her head away and rub the bridge of her nose to try to dissipate the discomfort.

The bouncer had probably hurt her subconsciously, because he didn't even seem to notice. He just pursed his lips sourly at Satara and shrugged. "I don't know what to tell you. You're not on the list."

Edie turned her head back in time to see him reach under his coat and grab the weapon concealed there. A surge of panic fled from her stomach up her spine. Without thinking, she lashed out and seized his forearm.

Their eyes met, and for a moment, she could see him for what he was: his eyes sunk in his skull, milky and lopsided in a bruised and peeling face. His torn lips stretched back, parched and blackened and revealing long teeth meandering in sallow gums. Edie balked, but didn't move her hand.

Mercy squealed. "Oh my god!"

The bouncer inhaled shudderingly and jerked his head to look from Edie to her companions, and back again. He seemed stunned for a moment, then he regained his composure and pushed Edie away.

"Get the hell off me!" he snapped, taking a couple steps back and glaring at her. He withdrew his hand from his coat, but there was no gun there—just an old PDA device with an attached stylus.

Edie inhaled sharply. "Oh. Sorry. I thought—"

"Who the hell do you think you are?" the revenant demanded, the glamour returning with a shimmer.

Edie looked back at Satara, unsure if the truth would help or hurt the situation. Satara only looked back at her with the same unsure look. In almost every other case, when she'd said her name, she'd gained some sort of respect, or at least fear. Would it work now, too? And even if it did, did she really want to go around invoking her father's name? Sure, it might get her what she wanted, but it wasn't … right.

The dull mumble of Cal's panicked brain still thrummed through her head, clinging to the back of her skull and radiating to her temples. She couldn't let him get hurt because of her. Again.

With a sigh, she looked the bouncer in the face. He was glaring at her with disgust, and she felt a dim wave of anger wash over her heart. "My name's Edie Holloway. Is *that* on your list?"

There was a tomb-silent pause. The revenant studied her features, his look of disgust dissipating somewhat and giving way to one of unease. Slowly, he lifted his PDA, using the stylus to scroll down his list. "Holloway?" he mumbled, never taking his eyes off the screen.

"Edith Holloway."

Still looking uneasy, he lowered the PDA, trying to glance anywhere but her. "You're ... not on the list, but you're right. We've been expecting you." He sounded angry, and his brow twitched like he was trying to correct the glare of complete loathing and disgust that shone through anyway.

Edie didn't think he was scared of her—the way he looked at her told her that much—but he looked afraid of something. She, too, failed to school her features. She was sure she looked as surprised as she sounded. "We— You have?"

Satara shifted and grabbed Edie's wrist tightly, keeping her from going forward. "You have?" she echoed. "Who? Who has?"

The bouncer moved to unhitch the velvet rope denying them access. "Just go in. That's what you wanted, isn't it?"

"Edie." Satara came close, speaking right into her ear. "Have you spoken to anyone from the Gloaming?"

"No," she whispered back, "never. I don't think?"

"They knew you'd come. We need to leave."

"But Cal—"

"If he's here, they only brought him here to lure you out."

Edie clenched her jaw so hard she thought her teeth might shatter. The bouncer was looking at her tensely, impatiently. "On second thought," she murmured, averting her eyes, "it's getting late, so we should go—"

"I said *go in*." In one smooth movement, the revenant reached forward and clamped an impossibly strong hand around her upper arm, yanking her toward the door.

The sound of distant screeching tires and blaring horns barely registered in her ears as blood roared through them. Whoever was waiting for her past those doors, she had a feeling they had sent those wraiths after her; they had ordered Scarlet to take Cal and do god-knew-what to him. Satara was right: whoever had "invited" her to The Ash Wyrm Club wanted to trap her, or worse.

And even before the wraiths and Cal, she had a feeling they had meddled in her life before. *Dad....*

Could it be the same people who had killed her father?

Somewhere nearby, maybe a couple blocks over, someone was laying on a car horn.

Edie tried to pull her arm away from the bouncer, but he only held tighter. She could already feel herself bruising. "Let me go!"

"Stop it!" Satara ducked under one of the adjacent rope barriers, flanking the revenant and grabbing his shoulder. When Edie looked, she saw fear and determination shining in the shieldmaiden's eyes.

The hand on his shoulder didn't do much to impede the bouncer, but he was distracted enough that he loosened his grip on Edie and turned to look at Satara. When he did, the shieldmaiden was waiting with a punch lined up.

A crack resounded, then a muffled grunt, and Edie was finally free. She tumbled to the ground.

Mercy gasped and went to her side. "Edie! Are you okay?" she asked, trying to help her up and losing her wool coat in the process.

The revenant roared wordlessly at Satara. The commotion was already starting to draw attention. People passing on the street slowed, and some stopped; some patrons from inside the club had apparently seen them through the tinted windows and were now starting to creep out the doors. Blearily, Edie managed to sit, glancing around at them. There were a couple human-looking people, an ethereally beautiful creature with pale hair and a tail, and a diminutive hooded figure, to name a few.

She looked at Mercy. "I'm all right." Grabbing one of the silver posts connecting the rope barriers, Edie managed to pull herself up. "Go."

"I'm not leaving you," Mercy insisted, her voice desperate.

Behind them, Satara blocked a swing from the revenant with a gasp before shouting, "Get back to the subway!"

Edie mouthed, *What?* Did Satara really think they'd just leave her there? But there was no time to question her commands, especially not when a super-strong zombie was moments away from tearing her arms out of their sockets. Instead, she grabbed Mercy's wrist, leaving her coat behind, and began to run across the street.

But Mercy was tugging against her hold, gasping. *"Edie!"*

Why was she resisting? They had to get—

The screeching of brakes finally managed to penetrate her panicked thoughts, and Edie stopped dead in her tracks, frozen to the spot as a pair of headlights sped toward her at top speed.

The car was so close that she could practically feel the heat coming off the engine; there was no way she was going to avoid it, even if she started running now. She was going to die, and this time not to some otherworldly monster, but because she hadn't looked both freaking ways.

She released Mercy's wrist and held out both her hands, as if that could stop the momentum of a two-ton vehicle.

At the last second, with a great roar from the engine, the car turned sharply and avoided her. It skidded to a halt near the opposite curb, almost tipping; then it lurched, and the metal frame protested loudly as the left tires hit the pavement again.

With a groan, the car settled, the headlights flickering for a moment before coming back in full force.

Edie still couldn't move. She felt her knees growing weaker as the onlookers, as well as Satara and the revenant, turned their attention to the near-accident. Numb, she watched Mercy run over to the driver's side door of the car, Satara following close behind—fortunately with both her arms still intact. The bouncer was nowhere to be seen, but the swinging glass doors of the club indicated he'd stormed inside.

After a moment, Edie slowly let herself go. She gave in to her shrieking blood and weak body and slowly sank down, sitting heavily on the pavement. Couldn't she go a day without almost dying? At this rate, she was going to have a heart attack at thirty-five—*if* she wasn't murdered before then.

Though Edie sat turned away from the scene, chin tucked up against her chest, Mercy's voice reached her: "Hey— Edie! Edie, there's no one...."

"What?" She turned her head.

"There's no one driving the car," her friend replied helplessly.

"Edie," Satara said, urgency mounting in her voice.

Brows furrowed, Edie turned to take another look at the car. It had just looked like any white convertible when it had been careening down the street at vehicular-manslaughter speeds. But now she recognized the make of the car: a '63 Eldo.

No ... she didn't just recognize the make. She *knew* that car.

A thrill of genuine joy shot through her body, and she was able to harness the feeling and pull herself to her feet. Moving Mercy to the side, Edie laid her hands on the driver's side door to peer inside for herself. She was right; there was no one.

The car purred when Edie touched it, and after a moment, it beeped once and shone its brights.

She gripped the door for dear life and breathed, "Ghost."

CHAPTER TWENTY-EIGHT

WHEN CAL WOKE, it was like waking from a vivid dream. He could feel the loss of a thousand memories of a past life; mere seconds after he became lucid, they flew completely out of reach. It almost seemed like a life that had belonged to someone else. He couldn't recall any details, he just knew there had been *something* ... and there wasn't anymore.

Freezing pavement bit into his back through his shirt, and a light rain fell on the torn planes of his face. He could smell exhaust and ozone and the aftertaste of something stale on his tongue.

What had he done...? A night of gambling gone wrong? Had he somehow gotten shitfaced and mouthed off to someone?

He lay there, still, for a long time. His head ached like someone had driven a spike through it, and trying to open his eyes only made it worse. Lying there so still, just listening, things began to come back to him. The city noise and the smell were so different here. Dread crept up his spine as he remembered he wasn't in Vegas anymore.

Anster. Holloway. He was on the East Coast. The kid had sent him to look after some broad in a nightclub, and...

He had no idea. In place of a memory, there was just a gaping blackness. There was nothing. The feeling made his skin crawl, and he forced his eyes open, staring up at the hazy night sky for a while. Nothing, no memory. He couldn't even remember if he'd had something to drink, or where the girl he was supposed to be watching had gone.

How was that possible?

With a groan, he eased into a sitting position, dragging himself backward a bit so he could rest against the nearby brick wall and take in his surroundings. He was in some sort of shipping area, in an alley—two thoroughfares on either side of a wide brick building, leading to an open space filled with boxes, a couple of dumpsters, and him. Cal craned his neck and looked upward and around, hoping he'd spot a street sign.

Nothing.

He tried to stand, but found he felt ... weak. He was shaking like a naked tree and an empty, miserable feeling gnawed in his chest, like something was eating away at his heart. He couldn't remember anything that had happened, but somehow, he knew it had been humiliating—had to have been. Someone had done something to him, then dumped him back here like a piece of garbage.

Cal didn't remember his father—he didn't remember being alive, let alone *raised*—but dammit, he was a man. Men weren't supposed to feel so ... vulnerable. *Violated*. Not men like him, anyway. That wasn't the way things worked.

Was it?

Managing to rise to his feet, he shuffled over to a nearby crate and sat, clutching his head in both hands.

What had happened to him? Thinking hard at the memory and trying to force it to reveal itself only hurt. And the more he did it, the clearer it became that he wasn't going to get back what he'd lost.

But where was— Ghost should have been waiting for him outside the club.

I swear to Christ, if those fuckers took her...

Stealing memories was one thing, but no one touched his car. The sheer rage that thundered through his body now was enough to spur him to his feet. He peered hard down one of the alley thoroughfares. He was definitely not in the same place, and he didn't recognize any of the storefronts across the street. Why the fuck had this place changed so much in the past ten years?

"Bullshit," he rasped. Jesus, he felt like he was about to fall over. Sometimes, if he exerted what magic he had too quickly, he felt like this— completely drained and weak. But he hadn't been exerting himself ... that he could remember.

And there was the goddamn *fucking* problem.

Cal reached up and touched his face. Somewhere along the line, he'd lost control over his glamour—not enough energy.

It's going to be okay. Just hold on, and she'll be here.

"What?" The sudden, strange, intrusive thought surprised him enough that he said it out loud. For some reason, he got the distinct feeling Edie was already looking for him. *Just stay put*, came another thought.

The wall. The wall he used to block her out of his thoughts had been reduced to rubble somehow, and she could feel him, was sending reassurances down their connection.

"Oh, *fuck* that." He tried to think harder, tried to push back against her and contain the panic escaping him like a horde of cockroaches, all tumbling and running over each other's backs to get out first. He'd had enough of people getting inside of him to last a lifetime. *"Fuck* that!" he repeated, his voice raw as he sat heavily on the crate again.

Somewhere in the distance, he heard the squeal of brakes and a long horn.

It was no use. He didn't have any energy left to deal with this shit. Laid bare like this, leftovers in an alley, he let his mind go limp and just closed his eyes, laying his forehead against his knees.

He wasn't sure how long he kept his head down. Mostly, he counted the moments by slow breaths, trying to quell the nausea. It could have been minutes or an hour; he barely registered the sound of squealing tires and two car doors shutting hard in quick succession.

"Cal?" It was her voice, so sweet and soft that it scared him. Didn't seem like the kid of someone like Richard Holloway had a right to be so gentle.

"I'm fine."

"What happened?" She knelt by him. When she touched his arm, her hand was so cold it burned, but he didn't say anything—didn't even move away, even though being touched at all was making his spine tingle with anxiety and anger.

"Don't know," he managed, sitting up straighter but keeping his eyes on the pavement. "Can't remember."

"What's the last thing you remember?" someone asked.

Other voices? He raised his head and spotted Satara, lingering nearby but keeping a respectable distance. And then, behind her—

Mercy.

"Shit." He ducked his head, blocking the view of his ruined face with one arm. Eyes wide, he looked to Edie and demanded in a hiss, "Why the hell did you bring her here? My ... face isn't working."

"It's fine," Edie said, frowning and taking her hand from him. "She knows."

Well, shit. Not only had he been captured by someone, but he'd failed his task. With an exasperated exhale, he lowered his arm and turned to glower at Mercy. "Great."

"What's the last thing you remember?" Satara repeated, her voice gentler this time.

Cal strained to figure out where exactly his memory went from fuzzy to completely gone. Slowly, taking his time with each word, he said, "I remember ordering a drink from the bar and then sitting in a booth in the corner. I was watching the stage..."

Had he finished his first drink? He couldn't remember. But no way he'd gotten blackout drunk off one glass of Scotch.

"I don't know what happened to— I can't remember." He gritted his teeth and looked away, like he'd find the answer somewhere on the ground.

"It's okay," Edie said, rising from where she'd been kneeling. He looked over and down, noticing that she had been on her knees, one knee in a puddle and the other in a pile of glass shards. She either didn't notice or didn't care; she simply brushed herself off and looked at him grimly. "We know."

He paused. "What?"

"We know who took you."

A wash of anxiety and fury spread through Cal's upper chest. "Yeah?" he rasped. "Well, let's go fucking get them, then."

But she shook her head. Why was she shaking her head? Did she think he was just gonna sit there and let this … whatever this feeling was … happen to him? "We need to go see Astrid and tell her what happened," she explained calmly.

"Since when are you the fucking voice of reason?"

"Before anything else, we all need to rest." She turned away from him.

Cal reached out, hovering off the crate far enough that he could take her smallish wrist in a firm grip. When she turned, their eyes met. She looked scared and exhausted.

"Edie. I need to know."

She hesitated. "I know. I'll tell you, but you have to promise me you won't run off to go break heads."

Her plea was frustrating, to say the least. Someone had got inside of his mind and screwed around, and she just expected him to sit back and bide his time? He couldn't hurt Richard Holloway for the things he had done to him, but he had this mystery asshole—someone living and tangible. Someone with 206 bones, all waiting to be broken.

With a raw throat, he asked, "Why won't you let me?" It was like someone had taken a sledgehammer to the part of his brain that kept a barrier between how he felt and what he said. He was furious, embarrassed. He sounded like a toddler trying to parse why the world was so damn unfair.

Edie turned and stood in front of him in such a way that the other two women were blocked from view; she wiggled her wrist from his hand and looked at him seriously. "Cal, come on."

Those were the words of someone asking to get punched in the face. But somehow, it was different, the way she said it. She wasn't trying to get him to shut up; in this moment, she was acting as that part of his brain, the one that protected him. She was stopping him from saying something he might regret in front of Satara or Mercy. Something weak.

"Okay," he mumbled. Fury still slithered through his pectorals and down his arms, rage so vast he couldn't place it all on one person. There would be plenty of time—later, when no one else was watching—to yell at Edie and demand that justice be served.

He was sure she didn't need to be told how he was feeling. He could feel the pain radiating from himself. For a second, as she helped him up and directed him toward the car, he thought he saw her tearing up.

Thank god Ghost was fine, without a scratch on her. Cal slid into the driver's seat with a thump, and the engine started up, purring under him without him even turning the key.

"Thanks, baby," he said, stroking the wheel. Behind him, he could hear people piling in; after a second, Edie climbed into the passenger seat.

"We ready?" she asked, peering at him carefully.

"Yeah." Cal wasn't sure how to feel about the concern in her eyes. It was easier to ignore it for now. He gripped the wheel a little tighter, dreading the thought of navigating the city with his head still spinning like it was. For a second, he wondered if anyone else in the car even knew how to drive, and if he would have to ask them.

But Ghost growled a little louder under him, and with a jerk, she started ahead and pulled out of the alley completely of her own accord. Cal put his hand on the shifter, just resting it there while it worked itself into first gear.

Maybe pretending he was well enough to drive wasn't fooling Mercy or Satara—he knew he wasn't fooling Edie—but it made him feel better, at the very least. Shouldn't have expected anything less than this; he took good care of Ghost, and she took care of him. She was the only thing he'd had in a long time.

Until now.

The realization that Edie cared—and he was still keeping things from her—made him itch.

. . .

The Wounded finally broke the silence with words that burned like hot coals: *"And here you stand before me, yet again, with no hellerune."*

Zaedicus, on his knees, looked into the eyes of the conjured vision and saw nothing but hatred radiating from them. They were red as the flecks winding up the Wounded's arms, following the avenues of those deep, sunken scars. The high-wight had been alive for many centuries and seen many things; yet when he looked at those markings, he still went cold.

"My deepest apologies, my lord," he mumbled. It wouldn't make much of a difference, standing or kneeling; he would be punished the same. He could only hope he made it through this encounter intact.

"I am not one of your diplomat friends. Your apologies are worthless." The Wounded stepped closer and crouched so they were level. *"And I'm beginning to think you are, too."*

Zaedicus knew better than to refute that.

The vision straightened up and looked away from the high-wight, as though Zaedicus was so utterly insignificant that he need not acknowledge him. *"I have heard that she came to your den of her own free will, that you had her revenant in hand. You had every opportunity to seize her, yet you squandered it."*

"The idiots who erred in those endeavors have been dealt with." Zaedicus had not killed Scarlet, though he'd wanted to. And she'd have deserved it for throwing the revenant, something suddenly so valuable, away as soon as she was done with it. Perhaps he should have made his plan clearer to her. Perhaps he had become too attached to her. Her, a lowly human-wight. That abomination guarding the door, on the other hand—

With a roar, the ethereal flames surrounding the image of the Wounded leaped higher, and even through the shadow shrouding his face, Zaedicus could see the vision's eyes flash. *"Refusing to take responsibility for your sycophants yet again, are you? You are like a child."*

A child! Zaedicus could not overlook that slight. Annoyance at the tedious situation turned gradually to a stunned rage. "I am centuries your elder ... my *lord.*"

There was a brief silence, then a laugh filtered through the vision's haze. It was low and private, the way one laughed when one was amused by someone much dumber than oneself and only barely trying to hide it. Fear alone kept Zaedicus from scrubbing his blood from the floor and ending the exchange. He knew that, though the Wounded was young, he was more than capable of dispatching those who offended him.

And even if the Wounded were somehow to fail, there were beings above both of them, engineering all of this, who would not.

Zaedicus hugged himself, fingers digging into his upper arms. The thought of what powers lay beyond even the Wounded chilled his already-dead body.

Something changed within the fire: two forms now flanked the Wounded, lower to the ground and keeping close to his legs. The high-wight could feel their gazes fixed on him, and he thought he heard a snarl.

Wolves. And not just any wolves. Zaedicus's breath hitched.

The Wounded's anger seemed to come to a climax—or what Zaedicus hoped was a climax—and he growled, "*I want her!*"

One of the wolves raised its head, nosing its master's clenched fist. The touch seemed to calm him at once; he reached for both of them, scratching at the backs of their necks.

When he finally spoke again, his voice was quieter. "*Clearly, as those I command seem to be utterly useless, I will have to come and fetch the hellerune myself.*"

Zaedicus could not keep his eyes from widening. Seeing the Wounded's image was one thing; seeing him in person would be quite another. "Are you sure, my lord?"

"*I have little choice,*" the vision spat. Then, after a moment of thought: "*Luring her with her revenant was ideal, but the dying Reach will be on high alert now. I doubt the opportunity will present itself again.*"

The high-wight's spirits lifted tremulously. "What do you need, then, my lord?"

"*If I could secure the girl and destroy her allies in one maneuver, no one would come after her. She would have no choice but to join me.*"

Zaedicus felt relief wash over him. He had failed, but perhaps there was yet something he could do. A rare grin came to his face, and it shone through in his tone. "My lord, I have the perfect plan."

CHAPTER TWENTY-NINE

CAL DROPPED Astrid's leather journal on the table in front of her. "You said you found someone to replace the Little Mermaid, so let's get a move on, yeah?"

After their successful rescue mission, Edie and the others had agreed that they needed more than a night's rest, and so they had taken nearly two days to recover and regroup before going to Astrid. It had also been agreed that telling her about Mercy wasn't their best move just yet. Maybe it was in their best interests *never* to tell. In any case, for now, Mercy was safe at Drake's house.

The rest of them had been at Harbinger Trinket & Tome for a while now, updating Astrid but mostly officially introducing her to Fisk. The valkyrie had seemed less than impressed when he'd displayed his meager powers, but she'd admitted that he was pretty immense—and had the advantage of intimidation, not to mention brute strength.

The night before, Edie had told Cal everything he'd wanted to know about his kidnapping, and though he had kept his promise not to tear out of the apartment and go on a killing spree, he was ... *eager* to move forward.

"The faster we get through this, the faster I can pull my memories back out of Scarlet's fucking head."

Astrid looked at him, her mouth twisted sourly. She clearly didn't like being told what to do, but she simply brushed her hair over one shoulder and opened the journal. "Very well. I'm glad to see you're anxious to get to work, Calcifer. Perhaps the gravity of the situation is finally evident to you."

Ouch. Edie grimaced and glanced at Cal. The way he grunted, she thought he probably didn't like Astrid's tone either. It was awkward to see them angry at each other. When she'd first met Astrid, they had seemed so friendly.

The others could obviously feel the anger, too. Satara, who had finally had the opportunity to change into jeans and a floral shirt, sighed at the fire; Fisk, who was decidedly unclothed as usual, bristled with the tension.

Astrid worked her way through the journal until she reached a page close to the back. "I've been looking through these names, and I've considered many of my oldest allies and dearest friends ... but there was only one in the area whose powers eclipse Tiralda's tenfold."

"Who?" It was Satara who asked this time, just as eagerly—though not as grumpily—as Cal. Edie got the impression that she didn't know much about her battlemother's past, and that she cherished what little information she was given. Having a mysterious parental figure was something Edie understood, that was for sure.

"Her name is Indriði," Astrid answered. "She's a lesser Norn."

"You want us to recruit a ... Norn?" Edie said. "An actual Norn?" *Jeez.* Believing in the gods was one thing; talking about the gods like they were real *people* was one thing; meeting a being she was pretty sure classified as a demi-goddess was another.

Astrid smirked at Edie's skeptical expression. "It's been many years since we last spoke, but a thousand years ago, she was a high adviser to one of the old Reachers. It's not as if you're waltzing up to the Well of Fate and demanding to speak to Urðr herself, Edith. Indriði is very old, but she is still only a very minor goddess."

"Oh," Edie said. "No big deal, then. Just a *minor* goddess."

"You will need to get used to meeting people and beings not of the world you've known. Besides," she added with a chuckle, "you've already met a Norn."

"I have?"

The valkyrie nodded at each of them. "All of you have, though you didn't know it at the time. When a child is born, a Norn visits them and begins their tapestry; some guide the child through warp and weft, until the child's death."

Cal cut in: "So, where are we supposed to find this broad?"

Astrid's nostrils flared, and she glanced briefly at the ceiling before responding, "She lives in Anster. She prefers to keep up with the times and the fast pace of the city. The last I knew of her, she was living in a townhouse in Alderdeen."

Edie clicked her tongue. "That's a nice neighborhood."

"She's had a lot of time to become quite wealthy."

"If she was an adviser," Satara said, "why did she leave the Reach in the first place?"

With a sigh, Astrid pushed her chair out and brushed past Cal, going to look out the window. There was a pause before she spoke. "It's ... complicated. And it's the reason I don't think she'll speak to you if you just show up at her home."

"You're not great at keeping friends, you know that?" Cal grumbled.

Astrid either didn't hear him or chose to ignore him. "It must have been a century ago. We were close, but she was ... fixated on a certain Russian soldier. I warned her that caring for a mortal, especially a man going to battle for the Red Army at that time, was only going to end poorly."

Fisk gurgled sadly. Edie looked at him, then back to Astrid.

The valkyrie was looking down at her hands, and she knotted them and smiled cheerlessly. "I was right. And it was I who watched as he fell, who saw that he was carried back across his lines and into her arms. She begged me not to take him, told me to take anybody else, but I couldn't. He had to die. She, of all people, should have known I took no joy in it."

There was quiet for a while before she turned back to them.

"So, it's better if I stay away. And if you went to her home, Edith, she'd throw you out as soon as she realized you were with me. No." She walked back to her chair and slowly sank down, thoughtful. "It needs to be somewhere where the playing field is even, somewhere she wouldn't dare to cause a scene."

She said it as though she already had somewhere in mind, so Edie prompted her, "Where?"

"There is an elven wight. Zaedicus Oldine. He is a minor player within the Gloaming, but very wealthy. Favors throwing elaborate parties."

"Oh, Christ," Cal muttered.

Edie craned her neck to look at him. "Is he someone?"

"I've been to a couple of his parties. They're a fuckin' drag."

"*Drag* or not," Astrid said, "Indriði will be at the next one."

Edie frowned. "Why would she be there if she's not Gloaming?"

"Spirits of fate care little about factions and politics, generally. When their sisters and mothers have preordained the entire lives of the people around them, they see no point in taking sides, as they have no sway. To her, advising the Reacher was a curiosity, something to do in her spare time. But she loves parties. If the Aurora threw any, she might try to go to those, too. And who would say no to her?"

"How can you be *sure* she'll be there?" Edie pressed, then added suspiciously, "When is it?"

"The fact that we parted ways doesn't mean I haven't kept close track of her. It is wise to watch your allies, and even wiser to watch your enemies. I often scry for her, or mutual friends bring me information." After a moment, Astrid continued, "This time, I heard by raven when Zaedicus announced his latest party. She has never missed one."

"He just announced it?"

"Only a day ago."

The group exchanged glances, and Cal said, "Yeah, I'm *sure* we can trust that. Nasty vampire throws a party right after we give some Gloaming the slip and just happens to invite the chick you've been looking for. Sounds safe as can be."

Astrid wrinkled her nose. "Even if someone were to somehow find out that I was sending you after Indriði, I wouldn't worry about *Zaedicus*. He's insignificant. He was exiled from his coven in Europe and became a sycophant of the Gloaming Lord Fahraad. Now that Fahraad is dead, he's toothless. Their hierarchy has fallen apart. They're shiftless, disorganized. This is the perfect time for us to scout, because there is no one *to* lay a trap for us."

"Even if he's just some party boy," Cal said, "we better be careful."

"Indeed." Astrid nodded in agreement and moved to a pile of mail on the fireplace mantle. She shuffled some things around before producing a small stack of envelopes, each sealed with deep purple wax. "I had a friend procure these for me. Invitations. Once you are inside, ideally, keeping your cover will be your only challenge."

"When is it?" Edie asked again, accepting her envelope.

"Tomorrow night."

"Wait." Satara looked almost horrified when Astrid held one of the envelopes out to her. "You're making me go?"

"Of course, darling."

The shieldmaiden bit her lip. "Without you?"

Astrid shook her head. "They would surely recognize me, Satara. Besides, you will do fine. You've proven that you can fight without me by your side. Don't you think so?"

Hesitantly, Satara took the envelope. "But ... I've never been to a party before."

Edie could see how uncomfortable she was with the idea. She hated thinking that Satara would be forced to come along just to babysit her. "If you don't want to come, you don't have to."

Astrid gave her a look, but Satara spoke before she could say anything. "No, Edie, I want to go. If there's a battle, you'll need me. And after all, even if we don't find the Norn, it will be a ... useful trip. For intelligence." She managed to smile despite how nervous she seemed—probably about both social interaction and any potential threat.

Edie looked at Cal. He was glaring at the envelope Astrid had handed him, looking like he wanted to crumple it up and chuck it into the crackling fireplace.

"You don't have to come if you don't want to, either, you know."

He tucked the envelope into one of his back pockets and crossed his arms. "Like hell I don't. That bitch Scarlet went all in, but I'm holding a full house."

"Can I come?" came Fisk's dark, burbly voice from behind Satara. He had sat down next to her and curled up just out of the reach of the fire.

Astrid and Cal both snapped, "No," just as Edie and Satara were saying, "Yes."

"Why not?" Edie demanded, frowning as she looked between the naysayers. "If he wants to help, we could use it, couldn't we? It's not like we have a lot of backup. Plus, he helped us when we lost your stuff, Astrid."

The valkyrie didn't look happy at being reminded of that, but she remained silent.

"Kid, listen," Cal said, pressing his hands together and pointing them in her direction. "Much as it sucks, right now, *you* can't do much for us. You barely know what your powers are, never mind how to use them. So, at any given moment, I'm spending most of my energy makin' sure you're not about to get your fucking head cut off. I can't take care of you *and* the maki roll."

"I do not *want* you to watch after me, stupid man," Fisk hissed, his spines prickling slightly. "You dishonor the spirits by mocking me, and you dishonor yourself by contradicting your master's will."

Edie grimaced. "Don't call me that." She glanced at Astrid, then back at Cal. "The 'maki roll' is a lot bigger than you, Cal. I doubt he'll have any trouble defending himself if he needs to. Just 'cause his magic is, um..."

Fisk blinked at her with big, innocent eyes and a grin of approval.

"Uh, you know, isn't ... fully developed ... doesn't mean he can't throw down and eat a dude." She shrugged.

The revenant crossed his arms again and muttered venomously, "As you wish, *Master*."

Oh, Christ. She didn't mean to boss him around, but why leave Fisk behind when he really had a chance of helping? She had to let it go, though. Getting into a giant fight with Cal wouldn't help at the moment. If they weren't all focused and on the same page during this mission, she was pretty sure it would go completely freaking pear-shaped.

Satara drew Cal's attention, turning her invitation over in her hands. "These all have a plus one. We can get him in with that."

"Remember," Astrid said, looking around the room at them, "the party will mostly be attended by the Gloaming. They will far outnumber you, so *do not* make any scenes. Don't give anyone your real names. Most importantly, find Indriði quickly and discreetly."

Satara answered for the group: "Yes, Battlemother."

"Good."

Cal groaned and looked down at himself, picking at his blood- and dirt-stained T-shirt. "Anyone know a good dry-cleaner?"

Marius looked into the mirror, adjusting the cloak chain lying across his chest, focusing on the gold brooches covering the clasps. They shone, engraved with sunbursts and decorated with tiny pearls and sunset tourmaline. He took a slow, measured breath as he smoothed out the cream fur mantle, the fine black wool of the cloak, the golden silk lining.

The person looking back at him in the mirror was a complete stranger —a ponce in fine clothes, dressed for an event he did not want to attend.

He'd almost rather storm the mansion and risk death than go to the party.

Marius recognized this cloak, though he wasn't sure from where. He tried to focus on that, instead of the very real possibility that he would die wearing it. It wasn't a question of skill—he regularly took down monsters of all kinds, had trained his entire life to do just that—but rather odds. The odds that one Auroran vivid could even escape, let alone fight through, a ballroom full of Gloaming if need be.

The odds weren't in his favor.

But he appreciated his father's confidence in him. Eirik had had a vision that the hellerune would be at some high-wight's party. This would be another chance for Marius to bring her back, and to see what the Gloaming were up to. Another chance to prove himself. Hopefully.

The hellerune. Edie Holloway had eluded him three times already. Bringing Tiralda back had been a victory, but bringing the necromancer back would have been better. The last time he'd seen her, she had even been injured—bleeding from internal bruises, as he'd felt when he'd reached out to heal her. It would have been easy to capture her. And once he did....

And once he did, he wasn't sure. Maybe his father would destroy her. It wasn't the first time a Holloway had eluded them, and Marius was sure Radiant Eirik would want her executed.

But, despite himself, the thought of that sent a twinge of guilt through his heart. Even though she was now apparently attending Gloaming parties, Marius had seen that she was just an oblivious girl. She seemed completely clueless to the breadth of her father's crimes and the extent of her powers. *These unfortunates would thank us if they could comprehend that we are cleansing them.* His father had always said that and insisted it was true.

Clueless or not—maybe especially when clueless—she was dangerous. One way or the other, she had to be stopped before she hurt somebody.

The vivid smoothed down the cloak again and lifted his eyes as, in the mirror's reflection, the heavy oak door of his bedroom opened. His father stepped in a moment later, dressed down from his usual full suit of armor, instead wearing leggings and a linen shirt.

Marius said nothing as his father came up behind, observing his reflection closely.

"How does the rest of the clothing fit?"

"Well."

"Good." Eirik folded his arms behind his back and, though he looked straight ahead, met Marius's eyes in the mirror. "You have the invitation?"

"Yes. I should be set." He turned to look at his father. "But I'm only one warrior. How can I face so many of those rats on my own?"

"Your task is meant to be completed discreetly. If all goes to plan, they won't even know you're there. That isn't an issue, is it?"

"No, sir," Marius replied, bowing his head.

Eirik seemed to contemplate this for a moment. He caught one of the golden clasps braided in his hair between his fingers and peered into its reflection thoughtfully. "Perhaps you are right, though. Your safety should be our first priority, and if you're worried, you should at least have some backup."

Marius agreed, though his heart sank at the thought of having to share the credit. "Did you have anyone in mind, Your Grace?"

His father paused and looked into his eyes. If Marius didn't know better, he'd have said that he almost seemed ... sad? Or was that disappointment again? And if so, why? "There is one adherent who has been eager to prove herself. I think you know her. Ynga Widearms."

Marius blinked. "I didn't know she was gunning for rank. She seemed satisfied with where she is now."

Eirik managed a half-smile. "She has ambition and natural talent. And though her talent lies more with physical weaponry, light comes easier once Tyr's Rite is done. She would make a fine vivid. What do you think?"

Marius looked away with a stiff nod, turning from the mirror and unclasping his cloak chain, tossing the garment on his bed. His father's words stung, though he would never say it and couldn't quite understand why. Perhaps he was convinced that the Radiant never spoke of him the way he now spoke of Ynga.

Eirik's voice was soft when he said, "Well? Will you have her?"

I don't have any choice, do I? "Yes, Your Grace."

His father paused. It was almost as though he wanted to say something more. He moved half a step closer and lingered. But then the moment of uncertainty, it seemed, was over, and he retreated.

When Marius looked back up, Eirik had turned away, shoulders sunken; he was nodding, moving toward the door. "Good. Tomorrow night, I expect triumph. Get some sleep, son."

The oak door thumped closed with a sound as heavy and hollow as Marius's heartbeat.

CHAPTER THIRTY

EDIE TURNED the rearview mirror toward her and wiped the corner of her mouth with a tissue, clearing away a smudge of deep purple lipstick. Her hands shook. Was this really about to happen?

"It's going to be okay, kid," Cal said from the driver's side. He looked pretty sharp wearing an actual tuxedo, even if the coat was a size too big for him and unbuttoned. Easier to hide his guns, so he said; Colt Trooper MK III under one arm and Stoeger Bear Claw (barely) under the other.

Edie tried to smile at him and realigned the rearview mirror to look in the back seat. Mercy, Fisk, and Satara had all managed to squish in together, with Fisk in the middle, in a tux of his own. Well ... the shirt, jacket, and tie. They'd tried for hours to talk him into putting on some pants, with no luck. Satara had surprised everyone by showing up in a slinky, bright-red number, and Mercy had surprised no one by wearing her tea-length sequin and tulle monster. At least Fisk seemed to like it. Instead of complaining about the glitter now shedding all over him, he was rather fascinated.

Edie lowered her eyes and looked out the passenger-side window, just barely able to see the outline of her pale face and bare shoulder. Beyond her reflection was a long drive lined with little LED pathway lights, leading up to what could only be described as a leviathan of a house.

Zaedicus Oldine's manor.

Anxiously, she dug her fingers into the scratchy chiffon of her black sheath dress. The damn thing barely fit, and the shimmery epaulet of beads sewn onto the shoulder of its one angel sleeve did nothing to help the itching.

They passed a blue-and-purple-lit fountain in the center of the enormous roundabout driveway, and soon found themselves sitting behind three or four cars waiting to dispense partygoers under the porte-cochère. From where they sat, the group was offered a good look at some of the vehicles already parked in the stone-paved lot to one side of the mansion.

"Oh, god," Cal grumbled around his cigarette.

"Can you put that out?" Edie asked. "We're all going to smell like a minty asshole now." She waved some of his smoke away and added, "What are you *oh-god*ding about?"

Cal cranked his window down and ashed his cigarette, then used it to point to one of the cars pulling into the fancy parking lot.

Edie squinted as she watched the car tuck itself snugly between a Bugatti and a silver Lamborghini. It was a long, luxe old car that looked like it had just taken a wrong turn at Fifth Avenue and missed the Rockefeller Center by a couple states and about 80 years.

"What's that?" she asked, assuming he was admiring the car itself.

"1930 Mercedes-Benz SS Tourer," he rattled off without missing a beat. "Champagne pink paintjob, New York pink and cream leather interior, rose gold trim."

Edie looked at him, blinking rapidly. "You should really start charging for that."

He grumbled and gripped Ghost's wheel tighter, glaring at the other car as its lights flicked off. "I couldn't tell all that from just looking at it, doofus. I worked on that car."

"Whose is it?" Edie watched as someone stepped out, but it was just a valet.

Cal's shoulders relaxed, albeit infinitesimally. "My ex."

Mercy snorted, and Cal seized the rearview mirror, focusing it on the back seat so he could glare at her.

"Your ... ex? Ex-*girlfriend?*" Edie asked.

"No, Edie, my *ex*-tended edition of *Terminator 2: Judgment Day.*" He threw a hand up. "*Yes*, my ex-girlfriend. Matilda. She's probably inside. Fuck sake, I knew I'd run into her at some point." He hissed and dropped his cigarette out the window as they pulled up to the porte-cochère.

The mansion was even more impressive up close. It was made of stone and looked almost Georgian, but with heavy Gothic influences: blind arcading, angle-buttresses, and a pretty vicious-looking spire on the far wing. Golden light poured through the arched windows onto the lawn. Edie studied them in awe; their tracery looked almost organic, more like leaves than stone. Anster had some impressive old buildings, but she'd never seen anything like this.

Cal stopped the car and mumbled, "Stay inside. I'm gonna let you out." He slipped out, letting Mercy climb from the backseat first. He offered her a hand, and she took it, heaving her bulky gown after her.

Edie watched Cal closely, noticing how easily he took on a subservient role in this environment. She guessed that sort of thing was hard to shake, but the fact that he was still struggling—and the fact that, tonight, they all had to play along with it—made her more than uncomfortable. A thick shard of guilt punctured her heart; after all, she'd dragged him back here.

The valets and a few guests loitering near the entrance stared as Fisk exited the car next, causing the shocks to groan with relief and spring up. Satara climbed out, too, squeezing Cal's hand tight before she rounded the car and started up the stairs.

Edie's turn was coming up, and if she wasn't ready, no one was going to stop time for her.

Finally, Cal made his way over and opened her door, holding out a hand for her. She'd already warned him about her ineptitude in heels, and his arm was as stiff as steel while she practically used it as a crutch.

"I should have worn high-tops," she mumbled.

"I thought the plan was *not* to call attention to ourselves," he mumbled back, tensing a bit as a young valet approached him.

Uh oh. Edie watched as Cal's grip on his small key ring tightened.

"Your keys." The valet looked at Cal for a moment, then bypassed him, looking instead to Edie. "Your keys, ma'am?"

"Uh, sure," she said, laughing nervously to try and dispel the tension. She waited for Cal, and so did the valet, though he looked mightily unimpressed.

Cal's grip on the keys tightened.

Edie nudged him. "Cal."

The revenant seemed almost to come out of a brief fugue—probably of anger—and practically threw the keys at the kid. "Not a scratch," he warned, before pulling Edie away to follow the rest of their group up the carpeted marble steps.

Edie could feel the frustration rolling off him. It probably took all the strength he could muster not to come in guns blazing. Maybe there was something she could do to help, if even a little; if she could get him to lighten up, he might be less likely to blow a fuse.

She nudged him, gentler this time, and teased, "The way I'm clinging to you like you're a pool noodle, people are gonna think we're dating."

"No, they won't," he replied, tone deadly serious.

Okay, not a good time for jokes. She cringed and made a note to offer more *silent* support. Being here made all of them nervous, but for him, it was extra fraught. The people here would feel safe in assuming he was her thrall. For right now, theoretically, that worked to their advantage, but it was pretty sickening.

She was already tired of the Gloaming.

They followed Mercy, Fisk, and Satara into the vestibule, where a man in a dark suit was carefully patting down a guest, and a woman dressed similarly was looking through peoples' purses and taking their invitations. Edie knew that Fisk and Satara were unarmed, a fact that had everyone on-edge, but Mercy had whip-stitched a pocket into the inseam of her Spanx, big enough to hide one of her switchblades. It wasn't clear how much use a

Hello Kitty switchblade Mercy had never actually *used* before would be, but it was a nice gesture.

Edie held her breath as the man patted Mercy down with the backs of his hands, but there was no way he was getting anywhere close to her inner thigh without actually lifting her skirt. He let her go without much of a thought, and Edie relaxed a bit.

Cal wedged Edie between him and the man next, but her pass was brief; the guy was mostly busy eyeballing the six-foot-four revenant. When he was done with Edie, he moved on to Cal unceremoniously, reaching out to pat him down.

Cal looked like he might let him—he didn't have much choice—but Edie cut in. "Um, excuse me … his anti-decomposition charms are very volatile, so please don't touch him." *Oh, god—gods?—please let that work.*

The man paused, hands hovering over Cal, and looked at Edie. "I have to check everyone."

Whatever she did, she couldn't let him take Cal's guns. Harnessing her panic, she tried to sound as irritated and imperious as she could. "Leave it. Do you think I don't have him under my control?"

The words made her feel disgusting the moment they left her mouth, but they worked. The man slowly lowered his hands. For a moment, it seemed like he would protest, but apparently his desire to keep things running smoothly won out. He simply shrugged. "Very well. My apologies, madam."

Cal huffed as he rejoined Edie, tugging his lapels tighter with a stormy glare. "Security's tight."

"It probably makes them a pretty easy target, having so many Gloaming in one place." Quietly, she added, "Sorry that was … uncomfortable. But, y'know … you'd probably be even more uncomfortable without your weapons."

He just grunted in response.

They crossed a checkered floor to the foot of the grand staircase. The interior was all dark wood and marble from what Edie could see, decorated with statues of tall figures wearing armor and adornments straight out of

Lord of the Rings: flowing and strangely organic, like the tracery on the Gothic windows.

Relying less on Cal now that she was getting used to the heels, Edie followed the others up the grand staircase. On the first landing, she passed a wood burned mural of a family of elk under a yew tree before starting up the second, narrower staircase. She kept a firm grip on the twisted banister, so beautifully imperfect that it looked like it had been grown rather than crafted. Finally, the blood red carpet ended at the second landing, where huge double doors were propped open, granting a view of the ballroom.

"Oh my god," Edie heard Mercy breathe as she came up behind her.

It was enormous, with three huge, arched windows on the north wall and great glass chandeliers hanging from the vaulted ceilings. A dais was raised before the windows, overlooking a dance floor already filled with guests. The intricately-tiled floors were polished to a shine, and everything glittered, a joyous orange-yellow light filling the room. Not really what she had expected from a Gloaming party, but it was a pleasant surprise. She stepped through the doors, practically turning in a circle to take everything in.

Behind them, on either side of the door they had just come through, were a set of golden stairs which led up to a large landing and mezzanine. An entire second tier of ballroom, hugging all but the north wall, was full of people milling away from the food and dancing, some looking down and observing those on the ballroom floor.

Edie's heart beat faster at all the different faces and shapes—creatures she'd never even dreamed of before, let alone seen. Men and women at least eight or nine feet tall mixed with people half their height or smaller. Giggling balls of light wove between crowds and danced around chandeliers. Nearby, a skeleton in an ornate blue robe spoke animatedly with a death-pale woman whose skimpy dress revealed a ragged hole in her back, edged with moss and fungus like a rotten tree trunk. Beautiful, sharp-eared and sharp-toothed people of all shades—glossy ebony to powder blue, pearl-white to plum, even multicolored scales—danced and drank and laughed.

Edie was beginning to think that maybe coming here had been a bad idea. That maybe trying to look as plain as she did had been a fatal error.

An unveiled valkyrie wearing a double-slitted dress of swan feathers passed in front of them, and Mercy mumbled, "At least you're not wearing that. *Mega* itchy."

"So many people. Looks like there aren't very many humans here, though."

"We should start looking right away," Satara said, her voice strained as she approached holding her clutch tightly. Her necklace and cuffs—engraved with dragons and tiny runes—shone brilliantly in the honeyed light. "The sooner we find Indriði, the sooner we can ... leave."

Edie nodded and looked around the room. The mezzanine lined the ballroom in a U shape, with the door from which they'd just entered at the lowest point of the U. Held up by stone columns decorated with gold leaves, the cover of the mezzanine gave the recesses of the ballroom under it a darker, more private feel—a perfect place to gossip.

"I'm going to check around the perimeter," Satara mumbled, still eyeing the crowd warily.

Edie nodded and looked at the others. "Fisk, you search the second tier."

"What should I do?" Mercy asked eagerly.

Edie sighed. The danger here was unspeakable, and she really wished Mercy hadn't come. They'd fought over it for a whole day before Edie had finally accepted that there was nothing she could do to keep Mercy from coming. Guilt over how she'd treated her friend the past week weighed her down, too. She didn't deserve someone so dedicated. If Edie were as brave and selfless as Mercy, this whole situation would probably seem a lot simpler.

To top it all off, this whole *leadership* thing was already giving Edie a headache. Thank god Cal and Satara were here to tell her when her ideas were stupid. The most she'd ever been in charge of was a four- or five-person band for a set with DYSMANTLE, and even then, Mercy usually took point.

"Um ... you stay with me and Cal for now," Edie answered after some thought. "We can check the ballroom floor."

Their group splintered, and the two young women stepped further into the ballroom, Cal trailing behind.

After a few more moments of thought, Edie finally blurted out what she'd been thinking for the past three days. "I can't believe *I'm* the one who ended up having magical powers, out of the two of us."

Mercy laughed a little. "Why not?"

"Well, considering I'm sort of ... the sidekick." It wasn't quite the right word, but it was the closest comparison she had. "It's just weird."

Mercy's face fell, and she slowed to a stop next to one of the tables. It held a wide variety of food: a whole roast boar, a platter of baked apples stuffed with wild rice, fish—and further on, a barrel of mead and a flaming punch bowl.

"What do you mean, the sidekick? You're my friend."

"I know!" Edie said quickly, wringing her hands. "I just meant, you know, you're usually in charge of stuff, so it's just ... a really weird change."

She could see she'd hurt Mercy's feelings somehow, but she only seemed to be digging herself a deeper hole.

"You've just got the *pink-haired magical girl* vibe, and I'm just ... grungy. That's all. It's just weird. You know, like, if this were a comic or a book, you'd definitely—" Edie turned and tried to look like she was carefully selecting an apple. "You're just more capable. I'm not good enough to deal with all of this."

"Right," Mercy said, her tone flatter. "So you think I'm a stereotype—"

"I didn't—"

"—and bossy?" There was silence between them for a moment before she continued: "Edie, I love you, but I ... I don't know what to say. I have *never* thought you were inferior to me."

"No! I didn't mean it like that."

"It— it's fine."

It didn't sound *fine* to Edie.

"Now isn't the time, anyway." Mercy looked away. "I'm gonna try and find Fisk and make sure he doesn't undress himself."

She was already out of Edie's reach by the time she finished her sentence, and Edie didn't dare call out to her and risk drawing attention to them. Now she was stuck without her best friend, and with a baked apple she really didn't care to eat.

Cal came closer, hands in his pockets. "Women," he mumbled.

"You know I'm a woman, right?"

"You're a girl. It's different." He was trying to act cool as a cucumber, but Edie noticed how his eyes darted around the ballroom and how he bounced his leg.

She raised a brow. "I'm twenty-three." When he didn't reply, she offered him the baked apple. "Hungry?"

"Ugh. Get that out of my face."

She sighed. "Hm. You look too nervous to eat anyway."

Cal snorted indignantly. "I am *not* fucking nervous. What the hell would I have to be nervous about?"

Before Edie could respond, someone cut in to their conversation: "Cal?"

Edie didn't recognize the woman's voice—a bright, sweet voice with an Eastern European accent. It was the voice of someone who couldn't quite believe what they were seeing.

When Edie turned, she couldn't either.

CHAPTER THIRTY-ONE

Matilda was a petite woman, just over five feet tall, with delicate features. Her bone-white hair, the same color as her skin, was done up in two thick buns and adorned with a silver hair chain and teardrop pearls. The champagne-colored dress she wore was long and flowing, with the hint of a tasteful slit up the front, just wide enough to catch brief glimpses of her legs as she walked. The deep V-neck bodice appeared to be made of diamond-encrusted leaves of silver thread, creeping down her hips and onto the skirt like a living thing.

Edie hadn't really known what to say when Cal had mentioned his ex-girlfriend, but considering the kind of guy he was, she'd envisioned someone ... different. This swan-necked beauty was a far cry from the dishwater-blond cowgirl she'd been expecting.

"Cal?" the woman ventured again. "Is that you?"

Cal was stiff, and turned as if in slow motion to face her. Edie watched him take a deep breath. "Hey, Tilly."

Matilda glanced at Edie for a moment, but her gaze—the black-eyed gaze of a human-wight—was pulled back to Cal's face quickly. They both sucked in a breath and held it at the same time. "I had ... heard that you had come back from Vegas, but I didn't dare believe it," she said quietly, unable to conceal her wide-eyed astonishment.

The honesty and hurt in her face made Edie feel like an intruder, like she was watching something she shouldn't. Quickly, she turned away and focused on the banquet instead, though she still listened.

"Yeah," Cal said. "I had some business to take care of."

"I hope everything went to plan?"

"I did what I had to do."

"Ah." There was a pause. "So you'll be leaving again...?"

An even longer pause. "I dunno. I might stick around. Weird shit's been happening."

Somehow, Edie could *feel* Matilda's gaze turn to her, and a shiver went up her spine. The vampire's words only made the room chillier: "Who is this?"

Well, fuck. In an act of quick thinking that she immediately regretted, Edie took a huge bite of baked apple before she turned to rejoin the conversation.

Cal looked at Matilda, bewildered for a fraction of a second, before he said, "Oh," and turned. "That's Edie."

"Mmph."

"It is ... a pleasure to meet you, Edie."

Cal tugged at his bowtie and looked around the ballroom like he might see an emergency exit or somewhere he could just walk into the void, never to return. "Uh, it was nice seein' you, Tilda. I'll probably see you around," he said hurriedly. "I gotta..."

His sentence devolved into unintelligible grumblings, and Matilda bowed her head briefly as he left at a near-trot.

"Mmph!" With bug-eyes, Edie watched him go. What the hell was he doing?! They had agreed they shouldn't split up, since something seemed to go wrong every time they did. And not only had he left her alone, but he'd left her alone with a stranger.

A stranger who happened to be a blood-sucking wight, and was now gliding across the marble floor toward her.

Matilda's rose-painted nails were sharp like claws, Edie noticed, as she held her hand out and motioned for the apple. Edie handed it to her, and Matilda stared her down, murmuring, "Chew your food, girl."

Oh, god, what did he get me into? But she did as she was told, then swallowed hard.

"Good," said the wight. "We should talk."

As Marius ascended the staircase toward the ballroom, the phantom palm of his right hand itched.

When things became too much, it tended to do that; the anxiety of being surrounded by the Gloaming and their allies was getting to him. And the task looming ahead of him—to find Edie Holloway among the hundreds of partygoers, and to capture her without drawing attention to himself— seemed all the more impossible now that he was toe to toe with it.

At his side, Ynga seemed just as nervous. Her face was stern, her thick fingers knotted in the fabric of her flared-leg white jumpsuit. Tonight would be her chance to prove herself, to try to secure a place as one of the handful of vivids in the city. His own proving had been tough enough; between Ynga's past with the Gloaming, the importance of securing Holloway, *and* having to prove herself, he almost couldn't imagine the pressure.

Almost.

Marius shook his right arm a bit, careful to keep it concealed. Losing control was not an option. For both of their sakes, he had to keep a tight grip on his emotions. No matter what horrors he saw.

Just hold fast and don't draw attention to yourself, the vivid thought, flexing his jaw and closing his eyes briefly as he passed through the enormous gilt doors.

Lively chatter and warmth enveloped him at once. The room was alive with movement as the creatures there milled; the crowd twisted and writhed like a dark beast cooling itself in the mud at midday. Everything seemed golden and joyous, and to an outsider, it might have looked inviting. But it couldn't fool Marius, and it certainly wasn't fooling Ynga, tense as a wire next to him. The decadence on display here alone was enough to make him uncomfortable. The fact that it was Gloaming, that it had all happily been bought with blood and slavery and unholy pacts, made him feel ill.

"Where do we start?" Ynga asked under her breath, taking a flute of honey-colored liquid from a servant's passing tray.

Marius scanned the room further. This place was so deceptively bright, every horrible thing fully on display. It was hard to look at just one thing for too long. Here, the Gloaming didn't need to hide their shame. They *celebrated* it.

When he didn't answer, Ynga drifted closer to him and mumbled, "What does she look like?"

He took a breath, trying to imagine what Edie might wear to an event like this. "Five-foot-five, roughly. Pale white skin, raven hair, stormy eyes. Dark makeup. Probably wearing black." Black was a given. She favored the color, he'd noticed, and she probably wouldn't want to stand out.

"You've just described a third of the humans here."

"An expression of horror and confusion might clue you in. She's not skilled at hiding her emotions."

Ynga raised a brow, looking him over, but said no more. They eased their way deeper into the party, weaving past clustered groups of guests and dodging all manner of creatures walking the ballroom floor.

They were nearing the center of the room when something caught Marius's eye. A few feet to his left was a large semicircle of guests, clearly watching something but packed too tightly for Marius to see what it was. He stopped in his tracks, letting Ynga go on ahead while he lingered around the crowd before finally managing to squeeze into the semicircle himself.

Lying on the floor in front of those gathered was a human: a young woman dressed in a simple, long-sleeved cotton shift and a worn belt. Probably a servant or thrall. Her dark hair fanned out on the shining tile below her, and her skin was unnaturally pale. She was completely still.

Marius's stomach turned.

Laughter cut through his reverie, and he raised his eyes to the people standing above the human. They watched her with either gleeful smiles or keen, clinical interest. At the forefront was a human man with graying brown hair and thick-rimmed glasses, wearing robes of a fine, soft-looking leather. Marius could make out red runes etched into the skin of his throat, not quite covered by the collar of his robes. And the stench coming off of him....

The man thrust an arm out and leaned in, fingers splayed over the girl.

Just as Marius realized what he must be, the prone woman twitched. The gathered partygoers watched in awe—and horror, on Marius's part—as her back arched, bowing dramatically. Her legs shuddered and shook as they crept under her and somehow found footing, and without even using her arms to push herself up off the floor, she rose. Her torso jerked in the cradle of her hips as she did, as though her muscles couldn't quite accommodate the weight of her head and shoulders.

The leather-clad man smiled smugly and relaxed, lowering his arm.

Blood mage.

Beside him, unable to control its glee, stood a tréfolken—a formidable humanoid figure made completely of winding roots and branches, its body spindly and delicate-looking, almost skeletal. Its wooden, faunlike face was framed with wildflowers, and its scalp extended into a wide stag's rack covered in moss and small mushrooms. This tréfolken was etched in red runes like the mage, and its eyes and hollow chest glowed with an unnatural pinkish light. Someone was using its antlers to hold their drink; a wine glass was perched between two prongs.

The creature brayed and pointed at the human girl, the eerie light within its ribs expanding with every word. "Now make it dance! Make it dance!"

The blood mage obliged, barely lifting his hand this time. He simply twitched his fingers, his eyes, and his thrall followed unspoken commands. Marius watched in disgust as the human girl's arms jerked above her head and her hips began to shudder from side to side, like some sort of terrifying, death-pale exotic dancer.

The gathered partygoers tittered at the display—especially the tréfolken, who was laughing like this was the funniest thing it had ever seen. "Brilliant, Master!"

The blood mage, still controlling the human, cut the creature an irritated look and took the wine glass from its rack, taking a deep drink. "Someday, Dense-Elm, you're going to die laughing like an idiot."

Dense-Elm fell silent for a moment, its glow dulling to a blackened maroon. But the blood thrall leaned forward and began to throw her head in circles, arms spasming and feet shuddering right to left like some demented version of the Twist, and the tree-man's laughter soon resumed.

Marius tightened his fist, trying not to shake, trying not to draw attention to himself. He couldn't possibly sit by and let this happen. The smell, the sight…. It was an abomination.

And yet, if the crowd got even the slightest inkling he wasn't one of them, he would be dead in an instant, and Edie Holloway would walk free.

A woman in voluminous velvet robes and a male elf with a cascade of silky red hair sidled up to the blood mage. Coyly, the woman said, "Can you make her do anything besides dance?"

"Something more … useful?" the elf next to her asked. He carried a handful of red berries, and popped one in his mouth as he looked the blood thrall over imperiously.

Marius was unable to suppress a shudder, thinking of what the elf might mean by that. Thankfully, no one seemed to notice his slip-up.

The blood mage hung his wine glass in Dense-Elm's rack again and chuckled, though his eyes shone with an edge when he glanced at the berry-eater. Some humans could not help but feel inferior around elves, and Marius was sure a man so confident in his power didn't like it being challenged. "Of course," the mage said mildly.

With a snap, the thrall stood at attention. Marius was filled with dread. What in Asgard's name could the mage force her to do, here, in the light, with so many people watching?

The berry-eater—as well as everyone else—watched intently as the thrall jerked closer. Her color-drained hand disappeared within her master's robes, and Marius's mind reeled. Relief washed over him when she quickly drew her hand back out—but the relief was short-lived. She was gripping a bejeweled dagger.

"As you can see," the blood mage purred, "she'll do anything I want. Or, at least, her blood will."

Marius's gaze darted to the thrall's face. She was conscious once more, and she looked utterly terrified. Her circulatory system might have been obeying, but he had no doubt her mind was doing all it could to fight the mage's influence.

Her eyes met his as her hand jerked up, bringing the glinting blade of the knife to her throat. It pressed dangerously into her skin.

This ... *this* was blood magic. This was the reality of the Gloaming, and of everyone who meddled in the ebon magics: power-hungry beasts and evil people vying for power and hurting others. This was what he had been raised all his life to fight against, to stop at all costs. This was the grim history of the hellerunan.

And if he didn't stop her in time, before she came into her powers properly, this was what Edie Holloway would become.

Marius tried to keep her and all that was at stake in his mind as he watched the blood thrall jerk, about to draw the blade across her throat. This woman might die, but if he outed himself, he'd bring wrath upon everything he held dear. He *knew* the answer to the terrible choice he had to make in this split second. He knew what he must do.

But it was a little different when you were staring right at it.

He took half a step forward and began to raise his arm.

Before he could make a move to save the thrall, however— *Bong!* The ornate clock on the north wall chimed.

The blood mage's concentration broke as he and his companions turned their attention to the mezzanine landing, and the thrall toppled to the ground like a puppet whose strings had been cut. The dagger fell from her hand and clattered across the floor.

Another wave of relief flooded Marius, but it was soon replaced with apprehension. He held his breath, hoping no one had seen him falter, and followed their gazes to the figure looming above them.

"I don't know how I didn't see it before. You are like a ghost of your father. I feel like such a fool."

Matilda held her champagne glass close to her chest, head bowed. She and Edie had retreated to one of the darker corners of the ballroom and cozied up to a huge grandfather clock, where the vampire had thankfully listened to what Edie had to say before doing anything drastic.

"I get that a lot." Edie looked into her own champagne glass, wondering if things would be easier if she was buzzed. It probably wasn't a good idea to test that out at such a crucial moment. She wondered if the others had found Indriði yet. Hopefully, they could leave soon.

"Still." Matilda sighed and pinched the bridge of her delicate nose. "How silly to think that you two were ... together. And how ridiculous and selfish of me to react that way, even if you had been."

Edie smiled at the smaller woman. "It's not selfish."

"Thank you for saying so," she replied, looking deflated.

"I had no idea Cal had had a girlfriend. Especially someone ... like you. He makes it sound like my dad had him on a leash twenty-four seven."

Matilda peered at her warily. "Whatever Cal has told you about your father was not a *lie*. He would never lie. But no, there were times when they were separated. Cal has a gift for working on old cars, and for the past 80 years, always I am looking for someone to take care of my roadster."

"So you paid my dad for Cal's time," Edie said, smiling a little even though the thought of Cal working without compensation made her feel ill. Although ... if they'd grown close enough to be in a relationship, maybe he'd gotten a little more *compensation* than she thought.

The vampire grinned back, flashing viciously curved fangs. "Yes. And, mysteriously, my roadster began to have many problems that only Cal could fix! Thankfully, I have a large disposable income."

"That must have been a breath of fresh air for him."

"He appreciated the time off. Though he didn't like the idea of me paying to spend time with him." She shrugged sadly. "I tried to help him get away any way I could."

Short of killing my dad, Edie thought. "How long did you date?"

She shook her head. "Oh, I don't know. A few, maybe five years."

"Five years," Edie repeated in awe. No relationship she'd ever had (not that she'd had many) had lasted that long. She didn't think even her parents had known each other for that long before getting married.

"Yes." Matilda looked away. "And then ... your father died."

Edie frowned. It sounded like the story was about to take a sour turn.

"I thought that, with him gone, we could finally be happy, but Cal became ... restless. He said he had to go. Just *go*. Put distance between himself and this place, I suppose." The vampire shrugged, lips pursed tightly. "So, he went."

"But why not take you along?"

Matilda's shoulders hunched, and she looked down into her champagne.

Edie could sense that she was treading into personal territory—maybe a little too personal for their first meeting. "Sorry. Don't answer that."

"It's all right. He didn't *want* me to come with him. And I didn't want to leave. My whole life is here, has been for a hundred years. We parted ways. It was what was best for him, surely ... and it's been ten years, after all."

She looked away, and Edie followed her gaze. Nearby, a female giant—a *jötunn*, if Edie was remembering correctly—stood with a human companion, petting his hair and kissing his jaw. Edie had never had an overabundance of female friends, since most girls throughout high school had thought she was weird and creepy, but she knew the look on Matilda's face.

The unspoken words were heavy between them. Edie's expression softened, and she looked back at Matilda. "You should tell him."

The vampire looked over, raised her eyes. She was about to say something when the clock struck eleven, and complete silence fell over the room. Most of the guests turned to the south wall, looking up at the mezzanine landing, and so Edie did the same.

The clock was on its ninth chime when a figure finally came into view, resting his ring-heavy hands on the gilded parapet. He was an elf, very tall and draped in rich maroon robes. His skin and hair looked drained of all color, as did his shockingly pale eyes. As he scanned the room, his expression changed from one of disgust to a wide, pleasant grin.

"Late even to his own party, as always," Matilda whispered, shaking her head.

That had to be Zaedicus. Edie watched him closely as he spread his arms, addressing the entire room.

"My friends ... welcome! I hope you are enjoying what the night has to offer so far. You will be pleased to know that this is only the beginning."

He paused and scanned the room again, lowering his hands before continuing.

"I am sure some of you have noticed that this event is more ... diverse than usual. I am humbled to have Gloaming of all reaches here, and not just my fellow wights. Tonight marks a momentous occasion. It will be a night of new beginnings and alliances."

Momentous occasion? Anything "momentous" for this creep would definitely be something Edie wanted no part of. She raised her head, eyes darting around the room, trying to catch a glimpse of Cal or Satara.

"But," Zaedicus went on, raising a hand, "I digress on that point. My speeches—and our guest of honor—can wait for a while. For now, eat, drink, and dance. Here's to us, my friends."

The partygoers cheered and clapped. Zaedicus seemed very pleased with himself, and, still grinning wide, he gestured to the first floor of the ballroom.

Loudly and with authority, he cried, "Bring out the cattle!"

From the corner of her eye, Edie saw Matilda flinch. She opened her mouth to ask what the hell he was talking about, but her question was soon answered. Smaller oak doors near the corners of the ballroom swung open, and Edie watched as a finely-dressed serving staff filed into the room, dragging ropes after them.

Blood rushed from her face and into her heart, turning cold.

Attached to each rope was a line of five or six people barely strong enough to shuffle into the room on their own: humans, mostly, but also a couple elves and other, smaller figures Edie didn't recognize, all of them living.

The serving staff tugged them relentlessly; in the line nearest to Edie, someone fell, yet the staff kept pulling, simply dragging the fallen. They led the slow march to the dais at the north wall. Once all of them were lined up neatly, each of the serving staff drew long, sharp knives from the sashes at their waists.

Matilda covered her eyes. Edie knew she should look away, too, but she couldn't. She felt cold and numb all over. There could be no doubt what Zaedicus had in store for those people. But no one was doing anything; everyone just stood there.

Someone had to *do* something.

Edie took a step forward, inhaling sharply as if to cry out—but someone reached out and caught her wrist.

Matilda.

"Edie, what are you doing! Please … there's nothing you can do."

She knew it was the truth, but how could she just stand there and watch people being executed?

"Here, look at me."

Edie did. Tears pricked her eyes; she inhaled sharply, trying to subdue her own shaking.

"You're not part of the Gloaming, are you?" the vampire whispered, black eyes studying her.

She shook her head numbly and let her gaze flick back to the "cattle." More staff brought out large silver basins and set them before each of the prisoners. Those holding the knives forced them roughly to their knees and positioned most of their torsos in the basins.

"That's okay. I'm not Gloaming, either." Matilda squeezed Edie's shoulders, drawing her attention. "Edie, focus on me."

Edie did.

"I've heard rumors about the Reach. Are you really going to revive it?"

"I ... don't know. *Astrid* wants to. She says I would lead it."

Matilda nodded. "Then I want to help you. This sort of thing has been going on for too long, but people like me ... we have no place to go. No protection except for the Gloaming Lords."

Edie was still looking at Matilda when the servants slit the prisoners' throats, but she could hear blood spewing, beating against the sides of the basins. She shuddered in horror and looked over her shoulder just in time to watch as the "cattle" struggled hopelessly and eventually stilled. The majority of the partygoers clapped, and Edie heard Zaedicus sigh slightly from his perch.

She swallowed and closed her eyes for a moment. She had to put what she'd just seen out of her mind for a while. She had to focus. There would be time to deal with it later. "The Gloaming Lord of this area was killed, wasn't he?" she asked Matilda.

"Yes. And now it's more dangerous than ever to speak up. If you're ostracized by 'friends,' you truly have *no* protection against the Aurora, or even other Gloaming. It's dangerous, existing the way we do."

Edie scoffed and pulled her wrist away. "Yeah, well, it seems like it's pretty dangerous existing around here, *period.*" She spared a glance back at the dais, where many undead were gathering around to have their glasses filled.

"Yes..." Matilda agreed sadly. "But you could protect them, too."

"Enjoy yourselves, my friends!" Zaedicus called, spreading his arms again. "Let the festivities officially commence."

Edie looked back at the landing and realized he was descending, his eyes locked directly with hers. There wasn't any time to run.

Matilda followed her gaze and inhaled sharply. "Here, stay by me," she said, and linked one of her cold arms in Edie's. "I will think of something."

As Zaedicus approached them, Matilda schooled her expression like a pro, greeting him with a warm smile.

"Lord Oldine, very good to see you."

"Please, Lady Ardelean, the pleasure is mine entirely."

He'd just killed, what, twenty people? Yet he smiled so easily. Edie dug her nails into Matilda's arm, trying to keep her rage—and fright—in check.

"I don't believe we've been introduced," he said to Edie. His expression didn't change a fraction, but his voice seemed to darken, almost. She could sense that he knew who she was. But how? *Why?* Astrid had said he was insignificant.

"Ah." Matilda put a hand at Edie's back and smiled. "This is Sybil Crawford. I'm sure you remember, I brought her to last year's gala? Although she was a redhead then."

Zaedicus didn't even spare Matilda a glance, simply staring at Edie and never taking his pale yellow eyes from her. His smile never faltered as he offered his hand, chuckling lightly. "I don't recall. One forgets faces when one plans so many events. I do apologize."

Edie reached out numbly and shook his hand. The grip was stony, and she immediately wanted to withdraw, but he lingered. His smile had faded.

"Lord Oldine," Matilda said, loud enough that he had no choice but to acknowledge her. "I wonder, who is the guest of honor you spoke about?"

"Ah," he said, finally releasing Edie's hand, "all in good time, Matilda, my dear. For now, please, make yourself comfortable. You and your friend."

Edie squirmed, and he smiled again.

"I look forward to it, then," Matilda said. "Don't let us take up your time. I'm sure you have many important people to talk to."

With a cold, tight smile, he looked back at her and nodded. "Indeed. I hope you enjoy the night."

With that, the high-wight turned and drifted away, grabbing a silver goblet before disappearing into the crowd in front of the dais.

CHAPTER THIRTY-TWO

"Creep." Matilda squeezed Edie's hand. "Are you all right?"

"I ... I don't know." She shook her head. "I think I need some fresh air."

The vampire nodded sympathetically and gestured to the stairs. "There are balconies on the second floor."

That was all she needed to say. Edie nodded and left quickly, pressing a hand to her forehead. For the first time, the gravity of the situation gripped her—truly gripped her. A lot of these people were *evil*, and they didn't give a second thought to slaughtering other beings like animals.

Something *had* to be done.

She climbed the golden stairs, walking carefully in her unfamiliar pumps, and wove through the clusters of guests on the mezzanine. She spared a glance towards the north wall. The serving staff were cleaning up the dais now, bleeding the last from the bodies and removing them, probably so they could move the gore-filled basins to the refreshment table. The thought churned her stomach.

"Excuse me," she mumbled, scooting past the brawny form of what appeared to be an anthropomorphic salamander. Finally, she reached the arched double doors of the balcony. A shining crystal grille covered the glass, and in the ballroom's bright light, the exit gleamed like a beacon.

Edie slipped out onto the balcony. It was large and perfectly silent. Ferns grew from stone vases and onto the iron rail riveted to the parapet, obscuring it almost completely. She closed the doors softly behind her and took a big gulp of air, then crossed to the edge of the balcony. She was grateful for this place, so quiet and dark despite the horror that reigned in the ballroom and the throbbing chaos that reigned in her head.

Twenty people had bled out right in front of her face, and she hadn't done anything to stop it. No one had. *These* were the people she was supposed to be fighting. But how could she? She'd be dead—or worse—the first time she had to fight someone one on one.

That thought, and the fact that she knew the situation was inevitable—that she *would have to fight* at some point—made her extremities go numb with terror. She tucked her chin against her chest, looking over the parapet as tears welled in her eyes.

It was a good seventeen-foot drop, if not more, to the flagstones below. An urge she had never felt before rolled over her: *If I jumped now, I wouldn't have to be afraid anymore.*

She'd been clinically depressed for years, but she'd always had hopeless, lonely reasons for wanting to stop existing. This feeling ... it was different. The paralyzing fear of what was to come, what *else* she might have to see, was the cause of this panic. This grief. Grief for the life she'd lived before, and for the poor, oblivious girl that had been Edith Holloway a week and a half ago.

How can I save innocent people if I can't even save myself?

She gritted her teeth and carefully wiped away the tears with her fingertips, trying to cause as little damage to her makeup as possible. She tried to find new resolve in her anger and fright. She was being selfish, feeling bad for herself again. Like hell fear would kill her here, while she still had a chance to learn and help.

No doubt she'd die either way, and she'd never be prepared for it—but not like this.

She doubted falling from two stories would be enough to kill her, anyway, unless she landed directly on her head like a Looney Toon.

A skinny shaft of golden light fell over her shoulder and onto the parapet beside her as one of the double doors eased open. Music and laughter filtered out from the party, but whoever had found her was silent. Edie closed her eyes briefly, steeling herself before turning to look.

It took her a moment to recognize him in the unfamiliar clothing. "*Marius?*"

He seemed surprised to see her, but not nearly as surprised as she was to see him. He was the last person she would have expected to meet at a Gloaming party.

He lingered in the doorway for a few moments before toeing a nearby chunk of crumbled stone in front of the door, propping it open just a sliver. Taking a few steps closer, he muttered, "Holloway."

When he said that name, the horrible guilt—paused momentarily by her surprise—began to fill Edie's heart again. She winced and looked down, studying his outfit to avoid his eyes. He looked ... different in the silk-lined cloak, black embroidered doublet and breeches, and polished cavalier boots.

Yeah. *Different* was a safe word.

Marius must have noticed her grimace, because he said instead, quieter, "Edie."

"What are you doing here?" she asked, turning more fully toward him and trying not to sound as nervous as she felt. Risking someone from the Gloaming recognizing her was enough; she didn't need him coming after her, too.

"Here"—he gestured around them with a sweep of his cloak—"or the party?"

Edie shrugged. "Both, I guess."

Marius came a little closer, still standing in the shaft of light he'd let onto the balcony with them. Backlit as he was, she could only vaguely make out his features, but his eyes were as bright as ever. "I needed fresh air."

"Me, too."

Neither of them said anything. They didn't have to. They were no doubt fleeing the same guilt—and if Edie thought hers was bad, she couldn't imagine being Auroran, someone oathbound to protect the good and slay the evil or whatever.

Coming to stand beside her, Marius rested his wrists on the railing and looked out at the dark blue horizon.

Edie watched him, tracing his profile with her eyes. "And why are you at the party?" she finally asked.

He didn't move his head, but he glanced sideways at her. "I'm sure you already know."

Taking another big gulp of air, she nodded. He'd come to capture her. And now, here they were, completely alone together. Two stories was probably nothing for someone with his powers. It would be no biggie to knock her out and slip away.

But he didn't make a move to grab her or even threaten her. He just kept his eyes on the horizon. The music filtering in from the ballroom swelled—a lively flute, a harp, drums, and something else Edie couldn't quite pick out.

"The music is nice," Marius remarked suddenly.

"Uh ... yeah." She looked at him oddly, trying to figure out what his angle was. After a moment of silence, she added, "Besides the ... you know, the senseless killing, it's a nice party."

"You're a musician, aren't you?"

She was about to say the same thing she always did: *I just play bass.* But that wasn't really true, was it? She played bass, and keyboard, if it came down to it; she sang; she wrote at least half of the music and lyrics for all of DYSMANTLE's original songs. Mercy got most of the credit, but ... maybe that wasn't Mercy's fault after all. Maybe it was because *Edie* never took any. Maybe she was so insecure that she hid behind Mercy, so she could blame her instead of taking responsibility for her own failures.

Edie took a breath, coming to lean against the railing next to Marius. "Yeah. I am. Fisk insists on calling me a *skald*, though."

Raising a brow, he looked over. "The sea spirit?"

She nodded. "We brought him home. So I guess if you come across some sirens singing 'Friday I'm in Love,' that's my fault."

Marius actually laughed at that—and his laugh made her smile, too. It was quiet and deep and private. She got the feeling he didn't have much to laugh about, wherever he came from.

They fell into silence for a few more moments before he straightened up, turned to her, and offered a hand. "Do you want to dance?"

Well. That was unexpected.

She almost declined out of instinct; in fact, she almost looked around to see who else he could possibly be talking to. "What— You want to *dance* with me?"

He shrugged one shoulder, hand still extended. "It *is* a party. Everyone else is dancing."

"If everyone jumped off a bridge, would you do it, too?" she asked, taking his hand.

"If everyone here jumped off a bridge, my job would be a lot easier." He smiled and drew her close, closer than she had expected.

He was warm, and the fur and silk lining of his cloak was soft as it brushed against her arms. She hadn't danced with a boy since ... probably since senior prom in high school, although it wasn't wholly accurate to think of Marius as a *boy*. He was probably, what, twenty-five?

With his left hand, he kept hold of hers; he rested his right wrist, covered with a simple black sleeve, at her waist. "Sorry. I don't have all the usual equipment."

"It's fine." She adjusted a bit, placing her free hand on his shoulder. Once she was settled, he pulled her waist a little closer and began to lead her capably across the balcony. "When I first noticed your hand, you hid it from me. What ... happened to it?"

"I sacrificed it," he said simply, raising a brow at her like she should know.

"Sacrificed it?"

"Did your father tell you nothing about the Aurora?"

Edie shook her head. "I had no idea any of ... this ... even existed until a week and a half ago."

Marius seemed surprised and intrigued but didn't push, answering, "Our people follow the Pantheons, the Aesir and Vanir—"

"*Two* pantheons seems a little excessive."

"The Vanir are more ... primal—gods of the elves—where the Aesir are holy. The Vanir warred with the Aesir—the Asgardians—eons ago, but now they're more or less banded together." He seemed to study her face as they spun and swayed slowly. "The Aurora revere them all, but Tyr above the rest. He's the god of law and justice, bravery, and glory in war."

"Right." She raised a brow. "What does this have to do with your hand?"

Marius snorted. "I'm getting to it. You've surely heard of Fenrir?"

"The name sounds familiar."

"The wolf-son of Loki. Tyr loved him, became attached to him, so he convinced Odin to let Fenrir stay in Asgard with him. But only Tyr was brave enough to feed the wolf. Then the gods' favored seer foretold that Fenrir would eventually become vicious. He was growing rapidly, so they decided to fetter him. The gods tricked Fenrir into the bonds by assuring him that a wolf of his size and strength could surely break through them— and if he couldn't, they would set him free."

"Trying to trick the son of a trickster god?"

Marius smiled. "Exactly. Fenrir insisted that one of the gods show their good faith by putting their right hand in his jaws. Again, Tyr was the only one brave enough."

"Ah," Edie said. "Then I'm guessing he lost his hand."

"And his honor, in breaking an oath. But he did it for the greater good, and Fenrir remains where he was bound to this day," he finished, glancing down at his right wrist. "It's a rite of passage when someone graduates from an adherent to a vivid. It's a show of devotion, and it helps in channeling our powers."

"Right. The radioactive man," Edie mumbled, smiling and letting herself relax a little. "What if you decided you wanted to do something else with your life?"

He said nothing, just continued to lead her.

"I guess you couldn't get your hand back."

Still, silence.

After a while, Edie brushed her bangs from her face and came closer, so her chin was almost resting on his shoulder. It seemed easier, that way, to keep her voice quiet when she asked, "You all right?"

Marius didn't change pace or pull away, simply leading her along to the slow music. Finally, he said, "I should kill you," and even though his words were concerning at best, his tone told her that his heart wasn't in it.

She didn't move away. "I'd prefer it if you didn't, to be honest."

Her comment didn't garner the laughter she'd been hoping for. He remained quiet and troubled, his thick brows furrowed in deep frustration. "I should bring you to the temple, bring you to justice."

" 'Justice?' I haven't done anything wrong."

"You're not supposed to exist. You're a hellerune. Your kind has proven that you're dark. Light is supposed to wash out the dark." Marius's head moved a fraction, so their cheeks were practically touching. He was so warm. He was talking in her ear now, and it made her shiver.

"I didn't ask to be this way."

"Neither did Zaedicus. He was a light elf, once. The darkness twisted him."

Edie moved her head back to look at him, brows and mouth drawn, but didn't pull away. "You have to know that's not true. 'Light' and 'dark' … they don't *mean* anything. You have to see the difference between me and him…."

Marius's face, his eyes, said that he already did, but he mumbled, "I don't know."

She almost couldn't bear the sadness in his face. What the hell was going on in that head of his, that he had to do these backflips to justify what he'd been taught his whole life? The hand on his shoulder crept to the collar of his doublet, which peeked past the cloak's wolf pelt. "Not everything is so black and white," she whispered.

"Some things are."

Edie was about to protest. There were so many things about this world she didn't know, and maybe he was right; maybe there *were* some things that were cut and dry. But not this. Not her, not Cal, or a thousand other innocent creatures of "darkness." She wanted to convince him—thought maybe she had a chance, now, alone with him in the silence.

Then the silence was broken.

CHAPTER THIRTY-THREE

THE EXPLOSIVE SOUND of shattering glass in the ballroom ruptured the quiet on the balcony and filled the air with shrieks and panic. Edie and Marius jumped away from each other in surprise.

"What the hell?" Edie breathed, looking toward the doorway. They both listened as glass continued to shatter and screams spread. The shaft of light pouring onto the balcony was interrupted as the forms of fleeing guests rushed past the doors.

Marius rushed through the doors first, with Edie following close behind. They both kept close to it, pressed up against the crystal grille as panicking partygoers stampeded past them.

"What's happening?" Edie asked over the commotion, furrowing her brow as she looked to Marius.

"I don't know. But look." He nodded to the golden doors ten yards from them on the second tier, the ones from which Zaedicus had entered earlier. People were crowding around the doors, unable to go through, trampling and climbing over each other. "Someone locked us all in."

Edie was finally able to find a break in the fleeing crowd and tore through, leaning against the railing of the mezzanine. Looking out onto the ballroom floor, she tried to find the source of the exploding glass. It took only a second.

The massive arched windows on the north wall had been shattered completely, and though shards still stuck in the pane here and there, most of the glass was spread across the ballroom, either on the floor or embedded in furniture and people. Smoke—a horrible, hazy, unearthly smoke—seeped in through the windows, seemingly from outside.

Edie's mind began to race. Where were Satara and Cal? More importantly, where was Mercy?

She left Marius without a word, her momentum the only thing keeping her steady on her high heels as she ran. She pushed past the valkyrie in the swan dress, who was nursing amethyst-hued cuts on her arm, and rushed down one of the golden staircases. Her eyes darted wildly around the room. Above her, she could hear the chandelier tinkling, swaying gently; all around her, people whimpered and cried out for their friends and wondered aloud what was happening.

"Edie!"

She whipped her head around when she heard her name. Relief washed over her when she saw Mercy standing there, held tightly in Fisk's arms. Edie rushed to her friend and looked around, spotting both Satara and Cal coming toward them from opposite directions.

"What happened?" Edie asked, looking from Mercy to Fisk.

Mercy shook her head. "Those huge windows just ... *exploded* inward all of a sudden."

"Are you all right?"

She half-smiled and held up her arm, which had several nicks on it but seemed to be the only part of her that was injured. "I'm fine..."

"That smoke's bad news," Cal rasped as he came up behind Edie. "You smell that? It's like acid."

The chandeliers began to flicker, and the large one above their heads died completely, throwing the ballroom into partial darkness. Shouts rose in a wave. While everyone looked up, trying to make sense of what was going on, Edie trained her eyes on the smoke as it billowed higher and crept closer. In the darkness, she could see little lights peering out at her within the mist, almost like...

A howl pierced the panicked murmur of the crowd around them: a long, high-pitched cry that was somehow so familiar it sent a chill up Edie's spine. A shadow crouched there in the thinning smoke, larger than she'd imagined a wolf could be, tracking her with eyes like tiny suns.

Then it emerged. Hot sparks hit the floor, and the acrid smoke recoiled as the creature lunged forward—a wolf with a coat that looked more like fire than fur, golden yellow tongues fading to a deep orange. The flame curled off its withers, shoulders, elbows, and tail. Strange, round markings on its fur burned brighter than the rest of it, and its gaze seethed like fanned coals.

Another figure stalked nearby, still covered by smoke and flanking the crowd. After a few moments, it, too, emerged with hackles prickling.

A second wolf. Similar to the other, its coat was vaporous, as if made of fog. Its silvery white fur shifted to an umbral blue at the ends, and its eyes were cold and steely like liquid mercury. Its own markings were more angular than the other's, blazing azure. As it joined its companion, its mouth spread in what looked like a wicked grin, and a low, vibrating whine issued. Edie watched as its steely eyes constricted and changed color to a vibrant blue topaz, the iris distressed like a cracked mirror. The first wolf was majestic; this one looked demented.

Edie gasped and stepped back, letting Cal slide in front of her. She reached back and seized Mercy's wrist, then pulled her close.

"What's going on?" her friend asked, voice shaking. "What are they?"

"I don't know—"

Edie squeezed her eyes shut as another explosion sounded, destroying what was left of the beautiful Gothic windows and sending a tremor through the entire mansion. When she opened her eyes again, the chandeliers thrashed menacingly above their heads, and several of those still glowing flickered out.

Another brief wave of screams rushed through the ballroom, and it only seemed to spur the wolves on; they circled, tails low, biding their time. Edie tried to quell her fear.

And then a third figure emerged from the smoke on the dais, just beyond the wolves. A man.

He was tall and broad, carrying a claymore almost effortlessly in one hand. The mist still partially obscured him, but Edie could see his armor: A tough, black leather cuirass, sleeveless and trimmed with raven feathers; a dark steel breastplate and wicked, clawed gauntlets. A cloak with a wolf-pelt mantle was draped across his shoulders, but he discarded it on the dais as he stepped forward.

"Our guest of honor," boomed a voice from the second-tier landing. Every head turned to see Zaedicus, completely unharmed, not looking even a bit perturbed at the mess in his ballroom. He grinned widely and spread his arms. "Welcome, my lord."

The strange man raised his head, and the smoke dissipated enough for Edie to make out the rest of his features. His skin was brown, but pale and ashen in a way that told her he didn't see the sun often. Stark white hair fell to his jaw, tucked behind his ears. His eyes were gray and cold, and his face, with a long nose, thick brows, and a handsome mouth, was twisted in a lupine scowl. Despite how deadly he looked, he couldn't have been more than a few years older than Edie.

His skin—from his chin down to his neck and exposed biceps, arms, fingers—was marked with runic coils. There was something so ancient and primordial about the tattoos that the mere sight of them made Edie shudder. She wanted to look away, but she couldn't.

The two ghostly wolves flanked the man, waiting for his command.

"Esteemed guests," Zaedicus announced. "I present the Wounded, Lord Sárr."

There was no time for panicked whispers, no time for the crowd to acclimate to the strange introduction. Sárr stomped down the steps of the dais with purpose and raised his claymore.

His markings flashed blood red, and a thousand ruddy wisps flew up his arms like a colony of ants. The red reached his chin and blazed in his irises, turning the cold gray to a flaming scarlet. Lit up as they were, Edie could see that the markings were less like tattoos and more like ... scars. Like carvings in his flesh.

He brought the claymore down heavily, cutting down two nearby partygoers without so much as a glance. They fell to the floor in a pool of dark blood, and he continued on, his sabatons tracking it across the floor like ink. The ballroom fell silent, save for the tremors still vibrating the mansion. Shock paralyzed everyone.

It wasn't until Sárr moved on to another group and cut them down effortlessly, too, that the shock dissipated and panic began to set in again. Screams erupted all over the ballroom. People banged at the gilt doors, crying to be let out; others ran and clung to their friends, some tripping and becoming trampled in the layer of crushed glass at their feet.

"No fucking way," Cal said, whipping off his tuxedo jacket and reaching for his revolver. Satara's hands tightened into fists, shaking, every muscle wound tight. Fisk's spines prickled and stood on end.

Edie held Mercy's hand tight and edged closer to the wall, trying to keep to the shadows.

Things were being thrown and toppled, chandeliers shuddered and burst, lights flickered. Chaos reigned, but the Wounded seemed unfazed. He raised an arm, and his wolves lashed out, bringing down several of the fleeing guests. They tore at their flesh, arcs of blood spraying the floor, the walls, coating the wolves' fur. Still he retained his laser-focus, striding calmly to the center of the room.

Then he spoke. With one snarl, Lord Sárr managed to drown out the madness around him: "Enough!"

People still wept and shuddered, but now, they watched him with wide eyes. Even Edie's party stood still, tense but stunned into silence.

He swept his gaze, gray again, around the room. "I know she's here," he murmured. Then, louder: "I can feel you here, hellerune."

In front of Edie, Cal shifted, blocking their group a bit more. Mercy gripped her best friend's shoulders tightly and looked at her, terrified.

"Yes." Zaedicus, his voice slow and thoughtful, scanned the crowd from where he stood on the second landing. "She is here, Lord Sárr. In fact..." He turned, smiling pleasantly as he motioned for something behind him.

"No!" a familiar voice whimpered from the mezzanine. Edie gasped as Matilda was wrestled into view, arms forced behind her back. Scarlet stood there behind her, holding her tightly and kneeing her forward. Matilda cried out with a grimace, but Scarlet simply grinned.

Cal gripped his gun hard, shaking in front of Edie. "Move," he rasped, shoving her back further in the crowd.

Zaedicus shushed Matilda almost gently and turned, taking her chin in one hand. "Behold," he announced to the room, "Lady Matilda Ardelean. A loyal member of the Gloaming, so she'd have you think. And yet she has been conspiring with the hellerune, keeping her from us, helping her to elude us even as she stands in this very room."

"For the Gloaming!" Scarlet cried excitedly, tightening her hold on Matilda and making her cry out again.

The wolves whined and arched their backs, and Sárr heaved a great sigh. "Kill her."

Cal pulled back the hammer of his revolver, and its click reverberated through the room. "Lay a fucking finger on her"—he aimed for Zaedicus—"and I'll blow your eyes outta your goddamn skull."

Sárr barely glanced at Cal. He raised his hand, and the silver wolf let out a shivering bellow that sounded almost like a cackle. It lunged forward quicker than Cal could get a shot off, tackling him to the ground and sending the revolver skittering across the tiles. Snagging the back of his dress shirt, the wolf clenched down and shook him hard, fighting to drag him to Sárr's feet.

"Cal!" Matilda cried, only to be silenced by another tug from Scarlet.

"Thank you, brother," the Wounded said softly, reaching down to scratch the wolf's withers. Then he turned his attention to Cal, planting one bloody sabaton in the center of his chest and crouching so their faces were only inches away from each other. Sárr inhaled, his markings and eyes flared murky blue, and he nodded. "I can smell her on you. You must be the thrall."

"Fuck you," Cal managed.

Sárr looked up at Zaedicus and muttered, "Find her or no one leaves here alive. *No one.*"

The high-wight gripped the parapet of the second landing, setting his jaw. "Do you see what destruction your cowardice has wrought, Edith?" he announced. "No one else need be harmed. If you step forward and give yourself to us now, all will be forgiven."

Adrenaline hissed through Edie's body, the sudden rush of blood rendering her world wavy and off-kilter. Black spots threatened her vision.

No, no, no, no, no. Cal couldn't get hurt. Mercy couldn't get hurt. Satara, Matilda, Fisk…. She couldn't let it happen.

"Edie," Mercy whimpered, holding Edie's arm as if for dear life. "Don't do it. He'll hurt you!"

"I know," she whispered back, trying to pry herself from her friend's grip.

Every muscle in Satara's body looked as tense as stone. Her terrified brown eyes said that she understood the choice Edie had to make, and already knew what had to happen, but she still shook her head. "We can fight him. We can kill him."

"Not quick enough," Edie answered numbly, gently separating herself from Mercy and stepping forward.

It was too late for the twenty people Zaedicus had murdered for their blood. She'd just stood by when that happened. She wouldn't stand by again.

The room was as still as a lake, everyone watching the Wounded. As Edie pushed past the crowd and stepped to the front, there was a ripple of heads and gazes turning to her. And there she stood, no one by her side, shuddering in her borrowed heels.

Sárr turned his head and ran an awestruck gaze up and down her form, his markings and eyes burning a dull purple. Then he smiled grimly and raised a hand.

CHAPTER THIRTY-FOUR

EDIE FLINCHED, expecting the wolves to attack on their master's command.

This was the part where she died, right? She'd been forced into a corner that no amount of cleverness could get her out of. The inevitable death she'd been dreading on the balcony earlier had come sooner than she thought.

But instead, Sárr only held out his hand, clawed gauntlets glinting in the flickering lights. It took her a moment to realize he was reaching for her, asking her to come stand with him. She shuffled forward unsurely, kicking glass out of her way as she did. The wolves kept their distance, and their master lowered his hand slightly as she approached, fingers flexing, insisting she take it.

She did. His skin was cold, but the brands on his palm were burning hot to the touch.

The Wounded seemed to relax a bit, curling his hand around hers and pulling her closer until she was standing at his side, their shoulders nearly touching.

He released her hand after a moment and grinned. The way he stood over the crowd, his stance open and his chest thrust forward, he looked like he'd just won a battle.

Clearly, there was something she was missing.

Cal was still lying at his feet, unmoving, his white collar damp and red from the wolf's jaws. Edie glanced sidelong at Sárr, wanting to kneel down and help her friend up, but who knew what Sárr would do in retaliation? Kill her right away, chop off Cal's head? She stood still even though she was screaming inside.

She wanted her dad. If Dad was here...

What? What could he possibly do? When would she finally accept that he was gone—that he'd never really been there in the first place? Just a fucking ghost of himself, a complete lie; someone who had done unforgivable things and hidden them from her, then left her in the dark, weak and vulnerable.

Edie glared at the toes of her pumps as Sárr stepped over Cal's still form and spoke.

"Brothers and sisters. I know that none of you know who I am, and you fear me. But I know you. I have been watching from the shadows for many years, witnessing the decline of our faction. It is sickening and pathetic." He raised his chin. "Those of you who are members of the Gloaming ... your lives, your beliefs, have all been challenged by the Aurora in their false crusade. For thousands of years, this has happened—and too often, of late, I have watched your leaders respond with fear and weakness!"

Some of the crowd members, though still frightened, seemed more intrigued now. People looked at one another, whispered, watched the Wounded warily.

"It isn't just here, in the Americas; it is the entire globe. The Aurora would have you relinquish your power, your wealth, your very lives, and have already obliterated thousands and millions like you. Hundreds of sects of the Gloaming around the world. It. Ends. Tonight!" he cried, clenching his fists tight. "Forget the Gloaming you pledged your allegiance to. They have surely forgotten you! Your leaders are dead or dying or trapped. Corrupted, useless. It is time for a *new* Gloaming, one more united and powerful than we have been for a thousand years."

Stronger murmurs flooded the ballroom, and Sárr stomped past Edie again to elevate himself on the dais just behind her. He turned and raised a fist.

"The false crusade will end! We will seize power once more. The world will be ours again, as it was for thousands of years. And it starts here."

To Edie's horror, the crowd that had previously been so terrified rallied in Sárr's favor. People began to applaud and shout affirmations.

"Yes! It starts with us, brothers and sisters. No more cowering in caves and forests, no more tolerating the weak, no more languishing in obscurity while the Aurora closes in on us. *I* will lead us to honor and victory, in the names of the gods!"

The applause became overpowering. Creatures yipped and howled, cheers and roars and shouts echoed. Sárr was suddenly by Edie's side again, and he grabbed her wrist with a grim smile, raising her fist with his.

Zaedicus cried from the mezzanine landing, "Hail Sárr! Hail the Wounded Lord! Hail all the gods in their enigmatic glory! Hail the New Gloaming!"

The realization hit Edie, and she struggled to remain on her feet. She remembered something Astrid had said. The Gloaming didn't want to kill her like the Aurora did; that had never been their plan. For god-knew-what reason, they needed her.

They wanted her to join them. They wanted to use her.

Surely death was preferable.

She yanked her wrist from Sárr's grip and took a step back, trying to put a little distance between them. But the Wounded seemed to barely notice, looking up at Zaedicus with a smirk.

"My brothers and sisters, if you'll have me as your general now, my first act will be to give you back the protection your families enjoyed under Fahraad. New Gloaming, I hereby name Zaedicus Oldine Gloaming Lord of this province."

There were fewer shouts at that; the applause was more polite than passionate. Edie watched as people turned to one another, confused but too intimidated to say anything.

So much for Zaedicus not being a player.

Still, there was enough celebration that Sárr and his high-wight lackey were utterly pulled into their little play-act from the Dark Ages. No one but Edie noticed when, a few feet in front of them, Cal shuddered and shook some glass off himself.

The Wounded stepped forward again, probably poised to start another spiel. But as he stepped over Cal's discarded body, the revenant suddenly jerked upward, swinging one arm. Something in his hand flashed in the dim light, and his blow connected.

When he pulled away, a long, ragged shard of glass protruded from where he'd shoved it into Sárr's lower back.

Before Sárr even had time to cry out, Edie had darted away from the dais. She dove into the nearest crowd, knocking partygoers out of the way. Cal skidded across the floor, grabbing his Colt on the way, and joined her a few seconds later.

"Sorry," she whispered as she struggled through the crowd.

"Raise them," Cal said gruffly, his revolver aimed toward the ceiling.

Edie's head still spun. Was she hearing things or was Cal telling her to *use* her necromancy? "What?"

"Those Gloaming bastards he killed. Raise them, throw 'em at these assholes, and make a break for the windows while they're distracted." Cal grabbed her shoulder and spun her around, pushing her further into the crowd. As she stumbled forward, he threw his head back and shouted, "Eat glass, fucker!" aiming for the chandelier above Sárr's head.

He fired two shots and crystal shattered. Bedlam broke out around them. People scattered, fleeing the sound of gunfire and the raining glass; the two wolves' howls reverberated through the mansion, shaking it.

The chandelier swung dangerously. Cal fired two more shots.

With a horrible groan, the chandelier slumped. Then it slipped from its abused fixtures and plummeted toward the ballroom floor.

Edie hesitated, at a loss for a moment, before breaking into a run. The floor shook with the chandelier's impact, and the chaos escalated. Guests flew past her, toward the ruined windows. She had to find Mercy and anyone else who needed protection and get them the fuck out of there.

And considering she didn't even know *how* to use her powers the way Cal had told her to, she'd have to do it without undead backup.

She floundered through the discord for a while, trying to find her way around or spot her friends. It was like drowning all over again. Finally, someone grabbed her upper arm, and when she spun to see who it was, relief washed over her. "Mercy."

"Edie! Oh my god, you're okay!" Mercy pulled her close, burying her face in the crook of her neck for a moment before quickly pulling away again. "What is going on? Who *is* that guy?"

"I don't know. No one seems to know," she said, looking around. "Where are Fisk and Satara?"

"I— I don't know. I lost them when the chandelier fell. It was so loud, Edie."

Edie looked over Mercy's shoulder to the center of the ballroom, which was partially obscured by the partygoers rushing to get past the chandelier. Its body stuck up haphazardly, collapsed in on itself, the gold chains and crystals tangled. There was no sign of Sárr, but his wolves were going absolutely mad, tearing up the floors as they skittered across, ripping out throats. About ten yards from where Edie stood, the fiery one brought a shrieking elf to her knees with its claws in her back, stripping the skin.

"We have to get out of here." She took Mercy's hand again. "Come on, before one of those things sniffs me out and comes after us."

"Where are we going?" Mercy asked unsurely.

Around them, the chaos had turned to fighting; some of the Gloaming tried to force their weaker companions to stay and some saw the panic as an opportunity to revel in bloodshed. Edie thought it was probably likely that a lot of them were frantically looking for her, too, now that they knew she was worth something to their new masters.

She and Mercy staggered forward, trying to find their way in the dark, battered by people struggling and pushing past them. Those who could were rushing to the Gothic windows on the north wall, and some had managed to climb out of them and drop down.

Edie pointed wordlessly.

Mercy followed her finger and balked immediately, letting go of Edie's hand. "What? I am not jumping out a two-story window!"

"You'd rather get eaten by a wolf?"

Mercy opened her mouth to respond, but something came flying towards them—an end table, still covered in a tablecloth—and they both ducked instinctively. They turned and watched as the table splintered against the marble-tiled floor just behind them.

Mercy looked back, her brown eyes wide. "Uh, okay ... I'll try."

Keeping their heads down, they worked their way through the pandemonium, toward the windows.

Nearby, Edie spotted Satara with a spear-ended tapestry rod in one hand and a serving dish in the other, blocking blows from a huge, heavy-set man. The shieldmaiden didn't even blink when the man roared and turned into a massive white bear; she simply leveraged the time he spent transforming to bolster her defenses with a magical battle-cry. A couple yards to her left, Matilda and Cal were standing back-to-back, a pearl-handled handgun in the vampire's grip and the revenant's Colt Trooper in his. They were tossing ammo back and forth, picking off wisps that a skeletal sorcerer was conjuring.

Mercy gasped and pointed up ahead. "Look!"

Someone had beaten Edie to the punch when it came to raising the bodies of the people Sárr had killed. A vættr woman with long ears and mauve scales sprinkling her olive skin stood on one of the banquet tables, gathering noxious blue energy between her fingers. The pale, limp bodies of the fallen were drawn to the energy, to her target: Fisk, who was struggling under their dead weight as he tried to claw his way to the necromancer.

Edie noticed that he had also managed to completely undress himself, and sighed.

"Come on, let's go." She and Mercy kept low, creeping behind the banquet table.

"You should never have crawled out of your disgusting hole, baseborn!" the witch cried over the chaos. Around her palm, small molecules of water separated from the air and merged to form an icy ball pulsing with energy. She flung it at Fisk, and it connected, shattering against his chest and embedding in his scales like glass.

Edie and Mercy had inched closer until they were almost behind the witch, and Mercy gasped when she saw Fisk stagger back, sagging under the weight of the bodies piling on him and tearing at his flesh. Though he was shaking them off as best he could, his strength wasn't enough. There were too many.

"We have to— Mercy?" Edie looked to where her friend had been crouching half a second ago, but she wasn't there. It took her a moment to realize Mercy had jumped up onto the table, behind the vættr woman.

The witch barely had time to turn around before Mercy drew her hidden knife. With one click, the Hello Kitty stiletto flicked out, and Mercy lunged without warning, sticking the witch right in the stomach.

Purple-red bloomed on the woman's midsection and stained her toga dress. With her concentration broken, Fisk had enough time to shake off her minions and tackle her to the ground, crushing her windpipe with one massive forearm.

"Oh, for the love of god!" Edie shouted up at Mercy. She looked between her and Fisk. "I'm supposed to be the one protecting *you*!"

"Sorry." To her credit, Mercy really did look embarrassed. Not to mention shaken up, considering she'd just stabbed someone. She sat on the edge of the banquet table, shuddering, and eased off with Edie's help. Looking to Fisk, she said, "Are you all right?"

"I will be fine, my pearl," the vættr snarled. "Go!"

They didn't waste any time, taking off toward the windows again. As they reached the north wall, avoiding anyone who might push them out in their haste, Edie slowed down a little and looked at Mercy skeptically. "*My pearl?*"

"Yeah ... I think he's into me."

An intense gust of freezing night air blew through the window and drew Edie's attention back to what was happening below. Weapons clashed, magic flew back and forth, blood watered the lawn. Somewhere in the distance, she could hear an ambulance siren. Apparently, those who had managed to fight their way outside were being met with resistance—but from whom?

"Uh," she said, "maybe the lawn isn't the best place for us after all."

"Edie!" Mercy shrieked, grabbing her arm. When Edie turned, she saw the two ghostly wolves. They were ignoring the chaos in the ballroom, now, their heads bowed and teeth bared. And they were making a beeline for the ruined windows. She and Mercy were sitting ducks.

"Freaking hell." Edie looked at Mercy and took her hand, squeezing it. "Ready?"

"Not really." Mercy shook her head. "But I am so not getting blood on this dress." She kicked off her heels, and Edie followed suit.

They both took a big breath, glanced at each other, and jumped.

CHAPTER THIRTY-FIVE

THE FIRST THING you learned in cheerleading was how to fall. It was a combination of knowing where to land and how to release the energy of the fall after impact.

Unfortunately, after their inelegant performance during tryouts, neither Edie nor Mercy had made the squad.

The fall from the window to the garden below was over a lot faster than Edie anticipated. She landed clumsily on her feet for a split second, then bent her knees and tried to tuck into a roll. The result was more of a tumble than anything, and pain shot up her ankles and arms as she thumped into a bush.

She lay there for a moment, looking up at the spinning sky, wondering if Mercy had made it all right.

A groan next to her answered her question.

"What's wrong?" she managed, grimacing as she pulled herself up on one elbow. She was wet for some reason, all over her arms and legs, but she assumed it was dew from the garden and grass.

Mercy was lying nearby with her right arm cradled to her chest. Even though tears welled in her eyes, her face was blank. "I hurt my ... my fucking arm or something. I can't ... move it." She tried to sit up but yelped and fell on her back almost immediately. "Something's wrong!"

Edie's heart leapt, and she crawled on her hands and knees over to her friend, laying a hand on her uninjured side. "It's going to be okay."

The sirens were louder out here. At the end of the drive, flashing red lights refracted off the tree line and the wet grass.

"You're hurt," Mercy said, wiping her good hand down Edie's arm. It came away pinkish, streaked with blood.

Guess it wasn't dew after all.

"We'll be okay. Someone called the paramedics," she breathed, though her focus wasn't on Mercy anymore. The battle on the lawn was a lot hotter, louder, and more frightening up close. Now that she was down here, she could see warriors and mages dressed all in black and silver, adorned with raven feathers, picking off those who tried to flee the scene.

Thump. With a horrible braying, a large stag reeled and fell to its side before them, going still. After a moment, the great beast shimmered and morphed back into a man, his party clothes drenched in blood from his throat and stomach.

Mercy screamed and squeezed her eyes shut, looking away. These assholes were killing people just for running away. Sárr must have sent them ... but why? And how had he amassed followers without anyone knowing who he was?

Something heavy landed easily behind them. Steel clanked against steel. "The culling of the weak," came the Wounded's voice. "Isn't it marvelous?"

Before Edie could turn, he had reached around her and grabbed Mercy's hair, pulling her up. Blood from his gauntlets mingled with her bubblegum-pink locks as she cried out in pain, struggling to come to her feet. But he didn't give her the chance, throwing her aside like a ragdoll.

"No!" Edie lunged after her, but only got so far, stretching a hand out in her direction.

Sárr looked between them, smiling before walking calmly toward Mercy. The battle bent around them, avoiding him. "Who is she to you, Edith?" When Edie said nothing, he turned and barked, "Answer me!"

Her voice trembled with rage and terror. "She's my friend. Don't lay a fucking finger on her!"

He snorted and dropped his claymore, raising his hands as if in surrender. "Not a finger," he promised in a purr.

Then he turned and stomped hard on Mercy's right leg.

The crunching of bone could be heard even over the battle raging around them. Mercy's shriek pierced the air, her face twisted in pain.

"*Stop it!*" Edie inched closer, ignoring her own aching body. "Stop hurting her!"

"You had a chance to surrender, woman, and you elected to defy me." He stomped on Mercy's left leg, and ground his foot into her. "This could have been so much easier for you."

This time, Mercy didn't scream; her head just slumped to the side.

"Mercy!" Edie screamed, trying to get her attention, to wake her up.

Her desperate cries only seemed to spur Sárr on, but Edie couldn't help crying out as she watched splintered bone penetrate her friend's skin. She covered her mouth, trying to quell the sobs, her vision pounding with her head. She struggled closer, fingernails digging into the soil. If she had to throw herself on Mercy to make him stop, she would.

Before she could reach them, he stopped and rolled Mercy over with the toe of his sabaton. She was completely limp.

The Wounded rounded on Edie, markings blazing red. "Look at you, at how pathetic your ignorance has made you. There's so little you can do."

Edie slowly brought herself to her feet, trying to tune out how her bones begged her to stop moving, and spared a glance over her shoulder. The paramedics had also called for police backup, and those that had arrived were clueless, completely vulnerable to what was going on around them.

Two streaks of silver and gold tore past her and dove into the small team of humans, making short work of them. Blood coated the pavement. The wolves shook the bodies by their necks like squeaky toys. The golden one tossed a young woman to the side, and she slumped face-first into the sparkling fountain at the center of the drive. The sight drew another cry from Edie.

"Look at how weak they are," Sárr said, coming closer. "Why would you ever want to be like them? Why would you not seize your birthright?"

She looked at him, cursing him for blocking her path to Mercy. The urge to tear him to pieces mounted. "And what the fuck are you doing?! Is this you seizing your birthright?"

"Yes," he growled.

"I don't care if I'm weak. I am never going with you." Her anger was overwhelming. It bubbled over until her head was swimming with a thousand nasty things she wanted to shout at him, all mostly incomprehensible, furious gibberish. A strange, numbing coolness enveloped her arms, and she could somehow feel that she was on the verge of tapping into something. But no matter how she pushed, she couldn't reach that crescendo, couldn't push the power past her physical form.

Sárr watched her, snorted, and picked up his claymore. "Enough. This has been amusing, but it's time we left."

A battle cry rose over the commotion around them, loud and full of power. Edie watched as Satara and Cal charged toward where she and Sárr stood on the lawn, mowing down the black-clad mages and warriors in their path. The revenant was still jacketless, and the shieldmaiden had tied her dress up around her thighs. The Wounded turned and snarled at the sight of them. As they came closer, Cal sprinted ahead of Satara and knelt, pausing for a moment to line up a shot from his sawed-off.

Sárr darted just in time, but the bullet still grazed his ear. He barely had time to recover before Satara's makeshift shield collided with his knees and he was knocked off-balance. He gave an otherworldly roar, markings flaring brighter.

"For the Reach!" Satara cried, taking her tapestry rod in both hands and swinging with all her might as she flanked the enemy.

It connected hard, hitting the Wounded in his lower back, where Cal had stabbed him earlier. But the pain only seemed to empower him, and he turned and swung his sword in a wide arc, grazing Satara's upper arm.

Blood splattered, droplets flying from the sword's edge, and hit Edie. Satara only shouted, bolstering her defenses with a brief flash of blue light, and went back for more, but Edie's heart raced.

The blood that had spattered on her ... sizzled. Her skin came alive, and suddenly, the pain in her legs seemed a bit more tolerable.

Sárr's sword clashed against Satara's weapon as she charged at him, but she held fast, gritting her teeth.

There was more gunfire as Cal crossed the lawn, but Edie wasn't sure if any of the bullets actually hit their target. She felt a few embed themselves in the dirt near her. "Cal!" she shouted, trying to see around Sárr and Satara's duel.

"Get the fuck back here, kid!" the revenant barked as he stepped carefully over Mercy's body. He was playing it fast and loose with his gun etiquette, as usual—sawed-off in one hand, aimed ahead, and the revolver aimed to the side, ready to pick off anyone who might charge his flank.

Edie glanced hurriedly at Satara, waiting until Sárr's back was turned to her to sprint across the lawn to Cal. He covered her once she reached him, edging in front of her and firing the second shot from his shotgun, then flicking it open to reload.

She covered her ears and knelt in the grass next to Mercy. "Cal," she said, her voice shaking, "how can I help?"

"You can stay out of the way!"

"That's not good enough!" she shrieked.

He didn't answer, running ahead a few paces and leaving her with Mercy. Edie crawled until she was sitting in front of her friend, gently rolling her on her back and cupping her face. Mercy's skin was quickly losing its color, and Edie shook as she carefully maneuvered her head into her lap.

There was so much blood. Frantically, she pressed down on Mercy's thighs, trying to stop the flow.

"Hail the New Gloaming!" roared a gruff voice. Edie looked up to see two of the black-clad warriors charging at her, one with a matted blond beard and the other wearing a dark steel helmet.

She yelped and held Mercy closer, but there was nothing she could do.

A flash of brilliant light blinded her momentarily. For a few seconds, all she could see were the white outlines of figures in front of her as they clashed. But as her sight slowly returned, she could see that the light was coming *from* one of them—and she realized who it must be.

Marius lashed out with a whip of pure light energy, and the helmeted warrior's armor hissed as the plasma made contact with the steel, turning it a deep orange. The warrior cried out and lunged with his axe, but the vivid anticipated it. A disk of sparkling light bloomed over his right forearm and deflected the blow, sending the warrior staggering back. The distraction gave Marius enough time to summon a lucent blade in his left hand and sink it into the man's throat.

Someone else joined Marius as he rounded on the other, bearded warrior: A large woman with a crown of flaxen hair, wearing a wide-legged jumpsuit. She dual-wielded short swords and, crossing them over each other, slashed at the back of the warrior's knees.

"Auroran scum!" The warrior turned and head-butted the woman, who was momentarily dazed.

Marius moved in to bash him with his shield of light. On impact, it burnt the dark furs the warrior wore, branding his skin and making it bubble. He yowled in response and turned back on Marius, slashing wildly with his own sword.

The vivid grunted as the edge of the blade scraped his chest, taking a step back before feinting to the left. When the warrior followed, Marius dove right and toppled him with a firm kick to the ribs. The blade in Marius's hand broke apart and reformed into a ball of light, and he fired it at the warrior's head, finishing him off—or at least knocking him unconscious.

Finally, Marius turned to Edie, his breath fast. He'd discarded his cloak and doublet, revealing a flowing white shirt. With the high-waisted breeches, he looked like he'd just stepped off of a pulp romance cover from the 70s.

His still-glowing eyes traveled to Mercy, widened, then met Edie's gaze. "*Váði vitnis*, what happened?"

She shielded her eyes from the light of the bright weapons he wielded. "Sárr. He ... hurt her. Satara and Cal are trying to hold him off."

As if on cue, the shieldmaiden cried out in pain nearby, drawing Edie's panicked attention. Cal was dealing with some mages trying to flank them but was slowed down by having to reload his weapons, and Satara was bleeding from a wound on her scalp and one on her thigh. They were up against the wall, but Edie knew they would fight until they stopped breathing.

She couldn't let that happen. If she couldn't do anything useful, she could at least convince someone else to. She looked at Marius wildly. "Please ... you have to help them. *Please.*"

The blonde who had helped Marius take down the two warriors looked affronted. She hazarded a furtive glare at Edie. "Vivid Marius, remember what we're here to do."

"I remember!" he barked back, his brow knit tightly.

He only hesitated for a moment. Then he held his right arm out, concentrating on summoning something new. A bladed bow materialized at the end of his wrist, steady as if he were gripping it. It shone bright like his other weapons had—and when he reached for his shoulder, as though to grab an arrow, one appeared between his fingers. It sparked and popped like a solar flare as he nocked it.

"If you want," he said to the woman, "you can run back to Eirik with your tail between your legs, Ynga. But I will not let innocent people die."

The woman's face hardened, and she gripped her swords tighter. "*Innocent people?* I'm following orders, Marius!"

"Do it, then!" he snapped. He glanced at Edie, then looked ahead and squinted, aiming for the Wounded.

He took a deep breath, then loosed the streak of plasma.

It hit home. The arrow penetrated the tough leather armor of Sárr's shoulder. Sparks flew.

The Wounded turned with burning eyes to face Marius.

CHAPTER THIRTY-SIX

MARIUS COULD SEE that the shieldmaiden was slowly losing her duel, her defensive magic weaker by the second, but the Wounded Lord was bloodied. When he faced Marius, claymore held tightly in both hands, his white hair was matted with red and clinging to his scratched face. But, if anything, the battle seemed to fuel him. When he saw that he had another challenger, he grinned wickedly.

"Aurora," he snarled, his hot breath visible in front of his face. He studied Marius for another moment before laughing. "And not just any Auroran whelp, but the Radiant's son!"

Marius's heart sped as his opponent came forward. How was it that this demon whom no one, Reach or Aurora, seemed to recognize knew who Marius was? He lowered his glowing bow. "That was quite the speech you gave earlier. If you truly have your faction's best interests in mind, why kill them?"

Sárr swung his sword down with one hand and pointed it at Marius. The vivid couldn't imagine what kind of strength this mysterious man possessed if he was able to throw around a sword that big so easily. "Reform comes at a price. Their cowardice and vice are what made the Gloaming weak to begin with."

"Killing the innocent, then? That's what makes your faction strong?"

Sárr cocked a dark brow. "Is it not what makes yours strong?"

Marius gritted his teeth, poised to nock another arrow if he had to. "Your fight is with the Aurora, so come. Let's fight."

Nearby, Edie's revenant had gone to the shieldmaiden's aid. Marius cast a glance over the Wounded's shoulder and watched as they both eased down onto the grass and began to dress her wounds with torn bits of clothing from fallen warriors. But the zombie didn't look so well either; he was singed from magefire and bleeding in several places himself.

And beyond the burnt and bloodied grass, past the broken bodies, the two wolves had finished feasting. With red-slathered maws, they prowled forward, approaching their master.

Sárr took advantage of Marius's wandering gaze, and struck. He charged forward, swinging his sword down, and Marius just barely had enough time to deflect it with the bladed edge of his glowing bow.

They struggled, straining against each other. "Worried?" Sárr taunted. "Not sure your friends can handle my brothers?"

The bow sparked under pressure, and Marius gave a final push, throwing Sárr off-balance enough to buy him time to duck out of the way of his sword. The vivid's bow dispersed, then coalesced into a shield just in time to block another swing.

The shield flared and sang as the sword clashed against it. Marius tried to hold fast, blocking as he observed how his opponent fought. But Sárr was unpredictable. One moment, he seemed to be in a berserker's rage; the next, he was defensive and precise.

If Marius was to overpower him, he would have to break his focus.

The wolves were closing in on Marius and Sárr, and if there was one thing Edie knew, it was that Sárr was not going to fight fair.

She had to keep those things off Marius while he dealt with their master. But Mercy was growing colder by the second, her pulse becoming weaker. Edie had managed to staunch the blood with someone's discarded wool cloak, but she knew it was the shock that would kill her friend.

She looked up frantically and spotted Satara limping over to her, her legs and forehead wrapped in makeshift bandages.

"Hey!" Edie called, waving an arm.

The shieldmaiden approached, pushing past the woman Marius had called Ynga and dropping hard to her knees next to Edie. "Blessed Mare's tears, he mangled her."

"How are you doing?" Edie asked, her voice cracking. "Where's Cal?"

Satara shook her head. "I can't fight any longer. That man is like a monsoon. Cal's ... I don't know. He helped me wrap my wounds and took off."

Edie pursed her lips and looked toward Marius. He was holding his own in the fight, but the wolves were quickly losing interest in the bodies strewn across the lawn and beginning to circle him, waiting for their opening.

She looked down at Mercy—poor, broken Mercy. She almost couldn't bear the thought of leaving her side when she was in this state ... but if those wolves jumped on Marius? He wouldn't have a chance. They'd *all* die.

"Keep pressure on this," Edie said, voice wavering, and moved over so Satara could kneel by Mercy.

"Where are you going?"

"I have to do something about those wolves. Look."

Satara followed her gaze, but shook her head. "Edie, you don't know how to fight. And if those wolves are who I think they are, they'll kill you in a second."

"I don't need to kill them, I just need to keep them off Marius."

She looked around for something she could use, and her eyes fell on a nearby mage's staff. It was made of oak that twisted to encase a large ball of amber at the end. She lifted it, testing the weight before gripping it like a baseball bat and trying a swing. She could probably hit something pretty hard with it if—

A fireball shot out of the end and singed the grass in front of her with a booming sound, and she squealed, almost dropping the staff. "Did I do that?!"

Ynga, apparently engaged in her own personal battle, stood nearby. She glared at Edie and snapped, "That's a runic staff. It's already imbued with magic; you just have to wield it. You don't have to be a witch to know that."

Runic staff, huh? It wasn't shadow or plague magic, but it was something. She steeled herself and passed Ynga, muttering, "Well, *someone* has to do something."

She stole a pair of boots from a nearby fallen mage and pulled them on roughly, then focused on the wolves as she trudged forward. The boots were adorned with steel points on the ends, perfect for making as much sound as possible as she stepped over fallen warriors, kicking their helmets and shields aside.

As Edie approached, the wolves' attention turned to her. The golden one lifted its head, eyes burning brighter and ears perking up. Its silver companion lifted its head as well, sniffed the air, and emitted one of its shivering cackles. She saw those cold eyes constrict, and a shudder went through her.

Don't freeze up. Just get them chasing you. Find Cal.

She took a deep breath and glanced to make sure Marius was still all right. He had summoned a lance in his left hand but was mostly blocking, probably trying to pick out Sárr's weak spots. From the look on Marius's face, it didn't seem like he had many. Edie had to act quickly.

"Hey!" she shouted, surprised at the volume of her voice. She held the staff up over her head, and it ignited with a *whoosh*.

The wolves lowered their heads, hackles raising. Dread choked her. Shit. This was a mistake. What could she even say to taunt them off Marius and to her?

Suddenly, it came to her.

"All right, you primitive screw-heads," she barked, mustering her best Bruce Campbell impression, "listen up! You see this? This ... is my boomstick!"

With a fluid motion that surprised even her, she twirled the staff down under her arm and aimed it at the silver wolf's feet. It erupted, causing her to stumble back a bit, but hit its target with delicious accuracy—just close enough to singe them and successfully secure their attention.

And then she turned tail and booked it.

She swerved onto the driveway, streaking past the fountain and the ambulance. In the grass, she might trip on a body or something, and she really didn't need that at the moment. At least on the pavement she could see what she had to avoid.

The wolves were in hot pursuit. All she could think was that they ran a lot faster than she had anticipated.

She bought herself a little time by hopping over a bench, but the landing hurt her legs, and she almost collapsed right there. Not to mention it was pretty fucking inconvenient to have to keep hiking up the hem of her dress.

Edie ducked behind a low hedge and frantically tied her skirt up, knotting it around her knees as she tried to catch her breath. She could hear the wolves' heavy breathing nearby, but their footsteps slowed; she must have lost them, if only momentarily. But they were wild animals, probably used to tracking their prey in the dark, and she was just a stupid, loud, hairless ape.

The element of surprise wouldn't be hers for long; she had to act on it now.

She waited, listening closely as the wolves approached her hiding place —and at the last possible moment, just when they were about to round the corner and find her quivering there, she leapt from her crouch and swung the staff, flinging a round of three fireballs at them.

The wolves yowled as the fireballs hit home, but Edie didn't have time to admire her handiwork. She took off again and found she was falling into a cycle: run like hell, hide behind something, shoot at wolves, repeat. She let them chase her until she was almost where the road met the beginning of the driveway.

And then she fell.

She tripped, knocking the wind from her lungs, the shock of the fall reverberating up her arms. Once she was lying there, half on the grass and half on the pavement, feeling came rushing back.

Her cuts stung so bad it felt like her skin was on fire, and now that the power from the blood she'd come in contact with on the battlefield was fading, her ankles and knees ached. She gasped, trying to pull herself forward a bit. A bolt of pain shot up her leg.

Stop moving, her mind said, but that wasn't really an option. The wolves had already been on her tail, and the fact that she had fallen only seemed to excite them. They panted heavily as they advanced.

With a groan, Edie pulled herself into a sitting position and swung the staff, trying to buy herself a little more time by blasting them. It deterred them a little, and she could hear them whimper each time a fireball hit home, but it was no use; in a few seconds, they would be on her.

She turned, digging the staff into the ground and trying to lift herself up. If she couldn't run away, she could try to fight. She'd still be mauled, but better to die fighting than just lying there.

She was only about halfway upright when hot jaws closed around her ankle and pulled her to the ground again.

Somewhere behind her, tires squealed, and she could hear the trundling of a huge vehicle heading her way. Someone laid on the horn; it was so loud it left ringing in her ears.

She turned onto her back just in time to see Cal swerve past in a pirated ambulance and ram into the wolves on her tail.

She could feel the rush of wind as the ambulance sped by, close enough that she could have reached out and touched it. The wolves didn't even have time to whimper before they were tangled in the tires.

The ambulance screeched to a halt, tearing up the lawn as it went. Once the vehicle settled, its horn beeped what sounded like the beginning of the "Rock You Like a Hurricane" chorus: *Here-I-Am!*

Edie dug the staff into the ground again and, with a little effort, was able to lift herself to her feet this time. She leaned on it as she limped carefully across the pavement and onto the grass where the ambulance idled. Better not to look and see if the wolves were still alive. They were out of the way for now, and she had to get back to Mercy.

Cal leaned over from the driver's seat and opened the passenger door, then helped her up with one arm. "Good to see you in one piece, Ash."

"You heard that, huh?" She cleared her throat. "No Ghost?"

"Didn't wanna get her all bloody. She's already been through enough." He grinned, revved the engine, and spun the tires. Something yelped in pain beneath them, then they started forward with a *thud* as they rolled over it.

"Jesus," Edie said, wincing and slamming the door.

"We owe them a lot more than that, I'd say." Cal steered with one hand and reloaded his revolver with the other. "You ready to kick some ass?"

"Can't walk very good. One of them bit my ankle ... and I need to get back to Mercy." She eyed the EMT radio mounted beside the dashboard. "We need another ambulance."

"No prob."

Cal set his gun down on the dashboard and unclipped the radio. On the other end, someone was requesting a status update and becoming increasingly bothered by the lack of response. The revenant cleared his throat before speaking into the mic, keeping it close to his mouth.

"Send ... more ... paramedics," he rasped, giving his best impression of Radio Corpse #1 from *Return of the Living Dead*, then hung up and mounted the handset back on the transmitter. There was a pause. "I've always wanted to do that."

Sárr bore down on Marius's shield, teeth bared. The vivid was beginning to tremble under his opponent's immense strength, and the Wounded could see it.

"Where is Tyr's blessed justice now, Vivid?" he taunted, pushing harder against the flickering light shield. "Now that you *see* the wolf's jaws, you aren't sure you'd like to put your hand in them, are you?"

"You are no Fenrir," Marius managed, staggering back and letting Sárr's sword slide from his shield. There was only enough time to hazard a jab with the solar lance before he had to deflect another attack.

Sparks flew, but they didn't seem to faze the Wounded. He simply struck the shield again and again, relishing each time he caused Marius to stumble. "You're only delaying the inevitable. When the time comes, you'll be sorry you didn't lie down and die."

"So be it."

Finally, Marius saw his chance: His opponent moved to raise his heavy weapon again, and the vivid lashed out with the solar lance. Finally, he hit his mark.

Sárr's markings ignited, suddenly ablaze with white light, as the lance cut him deep enough to draw blood. With a yelp, he stepped back, his entire body trembling as though he was having a hard time containing the sudden unfamiliar energy.

It was as good an opening as Marius had had this entire fight. He lashed out again, this time leaving a long, molten-orange streak in the Wounded's breastplate. He struck again, then again, each time smiting his opponent somewhere new, until his movements were no longer precise but more like a blur fueled by pure rage.

He thrust his lance once more, this time aimed at Sárr's head—and it stopped suddenly, abruptly, almost taking Marius off-balance. The sound of burning, hissing flesh reached his ears.

The Wounded was *gripping* the end of the lance, staring at Marius with white-hot hatred. The light inside of his eyes and his markings shone so bright it was hard to look at, and his whole body shook, skin cracked. From every orifice, he gleamed like a star about to go supernova.

With a strength borne of what must have been horrendous pain, Sárr roared and planted a foot in the center of Marius's chest, knocking him on his back in the blood-painted grass. He gave another roar and bore down on him, hard. Agony radiated through Marius's ribs and down his arms, but the pressure just kept increasing without reprieve.

Tires screeched to his left; a horn wailed. There was a *boom*. The air around Marius became uncomfortably hot, but above him, Sárr howled in pain. The pressure on his chest receded.

"Get up, Marius!" he heard Edie shout.

His heart sped at the sound of her voice. This was his chance.

He closed his eyes and searched for the light inside of him, willing it to fill him; he would need it if he was going to stand up and deliver the final blow. A horrible burning sensation filled his chest, and he could feel his broken bones grinding back into place as the sun's power enveloped him.

With a long, loud shout of pain, the vivid raised himself to his feet and grabbed Sárr's shoulders hard, pulling him close.

He looked at the sky and unleashed his aura.

CHAPTER THIRTY-SEVEN

A BLINDING golden light burst from where Marius had stood, a white-hot gleaming bubble that expanded and swallowed everything around him. Edie fell to her knees and covered her face, eyes closed tight. Last time she'd been in range of that kind of explosion, she'd gotten a sunburn—and she really didn't need to add that to her list of injuries at the moment.

A horrible noise filled the air: the low, throaty moan of some great beast. It was so loud, so all-encompassing, that it shook the earth beneath them. Edie raised her head just in time to watch as Marius's aura faded. He was on his knees, and Sárr had collapsed next to him, markings fizzled out.

As the bone-chilling howl also faded, two bright flashes whizzed past Edie and Cal, one orange and one azure. They raced toward the Wounded before engulfing him in a helix of light.

And then they—both Sárr and the wolves—were gone.

Everything was silent. Edie and Cal said nothing to each other as they limped over to where Mercy's body lay.

"I can't feel her pulse anymore," Satara breathed, moving aside, her own hands shaking.

Edie collapsed to her knees and gently pulled Mercy closer, minding her legs. The rags she'd been using to staunch the bleeding had been bled through, but Satara had torn them up, fashioning them and a broken axe handle into a makeshift tourniquet.

"Mercy..." Edie's fingers ghosted over her friend's cold, gray face.

Cal sat on his knees across from her and laid a hand on Mercy's chest, still for a moment. "She's still alive."

"Her heart's barely beating, she's in shock..." Edie shook her head. "The paramedics will never make it in time."

He stared up at her, his gaze hard. "You don't need no paramedics."

Edie shook her head again. She'd raised Hervey from the dead, sure, but Mercy was still in there somewhere. Forcing life back into a corpse was one thing; pushing back against Death itself was another.

Tears welled in her eyes, and her voice trembled and cracked as she spoke. "Cal, I don't know how. I don't know how to do it." She looked down at Mercy, brushed her blood-matted pink hair out of her beautiful face. She couldn't lose her. She couldn't lose a best friend, a sister—the only person she'd had for so long. And Mercy still had so much to do. How could the world keep going without her in it?

Not her. Please, not Mercy.

"Come here." Cal's voice was gentle as he took Edie's hands, laying one on Mercy's chest and the other on her forehead.

"But—" Edie sniffled, looking up at him. "But how do you know—"

He shushed her. "Close your eyes."

She did.

"You remember how you healed me? You had to put the energy in to see the lines, didn't you?"

Edie concentrated hard, remembering. When the witchwolf had burnt up Cal's face, she'd had to feed her own energy into him, almost like she was coaxing the membrane of his aura to open up so she could manipulate what was underneath. "Yeah, but ... that was healing dead flesh. This is—"

"Just trust me. First, stop the bleeding."

Blood magic. If she could draw energy from blood, she could stop it from escaping Mercy's veins, too, couldn't she? With Cal guiding her hands, she tried to envision the flow stopping—envisioned the open veins cauterizing and closing up, the blood coagulating. Her fingers shook, pressure building up in her arms until the force of it was almost painful.

"Good!" She could hear Cal draw in a shaking breath—or was that her? "Now, tell Death to fuck off."

She inhaled deeply and held it, searching for the power. In her mind's eye, she reached inside and could see the stream of magic thrumming through Mercy's body, surging against her skin, looking for a release.

The magic reminded Edie of the dark waves on the coast of Maine, or of the unquiet river in her nightmare, and that thought scared her. The waves became more excited as she acknowledged them, pounding against her skin. Vaguely, she was aware of a strange, dim heat under her palm, fading fast. Mercy's life.

Edie dove into the dark water—through her chest and out her palms, into Mercy. With a gasp, the floodgates released. She opened her eyes and watched as Mercy's aura responded to the touch of her magic.

As if someone had cut the ropes of a theater backdrop, the world fell away. The faraway drone of Cal's voice, Mercy, and the power were all that were left. Cal was saying something, but Edie couldn't make it out ... she just looked from him to the body under her hands. The new, dark world seemed to shake around her as she fought against the grip of Death. Or was that *her* shaking?

A hazy, almost moldy blue was covering Mercy like an exoskeleton. When Edie got under the skin of it, she found she could push it back. Her magic pounded against it and wore it down, forcing it to ebb. Cold seeped from Mercy into Edie and took hold of her heart. She sucked the death and fed it into her own body.

Blackness threatened her vision; her head felt weak. Then she felt Cal's hand enveloping hers, moving it. She could sense another bright spot of heat, of power. The coppery smell of blood invaded her nose as her hand tangled in something soft and wet, and miraculously, the blackness receded. Blood ... the blood all over Mercy's clothes, the grass—

"Keep going."

Who was that whispering? *"Dad?"* she croaked.

"Don't talk. Take it out of her and into you."

There was a scream of anguish and frustration. Was it her? Her throat felt raw, and the sound wouldn't stop. Death crawled inside of her; her skin was wrong, all wrong on her bones, and her nerve endings cried out for an end to the shuddering pain.

Under her fingers, the blueness broke apart and rolled off Mercy's body like smoke.

Edie's heart seized up in Death's grip. Unless she wanted to die here, too, she had to let go. There was nothing more she could do. She could feel that, *knew* it somehow.

Screeching. There was screeching on the horizon.

Edie raised her eyes and saw that the world was there again, though it swam like an impressionist painting. She tried to blink away the exhaustion, squinting. The sky was lightening.

Surely they hadn't been here all night? She collapsed on her back, watching the horizon through slitted eyes. No ... it wasn't the dawn breaking.

As the light came closer, she could discern figures—enormous figures of silver and blue, some mounted on wolves and others on great ravens, their wings outstretched and armor shining. Valkyir overtook the sky, riding it in a spiraling current like it was a giant whirlpool.

It was over. The battle was done, and the choosers of the slain had arrived.

Edie's body, broken and humming with pain, finally surrendered. Darkness swallowed her vision.

CHAPTER THIRTY-EIGHT

It FELT like it was days before sound finally pierced the silent darkness. Something near her breathed quietly like a huge beast, and she could hear a soft, soothing beep at intervals. Voices murmured nearby, though she couldn't make out what they said.

For a long time, there were only sounds. Even if she could have opened her eyes, she didn't want to. She just wanted to sleep.

There was no pain, only a cold feeling in her arms and legs. Edie knew she must be dead. And somehow, that was the biggest relief of all. There was nothing more for her to do. She didn't have to feel guilty for just lying there.

Sometimes she lay still, feeling strangely lucid, but the boundless darkness never became boring or scary. It was comforting, almost homey. Mostly, though, she slept. She dreamed she was walking with her father, having lunch with Mercy, playing guitar in the park—but she found she forgot the details of the dreams almost as soon as they happened.

Then, eventually, the darkness seemed thinner. Sometimes it was still pitch black, but most of the time, now, she could feel light on her face, could see it through her eyelids. It didn't seem like the sun. It was too cold and white. The murmuring that she sometimes heard took shape. She knew those voices from somewhere.

In the end, it was hunger that woke her. Where she had felt nothing before, there were suddenly acute pangs in her stomach and an unbearable dryness in her throat.

Once the hunger pangs broke through the dark, it was only a few hours before she was aware of the rest of her body—of the papery sheets underneath her, the way her bandages felt as they scraped against the waffle-weave hospital blankets. Every time she moved her arm a certain way, a way that felt mightily superficial, the voices on the outside reacted.

God, she was tired. She ignored the hunger and went to sleep again.

But the next time she woke, she opened her eyes.

The light hurt at first. It was like she had just reached the end of a long, long tunnel, and she winced at the brightness. When she tried to lift a hand to shield her eyes, her arm wouldn't move. She gave a whine of annoyance. The darkness had been a lot less annoying, that was for sure.

Squinting, she looked around. She was in an austere hospital room, with seafoam-and-gray linoleum and matching walls. Teal curtains were drawn to her left and right, and directly ahead of her, on the wall, was a whiteboard with her name on it. She couldn't make out what was scribbled underneath.

The huge beast who had slept next to her all that time was still breathing somewhere nearby. Slowly, she turned her head to look at the curtain to her left. The breathing was coming from in there, and with a shudder, she realized what the noise must be: someone else's life support.

"Edie?"

She looked toward the voice. Cal had just entered the room and was eyeing her now. He must have sensed her waking up.

"Hi," she tried, but it came out more like a wheeze with her parched throat.

"One sec." The revenant came to her side and crouched, taking a bottle of water out from under the rolling table next to her bed. He twisted the cap off and handed it to her.

Edie's hands shook, but she held it tightly so she wouldn't spill any.

Cal pulled up a chair. "Good to see you bright eyed and bushy-tailed, Sleeping Beauty."

"I feel like shit." She rubbed her eyes with the back of one hand as she nursed the bottle of water. She thought it tasted strange, then realized it was her mouth that tasted strange, not the water.

"You've been out a few days. No coma or anything, just sleeping. They had to feed you through a tube. And apparently"—he rolled his eyes— "hospitals haven't had a smoking floor since the 80s. *Phff.*"

Edie groaned. But her self-pity was short lived as the memories flooded back, and her heart sped. "Is Mercy okay?"

Cal nodded and stood from his chair, pulling back the curtain to her right. Mercy lay there, looking like death but definitely breathing. Nasty cuts marked her face and arms. Her bottom half was elevated with pillows, and she sported a pretty gnarly-looking cast that covered both legs and her waist. Her arm was in a cast, too, strapped to her chest.

Edie felt tears threatening her eyes again, and she looked at Cal. "The magic worked."

The revenant smiled a little, his gaze surprisingly soft. "Yeah, kid. Good job."

"What— what did I do?" She barely remembered how it had all happened. She'd been delirious, almost half-dead herself.

He sighed. "It was death magic. Once she was toeing that threshold, you had a lead; you sacrificed some of your own life-force to suck the death out and replace it with … not-death. It's not exactly healing, but hey, it worked." After a moment, she noticed his eyes flick to her wrist.

She followed his gaze, and her heart skipped a beat at what she saw. Sitting just below her IV was what looked like a tattoo. It was solid black, stark against her sickly white skin: an angular, unmistakable shape. A rune.

"I told you they would show up the more you used your powers," Cal mumbled.

Edie could feel shards of fear pierce her body, but she was so tired they were easy to brush off. She relaxed into the pillow behind her, looking up at the ceiling, already wanting to fall right back asleep. But there were other questions she had to ask. "Is Satara okay? And Marius?"

"I dunno about Sunshine, but Satara's fine. Only had to have stitches."

She let out a breath. "What about Fisk?"

"Back at your apartment. He begs every day to come see you and Mercy, but like that's gonna happen." Cal rolled his milky eyes. "These pricks get pissed off enough with regular visitors, never mind seven-foot fucking fish men."

Edie closed her eyes. She hoped he was okay.

"Actually, Satara's gonna want to talk to you before the nurses do," Cal added. "I'll go get her."

Edie wanted to ask him to stay, but she didn't stop him. She just nodded and let her head loll to the side as he left. Mercy looked so peaceful, even with how beat-up she was. The fact that she was alive ... and that it was because of Edie...

"I guess you owe me one," she teased in a whisper, reaching out. Mercy probably couldn't hear her, let alone reach out and hold her hand. She dropped it.

A few minutes later, Satara and Cal came back. Cal leaned against the wall across from Edie while Satara sat in the chair next to the bed. She was wearing cotton leggings and a loose T-shirt, and Edie smiled at the sight. It was good to see her relaxing and out of her armor. Hell, it was good to see her alive.

"We'll have to tell the doctor you're awake soon," the shieldmaiden began, avoiding eye contact. She fiddled with the edge of the hospital blanket, then smoothed it out.

Edie nodded. "Yeah. But Cal said you had stuff to tell me."

"It's about the Wounded."

Edie straightened up in bed and nodded, raising the water bottle to her lips again.

"Astrid and I have been working to try and figure out who he is or where he came from, but it's ... difficult. There's no mention of him anywhere, but it makes no sense that someone unknown could have soldiers already at their command."

"Maybe he's working for someone else," Edie suggested quietly.

"Perhaps." Satara grimaced. "Several international leaders of the Gloaming died last night."

Edie's thoughts turned grim. What had he called it? " 'The culling of the weak.' "

"Whoever Sárr is, his influence has great reach. And it seems like the remaining Gloaming Lords and their followers are either surrendering to him or really buying in to this idea of a New Gloaming."

Edie ran a hand through her hair, which was unpleasantly greasy and smelled like hospital. "Did you figure out why he wants me so badly? Anything about his markings ... or those wolves?"

Satara gnawed on the inside of her cheek. "Hellerunan are very powerful. If war with the Aurora is what he wants, he surely thinks you'd turn the tides in his favor. We aren't certain about the scars. Astrid is still looking into it." She looked away again.

Edie could tell she was leaving something out. "And...? The wolves?"

There was a pause. "Yes. I think I know who they are." The shieldmaiden heaved a big sigh and looked down at her palms. They were still scratched from the battle, and Edie could tell she had been picking at the scabs. "Have you ever heard of Hati and Sköll?"

Edie shook her head.

"They are two of Fenrir's sons. Hati, *He-Who-Hates*, is a wolf of fire. He chases the moon, trying to eat it. Sköll, *He-Who-Mocks*, is a wolf of icy moonlight who chases the sun. The prophecies of the gods' fates say the two will succeed and devour Máni and Sól at the end of the world."

"Ragnarök," Cal said, biting on an unlit cigarette, "which I always thought would be a decent nickname for my—"

"You're saying that Sárr has two ... what, gods, demigods? ... at his disposal, following his orders? And me and Cal beat them?" Edie closed her eyes and took a deep breath. She didn't even know if she could muster a panic attack, she was so exhausted. "I guess he really is as important as he says he is."

"Yes. Which is why it's strange that we can't find any information about him." Satara peered at her. "You're pale as a fish."

"Thanks." Edie relaxed back on her pillow and looked at Mercy again.

Speaking of fish, they'd have to figure out something better for Fisk, long-term. He couldn't live in her bathtub for however long he stayed in the city. She hoped Marius was okay, too, even though he was technically supposed to be out for her blood. Whatever he had done to hurt Sárr bad enough to scare him away was sure to have taken a lot out of him. But she had a feeling she'd see him soon enough.

"One last thing before I let you rest," Satara said. "Indriði must have heard that we were looking for her at the party. She left a calling card at your apartment."

Edie opened her eyes again and looked at Satara skeptically. "I thought she hated Astrid."

"She does. But she didn't ask for Astrid. She asked for you alone."

She laid her head back down on the pillow and closed her eyes again. "Great." Admittedly, it was an unsettling thought, that a Norn wanted a private meeting with her. But after all they had gone through to find Indriði, Edie was glad it hadn't been for nothing.

Right now, though, she was too tired to give a damn about *who* wanted to see her or what they wanted to talk about.

Satara and Cal had gone quiet. After a few minutes, Edie cracked one eye open and saw that they'd left.

Beside her, there was a weak moan.

She sat up a little too quickly and tried to ignore how her head spun as she leaned to the side. "Mercy? You awake?"

Mercy shifted where she lay, obviously uncomfortable from all the cords connected to her. But, finally, her eyelids fluttered. "I'm awake..." she croaked. "Edie? Is that you?"

"Yeah."

Mercy opened her eyes and smiled, and Edie felt her heart soar. She hadn't been sure she'd ever see her friend smile again.

"How do I look?" Mercy asked.

"Like crap."

"Hah. You're just jealous. I'm always gorgeous." Her face fell a little. "I woke up the day before yesterday. The doctor says she doesn't know if I'll ever be able to walk without help again. My pelvis got all fucked up in the fall, and my legs ... ugh."

"It's going to be okay," Edie said. "I'll help you get better."

Mercy smiled. "No, I'm gonna make you carry me on your back like Yoda."

Edie tried to smile back, but the misery was too heavy. She'd put her friend in danger. She'd been a coward when Mercy had been nothing but brave from start to finish. And now ... now Mercy was hurt, maybe forever. Her life would be harder and all she'd done was try to help.

Edie looked away when she felt tears pricking her eyes—tears of anguish, of guilt, of embarrassment.

"What's wrong?" Mercy's voice was soft.

With a shudder, she replied, "I was useless. I don't deserve you."

"Don't say that." With a little effort, Mercy untwisted herself from her IV cord and reached out a hand. "Don't say that."

Edie recoiled, shaking her head and forcing herself to stop crying. She had to take responsibility for this, if nothing else. "I've treated all of you like garbage from the start ... Cal, Satara, you. And you're hurt because of me."

"Edie...." Mercy's eyes were filling with tears, too, her brows knit. "Friends are supposed to be there for each other. And you *were*. You saved my life."

"But after keeping all of this from you for so long, and blowing you off ... and after how I acted at the party—"

Mercy withdrew her hands, watching her tearfully.

"I hurt you. I've *been* hurting you." She wrung her hands. "But I was *wrong*. And I'm so, so sorry."

Mercy's face scrunched up a bit as tears began to fall. "I get it. And you're not my sidekick, Edie ... you're so much more than that." She stretched her hand out again, struggling for Edie's. "Don't you forget it again."

Edie would do better. She wouldn't let Mercy's support go to waste—or Cal's, or Satara's, or anyone else's. Her heart swelled as she took her friend's hand and managed a smile.

They were only close enough to hold each other's fingertips, but it was enough. It had to be, for now.

ACKNOWLEDGMENTS

Nothing you just read could have happened without the help of everyone who has supported me through the grueling process of finally getting this behemoth written and published. In particular, I want to acknowledge these people:

Tammi Labrecque, who made sure I was fed and housed while I muddled my way through this, who continues to answer every tedious question I have about writing and the industry (of which there are many), and who patiently listened to my every insistence that this book would be garbage and I should just give up.

Audrey, my boyfriend, who has not only lent insight but *actual, entire* characters to this story, such as Matilda.

My friend, Danny, for helping me figure out my main characters and always encouraging me—Edie would be incomplete without him.

Marina Finlayson, whose stories I have enjoyed immensely not just as a reader but as an editor, who is always ready with words of encouragement or a sharp beta read, and who is, overall, just one of the smartest, sweetest, best people I've ever known.

C. N. Crawford, in particular Christine, whose company I always enjoy when we get to hang out in person—whether we're slumming it in London or climbing extremely steep hills to find hanging trees in Salem, Massachusetts; whose books have always made me cackle (or choke up), and who is always ready to jump in and help others with their careers because she truly, deeply wants other people to be successful and fulfilled.

My therapist, Larry, for giving me that look he gives me when I am, yet again, saying stupid shit.

Finally, the one person I wish I could thank but can't: Blaze.

A year and a half ago, a long-time friend and ex-boyfriend of mine passed away suddenly in a car crash. I am a very young adult and so had never had a good friend pass away before. It was the most utterly shocking thing I had ever experienced, more so because it was *him*. People *say*, whenever someone dies, "They had such good energy. They were a light wherever they went, everyone loved them, it couldn't have happened to a nicer person."

Blaze was one of the few cases where this was 100% irrevocably, indisputably true. He was a dork and could occasionally be a total idiot, but I'm convinced that he was some kind of angel on earth, and he really did touch the lives of every single person he ever encountered. He talked me out of and down from some really stupid shit as a teenager; we were each others' only friends for a very long period of time. He had such a strange, magical, immense love for everyone and everything. He was one of the few people I've met that I would call truly beautiful right down to the core of his soul.

In June, I had already started *Rune Awakening*, but it was not going well. Frankly, it was shit.

Then he died. I took a few weeks, and even though he and I had fallen out of touch, I could not stop thinking about how young he had been. I couldn't stop thinking about all the things that he would never experience. I started thinking about my own life—what could *I* do to honor him? What could I do to make it so that he lived on in this world, in some little way? How could I just sit around and not *do* anything with my life when I still had a chance and he didn't?

I started writing down my feelings about what had happened. Then I started to look at *Rune Awakening* again, and all of a sudden, I had a much deeper understanding of what needed to happen.

A lot of the words I wrote in that session, where I wrote down all my feelings about what had happened, can still be found in the book somewhere. There's a lot of Blaze in Mercy, too. But in the end, he didn't inspire one particular character or scene in the book—he brought it all to life. It's because of him that I said, okay, I need to make up my mind; I have no choice but to *do this*, and here's how it needs to happen.

I wish you were here. Let's get this bread, buddy.

GLOSSARY

I use a lot of crazy words in this book that you might not know how to pronounce, so here's a small list of all of the Norse words in *No Earthly Treason* and how to say them.

Some things to keep in mind before you read this guide:

1. Some words have been adapted from Old Norse rather than taken from Old Norse, so their pronunciations are different. It's also important to note that any "authentic" Norse pronunciation is reconstructed.

2. Some words are pronounced different contemporarily, so they aren't widely pronounced the way the Norse would have said them. In fact, I mix and match a lot—sometimes I use the legit Old Norse words for things, and sometimes I use the more contemporary forms. In the case of **valkyrie/valkyir**, I literally just made up the plural "valkyir" because it sounded cool.

3. I've had to cobble together words like "**hellerune**," etc., from other languages, so their pronunciation is a little fudged. As for

the full sentences, I'm absolutely fudging vocab and grammar. If you know someone who can hook me up with an authentic Old Norse translation, I'll take all the help I can get.

4. Pronunciation basics: the Norse almost always **rolled their r's**. The letters f and v, when they don't start the word, are pronounced as a v sound and a w sound respectively. The "aw" I've written to express the letter á is a round-mouthed almost-o sound like the au in the English word "**maul**" as opposed to "ow." The letter j is pronounced like y is in English. The letter thorn (Þ, þ) is pronounced like the "th" in "Thor," while the eth (Ð, ð) is pronounced like the "th" in "father" or "this." I've expressed the eth sound as "**dth**" because that's what it sounds like to me.

CHARACTER NAMES

- Marius – MAH-ree-us
- Eirik – EY-rick
- Sørensen – SUH-ren-sin
- Ynga – ING-ga
- Tiralda – teer-AHL-da
- Fiskbein – fisk-bane
- Indriði – INDRI-dthee
- Sárr – SAWR-ur (a very hard name to say, I've come to find...)
- Hati – HA-tee
- Sköll – skohl

MISC:

- Ván – vawn
- Ljósálfr – LYOES-awl-vur
- Døkkálfr – DEUHK-awl-vur

- Hellerune – HELLA-roona
- Hellerunan – HELLA-roonen
- Jörmungandr – YOUR-mun-gaahn-dur
- Valkyrie – VAL-kur-ee (in reconstructed Old Norse, "valkyrja" or VAUL-keer-ya.)
- Valkyir – VAL-kyur
- Sól – soul
- Máni – MAW-nee
- Fenrir – FEN-reer
- Valhalla – VALL-halla or VAHLL-halla (Old Norse "Valhöll" or "VAHL-holl.")
- Sessrúmnir – SESS-room-neer
- *"Nøkkviðr minn sár, rjóða minn knífr"* – NEUHK-we-dthur min sawr, R'YO-dtha min K'NEE-vur. (**Rough** translation: "Naked my wound, red my knife.")
- Seiðkona – SAYdth-conn-ah
- Seidr – SAY-dur (Old Norse "Seiðr" or "SAY-dthur.")
- Fólkvangr – FOALK-van-gur
- Freyja – frey-ya (Or, with reconstructed Norse pronunciation, "FROY-ya.")
- Aesir – ICE-eer (Old Norse " Æsir" or "ASS-eer," which for obvious reason doesn't sound as cool…)
- Vanir – VAH-neer
- Vættr – vaa-tur (where "æ" is pronounced like the a in "had" or "mad.")
- Sjóvættr – SYO-vaa-tur
- Njord – n'yord (Old Norse "Njörðr" or "N'YOAR-dthur.")
- Sandgerði – sant-gyer-they
- Wyrd – weird
- Urðr – OOR-dthur
- Tréfolken – TREY-vol-ken
- Jötunn – YO-tun

- Tyr – teer (Old Norse "Týr," where the y makes a rounded "ee" sound like the u in "tune")
- "Váði vitnis" – VAW-dthi VIT-niss. Translation: "Foe of the wolf," a kenning for Odin.
- Ragnarök – RAHG-nah-rohk

ABOUT THE AUTHOR

Genevra Black is an author, a video game and movie nerd, horror buff, and lover of all things odd. She lives in Maine with her partner and her pitbull. She has always been enamored with mythology, folklore, and the paranormal. Her favorite pastimes include playing Dungeons & Dragons; gaming; watching slasher films; and designing and creating costumes/cosplay. She loves spending time in epic, exciting worlds, and each and every one of her stories is a personal invitation for readers to join her!

Find her at:

genevrablack.com
fb.me/GenevraBlack
twitter.com/GenevraBlack
genevrablack@gmail.com

And if you join her mailing list at GenevraBlack.com you can download the exclusive short story "Night Vet of the Living Dead"—the tale of exactly what happened to Hervey at the emergency vet.